# The Greener Trees

Robert Hilliard

ISBN: 0984248943
IBSN-13: 9780984248940

Pubished by
PARLANCE
P.O Box 391114
Cambridge, MA 02139

to those who dared to open the closet doors
and to those who still must decide

Greenwich Village, 1960s.  Before Stonewall . . .

# Chapter 1

The faces of Ezio Pinza and Mary Martin peered out over the words SOUTH PACIFIC on the cover of the music album leaning against the side of the hi-fi. The refrain "There Is Nothing Like a Dame" filled the apartment on Barrow Street in Greenwich Village. A male chorus was singing, emphasizing the words and making them sound more important and impressive than the music. The music resonated against the high walls of the living room and through an open door into the bedroom at one end of the apartment.

A voice shouted from the bedroom through the living room and into the kitchen at the other end. "Turn that damned thing off, will you?"

A man in a dark blue dressing gown darted out under the paneled, rounded archway entrance of the kitchen. "What the hell for?"

"It's bad enough having to get up at nine o'clock in the morning without having to hear the hi-fi," the voice answered, "and it's bad enough having to hear it without it singing something about dames." The emphasis was on the word "dames."

The man in the kitchen stepped further into the living room, brushed back a lock of black hair from his forehead, started to say something, instead walked quickly to the hi-fi and, with a great flourish, turned the volume up.

"Hey, Tony," came the voice from the bedroom. "I said to turn it down."

"When you hear music by Rodgers and Hammerstein," Tony called back, "the best thing that can happen to you is to turn it up."

"Shit!"

The voice from the bedroom stopped and there was the sound of footsteps and then running water from the bathroom. Tony walked back to the kitchen. A moment later he came out, a tumbler full of ice cubes in one hand. He stepped to the small bar at the side of the living room, looked for a moment with satisfaction into the rounded mirror above the bar, reached down to an open shelf, came up with a bottle. "You want some bourbon?" he called.

"What?"

"Want a drink?"

"Yeah!"

The sounds from the bathroom stopped.

"Straight?"

"Yeah."

Tony poured one for himself, tasted it, put a little more liquor into the glass, then poured another one, left it. "It's on the bar," he called. He sat on the sofa, put his drink down on the cocktail table and waited.

The living room was typical of the old, high-ceilinged brownstones of the 1920s, retaining the ultra-respectable conservativeness of form and adding the lacquer of Village bohemia. It was well furnished, seated on thick grey wall-to-wall carpeting. The walls were papered light grey on three sides, a reddish-brown on the fourth. The ceiling was

white, giving the room a feeling of width and depth as well
as height. Directly in front of the two tall, thin windows at
one side of the room stood a baby grand piano. The cover was
up, the lid of the piano lifted on the single prop. It was clear
that it was in constant use. Along the right wall was a couch,
modern, flat on the ground, with hard, square lines. The soft
deep cushions belied its look of coldness and uncomfortable-
ness. In front of it was a blonde mahogany square-shaped
table. The kitchen entrance was next to the couch, to the
right, then more wall and the front door. Past this door was
a hallway leading past the kitchen at the far end, past a telephone table, a jog right past the bathroom, and to the other
end of the apartment, the bedroom. The piano dominated
the living room. There was no doubt that this was the most
important piece in it. Bookcases lined the wall space of the
room at the left. Directly across from the couch, in front of
the bookshelves, was a large easy chair in the same blue-green
color as the couch. In front of this a bar, four feet tall, with
shelf cabinets in front and wheels on the bottom. In back of
the chair, on a light-colored end table, was a high-fidelity
record player and audio-tape combination. Compact discs had
not yet replaced them. The open space on the table was piled
with records and tapes. There was no pattern in their selec-
tion. They included Chopin to Debussy to Tchaikovsky to
Moussorgsky to Beethoven to Shostakovitch. The five albums
of Stravinsky, more than of any other single classical composer, suggested that if there was a favorite, it was he. Next
to this, on one of the bookshelves, was a collection of some
fifty Broadway musicals. These were as much for study as for
entertainment.

The other man came in, walking carefully and lightly,
looked at the bar, went over and picked up the drink.

"What do we have to get up so early for?" he asked.

"I told you," came the answer. "My sister and a friend of mine are coming in to New York."

"An old friend?" He emphasized the word "old" and raised his eyebrows as he tasted the liquor and looked at Tony. He adjusted his trousers, stuffed in his undershirt. He was of medium height, light-complexioned with a fringe of brownish-blonde hair. The beginnings of baldness outlined a high forehead, making him seem older than his thirty years. He was thin. All over. His face, his hands, his body, even his voice. It was high-pitched, a high tenor. He spoke and moved in quick patterns, as if he were impatient to complete whatever he was doing, as if each thing he did was the most important, as if he would never get to do another.

"An old friend," Tony repeated. He made it emphatic. He didn't want any arguments. "Don't worry about it, Larry."

"I'm not worried." Larry walked to the kitchen. "Any breakfast?"

"No time."

"If it's only an old friend, why the rush?"

"I want everything to be proper." Tony accentuated the final word.

"I don't see why I have to leave," Larry insisted. He was annoyed.

Tony was, too. "My sister is also coming, that's why," he said sharply. "Get a move on and get out of here before they arrive."

Larry turned and gulped the contents of his glass. He walked toward the bedroom. "Okay." He stopped and put down the empty glass next to the telephone. "Only I don't see why you're being so bitchy this morning." He disappeared into the bedroom.

Tony stood up, made a motion toward the bedroom, stood still for a moment, his lean body making him seem taller than he really was, his 23 years carried with a confidence that made him seem older. He pressed his tongue against the inside of his cheek, letting the anger boil away. With quick steps, he walked to the kitchen, washed out the two glasses, and came back into the living room. Hurriedly, he straightened out the pillows of the couch, of the easy chair, took several periodicals off the cocktail table, stuffed them into the bookcase. He took the sheets of music that were piled onto the music rack, opened the lid of the piano bench, put them inside, then withdrew one piece, looked at it a moment, placed it carefully onto the rack. For a moment he was undecided. He glanced at his watch. Just a little after nine. It would take them another twenty minutes to get there.

He called to the bedroom. "Come on, Larry, hurry up."

"Bitch" was the single-word, high-pitched answer.

Tony ignored it, turned off the music, sat down on the piano bench and began playing from the notes in front of him. Penciled neatly under each music line were the lyrics. Tony hummed to himself.

He played the song all the way through, took his eyes off the music, watching his fingers on the keyboard to see if he could remember it by heart. His fingers made a pattern of black and white over the keys and, as he played, he remembered when he had played it for the first time: when the lyrics had been brought to him for the college musical in Des Moines. The song meant a lot to him, even now; it gave him a security of having. More, of owning. As he played, it was easy to move to a thousand miles and three years earlier, this song evoking a special memory.

He was always able to sit, abstractly, at the piano, letting the notes come and the memories follow, losing himself in a different world. It was a release of tension, a necessity for accomplishment. It didn't matter what he played. The music wasn't to purge his own soul; it didn't have the same empathy for him as it had for his audience. It was a means of going back in time and space without consciously thinking of it, not having to decide what had been right or wrong, good or bad, just or unjust. It was easy to lose himself in his piano playing and to float without recrimination, as a drug addict might lose himself in his own device.

It was easier to search for the meanings of existence this way, to find the understanding of his own life and needs through this transfer of emotion than to face it in a mirror of unbending facts.

Often he had run his fingers across the piano keyboard and drifted in his musical hypnosis. And every time the memory returned, it was the same. It was a most important one. It told him a great deal. But the self-analysis never quite told enough. He needed to know more. He would try again. But again and again the time machine would stop in exactly the same place. It did now.

He was in his second year at the College of Des Moines, a lonely 19-year old young man whose only friend was the upright piano in his small off-campus apartment. His only acquaintances were some of the dramatic club members during the two months of rehearsals each year when he wrote and directed the music for the annual college musical show. A person who is lonely is not a complete person. Tony thought this and knew it. What elements of background, what detailed frustrations that lead a person to accept a salvation for his or her needs are lost in the intermediate dark of the past? Only the specific set of circumstances remain. To Tony, these alone were his source of light.

It was to a concert by an artist from New York, a pianist, a man who he had not met before and never saw again and whose name he had all but forgotten, that his remembrance took him. The name was unimportant. The pianist's recital had drawn a meager crowd. Students at a college,

perhaps because they are taught passive appreciation of
music rather than actively experiencing it, usually have little
affinity for a piano concert. The faculty, although perhaps
inwardly compelled by the same motivation as the students,
were more bound by their duty and their position to attend.
The audience was seated sparsely, but advantageously, and
the applause filled most of the auditorium. Tony felt bitter
toward these people. He felt that most of them were insin-
cere, that they did not really feel and fully understand as he
did. Only he, who had sat alone at his piano, knew how this
man felt who touched the keys and made the music part of
his self. The concert was over and the artist was alone. The
people who had been given the privilege of hearing him were
walking out, perhaps to immediately forget what they had
heard. Tony, sitting in the front row, remained. He wanted
to go up to the pianist and squeeze his hand and thank him
personally. Instead, he sat in his chair, his hands grasping the
felt-covered, wooden arms. The touch was pleasant. The pianist came from the stage entrance into the auditorium, shook
hands with one of the professors, a teacher of music.

"Shall we adjourn for some liquid refreshment?" Tony
heard the professor ask.

"We won't embarrass some of the others if we do?"

Tony wanted to smile at the question in reply. It carried a
subtle bitterness that he himself felt.

"No, not at all." The professor laughed. He didn't understand, Tony thought. The pianist and professor began to walk
down the aisle, passing Tony's seat. He was, besides them,
alone in the hall. They stopped, turned to him.

"This is Tony Jordan," the professor said. "He's composed the music for some of our student shows. An excellent
pianist."

"Don't tell me my music so impressed you that you
can't leave your seat, young man." The pianist laughed. Tony

smiled, embarrassed. When he thought about this later, he knew that the pianist was not making a joke, but was secretly wishing that what he had said was true.

"I enjoyed it very much," Tony said. He got up, shook hands with the pianist, the professor making the proper introductions.

"Can't leave a music lover here alone, can we, professor?" The musician looked at Tony seriously, without smiling. He smiled when he turned to the professor.

"Why, uh, no—no, of course not."

"That's what I thought," said the pianist. "Come along, Tony." They went to a small bar near the college.

The professor virtually disappeared as they sat and drank and talked, at first slowly fading into the background of the conversation and then, finally, excusing himself to go home to bed. Tony remembered the word "bed" because the pianist had used it.

"Our friend is probably going back to a hot water bottle in his lonely little bed," the musician said, after the professor had gone. Tony laughed, not because the remark was particularly funny, but because, ironically, this was how he had always, in the back of his mind, imagined was exactly what happened to the music teacher every night.

Tony felt his own tenseness disappear as they talked and drank some more. He had been intimidated at first by the closeness to this important and, for his own satisfaction, renowned New York pianist. A relaxation replaced his self-uncertainty and gradually became a feeling of belonging. There was empathy between them, the partition of differences growing thinner and then disappearing as the liquor became stronger. This was someone Tony could admire freely because, in turn, this man understood his own ambitious dreams. Across the small table Tony could glimpse part of the future. He was not alone in the thought. There was much about this young man that the musician consciously saw in himself. Being able to see part of the past is sometimes more important than looking into the future.

Tony lost track of time. It was one o'clock in the morning, perhaps two. The drinks had stopped coming and the two men slowly finished the glasses in front of them. The musician got up.

"My hotel is up on the hill—if you can call any of this prostrate city a hill." He smiled. "I'd better get some sleep before morning."

Tony stood up, was about to shake hands, then decided he couldn't just yet. The hours had been too complete to end so abruptly.

"Suppose I walk you up to your hotel?" he suggested. He was unsure of his words, but felt certain of his judgment.

The answer was a look of surprise, then hesitation. "If you want to," the pianist told him. Suddenly, he, too, became certain. "It would be delightful," he said. "You're the only person," he confided, "I've met here all day that I could talk to."

Tony was elated as they walked slowly past the darkened shops that surrounded the college campus. Tony tried to make the trip interesting, pointing out dubious landmarks along the way. He conceded, finally, after the other acknowledged this information with a bored acceptance, that the surroundings weren't so interesting after all. The streets swerved away from the campus, one of them lined with the black outlines of large trees along a brick paved road rising slowly onto what was facetiously called "the hill." The area was remarkable for its flatness. They walked silently.

He felt the musician take his arm, instinctively wanted to pull back, then tried to relax. "Over there," the musician pointed. "That large tree." He kept his fingers tightly onto

Tony's arm. "Its tentacles reaching out, the branches trying to touch the greener tree next to it, but falling short by inches, by the width of perhaps a finger. By the split-hair of the brain's reason," he added.

Tony relaxed now. The street was dark and lonely. With the other's hand on his arm, he felt secure.

"It's a pity that the tree isn't able to find what it's reaching for," the pianist said.

"It is," Tony agreed. He had often thought in these terms, sometimes afraid to face it in reality, making it a philosophical observation. The searching tree was like his own loneliness. Now he heard the thought verbally and it made it easy to talk about. "I've felt like that many times myself," he said. He felt no strangeness in this confidence.

"So have I," the pianist confided. "It's so rare that you find someone you can share these little secrets with."

"Yes."

"It's a good feeling, sharing personal intimacies with someone."

"Yes." Tony wanted to say more. But he could only feel the words; he couldn't say them.

The musician understood what was happening. "When I started as a pianist, I had the trouble of uncertainty. I was a bad pianist. Perhaps it was a lack of confidence in my place in the world." He looked over at Tony, got no answer, then continued. "I was lonely. I overcame the loneliness and found confidence and it went right into my piano playing."

Tony interrupted him. "I know what you mean. I feel that way, too."

"I may not be the best pianist in the world, but I'm not too bad," the other smiled. "The important thing is I wouldn't be anything if I hadn't fulfilled the need." The musician held onto Tony's arm. Tony felt the fingers as something alive. "Do you know what I mean?" the pianist asked.

Tony wasn't sure and gave no answer.

"You think about it," the other said.

They arrived at the hotel. Purposely, yet not understanding why, Tony followed the other man into the elevator, up to the room. The pianist said nothing. For a drink, Tony reasoned, as the hotel room door was opened. The door slammed behind him and he knew this wasn't true. He didn't know what was.

Suddenly the musician was no longer gentle. "Go home," he said quickly, angrily. "Go home."

Tony tried to leave. He took a step toward the door and then stopped. He felt a pounding inside, as if a chain had been tied to his lungs, choking his breath, and a heavy weight was pulling his heart to the floor. "I would like to stay a while," he said, the words coming slowly, in gulps.

"You don't know. You'd better go. Go now while you can." The pianist turned away from him, had taken off his coat, and was unbuttoning his shirt. He was angry, not with Tony, but with himself. Tony knew this by the loudness of his voice.

"May I stay?" Tony asked compulsively. The words were calmer. He felt a confidence that was as strange as the setting he found it in.

"If you stay, you stay all night. You know that."

He didn't know. But somehow, emotionally, he felt that he did. "Yes, I do," Tony said.

The musician came over to him, by the door. He was gentle again. "Why do you want to stay?" he asked. "Do you know why?"

"Yes."

"Why?"

Tony watched the other man closely. He was trembling, too, just as he was. But he felt quite steady now, inside. "That need you spoke of," Tony answered. "I want to fulfill it." The pianist nodded, smiled, and turned toward the bed. Tony smiled, too, and followed him.

This was Tony's remembrance as he lost himself in his music. It was the beginning he always thought back to, perhaps because it was on the surface and easy to see. It made its impression and served as a landmark. It was a concrete plaque that made it difficult to go beyond, to dig underneath. Tony tried again, and again there was no passing.

Before the memory he had always been dependent in a world of dependency. That need that had begun its fulfillment in the hotel room with the pianist reached a fruition with the fellow student who had written the lyrics of the song he played now. After one year in New York he had broken completely from the coattails and had given himself the apron strings to dangle. It didn't matter how he held them or that above them, now, was the promise of the dollar bill. In his success, he had found the easiest means the most successful. Larry, in the next room, was proof of this. The man who searches in society must find his way in and the logical path was, at first, acceptance. But acceptance sometimes isn't necessary for the man who has the promise of the future and the blessing of the favored.

Not that Tony was not intelligent enough to think deeper. But his need of the present had become so great that any possibility of the negation of the validity of his actions in the present made anything else, even in thought, unacceptable. Alone at his piano he could liken himself to a tormented Henley writing "I am the captain of my soul, I am the master of my fate." This was the extent of his understanding.

"You scream at me to hurry up and you sit there and play that damn piano." Tony was startled from his reverie, suddenly realized that he was playing the song over and over again, automatically over and over. He stopped, saw Larry standing over him.

"Do you really want me to go?" Larry asked.

"Don't give me a hard time about this," Tony said angrily. He got up from the piano bench. "Do you need any money?" he asked more quietly.

"Can I have twenty dollars?"

Tony went into the bedroom, took a bill from the top drawer of the bureau, added another twenty from his wallet, and returned, giving the bills to Larry. The latter had gotten the bottle of bourbon from the bar and poured himself a drink. He leaned against the bar, pocketed the money.

"Thanks," he said. "It's sweet of you."

"I'm not made of money." Tony resented the sarcasm..

"I'll get a job. I'll pay you back," Larry answered hurriedly. "Must be somebody who can use a hat designer."

Tony looked at his watch. Nine-forty-five. "They'll be here any minute, Larry. How about it?"

Larry remained, leaning against the bar, finishing the drink in short, quick gulps. "Wonderful, this bourbon," he observed.

"Best breakfast in existence." Tony took the glass from him, took it to the kitchen, started to wash it. Larry walked to the arch, watched Tony, contemplated his nervousness. "An old friend," he muttered, letting the words slide out meaningfully.

Tony turned off the water, put the glass down on the sink, whirled toward Larry.

"I told you to get the hell out of here," he yelled.

Larry smiled. "Just watching you. You look like you were getting ready for your first date."

Tony walked toward him threateningly. "I told you to . . ."

He didn't get any further. The doorbell rang. Then, seconds later, a knock on the door.

"God damn you, get in the bedroom," Tony ordered. "And don't come out."

Larry smiled, satisfied.

"If there's a peep out of you while they're here, so help me, I'll kick you out for good." Tony was emphatic.

Larry turned, still smiling, walked slowly to the bedroom, closed the door behind him.

Another knock on the door. "Just a minute," Tony called. He walked to the door, rubbed his shoes against the back of his pants leg, giving them the slightest bit of extra shine, secured the sash on his dressing gown, adjusted the white ascot around his neck, tucked it properly into the top of the robe.

He felt his stomach tightening and the need beckoned, a little closer now and more expectant. He pushed the black lock of hair back from his forehead and opened the door.

## Chapter 2

The sun reached through the train window, drew John Thomas into it and disappeared for a moment. It returned again quickly, reflecting his face, twenty-two years worth of soft sunlight, through and across the moving railroad car onto the young woman sitting next to him.

The yellow brightness flickered on and off, the beams broken by the telegraphic interruptions of the high wooden poles that sped along the side of the tracks. It was like the silver mirror he had played with as a child, reflecting in staccato and uncertain fashion the messages of the far away sun.

At that moment he was far away from the woman who sat so close beside him. The wheels of the train sent up a steady sound that inserted an artificial distance between them. John stared outside the window, onto the moving brown telephone poles alternating with the tall yellow grass. As he watched, the two colors seemed to grow into each other, began to revolve until they blended. He let his eyes follow the whirling pattern and he became part of it. The stone of a ring pressed against his palm and he was conscious of the woman's hand in his. He concentrated on trying to keep his place as one of the pirouettes in the moving kaleidoscope.

The brown and yellow blended with the flashes of green and they fell into place like the bits of colored glass in the kaleidoscope and carried him back along the rails, speeding back through the calm, even-tempered fields of wheat, through the red-furnaced cities, across the blue and deep brown of the Mississippi, along the cornfields of Iowa, back onto a small street in the small town of Belleville in the suburbs of Des Moines, back a month, two months, a year.

He knew where he was. His eyes were open and the telephone poles still flickered by. The wheels of the train still moved loudly beneath and he felt the growing numbness of the woman's hand pressed into his. Everything was as it should be and where it should be—except himself.

He breathed in deeply the sharpness of autumn air and was walking down the street in Belleville.

He walked slowly, reluctantly, stopping to pull a large, pear-shaped leaf from a hedge, tore it carefully down the center, folded the thin seams of the leaf, judging it meticulously as it broke into even concentric pieces. He dropped it and pulled a handkerchief from his pocket, wiped off the wetness of the green that had stuck to his fingers. He looked at the pieces of the leaf at his feet, the glossy green reflecting, only dully now, the late afternoon sun. He felt ashamed. It was living, he thought. Now it's scattered into a dozen dead pieces. He ground his foot into several of the larger segments. Like a human being, he told himself. One minute bright and fresh and green, and the next ground down into the dirt. He forced himself to laugh and thought of a better analogy. Into the concrete, he mused, since it's the city. I guess Des Moines is a city, he muttered without sound.

He continued walking, reached into the pocket of his sport coat and pulled out a pack of cigarettes, lifted a cigarette out between his lips. He lit a match, puffed. Nothing. He lit another match, watched it blow out before it reached the cigarette, lit another and inhaled the smoke. "Too damned nervous tonight," he said, letting the words come aloud. "It's just as bad for him as it is for me," he insisted.

He stepped to the side of the walk, let two young women hurry by running for the bus on the corner. Transportation was a problem in Belleville, though it was not too far from Des Moines. It had just taken him thirty minutes of bus riding from the campus of Des Moines College to the center of Belleville. It was a nice place to live, this suburb. It reminded him very much of his own home town of Rockwood on the outskirts of Cleveland. A small town, Belleville, but its own master.

There were perhaps three hundred homes in all, all separate, in this section of the city, with their small plots of green yard, both back and front, some fenced in, others with well-mowed lawns, short, neat, open for the passerby to step across, to flip a cigarette butt at, the small child to play on. But in Belleville the passersby were too well-mannered, the small child too well-behaved. They were afraid not to be. It was that kind of town.

The houses were different, each one. Not the forced individuality found in the different colored window-shutters of the otherwise identical familiar rows of duplex houses, but the independence of construction and architecture. There were the low, picture-windowed ranch houses; the gabled, slatted three-story homes, newly built but winking back to another era; the square, squat brick houses that were built as a starter, to be added to in the unforeseeable future that never came. There were old blocks and new blocks, the newer houses resented in their freshness by the older ones, like upstarts trying to show off.

The concrete walk turned into cobblestones as John pushed open the small iron gate in front of a two-storied white frame house. The name "Jordan" was neatly printed in large capital letters on a square white card pasted on the mailbox at the entrance.

This was one of the older houses of the neighborhood. It had been started just before one of the country's frequent economic recessions and, rather than let it stand as an empty-shelled tribute to the economics that had abandoned it, it was completed with Harry Jordan's last penny. In the years following, when there weren't even any more pennies to be had, Harry Jordan insisted that at least he and his family had a place to live. "Which is a damned sight more," he used to say, "than a lot of people got." He was an insurance salesman and, except for a few years during the height of the Great Depression, had always managed to make a living. He was proud of it.

There was a small railed porch. The front door opened only a foot or two off the cobbled walk into the inside hallway. Two large windows, one on either side of the house, bulged it out, making it seem bigger than it really was. A second story, set back a few feet from the first floor, merged into the sloped triangle of an attic. It was a secure structure.

John brushed his shoes on the straw mat by the front door. Automatically, he began combing his hair, pushing a soft brown wave to the front, checked with a forefinger to see if the part was straight. He adjusted his tie, pulled down the back of his jacket. He rang the bell. The cigarette flipped hastily away from him onto the cobblestone walk.

The door opened quickly. "Hello, Tony." John greeted the tall thin man who stood in the doorway. His voice was low, almost inaudible. He said it again, choking onto his voice to make it louder. He watched small pin-pointed eyes open wide, the hollow cheeks bulging slightly as Tony washed the inside with his tongue. It was habit and John noted it gratefully. It was a sign he had come to know in the other man. It meant that he, too, was nervous.

Tony Jordan brushed a lock of black hair back from his forehead with one hand, beckoned with the other for John to follow him inside. "Glad to see you, Johnny," he said. "Glad to see you."

John watched the shoulders bend slightly as the man walked, almost bouncing with his quick, sudden step. It always surprised John, this walk. Otherwise, Tony looked older than his twenty-two years, the long, drawn, dark face, the intense, serious manner, the tall thin body making him seem closer to thirty. Tony was only a year older than John, whose soft, ruddy complexion and brown wavy hair made him look, by comparison, even younger.

The hall was dark, a single yellow bulb barely lighting it from the small lamp on a telephone table. On the right a large double door led into a dining room filled with light from its bay window. The kitchen was behind this, further back.

Tony opened a double door on the left, let the light slide out for a second from the living room into the hallway. They went in. Next to this room's jutting window was a baby grand piano, the first thing that met the eye. John pushed himself onto the faux-Louis XIV couch directly across from the door. The couch was the second most impressive piece of furniture, although the gold-trimmed edges of the finishing had begun to wear white and grey in spots. A matching chair stood next to the couch, a large bureau directly across. There were no other decorations, no pictures, as if anything else artistic might detract in some way from the piano.

Tony pulled a bottle and two glasses from a drawer in the marble topped bureau. He moved easily, too easily, John thought. Too damned comfortable, John thought, looking at the soft carpet slippers, flannel slacks, silk sport shirt worn loosely and freely. John pointed to the bottle.

"Not for me," he said.

"Come on, Johnny. No temperament tonight," Tony said. "Any other night, all right. But not tonight. Tonight let's drink." He walked across the grey, wall-to-wall carpet, placed the bottle and glasses on the small round cocktail table in front of the couch. "Pour 'em, Johnny," he said. "I'll get come ice."

John watched him as he began to walk out of the room, sat back obstinately for a brief second. Then he jumped up.

"What the hell do you have to go for? What the hell do you have to go a thousand miles away for?"

Tony stopped, almost at the door, looked at him slowly and deliberately. "Relax, Johnny, relax." He walked over to him. John sat down, deep against the corner of the couch. It gave him protection. Tony sat next to him, straight, slim, his posture making him appear unseemly tall.

"Why do you have to leave?" John asked again. This time it was quiet, almost a whisper.

"You're putting it all out of proportion," Tony answered. "We knew it was coming. For a long time. For the last year. From the first day. Don't fight it now."

"It's easy to say." John sat up straighter. "But it's not easy to do. You just can't wake up in the morning and find something that's been there for two years isn't there anymore."

"You want me to be philosophical with you, Johnny?" There was a hint of exasperation.

"I just don't want you to go."

Tony stood up, walked around to the front of the cocktail table, faced John. He wanted the evening to be pleasant. He had wanted the goodbyes to be happy ones. Not necessarily joyful, but certainly not angry. He hadn't wanted any enmity. This was his last day in Des Moines. A few hours more with John Thomas and he didn't want them to be angry ones.

"This is our last time together for a while, Johnny," he said. "Let's make it a good one."

John gulped the words. "Two years ago, when we first met, it might have been easy to do. It's not so easy now."

"It's not easy for me, either," Tony admitted. "But there's nothing I can do about it."

"You can stay a while longer."

"I wish I could, but I can't." He brushed the lock of black hair back into place. "Stearns says I've got to be in New York the day after tomorrow to start on the music. I can't mess that up."

John thought a moment, nodding his head. "Maybe I can come with you?" he offered. It was only half-said.

"We've talked about that," Tony reminded him. "There's no use going over it again. You've got another year of college. When you finish it, then we'll see."

"I could write your lyrics," John insisted. The words came quickly, almost frantically. "I wrote the lyrics for your shows in college. I could do it in New York."

Tony was angry. His voice showed it. "And what do I tell Gerald Stearns? That he should go off to the Thousand Islands and lose himself?" Tony rubbed his tongue against the inside of his cheek. He found it an effective way of stopping himself from saying what he really wanted to say when he began to get mad. It served the purpose of counting to ten and at the same time relaxed him just a little inside.

"Look," he said, moving closer to John. "I'm a little fish, a guy who was lucky enough to meet a big shot who wants me to do a couple of songs for his new show. It's a break and I'm lucky and I'm taking it."

It was definite and final and John knew it. He tried to find something to say, lifted his hands in protest, and found nothing. He let his hands find, instead, the bottle of whiskey. "Get the ice," he ordered. Tony stared for a moment, then walked quickly to the kitchen.

John listened to the steps disappear, heard the slam of the refrigerator door.

He felt weak. He always did whenever there was a crisis with Tony. He never wanted to, but there seemed to be no other way. Tony was always in command. This troubled him now, as it often had. But trouble requires a solution and there never seemed enough time or opportunity for him to find one. So he only thought about it. Too many things always weighed heavy. He wanted to be less weak now, to appear strong, even if he really didn't feel it inside. He made an attempt.

"I feel better," he lied, as Tony returned with the ice, dropped the cubes into the glasses of liquor.

"Good." The response revealed nothing.

"You know I wouldn't do anything to hurt your career," John continued. "I guess I was just feeling sorry for myself. There's no place for that for us, is there, Tony?" He had meant it to be a statement, but it came out a question. He didn't want to apologize, but he felt he had to explain in some way. Even as he spoke he knew he was asking Tony's approval, as always, for even the little thoughts.

"No, no place for that," Tony repeated quietly. He would let John talk himself out.

John drank down the whiskey quickly. It made him hot and even burned a little. It hurt him and he was satisfied because it would somehow ameliorate the larger hurt. He stood up. "As a matter of fact, there isn't even a place for us anyplace, is there, Tony?" He put out a hand to steady himself, touched nothing, and sat down again.

John poured himself another drink, gulped it down as quickly as he had the first.

"You're drinking too fast," Tony advised. He sat on the couch, sipped his drink easily.

"I thought we wanted to be happy. Be happy. Be drunk." John's voice was louder. He poured and drank down another without a pause. His hand shook. He tried to steady it. He peered at the empty glass, held it close to his eyes, looking through it. Then he began to twirl it, round and round, circling it nervously between his fingers.

"I don't want you to go," John thundered. "What'll I do? What'll happen to me?"

"I thought you were feeling better," Tony said gently, without moving.

"Go ahead. Talk nice and soft and sweet. You're smug. A helluva lot you care what's happening."

"I can't stay," Tony said firmly.

"But I can?" John was on his feet now. His voice rose almost to a yell. He poured another drink, forced it down. It tasted bad now. He didn't care. "You can go, I can stay," he hollered. "Good for Tony. Poor, poor Johnny. I go home to my own little bed and you get to fly to New York. So the world goes to hell on an airplane."

Tony stood up, angry now. "You're getting too damned drunk." He grabbed John by the shoulders, tried to move him back onto the couch.

John put his hands on Tony's, held them tight against his shoulders. "That's it, Tony, take care of poor, poor little Johnny." He swayed and smiled. "He needs to be taken care of by big strong Tony."

The hands jerked quickly away. Tony straightened up. "Maybe you'd better go home."

John heard the words and waited. His stomach felt weak, not from the liquor, but from the fear of being punished. His head began to whirl with the drink and the grey carpeting turned into green and yellow and blue and brown. He couldn't make out which.

"No," he heard himself say, "I'll be good. Don't make me go home." He wanted to cry. Tony paced in front of the cocktail table, carrying John's eyes with each step, back and forth.

Tony spoke as he walked. "How many times have I told you, Johnny? This thing, this whole business, it's only for a moment. For a year, even two years, even counting every minute of two whole years or ten years or twenty years, it's still only a moment. You live and you have fun and you do what you want to do, but it can only go so far. Do you understand that, Johnny? It can only go so far."

"I understand." John sat slowly, carrying the words with him.

The black lock of hair hung over Tony's forehead again, but this time he didn't bother to push it back. "Do you know why it can only go so far? Do you know why?"

The answer came, again obediently, in a whisper, the pupil responding to the master. "I know why."

"And so that's that," Tony concluded. "We live and we enjoy. And then we just end it. Just like that. You take what you can get while you can get it. And when you can't have it anymore, then you throw it away and forget about it."

"Is that the way you want it, Tony?"

"I want it?" He laughed. "I'm only one person. Out there, there are millions. It's the way they want it. Go ahead and fight them."

John didn't answer. He didn't have to.

The whiskey bottle tilted again. John abstained. He wanted to hear clearly what Tony said.

"There's plenty to do," Tony said vaguely.

"I don't want to forget about you."

"You don't have to." Tony got a sudden thought. "If you feel lonesome for me, you can always talk about me with Carol."

"Your sister?" It sounded incongruous. "Your sister, Carol?" John repeated. The impropriety was so sharp it almost hurt.

"Sure. Why not? If you're as lonely as you'll think you'll be."

John held onto the straw. "I could talk to her about you a lot," he admitted. It wasn't so bad on second thought. Even one alternative makes hope out of seemingly hopeless frustration. "I guess you're right, Tony," John said. "I guess I won't forget about you." He felt he ought to be able to relax now and he undid his tie, unbuttoned his collar. "It's getting kind of hot in here."

"You never have been able to drink so many so quickly."

"Open the window, will you?"

Tony walked around the piano, pushed open the double frames of the window. John watched, let his eyes meet the carpet again, trying to find the mound of nap that had gone in the opposite direction, trying to, but not understanding why it just couldn't stay the way it was. He shook it off as Tony came back and sat close next to him.

"I feel okay now," John said. "I think we're going to have a nice evening after all."

"Good."

John concentrated on the rug again, the heat from the liquor lending an auto-hypnosis, rising from his stomach up into his throat and swelling through his head. The grey carpeting faded into a vari-colored kaleidoscope, carrying him swiftly forward, the patterns changing from blue to deep brown, to green and to yellow, each pattern lined with cross patterns, with ties like a railroad track, then becoming stiff and round, the tall hard wood of the telegraph poles whooshing past a background of yellow in front of a moving window. John felt his body shiver, as if he were straightening his soul together with it, composing the myriad storms into a unified physical mass.

John was conscious of the woman's hand in his again. The sun was bright through the train window and he felt bathed clean. He shivered again, slightly, shaking off what he had just been thinking, unbelieving what seemed an impossible dream. He looked at the young woman. She smiled to him and he felt better.

"Are you all right, Johnny?" the woman asked.

"Sure. Why?"

"You were shivering. You looked as though you were far away and were afraid of where you were."

He didn't answer.

She reached over and brushed the brown wave into place, liked the way it planted itself high in front of his forehead. She looked at the soft chin, round cheeks, a little plump now with sleepiness. It was a gentle face and a gentle person, a warm person and she held what she saw in her mind's memory like quicksilver.

"I'm all right now," John told her.

She smiled, knowingly. "As long as you're not afraid." She wasn't worried. Even if he were afraid, she would give him her strength to hold and between them there would be no fear.

He grasped her hand tightly and smiled back. The train began to sweep around a curve in the track and the sun leaped from sight. He held her hand more tightly, his fist squeezing over her closed fingers. The railroad track swerved back and the sun loosed itself, showering them through the window. He leaned over and kissed her on the lips, lightly, then pulled her close to him, her head resting against his shoulder. He felt stronger. She knew this and let her head stay there, satisfied. They rode for a while like this, neither one speaking.

The sun grew thinner and gradually lowered itself into the protection of a graying evening. The young woman sat up quickly.

"I must have fallen asleep," she said, watching the flickering of the last few rays of sun. She looked at her watch. "Eight o'clock. We ought to be in Cleveland soon. Then just another twelve hours to New York." She repeated the words "New York." They sounded exciting and she felt she should be excited. Like a little girl. She let herself relax and be a little girl. She looked at him, her face reflected in his large brown eyes. She caught the reflection there, covered herself securely with it. There was good freshness in being alive, and she prayed thanks for it. For the train, for John, for all the good things that were to come.

"Another twelve hours," she repeated. "I'm glad we took the train instead of flying," she said. "It gives us more time together, to share the time, the feeling, the sights, the sounds of the places that we pass through. It's good to be alive, isn't it, Johnny? With my fiancé, on my way to New York City, to see my brother Tony and to make our fortune."

John didn't answer. He held her close, his face turned toward the window watching the quickly darkening kaleidoscope.

## Chapter 3

The New York skyline rose up and then disappeared as the train rushed into the blackness of the tunnel. John strained to hear the hollow sound of the river beating against the walls above them and, after a moment, all around them.

"It's the Hudson River we're under," Carol said. She sat up straight, her handbag clutched, ready to move the moment the train stopped.

"Under the Hudson from New Jersey to New York," John amended.

"It's so very exciting," Carol said.

Her voice was low, John noted, always low and gentle and soft, like Carol herself. Even when she was excited, she was calm.

"Pretty soon," she continued, "the lights of Broadway and Greenwich Village." John nodded.

"It'll be good to see Tony again," she said.

John nodded once more.

Carol shifted closer to him, put her hand in his. He felt the stone of the engagement ring rub against his palm. The awareness somehow bothered him.

"Is there something wrong, Johnny? You're awfully silent."

"Nothing," he told her. "Just getting steeled for the . . . excitement." He wanted to say ordeal.

Carol smiled. "It's hard to believe, isn't it? Just a few more minutes and we're finally in New York. It makes the whole trip worth it." She waited for him to say something, then laughed sweetly. "All right, Johnny, I'll leave you with the awe of the big city. I won't bother you."

"You don't bother me."

She held onto his arm, feeling against the muscle below his shoulder. It was good, being able to belong, to take care of or to be taken care of, to share with. She felt disturbed sometimes about John's moodiness, but the sadness that had been all of John when they first met a year before had gradually disappeared and had morphed into an eagerness for the new things and the good things of life that they had begun to discover together. She was happy.

John looked out the window and the darkness seemed to grow larger. It moved around him and his thoughts were someplace else, although he felt and heard Carol next to him.

"It's been a wonderful year and now we're in New York," she was saying.

It had been a full year, John thought, since he had said goodbye to Tony. And it was only one day after Tony's departure for New York that he had stepped again down the concrete walk in Belleville, pushing past the iron gate onto the cobblestone walk and rang the bell. Only this time there was no Tony to answer.

He had automatically begun to comb back his hair, to straighten his clothes. Then he had laughed. Tony wasn't there to see. Just Tony's sister, Carol. And he had come only because Tony had asked him to. Because it was Tony's house and it would bring him, in some way, a little closer to the man who was then so far away. He wouldn't stay long. He expected Carol would be a bother; he only came to talk about Tony, anyway.

The door opened. Without seeing, he looked up, almost expecting the long thin face, the dark eyes, the black lock of hair. It was all there. It was even the same voice.

"Did I frighten you?" the voice asked.

He blinked his eyes. "No," he answered. "Just surprised."

She laughed. "You didn't expect Tony!"

"No, of course not." He was embarrassed.

He looked at the young woman standing in front of him. Her eyes were dark, pin points on a smooth skin, bright, shining. Her face was long, not thin, but slender, graceful in itself. She was tall. Or perhaps because she was slender she looked tall. John felt he had said all this to himself before; then he realized that he had—about Tony. This was the first time he had looked at Carol so closely.

"Let's not stand out here all night. Let's go in, shall we?"

"Yes," he answered. "Thank you."

Carol brushed back the black lock of hair that hung against her forehead, turned and went inside.

John followed her down the hall into the living room. He sat down on the sofa, deep into the pillows at the side.

"Would you like a drink?" Carol asked.

"Uh . . . no, thank you."

"Don't be bashful. You can if you wish."

"Well, a small one, if you don't mind." He was uneasy and he was conscious of it.

Carol walked to the bureau, opened the drawer and took out a small bottle. It was a new one, John noticed. The large one had been finished the previous evening.

"Wait here," she said. "I'll be right back with some ice."

John looked around the room. It hurt him because it was exactly the same. Isn't there any relationship between space and matter that changes when a person who was, isn't any longer?, he insisted to himself. Or doesn't it count when the matter is a human being? Some laws just don't apply to human beings, he concluded. He wanted to be bitter about it.

Carol returned, took two glasses and filled them with ice. "Soda for you?" she asked.

"Yes, please."

She poured his glass half full with the liquor, then the soda. Carefully, she emptied the rest of the soda into her glass.

"You can't get very drunk that way," John offered.

"I know," she answered. "That's the purpose. I don't drink."

"Oh!" John smiled, began to fiddle with the glass, twirling it around and around. Carol watched him. He didn't stop.

"Nervous? Don't be on my account," she said.

"No, I'm not," John answered. "I always do this. Just a bad habit."

"Don't let it get the better of you. Bad habits are hard things to shake off," she said. "Sometimes they get hold of you so completely, it hurts dreadfully when you have to let them go."

"Yes, you're right," he answered. "It does hurt to let things go." He tried to smile in self-sympathy. He took a drink of the liquor. "How about good habits?" he asked.

"Are there any?" Carol countered. "Except brushing your teeth twice a day, of course."

"No, I guess all habits are bad, aren't they?" John offered.

The remark held no meaning for her, John felt. It was a private observation. Tony would have found an understanding in its meaning. But Tony wasn't there. It was only Carol. And she was alien. John was glad that she knew nothing about Tony and himself. He guessed she didn't. He felt guilty, told himself he shouldn't. Immorality was a word only for those who did what they shouldn't do. Tony and he had done only what they should have, he assured himself.

He felt the loneliness without Tony and wondered if he should try to speak to Carol, to find in her the laughter and understanding and friendship he needed. He remained silent.

He watched the twirling glass in his hands, wanting to stop, but not able to think of any reason why he should. The world went around in circles, he thought, why shouldn't a whiskey glass?

Carol wondered at John's silence, wanted to break it, and then hesitated, preferring not to disturb its seeming deliberateness. She tried to decide, casually, whether he was frightened or shy. There had been little but an occasional "hello" between them before; now it bothered her why there hadn't been more.

John stood up, pointed to the piano. The cover was up, the keys reflecting the yellow of the lamp light. "I thought it would be in moth balls," he said. He smiled, unsure that he had said anything worth smiling about.

"My soon to be celebrated brother isn't the only one who plays," Carol explained. "But I'm only an amateur compared to Tony," she hastily added.

"I guess Tony is in a class by himself," John suggested. It made him feel good to say it.

Carol agreed. "I could talk about him all night," she said. She watched John take his drink again, sip it slowly. It must have been the right thing to say.

It was. "So could I," he assured her.

Carol felt the stiffness begin to fade slightly. "I could tell you a lot about him you don't know," she offered. The subject would give the evening a purpose. Better than to sit in silence, she decided. She felt a responsibility for John's uneasiness. She wondered if he was always like this, shy and uncomfortable.

They sat together on the couch, John pushed into one corner, Carol upright at the other end. She told him about Tony, the little things he hadn't known before. John began to relax. The pattern of Tony's life was much like his own and this gave him a reassurance of closeness. It was a kind of certainty for what had been between them and what John felt still was.

"Tony and I have always been very close," Carol told him. "As a matter of fact, even though he's three years older, people sometimes mistake us for twins."

"You do look alike," John confirmed.

"I hope that's good," she smiled.

"Very good," John answered. Then, quickly: "Of course, you're much prettier."

"Thank you." Carol laughed. John joined her, not because it was really something to laugh about, but because they both grasped at the chance for relief from the stiffness. It was a necessary laugh.

"You're about twenty," John said.

"Three months ago, in July."

"I like the summer," he said.

"It takes you outdoors. Into the world. You're not so cooped up."

"Not only for that," he explained. "I just like it because it's warm." They found that incongruous and laughed again.

They relaxed. "About Tony . . ." she began.

John moved closer to her. This was all new, these things she said. He and Tony had exchanged thoughts and feelings. But it had all been subjective. This was objective history and he listened attentively. She told about her parents. She told it casually, as if it were something to say but of no particular importance. Her father met her mother when he was a young man just entering the insurance business. They had never explained just how it did happen. Her father had gone to Chicago on a business trip one weekend and when he returned to Des Moines he brought with him a wife. Her father had always laughed about it.

"Harry," her mother used to say, "you oughtn't to joke about it. It hasn't been so funny. Things might have been much happier if you hadn't come to Chicago that weekend at all." And Harry would roar that much louder.

Tony was born nine months after they came from Chicago, almost to the day. Carol blushed, then laughed: "I guess they worked pretty fast in those days." Her father did well in insurance and when she was born they thought they would build a new, modern house in the suburbs where, as her father said, the better class of people lived. Her father laughed at that, too. He was a large man, always laughing. Everything was a joke to him. Carol often wondered if she and Tony were the same kind of jokes. Her father never seemed to take them seriously. She and Tony had never known much about their mother. Her background was never mentioned, except that she had lived and worked as a salesgirl in Chicago. Carol and Tony never met their grandparents on their mother's side. On the other hand, they remembered their father's parents, who lived in an apartment in Des Moines from where they often visited, and later in a retirement community cum nursing home, where Carol and Tony often visited until some years earlier when both grandparents died. They had always appeared to be old people; quiet and sedate and older than their time. Their son was just the opposite.

Carol remembered vividly when her mother died. Carol was just ten years old. Her mother's constant sicknesses added to a life of constant complaining that led to an early grave. Her mother had been Methodist. "Daddy let them take her to a Methodist church for a funeral service," Carol said. "He never went to church himself before that. We never went afterwards."

"The casket was large, covered with flowers, I remember,"
Carol continued "Daddy bought a new suit. I never knew
why he had to go out and buy a new suit as though he were
celebrating something." She poured a little more soda into
her glass, put it down without tasting it. "We went to the
cemetery. The minister was there saying some things about
Mother. I stood and listened. Things about what a wonderful woman she was, how hard she had worked, how much she
had given to life and to her children and to her family. How
close she was to God. Everyone was standing around crying.
And the more they cried, the louder the minister talked. I
began to hurt inside. I kept asking myself, how dare he talk
about my Mother when he didn't even know what she had
been like? How did he know what she did for her children
or her family? I kept repeating the questions to myself and I
hurt more and more inside. It was almost like a circus. The
people standing around, dressed up new and shiny, and the
black veils and black and white handkerchiefs waving as if it
were a celebration. I was only ten at the time, but even then I
understood."

John leaned toward her. "You don't have to talk about
it."

"No, it's all right," she said. She smiled, brushed away
the moisture from under her eyes. "It's just that I still get
mad every time I think about it."

She continued once more. "Tony must have been thinking the same thing. He was thirteen and was very devoted to
mother. For some reason he couldn't stand Daddy. He didn't
like the practical jokes."

"I know," John said. "He's told me about them."

"Then you know about this."

"No. He never told this story."

"Tony suddenly told the minister to shut up," she continued. "It was funny, now that I think of it. But it was serious

then. I wanted to yell out, too. I remember Daddy had gotten Tony a new suit. I hadn't gotten anything. I was always kind of the extra one of the family and treated without much consequence. I suppose I should be a screaming neurotic."

"You aren't," John assured her.

"I got over it. I was lucky." She continued. "I remember what Tony said. 'You don't know my mother,' he screamed, 'you're saying these things and you never even knew her, you stand there and lie and say things that you don't know. My mother is dead. Don't torture her any more. Leave her alone!' Then he cried." Carol smiled at John. It was a difficult thing to talk about. She didn't mean to bore him.

"Go on," he told her. "I want to hear it."

"Well, there's not much more to tell. I said a few things too. Daddy took us both aside and the minister continued. I remember Daddy's parents were shocked, as was everybody else. But we went home and it was forgotten. Daddy joked a little bit less for a few weeks and then everything returned to normal."

"I've always had both my parents," John said, "so I don't really know how it is. You and Tony must have had a rough time. I can see why you and Tony were so close. With nobody else around, you had to stick together."

"We did. It was a very unhappy childhood for a long time." Carol reached for the glass, picked up the whiskey bottle. "Do you mind if I have some?" she ventured.

"I don't mind." He poured a little into her glass. "I thought you didn't drink."

"I don't, but I guess sometimes it's good to make you feel better."

John laughed. "Then by all means, try it."

She drank it. It was pleasing; a little bitter, but warm and comfortable.

"I guess Mother's death accounts for Tony's piano playing talent," Carol continued. "Mother had started him on lessons and after her death he practiced almost constantly, trying to become really good. To make up for something, I suppose. He never had any friends. And neither did I. We played together and I don't think there were more than one or two kids on the block that we knew well. We shared everything: food, money for entertainment, even clothes. Then, after about a couple of years, things began to change. And not in Tony's favor, I'm afraid."

"He should have been able to take care of himself better than you could take care of yourself," John said. He began to feel a closeness to Carol. He liked talking to her.

"I think now that Daddy began to have misgivings or pangs of conscience. At any rate, he began giving everything to me. Maybe because I was a girl. He had never given anything to Mother. I began to have the best. Tony sometimes was almost left out in the cold. I didn't want things that way, but I couldn't refuse. I worried about Tony because he had no other friends and was so alone. I suppose he should have gotten to dislike me. But he didn't. We got along fine. Sometimes I felt just a little bit that he was jealous of me. But that was rather foolish, wasn't it?" she added.

John wanted to suggest that maybe Tony really had been jealous. Perhaps that was why he had talked so seldom about his sister. She was very nice and yet forgotten by her brother as if she didn't belong. It had been, John remembered, as if the very mention of her would give her something and take something from Tony. John kept his thought silent.

Carol sipped on the drink, seemed to like it. "This might turn out to be a bad habit," she suggested.

They sat for a few moments, silently.

"There's little more I can say, I guess," she told him finally. "I'm boring you pretty well stiff as it is."

John assured her again that he was interested.

"Okay." Carol shrugged. "Things continued as they were," she said. "I tried to be as close to Tony as possible, but after I started high school and began to go out with boys he got very jealous. I used to tell him to get a date himself and he'd get mad." She shook her head, not understanding. "He seemed so shy, so insecure with people. He buried himself in his music." She stopped a moment, thinking in the past, then letting her thoughts move to the present. "And then, after he was rejected from the Army, he started college. Although it's not that far away by bus, he wanted to live on campus, so Daddy paid for that small apartment he has. You've been there, of course."

John nodded. "Many times," he said. "We compose our songs on his piano there."

"Oh yes," Carol acknowledged. "I don't think he made many friends at college. Just you."

"Very few," John agreed.

"And when he came home on weekends, he'd just sit and play the piano. I got along all right, then. I went out all the time in high school, to all the events, a lot of dates and . . . ." She stopped. "But this is about me. We don't want to talk about me, do we?" She looked at him matter-of-factly. "I'd like to hear about you now," Carol said.

"I don't like to talk about myself," he told her. "Sometimes I remember a lot of things I'd be better off forgetting."

"Like what?" She tried to pump. She got nowhere.

"Let's talk about the pleasanter things of life," John said. "The more recent things, I think, were pleasanter. Let's not go all the way back to Cleveland. That's my home town. Actually, it's a suburb, Rockwood, but nobody's ever heard of it, so I say Cleveland," he added.

"Okay," she helped. "The recent things. Only now you talk. You're on the stand."

He sat up, in mock pose, addressed her seriously as if he were a teacher lecturing to a class. She laughed

"I was born in Cleveland, raised in Cleveland, and three years ago I came to Des Moines College." He paused. "That's my life story," he concluded.

Carol tried to make it easy. "Do you like Des Moines?" she asked.

"The college or the town?"

"Oh, nobody much likes the town," she answered. "None of my friends who lives here does, anyway."

"It seems like an okay place to me," John said."

"I mean the college," Carol said.

"It's pretty good. A nice school, nice campus. Some good courses."

"You're a writer, aren't you, Johnny?"

"Tony told you?"

"He told me you want to write novels," she said. "That you write anything, though."

"It keeps me busy," he said. "Like the book and lyrics for Tony's shows. Not that I didn't like to do them. I did."

"You're modest. I bet you're very talented." She didn't mean to flatter him. She was being friendly. John became a little embarrassed again. She forced the conversation once more.

"That's how you met Tony, wasn't it? Writing a college musical." She already knew this.

"That's right." This was more of what he wanted to talk about. "I'd heard about what wonderful music he wrote, so I went up one day to see if he might like my lyrics. And he did and we wrote the show together. And then last year's show, too. It's been wonderful working with him."

Carol looked at him closely. She could see it had been a happy time.

"Two years ago. That's when you started coming here on weekends," she reminded him.

"Uh huh."

"It's surprising I didn't see you more often," she said.

"Well," he tried to excuse himself, "we were always busy, with the music or planning things."

"I know." She helped him. "When I started college last year, I remember every time I visited Tony at his apartment you two were always together, talking, reading, playing piano, or just sitting. It's a good thing I didn't room at the campus. I wouldn't have seen much of Tony, anyway." Then, after a moment: "But I'm going to room there this coming year."

"How come?" His interest was only academic.

"Well, with Tony away in New York, Daddy is going to spend the money saved on Tony's room for me. So it'll be easy. And I won't feel I'm imposing."

"That'll be nice." John was casual.

In his casualness Carol felt more and more understanding for John. She liked it. It was good, too, that John and Tony had been so close. It made it easier. She thought she was going to enjoy being friends with John.

"Are you hungry?" she asked.

"A little," John admitted.

"Let's go to the kitchen. I'll scramble up some eggs."

They walked through the dining room and into the kitchen. The interior decorating of the frugal 'thirties showed itself here in the smallness of the kitchen; the automobile and the movies had taken the family from the hearth and, later, from the kitchen to the radio and then to the television set. John sat at a table, Carol standing directly in front of him by the stove.

They talked some more, then ate and talked again. About little things, about anything. It was surprising to John how quickly the evening went. It was after midnight when he finally decided to leave. He stood at the door awkwardly. He didn't want to leave. Even without Tony there, there had, unexpectedly, been something good. He couldn't decide exactly what, but it had been calm and peaceful, more peaceful than with Tony and yet, somehow, very similar. He tried to understand this. There was much of Tony there, and yet it wasn't Tony. He looked at Carol, trembled slightly inwardly as he judged the eyes, the cheeks, the nose, the warm, wide, thin lips, the black lock of hair. He wanted to brush it back for her. She noticed him staring at her.

"Pretty bad?" she asked. She brushed the lock from her forehead.

"No. I didn't mean to stare. You look very nice." The words sounded strange to him. He wanted to rush out, but he didn't. "Carol . . ." he began. The words were hard in coming, but they reached his mouth, then blurted out foolishly. "Do you think we can get together again, sometime . . . to talk?" He hesitated. It was hard to say. "Maybe even the dance at college next week?" He felt his face blush red. He was fearful of her answer. He didn't want her to say yes and at the same time he didn't want her to say no.

"I'd love to."

These were new words to John. Asking a girl to a dance was something new. I shouldn't be afraid, he insisted to himself.

"But you don't have to wait until then to come over," she was saying. "You're welcome here all the time, you know."

"Thank you." John had decided quickly. "Thank you. I'll take advantage of your offer." He walked out the door.

"Good night."

"Good night."

The door closed behind him. He walked down the street thinking about the evening. He was confused. But it was not unpleasant confusion. There were no knots of frustration or self-accusation. He had done what he wished and felt good about it. "What would Tony say?" he asked himself. Enjoy life! Well, I enjoyed the evening! He passed the green hedge, tore a leaf from it, looked at it, left it whole and watched it glide back and forth as it floated to the ground. He walked along quickly, almost briskly. "It was a good evening," he said to himself. And then, as an after-thought, "we can always talk about Tony."

## Chapter 4

The darkness of the train tunnel turned light again as the florescent lamps of the station began to flash past. John stood and felt a suitcase bang against his knee as he moved into the aisle. A big male voice said "excuse me." "It's all right," John answered as he took down his own suitcase from the rack above the seat. A large woman bumped into him as she hurried along the narrow aisle toward the exit door.

"I've got it, Carol," John said. "You go ahead."

Carol held onto a smaller bag. "No, you first," she said. "I'll let you clear a way for me through this mob."

They pushed their way onto the platform.

"Now where?"

Carol pointed. "Over there. It says escalator." She followed John through the crowd again, got in line as the people moved gradually up onto the moving stairway. John stepped on in front of her, turning sideways to watch what was happening below. She looked at him, watching his large brown eyes. They seemed sad. For some reason, whenever she looked at him closely they always seemed to carry a sadness. As the escalator moved and people disappeared over the top, John's face remained steady in front of her. It was the same

face she had remembered a year before, the first night he had
visited her. It was sad then, but it had also been more afraid.
It worried her now. Some of that fear seemed to be creeping
through. John's face moved again and it became part of the
crowd of faces pushing through the main level of Pennsyl-
vania Station. Carol put aside her reverie and followed him
through the door to the lobby, fascinated by the beam of
light that opened the door in front of them as they passed
through it.

The feeling of the crowd was good. It moved in unending
patterns, in no particular direction, but nevertheless unceasing. It was like life, fresh and important and full of vitality.
She wondered how much of this life knew where it was going.
John disappeared under the alcove leading to the baggage
room. She didn't mind the waiting. It would not be long,
neither now nor in the future. Now they were engaged, she
and John. In a matter of months they would be married. She
thought about Iowa. She would return there in a week. Then
she would wait for the important message from John. She
thought about how it would be phrased. "Novel completed.
Advance paid. Take next plane." Or maybe something like
"Typewriter worn out. Publishers worn out. John Thomas
worn out. Hurry."

He had come a long way in the past year. He had written
a novel, a good one. Sometimes, as she read parts of it during
the time he worked on it, she didn't completely understand
its meaning. It was about two men wanting something in
life, but not sure exactly what they wanted, and their trying
everything and anything only succeeded in their burrowing
deeper into their own confusion. Like a ship without a rud-
der, John had described it. But it was good. A fine young new
talent, the publisher had told him and invited him to come
to New York to finish the manuscript and do the necessary
revisions under an editor's supervision. She had come with

him, to see New York, to visit her brother Tony, and then to return to Iowa to school, to eagerly await the time when she would come to New York for good. These were good plans and the feel of the crowd made them seem even more alive.

John came back. "I had the bags sent to the hotel," he said. Nothing like the efficiency of New York. He took her by the arm, carried the one small suitcase they had with them in one hand. "Feel good?" he asked.

"Feel wonderful," she smiled. "I was just thinking about the novel. It'll be soon, won't it?"

"Real soon," he said. He didn't seem too convincing.

"Something wrong?" she asked. She wanted to ask more, but didn't.

"No, nothing." He seemed less assured, uncertain of himself, like the person she had known over a year before but had seen only rarely since. "It's the excitement," he explained. He smiled, then dropped her arm. "I almost forgot. Since we're going straight to Tony's first, we'd better call now." He hesitated. "Do you want to call?"

Carol waited a moment, then started quickly toward a phone. "Sure, I'll call," she said. She returned a few minutes later. "He'll be waiting for us," she said.

"C'mon." He took her by the arm again. "We're off."

They walked up a long flight of stairs, found a taxi waiting in the narrow street passageway, got in.

"Barrow Street. Four-nine-four Barrow Street," John told the driver. "That's in Greenwich Village."

The driver leaned back, set the flag on the meter. "Yeah, I know." The cab lurched forward.

Carol looked out the cab window, watched the moving crowds, followed them along, trying to find an end to them and to the buildings that reached higher than her line of sight. It was a big thing, this new world. "It's going to be good, Johnny," she said. "I can't wait until you finish your book, and then . . . "

"Yeah," John interrupted her. He was embarrassed at being so quick to respond, smiled and turned away. He watched the meter disinterestedly, listening for its tick. It gave him a focal point for his thoughts. It intertwined with the tall buildings and the masses of people. It made him feel part of them and apart from them at the same time. It made him feel strong and he turned and took Carol's hand, held it tightly.

"I think we should have told Tony we were engaged instead of waiting to make it a surprise," she said.

"It doesn't matter. People have to get used to surprises."

"All right."

They didn't speak for a moment, letting the moving wheels of the cab carry their thoughts. "About the hotel," Carol offered.

"What about it?"

"I still think you should have taken advantage of Tony's offer. To stay with him at his apartment, at least until the book is finished.

John turned to say something, then stopped. He smiled and she felt better. He continued smiling. It made him feel better, too.

## Chapter 5

What was to happen in New York, indeed at his moment of entry into the Barrow Street apartment, was important to John Thomas. Not more important than moments of crisis are to any individual, but certainly not less.

He had come a long way in his own development since he had last seen Tony the year before. He had come a long way in each preceding year. Some of them were so strange that as he looked back upon the past he found it difficult to accept that they were truthfully part of him. Most difficult to reconcile were the personal freedoms he enjoyed now at twenty-two years of age, given the cloister and consecration of his youth.

John Thomas was born and raised in the small city of Rockwood, a middle-income suburb a few miles north of Cleveland, Ohio. Rockwood covered itself in moral prophylaxis and the townspeople walked the streets with their eyes off the ground, proclaiming themselves as having protected the virginity of their city. John's home was the sanctum sanctorum, a retreat of seclusion and obligation.

In his present year, at twenty-two, it would require extensive psychiatric treatment for an understanding of his formative years and their application to the insecurity that still possessed him. Had he been able to translate the past, instead of only read it, he probably would have hated his mother. As vehemently as do millions of other young men who experienced a similar youth. But he didn't. Or at least thought he didn't. Instead, the hate and resentment remained inside. The religious excesses and incontestable will and control of his mother were accepted as part of a necessary and normal, if unhappy, childhood.

The hate was given no outlet and the unhealthiness grew inside. It is difficult to admit physical truth that is contrary to moral insistence—and vice-versa. He didn't permit himself to understand his own emotion, the unhealthy emotion that is the cross to bear of the young man in a society that distributes health in bottles. John was raised in an atmosphere of hypocrisy where truth was dependent solely upon his mother's religious concept of it.

She had been married fifteen years when John was born, herself almost forty at the time. He was her first and her only child. She regarded the many years when she tried and was unable to conceive as the will of God, and when her fifteen years of child-prayers were answered it was, she knew, the will of God. At one time, in her youth, she had contemplated becoming a nun in the Catholic Church. Her parents had been Episcopalian and her Episcopal worship, she felt, was very close to the Catholic. After much thought she decided against it. If God would have wanted her to be Catholic, she concluded, He wouldn't have had her born Protestant. She devoted much time to charitable work, to social service and fund drives, to her prayers for contributions and to the distribution of the results of her prayers, the monies from the mansions of Shaker Heights to the huts and flats along the lake and factory districts. God took care of His children in ways strange and wonderful, she knew, and she made sure to thank Him for this help to the poor and sick.

Grace—she had felt, too, that God had somehow chosen this name for her—worked at a commercial job until
she was twenty-three. She had seldom thought of marriage
and though she often wondered what went on in parked
automobiles at the lakefront or in the night-darkened park
in back of the Art Museum or behind any drawn curtain in
any street, these thoughts became too alive and bitter inside
of her and she put them away from her eyes as the tempta-
tions of an anti-Christ. Consequently, her relations with men
were meager and never adequately normal. Her own pas-
sions strained and, afraid to satisfy them, she looked upon
all human relationships outside of marriage as immoral. She
met Gordon Thomas just before she turned away from life
entirely. He offered her the sanctity of the wedding ring and
at the same time left her free to her prayers and moralities
and she accepted.

Gordon was twenty-five, an English teacher in a high
school, and also had come from a religious family. But unlike
his wife, he would say he was determined "to live and let
live." He went to church, but only when there was nothing else to do. He prayed, but it was out of duty rather than
devotion. He wished only to live a happy, peaceful, settled
and, for the most part, uneventful life.

When they married they honeymooned for two weeks at
Niagara Falls and then returned home to Cleveland, Gordon
to teach and Grace to become a housewife. She devoted less
time, but no fewer prayers, to the unfortunates she had been
helping for the five years past. They decided to have a child
immediately. But they didn't. It was three months before
Grace permitted herself to consummate intercourse with her
husband. And then she prayed twice as hard for God to forgive her for her transgression. The extent of her psychological
fear upon her physical desire was enough to prevent her from
conceiving the child she wanted. Even during the years that

she prayed for God to permit her, through His will alone, to conceive, she prayed at the same time for Him to forgive the immoralities that were, to her, somehow inherent in the very act of conceiving.

Gordon tried to understand, but with each year the understanding became more difficult until, finally, he found more pleasure in staying late after his teaching hours to visit a bar or a house of prostitution than going home to Rockwood. He lived and let live.

Then the son was born, a fair, light, beautiful little boy, someone for Grace to take care of and someone to take care of her. It was God's will to make the child her life. She named him John, after the Saint. She read and reread the words of Jesus from the cross: "Woman, behold thy son!"; and to the disciple: "Behold thy mother!" Her only regret was that her name wasn't Mary.

It was in this environment that John grew. He saw little of his father, the latter having made his own mold for the remaining years of life, and home was not included in the pattern. His mother molded him. He could remember his early years crowded with church and more church. And as he grew it grew with him, coming into his home. He prayed and read the Bible, over and over again. He felt at times that he must have learned the Saint James version by heart. It was a fascinating world, the world of religion. He read unceasingly, books by and about men of the cloth. But it became to him a world without variety, it became a boring one, and he began to resent being told that it was the only one and the right one. He wanted to begin thinking for himself.

Shortly after his sixth birthday there occurred one of the seemingly unimportant but nevertheless vivid incidents that a child remembers. It was one that John still felt. He had begun the first grade of elementary school and he was lost and frightened in this new world of strange boys and girls.

His mother had taken him to school in the morning. He worried all the morning and then, after lunch, all afternoon about what would happen when the school day was over. He cried gratefully when he found his mother outside the classroom waiting for him. She had waited by the school all day. It was an important moment, to run to the protection of this deity, so secure against the rest of the world of human beings. She did this for a week and then he began to find adjustment. He even started to make friends with some of the other children. He particularly admired two boys in the back of the room (he could not remember their names now) who always talked instead of listening to the teacher and were constantly being reprimanded. Somehow, although he knew they were doing wrong, he liked them and envied them.

Another incident, one which in an unclear fashion coupled that of the first day of school, repeated itself to him. It was sometime during that first semester. A group of other boys had asked him to stay in the school yard and play ball with them. He was aware that his mother expected him home immediately after school, but the thought of finding a freedom among these first friends was more important. He played with them. He couldn't remember for how long, but he knew that the skies had begun to gray when suddenly his mother appeared. Before anything else, she slapped him, quickly, twice across the face, and angrily pulled him after her. The slaps didn't hurt as much as the laughter of the other children that seemed to follow him all the way home. He got a spanking and a lecture that day. And he diligently went back to his prayers and to his mother's words from the Bible. The rest of that year found his mother waiting for him after school every day; and not only that year, but through the second and third grades as well. When he learned to read, he began to read the Bible himself. His mother smiled and he was thankful for that small favor.

More often than not he would go to his second floor bedroom, lay across the bed, and only pretend to read. He would
think of the children playing in the school yard and would
stand by his window overlooking the street and watch them
pass by. He cried and then cried some more, not out of self
pity, but out of his own guilt and temptation away from what
he knew was the greater duty. His mother had said so.

He began to find little games to play with himself.
Bouncing a rubber ball against the head board of his bed
and catching it on the fly, much as the children did against
the curbstones outside. Flipping the picture cards he saved
from the bubble gum packages and matching them against
himself, like the big boys on the corner matched pennies
and nickels. Sometimes he would simply sit by the window
watching the people who passed on the sidewalk below,
making up a story about each, imagining who they were,
where they had been, where they were going. After a while
he didn't have to see people for these dreams, but lying across
his bed, his eyes open, go to far off places and strange lands
that did not exist even in his Bible. He did not want them
to exist any place else. They were his own personal lands.
They were unreal and that was important. Reality, for the
child, is always controlled, and only in his imagination was
he completely free. Adventure novels and magazines that he
bought at second-hand bookstores for nickels and dimes and
managed to sneak into his room became a part of his life. The
guilt of wrongdoing was always present when he read them,
but, like an opiate, their necessity overbalanced any other
consideration. He read incessantly.

But his make-believe life suddenly stopped shortly after
his tenth birthday. He came home from school one day, ran
hurriedly up to his room. He found his mother there, crying.
On the bed were all his books, gathered from the corner of
the closet, the bottom of his bureau drawer. He wanted to fall

at his mother's knees and repent for his great sin; and repenting he would try to find some way to get his books back.

"Is this what you do to me?" his mother demanded of him. "I bring you up righteous and good and this is how you repay God?" She pointed to a picture in a detective magazine showing a woman lying on a bed dressed only in a nightgown, this torn fully across one shoulder, a man standing above her with a gun in his hand. "This horrible, evil thing you look at and read," his mother cried at him. "My boy reads the Devil's works."

He wanted to cry, but he was too confused. He didn't understand. He had seen nothing bad in the stories or the pictures. Now, having been labeled, they seemed exciting. He feared them and respected them at the same time. He remembered his mother carrying the armload of books down to the furnace and making him stand and watch as she burned them. He tried hard not to hate her.

When he was thirteen he went to a party, for the first time alone. One of the girls in his class, the daughter of a friend and neighbor, had a birthday and his mother had felt he should go; this was the only reason he went. Otherwise, he would have been too frightened to do so. The house was on the same block as his, only was larger, with a full backyard with trees and several small benches. He was a good looking boy, not awkward at thirteen, but slim and fairly tall for his age. He had already parted a wave into his brown hair and his face was full and gentle, attractive to girls of equal years.

He sat alone during the party, trying to feel the empathy of the young dancers and at the same time trying to appear in deep thought about something important, too important to be disturbed by something as inconsequential as dancing. He wished he had the courage to join the others. The hostess, a freckled red-haired girl whom he remembered as Nancy, came up to him.

"Do you want to dance with me?"

He wanted to say yes. He said "no." He felt nervous inside and afraid. She was a girl. He felt there was an immorality in his excitement.

"Then how about a walk in the garden?" She was being friendly. She had watched him sitting alone and wanted to be nice to him. He hesitated, wanting to be polite in his refusal.

"Come on," Nancy insisted, smiling. "Just for a minute."

"Okay, for a minute."

They walked around the flower beds, stopped by one of the little benches. Nancy sat down. "It's tiring," she suggested. She pointed to the bench, motioning to him to join her. It was peaceful. He did.

"Don't you like the party?" she asked.

"I do—very much."

"But you're not dancing."

"I don't feel like it," he answered. "Just today," he added hastily.

She reached over abruptly, smiling broadly, and took his hand. He pulled away.

"I'd rather not." He started to get up.

She grabbed at his hand again, caught it, held it tight. "Oh, don't be a scaredy-cat," she told him. She pulled him back. He sat down, his heart pounding. He began to feel tense inside, not the usual fear of shyness that he knew, but something like the excitement of the pictures in the detective magazines. He didn't want to think about them. Nancy moved closer to him on the bench, then leaned over. John's stomach began to pound and he felt sick.

"You can kiss me if you want to," she said. She put her face in front of him and offered her lips. He looked at her for a moment and felt his body strain toward her and then suddenly it was all evil and he wanted to run to the bathroom and throw up. He pulled away and jumped up and ran from

the garden, through the back yard, onto the front sidewalk
and to his own house. He slammed the door of his bedroom
behind him and threw himself on his bed and cried. He cried,
on and off, all night. He tried not to think why. In simple
terms, he had committed a sin. Kissing, his mother had often
told him, was something good little boys didn't do. This
much he understood. In terms of memory it was even clearer.
When he was very small, almost beyond remembrance, his
father had kissed his mother and attempted to embrace her
in his presence. His mother had scolded and raged and a terrible verbal fight followed. The whole scene lived with him
as something ugly. This he related to his own experience with
Nancy.

But he felt something deeper, the confusion of which was
too great for his understanding. The girl was the woman, and
the woman was his mother. He had wanted to kiss Nancy. He
had felt it. But not in the way he kissed his mother. He never
wanted to kiss his mother. It was more a having to. It hurt
him deep inside. It was his own picture on the cover of the
detective magazine and Nancy was the girl in the torn neg-
ligee and the girl was his mother, and he ran from his own
feigned reality. He never told his mother about the incident.

He grew further away from the other children after
that and closer to his mother. She protected him. And the
closer their relationship became, the more unsatisfied he
was. It choked him, and yet he could find no other course.
He searched for a sanctity unto himself and after a few years
found it. He began to write.

A kind of self-satisfied freedom poured itself out into little pieces of prose. They were mostly adventures, improbable
and unimportant, of imaginary places and unreal personalities. The writing became part of him, as much as his reading
had been before and as much as his struggle with religion
before that. He had managed to put religion away from his

thinking, consciously avoiding it when he wrote and only talking about it politely with his mother when she spoke about it. He wrote without purpose. As yet, his creativity was only an escape.

In high school he was faced with the dichotomy of the will to independence and the inability to cope with it. His mother's control had lessened and though, intellectually, this pleased him, emotionally he blamed himself for growing older. He was not sufficient unto himself. He feared others and avoided the normal contact of high school life. No parties, no extra-curricular activities, no friends. There were only a few acquaintances. By the time he was seventeen he began to think about his inner self, seeking an understanding for his unhappiness. He was a bright young man, with good grades and the ability to reason. But his reasoning inevitably led him to blame his mother, and rather than allow himself to pass through a period of hate-into-understanding, he divorced himself from logic and put his thoughts into semi-fictitious writing. The writing allowed him more freedom and he delighted in introspection about sex. Deliberation tended toward objectivity and much of his seventeenth year was spent in avid descriptions of sex and ideas about sex, the exciting becoming lurid and, in turn, tending toward perversion. He had never gone out with a girl and since Nancy's party in his thirteenth year he feared and envied their strangeness and forbidden stimulus. The unsatisfied yearning for female relationship gave way to a purposeful condemnation of such relationship. Since he could not have it, he refused to acknowledge it.

Just before he was ready to graduate, he was invited by three acquaintances, boys with whom he spoke more than with any of the others, to join them in a pre-graduation party. "We'll make a big blowout," they put it. He didn't question whether their motive was pity or interest, but he felt that he wanted to go. He made up his mind he would, then consulted his mother. Surprisingly, she agreed.

"You're old enough to take care of yourself," she said. "You know the Will of God." Even as she spoke he was conscious that God had long since been too unkind a subject to him and had ceased to be in his loyalties. "Just remember to be faithful to Him and to me."

There were four of them, a week before graduation, in the new shiny red convertible of Willy Lewis. Willy was a big, hefty young man of nineteen who was a star football player on the high school team and whose father was one of Cleveland's leading contractors. The car was a graduation present. Willy was an insistent boy and what he couldn't get through his father he generally got through his own strength. Harold Bonner sat in front with Willy, the physical opposite of the latter. He was a small, dark-complected boy, making his thinness seem shadowy. He adored Willy and in turn Willy accepted him as an ego-satellite, taking him with him wherever he went. Harold was not a stupid boy; he knew full well that this closeness was solely an identification with the athletic and physical prowess that he would never have. He understood his predicament and then his need and this was his solution. It was Harold who had convinced Willy that John should be invited on their spree. When Willy was not around, Harold stood forth intellectually, in his classes and as the expert in resolving bull sessions. He wrote a great deal and had often discussed books and authors with John. John regarded him as an equal on his own plane.

The fourth member of the party was Guy Gabriel, a tall, thin boy with a large nose and a receding jaw. He was awkward in his height and his nose was the subject of teenager's jokes about Gabriel blowing his horn. His homeliness persecuted him until he found he could fight back with even a sharper wit and he became known as the class humorist, constantly striving for a joke, tending toward biting, sarcastic humor—anything that would get him a laugh. Willy liked him. Willy liked a diverse retinue about him. He even seemed to like John's close-mouthed shyness. It made him feel more superior.

They drove from Rockwood through Cleveland, along the drive next to Lake Erie. They drove south, on route 6 toward Cincinnati.

"Where shall we go on this wing-ding?" Willy's voice boomed into the back of the car to John and Guy. Guy suggested Lorain, a steel mill town about twenty miles south of Cleveland. "I know a place where the bartender can really mix the drinks and the waitress can shake them like nobody's business when she brings them to the table . . . and I don't mean the drinks." He laughed hoarsely, the others snickering with him. John joined in politely. Suddenly, John felt uncomfortable. He opened the car window and the cool breeze freshened his face and neck. He laughed a little easier and decided to make the best of it.

They talked about their respective futures after graduation. Willy was going into his father's business. Guy didn't know and, he insisted, he didn't "give a damn." Harold wanted to go to college. He didn't know which one, but he hoped to get a scholarship to a good one in the East and study psychology or philosophy. They got around to John.

"You going to college, Johnny?" Harold was interested.

"Hope so. I applied for one out in Iowa. A little school called Des Moines College."

"What the hell do you want to go all the way out there for?" Willy asked.

"Sure," Guy added. "Where's your patriotism to your good old home state?"

"I feel like getting away, that's all. Someplace new."

"Well, you always were a loner, anyway," Willy concluded. He really didn't care.

"Besides, they have a good writing program there. And I want to write." John felt he had to add a fuller explanation.

"I wish I was sure of someplace good," Harold added, sadly. "But my folks just don't have enough dough, so I've got to cross my fingers for a scholarship."

"You just stick with Willy, Harold old boy," Guy suggested meaningfully, "and you'll be wearing diamonds."

They all laughed and promptly forgot about the future. They placed it somewhere far back of girls and drinks and athletics and finally drove down the large, clean, two-lane highway, turned off onto a gravel road and stopped in front of the cottage-like roadhouse, green-shingled, wooden, with a small porch at the entrance. A row of windows draped in multi-painted designs faced them as they parked the car. On the second floor a parallel set of windows with contrasting dark shades tightly drawn let through occasional cracks of light around the edges. Inside the roadhouse was, first, a bar, then, under an archway around a long dance floor, closely packed small square tables. At the far end four tired and not very good musicians played disinterestedly for those who might have been in any way interested. The light-colored wood floor and ceiling enveloped the few couples who were dancing. John and the others sat at a table, unhappy by the lack of people. Guy seemed to feel personally responsible. The bartender hastened to explain: "Don't worry, fellas, it's always quiet around this time. In another hour or so there'll be plenty of girls coming in." That satisfied them and they ordered drinks. John hesitated, then compromised on bourbon and ginger ale. Willy explained, authoritatively, that it was mild and sweet, almost like a coke. The waitress served the drinks and John noticed grudgingly that she was, especially when she bent over to place the glasses on the table,

well-deserving of Guy's description. The drink, the first that
John could honestly remember having, tasted bitter-sweet;
then, as he sipped more of it, warm and gradually better tasting. It satisfied him, seeming to dispel some of the
tenseness and reluctance he felt. He felt a little guilty, but
the guilt disappeared into the heat of his stomach. The other
boys made jokes with the waitress and after another drink
the lightness sifted to John's head and he joined them. The
others were surprised, then interested, as he began to take up
the bulk of the conversation. It was a strange feeling to John
because, though he knew what he was saying, it was as if the
words were coming from someone else. He talked about the
stories he had written and carefully recited some of his pas-
sages on sex. They laughed and they encouraged him and the
more he talked the more he drank and the more he held the
center stage. He felt that suddenly they were all dependent
upon him.

A party of four girls entered and with clear deliberateness sat at the table next to theirs. John stopped talking,
momentarily angry at the interruption. He said as much. The
others laughed. "All right, so why be anti-social?" John stood
up, steadied himself against the table, and stepped over to
introduce himself to the girls. His inhibitions were gone and
in a few moments the two tables had been pushed together
and the eight people were sitting side by side. John wasn't
particularly interested in making friends with the girls, but
he decided they were, after all, a necessary part of the evening
that he had already used to such good advantage. He found
himself next to a tall brunette with short-cropped hair, a
sharp chin and nose, and an unsubtly lifted bosom. Her name
was Anne. She told him her last name but he quickly forgot
it. She was eighteen, she said. She was a husky girl and as
his chair pressed closer to hers and their elbows and knees
touched, he felt a sudden flush of desire. He didn't reject it.

The other three had divorced themselves from the group
and each of his friends quickly had an arm around "their
girl." There was little conversation. Every so often a giggle
from Guy or the girl he was with caught John's attention and
he felt unconsciously angry about both it and his observation
of Guy's hands continually moving, darting up and down
above and beneath the table. Harold had a small girl, a rather
stringy thing, John thought, who was not at all disturbed by
Harold's frantic attempts to pull her closer to him with each
word. Willy sat still and calm, giant-like next to the thin
little blonde who almost disappeared every time he put down
his glass to put an arm around her. Somehow appropriate,
John thought.

Anne told about herself quickly, giving him her pertinent facts in a practiced routine. She was a clerk in a mill
office, had left high school in her second year and, with much
emphasis, stated that she liked to have fun. John agreed. "I
like to have fun, too," he said aimlessly.

She nodded at his liquor glass. "I can see you're loaded
for fun."

He felt it necessary to apologize. "I never drink," he said.
She laughed.

"The first time," he added. He needed approval, though
he didn't know why. "I'm not a drunkard," he insisted.

She laughed again. "I don't care," she said blandly.

"Oh." John kept looking at her, at her knees, across her
bosom, up to her lips. She continued to laugh, delighted. He
could no longer distinguish between fact and feeling, and
feeling became most important. He didn't even mind her
unfocused laughing.

Willy whispered something in the blonde's ear, then
stood up. "C'mon," he ordered them, "we're going." Willy
paid the bill and they followed him out to the car. They all
somehow squeezed in and John felt himself pushed against

the back armrest, Anne on his lap. His hands suddenly seemed grotesque, held aimlessly at his sides.

"It's the fourth house, the white one, near the lake, right past the traffic light," the blonde with Willy said. The car pulled into the driveway and they walked down a stone path, across a lawn and to the back yard of the house.

"Who wants to stay here?" Willy asked. No one was interested enough in words to answer. "All right," Willy ordered, as though he were calling signals for a football play. "John and Guy take the house, Harold, you take the porch." He pulled the blonde after him. "C'mon, baby, you can show me the lake."

". . . and other things," Guy remembered to call after him. Guy walked into the house with his girl. John felt Anne pull at his arm, lead him to the doorway.

"It's all right," she said. "There's nobody home." He followed her. They stopped in the living room. John stared without purpose at Guy and his girl on the couch. Anne pulled his arm again. "Upstairs," she pointed.

"Where are we going?" Actually, he didn't care. His main concern, and even this wasn't important to him, was his difficulty in walking straight.

"Upstairs."

"What for?"

"Boy, are you stewed," she said.

He followed her up the one flight of stairs, holding onto the banister and taking one step at a time automatically. He felt light and wondered why it was so difficult, therefore, to negotiate a few steps.

"C'mon, lover boy," Anne said loudly, annoyed. "We ain't got all night, you know."

"Okay," he said. He wasn't sure what she was talking about, but it sounded reasonable. The entire evening began to get lost in a compact bundle in his brain and whirl into itself like a merry-go-round getting smaller and smaller. She led him into a small room, left the light off, and locked the door after them. He stood in the center of the room, rocking back and forth unsteadily.

Anne came to him, put her arms around him and pulled him close against her. He moved away, instinctively afraid, then let himself be drawn back. Anne took his hands, moved them carefully across her body. John liked it. He did it again without any help. It was like walking through a cloud, in a dense fog with nice, unreal things happening outside and inside without actually having anything to do about it himself. She pulled him over to the bed, sat him on the edge. He watched her, his eyes large, uncontrolled by him, as she began to undress. He followed the pattern of her movements as she threw one article of clothing after the other onto a small chair.

Moonlight through the window next to the bed mixed the blackness with silver greys, and then it, too, began to twist and turn like the feeling in his head. He suddenly felt the lightness become heavy. His stomach began to move up and down, and he reached out onto the bed to stop himself from falling back on it. His eyes didn't move from Anne and the longer he watched the lighter the room became. The dizziness began to clear. He rubbed his forehead with his hand and felt it wet. The room took shape and for the first time he saw clearly the girl standing in front of him, her body filling the entire view of his vision. His eyes moved down, onto her ankles, then slowly, with anticipated deliberateness, up to her knees. He began to look higher, stopped, closed his eyes, then opened them quickly onto the triangular black patch of womanhood, up to the breasts, not too straight and firm, but pleasingly large. He didn't want to see her face and looked up and down again several times, believing what he saw, but not understanding why he was seeing it. He looked up, saw her face smiling confidently.

"Now it's your turn," she said.

He stood up. "My turn?" He repeated the words, trying to understand what they meant. He faced her, his body brushing hers. Anne leaned over, began to unbuckle his belt. His body tightened. He felt the girl's hands move over him, at his waist, his hips, at his thighs. He wanted to run away and leave his body behind so that it could fall upon and lose itself into what he had seen. He tried to think and suddenly the words came from nowhere.

"Mother! God!" He pulled away, hurriedly fumbled at tightening his belt and moved toward the door. He shook with fear.

"Where are you going, lover?" Anne asked. Her voice was sweet and he wanted to stay with it. It was a nice voice. He kept thinking that it was like his mother's voice. It suddenly became ugly. He pulled at the doorknob, then pushed back the lock.

"What's the matter, lover? Don't you like it?" She moved toward him calmly, swaying her hips from side to side. "I think it's pretty nice myself." She ran her hands across her stomach, up and down her body. John stared, not moving. She reached him, put her hand on his shoulder. He twisted away, flung the door open.

"For Chrissakes, you don't think I went to all this trouble for nothing, do you!" She fairly screamed, and her voice was like his mother's when she scolded him. He shivered, wiped the tears from his eyes, took one more look at the girl and ran out the door.

He ran down the stairs, didn't even hear the frightened squeal of the girl on the couch and the curse from Guy. He stopped in the yard, found the direction and stumbled across the cobbled walk to the road. He stopped and looked back.

There was a light in the upstairs window now. He could hear
Anne's voice screaming after him: "Sonovabitch." He shut
it out of his ears; it disemboweled his insides, carrying with
it a heat and sweat and then cold. He closed his eyes tightly
and tried to shut out what he had seen. But the vision was
even clearer in the dark. He stopped, "I ought to go back,"
he said out loud. He touched his body, felt it tight and tense,
shivering, filled up, ready to go off like a loaded gun. He
looked back at the window. "I ought to go back," he repeated
to himself.

He steadied himself against the white picket fence, felt
his stomach double up and tried to stop it. It gagged him.
He leaned over, coughing, and vomited onto the dewy fresh
grass. He became more frightened and then the fear became
guilt. He stopped, coughed, and tried to steady his head with
his hand as he vomited again. He coughed some more, leaned
over and choked on nothing.

The cool air blowing in from the lake breathed into him
and he felt a little better. He took out his pocket handkerchief, wiped his forehead, cleaned his face, wiped a wet spot
from his pants leg. He stepped onto the highway, found a
lamppost, examined himself, and brushed the handkerchief
across his spattered shoes. He wadded up the handkerchief,
threw it back of a green hedge of one of the houses lining the
road.

He looked back at the house. The light in the upstairs
window had disappeared. He turned and walked to the corner
for the bus back to Cleveland.

He didn't speak to the three others when he saw them
again in school. He avoided them. He wasn't sure why. The
night had become a blur and the girl only some distasteful imaginary memory. He didn't deny what had happened:
He denied only its reality in relation to his own life. The
boy-girl, male-female normality of existence had come to

him quickly and just as quickly had been rejected. It was unwanted.

He was glad when he graduated the next week. He could forget this and, in fact, everything that had come before, and welcomed the trip to Des Moines in the fall. He could plan an entirely new existence.

His father had patted him on the shoulder when he left Cleveland in the fall. "It'll be good for you," his father said, "getting away from home for a while." His father looked at his mother, swallowed at his own boldness. "For a little while, anyway." He swallowed apologetically again, then walked hurriedly into another room. His mother cried; she didn't say anything. Only this gave John any feeling of reluctance about leaving. He consoled himself with the reasoning that she didn't understand him. He wanted to dislike her more for making it so difficult for him to leave. He tried not to; she was, after all, his mother. At the train station his father was kind once more. "Don't worry about money," he said. "I'll send you enough to take care of you."

He felt even younger than his eighteen years when he arrived at Des Moines College. He felt keenly of immaturity, and his fear of people made an adjustment difficult. He made an effort, mentally, to try to find an integration here in the new environment. He understood that it was here he would develop his personality to the highest peak of its juvenile life. But not having been a fighter throughout his entire life thus far, he was content to lose himself in his own small niche of university education.

It was not an easy thing to do, for though Des Moines College was in the center of a fair-sized city with a population of some 200,000, it was nevertheless a small school. It was partly a "street-car" college, the students who lived in the city commuting from their homes each day, and partly a "campus" school, with dormitory facilities principally for out-of-state students. It was a co-ed institution with a little over 4000 students in all, with more males than females enrolled.

The campus had an entity of its own within the city, although the outside world of stores, streets, bus lines and people walking and working was separated only by the width of an iron fence. The fence enclosed the college completely, circling the entire grounds of a quarter mile wide and a half mile long, pausing only briefly at each end for two large gates. One was the front entrance, on the main commercial street, so designated because it opened onto the men's part of the campus. The back entrance, hidden away in more of a residential section, was the women's area. On either side of the huge green lawn down the center of the front entrance were two men's dormitories.

In the center of the campus, halfway down the length of the lawn, were the college's buildings of learning, set in a quadrangle facing each other: engineering, arts and sciences, education, agriculture, the library, the administrative building and the combination chapel and auditorium. A winding lane and a grey-surfaced, remarkably clean-looking automobile road ran from this point onward to the back entrance, where stood the women's dormitories, the road passing on the way trees, lawns, and well-kept floral beds. There were three dormitories for women, large and comfortable-looking. The architecture of the college buildings on the whole was as diverse as the intentions of the people who had originally given the specific monies to build them, each donor apparently having decided the mode, style, and determination for their particular structure. What resulted was a conglomeration of inconsistency. On many of the older buildings ivy had begun to swallow up the hideousness of design. It was fortunate, as one of the art teachers pointed out in a commencement day speech, much to the discomfort of many of the faculty, that nature invariably takes a hand to cover up humanity's artistic mistakes.

John liked the college. It was big enough to offer a variety of academic programs and a variety of people one could meet or not meet, as one wished. It was small enough not to devour him or shut out his own potential in the hurry-up competition of self-anointed potential geniuses and captains of industry. He made a few friends, none close, and casually exchanged ideas about writing and school in general with the classmates he infrequently met at "Carl's," the soda shop just off the campus. He had no girl friends. Occasionally, he felt an attraction toward one or another, but he also felt a potential ugliness in any relationship, deterring him from thinking seriously about it. At first he had intended to room in one of the dormitories, but the idea of being close and confidant with so many people frightened him and he found a small, single room in a rooming house several blocks from the campus. He ate at a variety of the small restaurants in the vicinity that catered to the college trade.

His first year was spent in study. He had some desire to join the literary club, but felt a lack of confidence and concentrated instead on his textbooks. His first year grades were, consequently, good, and for his sophomore year he tentatively planned to force himself to enter some phase of extra-curricular activity. The concentration on school work had consumed his loneliness to some degree, but not sufficiently to make him think that he was not unhappy without some sort of people relationship.

The three months spent in Cleveland during the first summer recess convinced him. He had returned home feeling mature in himself and pleased with his academic accomplishments and somehow expected to find conditions in Cleveland changed as well. They weren't. After a first day of fond greeting, his parents made it clear that everything was the same. He spent the three months almost entirely in his room, reading and writing. Occasionally he went to a movie. He saw his father rarely. The latter had his usual full schedule of bowling parties, poker games and other away-from-home-amusements. John rarely spoke with his mother. She tried desperately to get him back to the dependency she had once nurtured, but rather than enter into verbal fights John politely and tactfully remained silent. He felt that he succeeded, finally, in pulling away from the apron strings without too much of a feeling of guilt. His mother became a part of his life to be put into a sealed box and away on an upper shelf. He let it pass.

He was more than glad to return to Des Moines in the fall. He joined the literary club and spent more time in writing than on his school work. But his grades remained good. The club advisor liked his work. The advisor gave him some advice. Talent alone isn't enough, he was told. "Find a philosophy of life first. A writer must have a point of departure for his work. You are living in a world and breathing of that world and until you find your own basis of security and your understanding of that world there will be no point to your writing. You cannot escape from life. Until you understand it fully, your writing will be no more than unrelated and unimportant particles of thinking."

John thought about the advice and he knew it was true for him. He had been so long within himself that his writing was all introspective. All his characters were one shade, all his thinking was one level. Most important to him was the idea of inner security. This, he knew, he lacked. And try as he might, he could not find it. Not in the present world. His only security was the night, his head deep into his pillow, buried into the protection of his bed. The more he examined his writing, the thinner it became, and he became disturbed over his mental loneliness as much so as his emotional one.

He began to dream of his mother and woke several times empty and sick in his stomach. She offered herself as the womb of security and he was torn between the growing need and the lack of an alternative. He and his talent needed a satisfaction. It was in the fall of his sophomore year, in these circumstances, that he met Tony.

Tony had just broken through the peak of physical energy. It was one full year since the New York pianist had visited Des Moines and after the suddenly new existence had just as quickly become a void he had buried himself in his musical compositions, writing endlessly for the college musical shows. During the summer just past he had virtually lived in his living room at home in Belleville, alternating between the dresser with the drawer full of whiskey bottles and the piano. Now the music was completed and he was enervated. The semester began and it seemed slow and drawn out. The music itself even lost its raison d'être. He thought more and more about the pianist and his loneliness became acute. He knew what to do about it; but it meant a positive action on his part and he was afraid. These were his circumstances when he met John.

John had gone one afternoon to the drama office. He thought, perhaps, he might try to learn more about people by writing about them dramatically. He had heard that the drama club was looking for sketches for the college musical to be presented in the spring. A tall, thin girl in jeans and a man's white shirt greeted him in the office. She sat deep into a chair, dangling one leg over its arm, a long cigarette in her hand. He felt immediately intimidated, then a little less fearful when he thought about what his psychology teacher might say of this girl's own fears and her obvious forced extroversion.

"So you're a writer," she commented after he told her what he wanted. She said it almost too casually, as if in the presence of an actor a writer was abjectly unimportant and required little more effort than the flick of a pencil to create a Pulitzer Prize play. "We can use a couple of sketches and some lyrics for the musical. Got any?"

"I've sort of fooled around with song poems." He was embarrassed. "And I've been working on a play scenario. Only it's not much good."

"Are you a freshman?"

He didn't understand. "What do you mean?"

"You seem so damned scared. Here." She opened a cigarette case, gave him a cigarette, lit it for him off the tip of hers.

He sat down in the chair next to her, felt better. "I'm a sophomore. I haven't been around here before. It's strange, that's all."

"Nothing to be afraid of," the girl said. "I'm only a sophomore, too." She looked at him closely, studied his face, fair skin, small eyes and mouth, the soft brown hair with the deep wave in front. Not short, but not too tall; thin, but still well built in this, his nineteenth year. He was dressed well. Light brown slacks, an open collar shirt, dark green sports jacket.

"You're a good looking boy," the girl said. "You don't do any acting, do you?"

John was embarrassed again. "What about writing?"

She smiled. "Okay, here." She scribbled an address on a piece of paper. "This is where Tony Jordan lives. You know him?"

"He did the music for last year's show?"

"Right. Go see him. If he likes your stuff you can work with him."

John took the paper. "Okay." He started to leave. "What about the play scenario?"

"Why don't you show it to Professor Waters? He's the head of the department. If he likes it, maybe you can make it into a musical comedy book."

"Okay." He started out the door.

"Hey."

"Yeah?"

"What did you say your name was?"

"John Thomas." He closed the door carefully behind him. He went to his room, took a number of his song poems, decided to take the play scenario, too, and hurried toward the address on the paper. It was on the opposite side of the campus, near "Carl's", a two-story house on Academy Street. An old woman wearing a housedress seemingly as old as she, a bent cigarette hanging from her lips, answered the doorbell. She was partially deaf and John had to ask her twice about Tony Jordan before she led him down the narrow hallway to a side door.

"That's it," she told him, flipped the ashes from her cigarette onto the floor and left him standing there. He knocked.

The first picture he saw of Tony was a lean, tall young man of twenty years without a smile, his thin face sucked in as though he had been greatly disturbed. He brushed back a lock of black hair from his forehead. It shone under the glare of the hall light bulb. He wore a tight-fitting white polo shirt left hanging over a pair of slacks.

"Yeah?"

"My name's John Thomas. The drama department said to see you with some lyrics. Said we might be able to work together on the musical." He said it as quickly as he could. He waited nervously as Tony slowly looked him over. It was a supercilious look. John objected to the other's apparent attitude of superiority and had just about decided that he didn't care to work with him, after all, when he was invited inside.

The room was a small one, a single, narrow window at the other end through which John could see clotheslines stretched across two poles in the back yard. In front of the window, against the wall on the right, was a small upright

piano where it could get the maximum light from the outside. Opposite, only closer to the door, against the left wall,
was a studio couch, the kind that opened into a bed with
a mattress. A small table stood next to it and on the table
a small clock-radio. Across, down from the piano, a single
bookcase filled mostly with textbooks. A door at the right
was open, showing a small kitchen with a refrigerator, stove
and a table with two chairs. That was all.

Tony noticed John looking over the apartment. "The
bathroom is in the hall," he volunteered. He laughed. It
broke the uncertainty and John laughed with him.

"Pretty nice place," John offered. "I have only a single
sleeping room." Tony asked him to sit down, went into the
kitchen.

"Bourbon and water okay?" he called. John hesitated,
remembering the last time he had a drink. "Okay," he said.

Tony brought him a glass. "Hope it isn't too strong."

"I don't drink too often," John suggested. He tasted it. It
seemed fine.

"I always keep a bottle around," Tony said. "It gets lonely
sometimes and drinking eases it off. This is a pretty lonely
college," he confided.

John agreed. He was pleased there was already a common
ground between them. For the first time since he had come
to Des Moines he had been able to meet a new person and
almost immediately relax.

"What was your name again?" Tony questioned.

"John Thomas."

"Good to know you, Johnny." They shook hands. It was
a warm handclasp. Tony appeared to be pleased. John seemed
to have brought into the room, with his shy manner, a gentle brightness that broke up the eternal grayish light that
crowded the room from the one window.

They clicked glasses and drank. Then, together, they both laughed. Neither knew exactly why. It was one of those intangible moments when two people suddenly feel an unaccountable happiness or closeness between them and feel the need to express it. Sometimes in laughter. Sometimes in tears. Sometimes in silence. They laughed.

John explained fully why he was there. Tony offered a toast. "To our partnership," he said. "And I haven't even seen your lyrics yet." After a moment he asked more seriously, "Are they any good?"

"I have them right here." John paused. "I don't know. Nobody's ever seen them before."

"There's always a first time," Tony said. "Here." He gave John his glass to hold, walked with the potential lyrics to the piano. John followed, eagerly stood behind him as Tony began to try various melodies on the keyboard. Tony sang the words softly, playing a tune. He continued the music, adding a bass, playing as though he were giving a popular recital.

"That's wonderful." John was overwhelmed. "They sound wonderful. Just like I hear them in my own mind. You make them really sound like something."

Tony swiveled on the piano stool, took his drink, sipped it and gave it back to John. "This could be a good song," he said. He looked at the other song-poems. "In fact, there are a number of good possibilities here."

John beamed, felt a profound gratefulness. Tony's words had given him a confidence he needed and, hearing the words he had written melt into the music, a belonging. As Tony continued playing, John felt shivers begin inside and then a gracefulness as if he were walking on air. The more Tony played, the happier John was that he had come. He studied Tony's movements, stood ready with the glass of whiskey to offer it whenever it was wanted. He wanted to find some way to thank Tony for the good feeling he had found there. Tony finished trying out the lyrics and eagerly looked through the play idea. John watched him closely, trying to determine by his face whether he was pleased. He was.

"There's some really good stuff here, Johnny," Tony said, finally. "This scenario, too." He took the glass from John, finished it, put it on the floor. He wrote some notes on a blank sheet of paper. "I want to jot down some of the melodies before I forget them," he explained. "First inspiration is sometimes the best."

"The music sounds terrific," John offered.

"Then you're satisfied with your composer?"

"Am I!" Then, after a moment, "We are going to work together, Tony?"

Tony sat on the couch. John followed him. "It's going to be a lot of work, but I think we can turn out a good show." Tony leaned back, John copying his example. It was relaxing. He found a cushion at the side, snuggled his shoulder against it. He felt well protected.

"I gather you're a writer by profession," Tony suggested. He was well pleased with John. From this new person had come the impetus once more for his music and he felt, not fully conscious of it yet, that here was the fulfillment of his need for companionship, too. John's shyness was welcome, Tony thought. His own determination was strong enough, he told himself, to reach out and hold him.

"I don't particularly care to write musical comedies," John answered.

Tony was surprised, but interested.

"I want to write good stuff," John continued. He apologized. "Not that musical comedies aren't good. I'm referring to novels and the like."

Tony smiled. "Someday maybe the great American novel?"

John felt he should be embarrassed. He wasn't. "Maybe," he said.

Tony felt a tightening growing inside. He began to feel the need of a release from the sudden energy that had come without expectation and was now threatening to leave him. He wasn't angry. It was the need that had kept him tense and melancholy before and at the same time served as the nervous energy that gave him life, that served as a drug to ease him and also drive him forward at the same time. He was glad John had come.

"Do you have many friends around campus, Johnny?" He made it sound casual.

"Not many. I haven't met anybody that I really liked well enough." John tried to emulate Tony's casualness. "I was always pretty lonely as a kid and I never did have many friends. I don't make them easily." He felt he could talk to Tony.

"Same with me," Tony said. "When I do meet people, I'm extra critical to make sure I like them."

John suddenly felt afraid. He wondered if there was a possibility that Tony didn't completely like him. He wasn't sure why it was such a great concern. In a moment, he knew. Meeting Tony had gone so well, he was afraid of anything that might send him back to his loneliness.

"I think we could be good friends," John said quickly.

Tony leaned over, patted John on the arm. "We already are, aren't we?"

John smiled in response. Tony pulled a pack of cigarettes from his pocket, offered one to John, took one himself, lit them. "I feel pretty much like you do, Johnny," he said. "I think I'm right. You like my company."

"Very much."

"You're different than most of the fellows around here." Tony thought carefully. He didn't want to run ahead of himself. "They're crude, most of them. All the time, thinking of nothing but women. Got any girlfriends?" he asked.

"I'm not particularly interested," John said truthfully.

Tony grinned. "Good. We see eye to eye."

"We ought to," John suggested, "since we're going to be working so closely together."

"Even better than that," Tony said softly. He watched John's face. There was only an affirmative nod; the words didn't have any special meaning for him. Tony was disappointed. He decided not to press it.

Tony stood up. "I'm a junior now," he said. "That gives us two years together."

"A good two years," John agreed.

"And a bigger and better friendship," Tony added. "There's some bourbon left in the kitchen. Shall we drink on it?"

John smiled happily. "Sure, Tony, let's drink on it."

## Chapter 6

John's own rented room, which for a year had been his sanctuary, was no longer needed. He began to spend almost all his time with Tony. They shared expenses and ate all their meals in Tony's apartment, the money saved on what would otherwise have been restaurant costs providing them with before and after dinner wines, cocktails and other liquors. Each meal became a party. John and Tony both looked forward to the late afternoons and evenings when, after classes, they would get together to work on the musical. John's script outline, with Tony's urging, had been accepted. After a few weeks, what started primarily as collaboration for creative work become secondary. They took pride in each individual meal and tried to surprise each other with a different kind of wine or cocktail or appetizer every day. Even so, they saved over their otherwise separate expenses and found pleasure in watching the sum mount week by week.

The apartment began to grow. John first brought his books and, after they piled onto the piano, Tony bought a small unpainted bookcase for them. Soon, some of John's clothes, too, found their way into Tony's closet. John's room gradually emptied and after a while he used it only to sleep in and wash in. He had a key to the Academy Street apartment now and every afternoon would hurry there, anxious for the evening. On the three days a week that Tony had late classes, John would sit at the kitchen table with his typewriter and try to write, waiting for Tony to arrive. Invariably, he found himself walking aimlessly back and forth across the front room. He couldn't work by himself. The collaboration had given him such complete security that anything less in any circumstance proved insufficient. He was happier than he had ever been. Sometimes a mood caught him and returned him to the old fears and lack of confidence and made him wonder at the validity of his happiness. But, always, Tony caught him and held him in proper balance. There was no doubt in his mind that Tony was emotionally stronger than himself. He was glad of it. It gave him the dependency he needed.

The collaboration went well. They rarely worked much after midnight. John had an eight o'clock class each morning and he reluctantly trudged each night the half-mile from Academy Street to his own room. By early December, three months after they had begun work on it, the show was almost completed. Tony took it one Friday afternoon to the drama office for approval. John waited in the apartment. He was too nervous to go, he insisted. He worried about what would happen, not particularly about the musical itself, but about his relationship with Tony. Now that their work was almost over, there was no overt reason for him to be so consistently in the apartment. He had no doubt that the deep and close friendship that had become theirs would continue. But he was anxious, nevertheless. He searched even the remotest possible reasons for a breakup in order to refute them.

At six o'clock John heard Tony's key in the door. He straightened his shirt, combed back his hair, pressing the wave in front with his forefinger. He didn't know precisely why, but he felt he must look his best. Tony came in, his hands concealing something behind him. He looked tired and grim. John asked the obvious question, "Did they like it?"

"You didn't think they would, did you?" Tony smiled, tried to shake back the black lock of hair that perpetually hung over his forehead.

"You don't look too happy," John said. Tony didn't move. Finally, he pushed forward a package he held in his hands.

"Here. I was waiting for you to ask, so I'll just give it to you."

John took the package. "For me?"

"A present. To celebrate."

"They liked it!"

"Loved it! Music by Tony Jordan. Book and lyrics by John Thomas! Casting and rehearsals start tomorrow."

John rushed to Tony, hugged him in a strong embrace. Tony held John closely. They stood like that for several minutes.

Finally, John pulled slowly away. "Hey," he said without apology, "I didn't even let you get your coat off."

Tony took his coat off, hung it in the closet. "Well, open the present."

John unwrapped the paper, found a long round glass container.

"What is it?"

Tony laughed. "I spend two hours running all around this town trying to get one and you don't even know a martini mixer when you see one."

"I'm sorry." John flushed. "That calls for cocktails, doesn't it?" He brightened, waited for Tony's approval.

"It certainly does." Tony pulled his shoes off, stretched out on the couch.

"You relax," John said. "I'll make them." He went to the kitchen, took the necessary ingredients from the shelves, ice cubes from the refrigerator. "No work tonight, huh?" he called to the other room.

"Nope. Tonight we celebrate."

John brought the drinks and Tony leaned back, feeling a richness of satisfaction. As John sat beside him Tony felt wealthy, a master in his own house. There was the successful accomplishment in his art and the fulfillment of his need. He glanced at John and felt the belonging that had come into his life. Tony wondered how much longer this could go on. With the musical finished, would there be a reason for the continuance of their relationship? He didn't doubt, but like John he found an assurance in the questioning. He knew John so well and yet, he told himself, not well enough. He wanted to know him even better, as close as two human beings can become.

It was after eight when they made supper, then returned, lazily and comfortably, to the martinis. Both wanted to talk, to say out loud what they were feeling, to assure each other that there was no doubt about their friendship continuing as it had been. They fidgeted with the drinks. Tony turned on the radio, twisted the dial for music.

"Pop music and pop music and pop music," he said with exasperation.

"No classical stations in Des Moines," John suggested.

"All commercial stuff." Tony switched the radio off. He remained silent for a few moments, then sat up with a sudden thought: "We've got sixty bucks in the kitty. Let's get a music system."

This sounded good to John. He agreed.

"We can buy a cheap one and start a music collection, too." Tony was excited. John felt it, too. "Okay, Johnny-boy?" Tony asked.

He had begun using the term "Johnny-boy." At first John felt he ought to object, then accepted it. It was rather pleasant. It made him feel he was under Tony's protection.

"We could build a collection together," John said.

"Sure."

They drank on it. "I was wondering what would happen when the musical was over," John suggested timidly.

"About us?"

"Uh, huh. But building a music collection will give us something further to do."

"We really don't need to do that to keep us together, do we, Johnny?" Tony's face was stiff, then broke into a big smile.

John reached over, put his hand on Tony's arm. He wanted to squeeze hard in thanks. Instead, he held it lightly, then smiled in acknowledgement. "No, we don't." They both understood and it was settled as quickly as that.

Tony wondered if he should say anything more. He had no doubt now at all of their relationship. His only uncertainty was about how much John understood. It had become more and more difficult to see him leave each evening. Several times he had wanted to suggest that he remain for the night, but he wasn't certain how John would react and he didn't want to spoil what was. He was afraid a sudden proposal might back John away entirely. He would let it come slowly, until the precise moment arrived. John, purely emotionally, felt the same way. He hated to have to leave every night. It was like leaving the best part of his life behind. But he didn't know what else to do. The solution that was ever-conscious with Tony did not occur to him. Even if it had, he would not have mentioned it or offered it himself.

Tony almost made the suggestion that night, sometime past midnight, as John prepared to leave. They shook hands, hugged each other tightly for a moment. There was the sensation of necessity. Tony looked squarely into John's eyes, trying to see what was there. He couldn't tell. He let the chance go. "Good night, Johnny-boy."

"Good night."

Tony closed the door. The moment would come, he knew. The one time when the question and the answer would both be inevitable. He decided it would be soon.

The next morning, on a Saturday, they went together and bought a hi-fi player. It cost them less than twenty-five dollars, but it was a good one and gave them the personal satisfaction of having something material between them. They were like children in a toy shop at Christmas and carried their purchase tightly, yet gently, eager to return to the apartment and use it. They bought two albums, one for Tony, and the other John's choice. They decided Broadway musicals would be appropriate to start with. John wanted to learn more about the medium.

"Rodgers and Hammerstein," Tony said. "We've got to start with one of the masters."

"Which album?"

"*The King and I*. Okay with you?" Tony asked?

"Absolutely. And I'll go for Cole Porter," John said.

"Which album?"

"*Kiss Me Kate*?" John sought Tony's approval.

Tony laughed. "Hmmm. I'm not so sure I go for the "I Hate Men" number, but on the other hand I'm all in favor of "So In Love With You Am I.""

They walked carefully, stopping for each light, watching the cars zoom by, crossing cautiously to make sure that nothing disastrous happened to their new purchases.

"We've got about thirty bucks left," Tony said. "We ought to get a few more."

"Okay." John had an idea. "There's a fellow who lives in the room next to mine who's got a bunch of recordings he might want to sell us cheap. He's graduating this February and has been selling a lot of things. You know, the tall fellow with the close cropped hair, redhead."

"Herbert Reese?"

"That's right, I think he's an engineer or a chemist or something like that.

"It's all the same," Tony observed. "Can we get in touch with him?"

"I can call now," John said. "That is, if that beetle-eyed landlady gets him to the phone."

They stopped at a drugstore pay phone. Tony waited outside, holding their purchases, leaning against the storefront to steady himself. John came out in a few minutes.

"He's got some," he said excitedly. He took the albums and they continued walking. "He's sold most of his albums, but he's got some symphonies and even some musical comedies left. He said he'd let us have the whole batch for twenty bucks."

"Sounds like a bargain. What are the pieces?"

"I forgot to ask," John answered apologetically. Then he brightened. "But I asked him to come over to the apartment with them this evening. If we don't like them, we won't take them."

"Good enough."

They hurried to Academy Street, delighted in their new venture. The album seller, Herbert Reese, knocked on the door some time after ten o'clock. They had almost given up.

"I'm sorry," he said. "Didn't mean to be late. But I had a date and she had to be in the dorm at ten for check-in, so naturally we took advantage of all the time we had." He winked at them. "You know what I mean!"

John felt uncomfortable.

Tony winked back. "Sure. It's not too late."

They examined the albums. Herbert sat on the couch, drinking the martini John had made for him. "You can play them if you want," the redhead offered. "I don't know if you like them all or not, but rather than sell them singly, I'll give

you the works for twenty. Don't want to carry them back to
Chicago with me."

They played parts of the symphonies. Stravinsky's *Rite
of Spring* and Beethoven's *Fifth* especially pleased Tony, the
first because it was, at the moment, an icon for young people
taking their first steps into classical music, and the second
because it was considered a basic essential in all music librar-
ies. They listened to the music, talked about the college and
personalities they mutually knew.

Reese pointed to some of the albums. "Some good dance
music here," he said. "Like dance music?"

"Not particularly," Tony answered. "But they'll do." He found
a Stan Kenton album. "This one I do like," he said. He played it.

Reese listened nervously for a moment, sat back and tried
to relax. "That music's all the same," he observed. He waited
for Tony to argue about it. Tony remembered him from a
political science class. He was a brash young man, eager for
argument, sometimes his eagerness carrying him forward
even after his reason was exhausted.

"Everyone to their own taste," Tony answered agreeably.
"I like progressive jazz," he observed about the Kenton record.

"That was a present," Reese said. "I'll be glad to be rid of
it." He was ready for an animated discussion. "It sounds like
a bowl full of alphabet soup. Gives me a headache."

"I like it," Tony said simply. He would have preferred to
have made the evening strictly a business deal, paid Reese,
and then relaxed again with John. He could see that John,
too, a half-interested spectator on the piano bench, was impatient. "It carries the whirling staccato of life, that music,"
Tony said. He let the term out, though he knew the pseudo-
philosophical words meant nothing in themselves.

"Kind of mixed up life," Reese countered. "No melody.
I like to see where I'm going. It has no purpose. I don't call it
music."

"Life is mixed up," Tony insisted. "This Kenton music expresses it. We can't run away from it."

Reese warmed to the argument. "That may be," he said. "But it doesn't mean it's right. There's a standardization, a normality of life, a moving forward of people and things. If we're to be part of progress, we ought to be like that. That music isn't progressive. It's retrogressive."

"Suppose people feel like the music?" Tony made the most of the opportunity. He looked over at John. "Suppose they're caught up in this whirlpool of life? Shouldn't they take what they find and make the most of it? Make it into a musical theme and let it blend with all the other facets of life. There's nothing wrong with discord. You can enjoy it if you know why it's there. Just fit into it."

He walked over to John, stood near him. "Don't run away from what you are," Tony said. "Life is a moving mixture of discords and so are we. Be yourself, that's my idea." He looked at John again and wondered whether the latter understood the point he was making.

Reese refused to accept the thesis. He gulped the rest of the martini. "Your philosophy only makes sense if a person's abnormal. If you're part of the phonies of society, then you can fit into what you said. But the average person needs something to grow on. A clear and peaceful world, not scarred up with shell holes . . . and atom bombs." He smiled. "That's an analogy. When the world goes cockeyed, it's like that music, and stops moving forward and just whirls around in its own confusion." He sat back, satisfied with the presentation.

"Then maybe there are two worlds?" Tony suggested. "Sometimes there's the person who is all alone, in a world apart . . . " He saw John look up, interested, and he hurried on, " . . . and he has to fulfill a need and there's no reason why he shouldn't fill it with something that doesn't follow this regular pattern you talk about that rejected him. If he finds happiness and security in his own world, then he is just as normal as anybody in any other society."

Reese didn't argue. "Looking at it that way, you're right," he said. "But," he objected, "that conformity is only a passing one. The abnormal person grows up or wakes up to see the real world passing in front of him and he's ready for a psycho ward."

"Maybe?"

"No maybes about it." Reese could see that the argument was coming to an end. "And if you're right, and a person has to resort to discord, it means that there is something wrong with the world that has forced him into this abnormality, isn't there?"

Tony smiled. He knew this so well. "That's right," he agreed. "But while this world exists, then we've got to find some way of being happy or we can just as well drown ourselves."

"Why not fight it?" Reese asked.

"It's easy to say and hard to do."

Reese laughed. "Yeah. It's a hard thing to do." He was ready to leave now. "You take the progressive jazz and I'll take the twenty bucks and I'll be in Scotland afore ye."

"Right." Tony laughed with him, gave him the money. John opened the door for Reese.

"How's the musical coming?" Reese asked before leaving.

Tony nodded. "Rehearsals are starting. I think it will be a good show."

"The guys over at the house have been wondering what happened to you, John. Never see you around anymore. But we figured you've been spending a lot of time here working." Reese seemed to have difficulty putting the words together the way he wanted, as if there were something wrong in saying them. It was more than a suggestion. "You know the way kids in a small college talk about things," he added, then regretted he had.

"We've been working pretty hard on the musical," Tony said quietly.

"Good night . . . and good luck." Reese went out quickly.

John sat on the couch, Tony close next to him.

"Do you agree?" Tony asked.

"About the kids talking?"

"That's not important," Tony said. "About what I said, I mean."

"I think so. I never tried to put it into words like that." John paused a moment. "But if I did, those are probably the ones I would use."

John sat thoughtfully, trying to think out a more definitive answer. It seemed so close, on the tip of his tongue, but he was waiting for another spark. His relationship to Tony was part of this nonconformity, this other world. He did not have to apologize to himself for that. Finally, he said so to Tony. Tony agreed.

"I feel the same way, Johnny-boy. We're one of a kind there."

"Is it enough, this kind of existence?" John wondered out loud. "It seems there should be something more." He wasn't dissatisfied, he explained. He only wanted to be more satisfied.

"How more?" Tony asked slowly. He tensed, groped to reach the end of the string and pull it the right way.

"Like with us, for instance." John grasped for the right words. "There's so much between us and yet there seems to be something lacking." He quickly added, "I don't mean that there's anything wrong. There isn't."

"Of course not," Tony assured him. "You remember what I said about abnormality not being abnormal."

"Yes." The picture was fuzzy.

"If we're part of that life, then there's no reason why we shouldn't take all of it. We shouldn't be afraid of it."

John got up, walked across to the opposite side of the room, walked back again. He hesitated to admit what was beginning to seem clear. He stood in front of Tony.

"I don't know." He said it slowly again. "I'm not sure."

Tony didn't answer.

John couldn't decide it himself. "Maybe I better go?" he suggested. "It's getting late." He watched Tony and felt the attraction to him. He wanted to avoid having it come to the point of decision. He didn't know why, he just wanted to.

Tony didn't move.

"Do you want to go?" He threw the words like a ball, leaving it up to John to catch or drop. He knew that it had to be John's decision.

John searched for an answer, then asked for help. "I've never felt like this before, Tony." He didn't know what good saying that would be, but he had to say it.

"I know how you feel, Johnny." Tony ached in his control over himself. He wanted to feel the security he had found for a brief moment over a year before. It had come back to rest on his doorstep. The hunger of loneliness also rested there. He didn't want to chase the wrong one away.

"It's a long way back to your place, Johnny, and a cold night. Why don't you stay?" He said it as calmly as he could.

John trembled. His stomach pumped against his body and he hesitated in fear of the unknown. He felt that there could be no compromise. He had to make a decision. On one side was the loneliness he had known too often. On the other was the closeness and security he needed. Between them was a wall he had to climb over; he could only guess how high the wall was.

"I don't want to put you out," John offered meekly. The protest faded. The fear was swallowed and the anticipation grew stronger. He thought of the girl at the lake-front house a week before he graduated from high school and knew that this was not the same kind of thing. That had been wrong. It was an ugly thing. This, in a way he could not completely rationalize but could only feel, was right.

"The bed is big enough for two," Tony said. He could say no more. It had been his decision with the musician; now it was John's with him. He mentally cursed the society that made these decisions so difficult. There was nothing wrong, he insisted; it was the world that made it seem so.

"I feel very close to you, Tony. If I stay I . . ." John stopped. He couldn't finish. "Do you know what I'm trying to say?" he asked. It was a plea.

"It's exactly what I've been saying," Tony answered. "I don't want to force you or influence you, although I want you to stay. If you want to go, go. But if you stay, you stay. Do we understand each other?"

John nodded his head. It was clear and his whole body shook. It was very clear and he wished the decision had been made and the initial step over with.

"You have to make up your own mind," Tony said.

John stood a moment, standing face to face with his friend. The tightness inside him grew and it reached out to the other to make him a part of it. He sensed the exhilaration of the other and they held each other's look, fully and overtly. John stood rigid and then suddenly the excitement in him burst loose. It grew, reached out between them and formed a common bond. They grinned, both of them together, and then they laughed. The wall had been scaled and the decision was made.

"I'll stay, Tony," John said. "I really couldn't do anything else but stay, could I?"

# Chapter 7

The crystallization of his relationship with Tony came slowly to John. But once it arrived it was total and freed him almost completely from the restrictions of the past and gave him a new plane of movement. He was freed physically, mentally, emotionally. He not only accepted what had become inevitable, but welcomed it.

He kept his own room, primarily so that there would be no questions asked back in Cleveland about a new address. Unconsciously, it retained for him something that was solely his; the rest, including himself, had been offered all to Tony. His landlady was interested only in the rent and not in the behavior of her tenants. She paid no attention to the fact that he no longer appeared to occupy the room, or if she did, she didn't mention it.

The apartment on Academy Street was never empty and never quiet. Even when he was asleep, John felt that he was awake. The feeling of belonging and the sensation of having for the first time in his life what he wanted and needed was too good to let go of even for a second. Paradise can be many things to many people. But to each, like John, no matter what form it takes, it belongs to him or her alone. And having known what life could be without it, one holds it tightly.

John held at tightly, although not without some trace of misgiving. It was not purposive. His formative years had stamped upon him their interpretation of morality and even his happiness did not prevent the occasional conscious tap of immorality. If he had been any less emotionally and physically satisfied, it might have bothered him excessively. As it was, it invariably passed. When the thought threatened to become virile, he helped stop it by talking to Tony, and in Tony's confidence he allowed himself to be dependent and accept the other's strength as his staff.

Tony, too, filled his need and, in fact, more. Not only was there the security of person in John, but in John's dependency an egotism of strength of himself. He reveled in it. He knew that basically, all else being equal, he was in most respects stronger than John. Now this strength exceeded natural bounds and it gave him a confidence he had not known before. Sometimes he took advantage of it, although not unreasonably. He carefully avoided any threatening of the structure that had been built up over the several months and had now become concrete. But he did hold the trump card of pressure, and if John was uncommonly reluctant, if he worried too much, if he protested or cried or called for moral self-satisfaction, Tony used this power. He could threaten and John would come to him and speak softly. He could bluster and rage and John would turn into the corner of the couch and brood and then return to him and act as though there had been no disturbance at all. He could demand and John would accede, first out of fear and then out of the realization that Tony was right, even if the truth consisted only in the latter's saying it was.

There was a strain, it is true, but only of the kind that exists when two people are in a constant relationship, sharing their lives. It was infinitely calmer than most. The loneliness, most important, had gone, and each found a shelter from the insufficiency of private existence. The struggle of life remained without, and within them it disappeared. Tony played the piano now better than he had ever played it before. The music he composed lacked nothing. It was his best.

John's writing did not fare as well. His completeness did not come as quickly. While he was with Tony, there was a fullness. When Tony was not with him, he felt the lack keenly. He began to fear being left alone, and when he was the uncertainties of the situation followed him. He would emotionally run and wonder whether these small doubts were in reality furies bent on overwhelming and punishing him. When he was alone he sometimes questioned the inevitability of the relationship itself. It was extremely difficult in the first weeks after he began staying with Tony to find the adjustment. But slowly he came to understand that it was not an antidote to loneliness that drew him to Tony, but a positive fulfillment of self when with Tony.

Once, while walking down the campus, he stopped in front of the men's dormitory and watched the students in the front lounge engaging in good-natured kidding and horseplay. This was normality, he knew, and it bothered him because he did not have it. On occasion, in the evening, leaving the library, he would feel an embarrassment for the boys and girls sitting on the library steps, hidden in the night shadows of the large round pillars. On Saint Valentine's Day he stopped at the gymnasium and watched the decorations being hung for a dance. These were normal things he saw. Normalcy, supposedly, means right. His relationship with Tony, all of it, from the playing of music to sleeping close together in the same bed, felt right to him. Why, then, wasn't that also considered normalcy? Why shouldn't it be? The more he thought, the more confusing the dual standard of society became and the more he leaned upon Tony for the answers. That was the strange thing: When he was with Tony, he didn't need any more answers.

John avoided people and yet he knew that they knew. Herbert Reese knew, he was sure, by the way Reese condescendingly smiled at him whenever they crossed paths on the campus. Reese had asked once why he kept his room when he didn't use it any longer, and then grinned knowingly and never mentioned it again. He was relieved when Reese graduated in February. In an English class one morning he came in late. The professor asked where he had been and John replied that he had overslept. One of the students, a next door neighbor to the Academy Street apartment, coughed loudly and the professor cut off the hushed reaction of the room by immediately resuming the lesson. He appeared to be somewhat embarrassed himself.

One evening John and Tony stopped in one of the small bars near the campus. Tony had gone to the men's room when two couples—boys and girls—came in and one boy, a classmate, seeing John alone, suggested to the others that they invite him to their table. "He's probably with Tony," another answered. "They'll want to be left alone." It wasn't malicious, but it was obvious enough for John to wish Tony would hurry back so that they could unobtrusively leave.

When they returned to the apartment, he told Tony: "Why can't we go out any place without people looking at us as if we'd committed some sin?"

Tony was bothered not at all by any of this. He was, in fact, annoyed that it disturbed John.

"How do you mean?" he asked, trying to make it seem totally unimportant.

"Those kids at the bar this evening. Did you see them look at us when we left?"

"Forget it, Johnny. They didn't mean anything."

John protested. "As if I were some kind of freak or something. I'm not complaining about us, Tony, so don't get me wrong. It's just that the whole thing seems to put me into an entirely different world."

Tony laughed it off. "They're hypocrites. Maybe they've got suppressed desires?"

"I'm not joking," John said. "It's disturbing. I feel so good being with you because for the first time in my life I feel really free. Because of that I want to go around with my head up and my arms open."

"Well?"

"Well, I can't. We seem to be caught in our own little cubbyhole. No friends, no parties, no nothing."

Tony decided not to argue. He knew there was no point in trying to convince him with words. "Is that the trouble?" he asked simply. "Parties?"

"It's not that . . ." John started to say, then stopped. "Are you laughing at me?"

Tony smiled. "I'm not laughing. I know you're serious. I'm not going to try to tell you this isn't a different world we're in. It is."

"But it's no world. It's empty. We're alone in it."

"We're not alone in it," Tony responded. "It's not just a world of the two of us. It's a whole society. With friends and parties and all the rest of it." He stopped and thought a moment. "Seriously, Johnny-boy, do you want to go to a party? Will that help you feel better?"

John didn't want to be misunderstood. "I don't really feel bad about it," he explained. "I'm just wondering."

Tony let him wonder. He waited for John to speak again.

"A party might be interesting," John suggested slowly. "I won't feel that there are only the two of us."

Tony felt a sudden resentment, wavered for a moment, then decided not to get mad. "Is it that bad?" he asked calmly. "Just the two of us?"

"No, Tony, that's not what I mean," John hastened to assure him. "You know how I am with you. It's when you're not here that I feel alone. If you disappeared, I think the world would just as soon vanish."

Tony was assured. The dependency wasn't threatened. "Let's go to a party," he said.

"Where?"

"Over at the dorm."

John was incredulous.

Tony laughed. "Didn't you ever read the Kinsey report on sexual behavior?" He went over to their music center, picked out a soft moody piece by Liszt. "Let's go to bed," he said. "I'll see a couple of fellows in the morning and find out about a party."

They arrived at the dorm at eight the next evening. John had never been inside. They walked through the gate, up the green lawn, past the slate grey walls of the building. The fluorescent lights outlined shadowy forms inside the dormitory windows, huddled over desks with opened books and moving pencils, accented by the single yellow bulbs burning from small lamps on the desks. The front door led into a lobby, then to the lounge that John had noticed through the high wide windows that opened onto the campus. The lounge was furnished with several settees, a radio, a hi-fi, some half-filled bookcases, and tables on which open chess and checker sets stood. At one table two students sat with their palms cupped over their chins, contemplating the life and death of their knights carved in wood. Pictures hung end to end on the huge walls, each one with a little plaque crediting its philanthropic, if not very discriminating, donor.

They walked through the lounge into a narrow hallway, newly painted light green, and up a flight of steps. The dormitory halls were long and narrow, running from one end of the building to the other with a staircase at either end. Tony and John stopped on the third floor, walked part way down the corridor and Tony knocked on one of the doors. A thin-faced boy no older than eighteen opened it. John recognized him as a freshman engineering student Tony had briefly introduced him to some weeks before.

"Come in. I'm Bernard Waite."

The boy's eyes shined with the anticipation of welcoming good friends, people he knew were more than just acquaintances, even though he may have never actually met them before.

John shook hands with him. "I'm John Thomas. We met a while back."

John felt at home immediately. It was a pleasant type of belonging. Only a few people were in the room, a square structure with a single bed in the right-hand corner, a desk with a wooden chair against the double window in the far center of the room. At the right, John saw a dresser on top of which were a hi-fi and a pile of albums. At the left corner was a leather-cushioned easy chair and next to it a wooden straight-back chair.

The thin-faced boy, Bernard, was the host. On the bed were two husky heavy-set men who John had never seen before, who looked as though they might be football players. John was introduced to them first, tried to remember which name was which, then forgot them. "I'll get to know you during the evening anyway," he said. The huskier of the two, who confirmed in the introduction that he was, in fact, a football player, laughed. "We'll become good friends."

John felt strangely at ease. These people didn't frighten him as parties and crowds had always done in the past. The other boy on the bed told him he was studying chemical engineering. In colleges introductions invariably are accompanied with an identification of the person's course of study. On the chair by the desk was a fellow John knew from an

economics class the year before. He was a quiet boy named
Henry Green who had never contributed much in class or
spoken to anyone outside of it. All John remembered about
him was that he had once mentioned he came from San
Francisco.

The introduction to the man in the easy chair was a
surprise. Although he had never met him, John recognized
him as a teacher of psychology. He was neither young nor old,
a full head of black hair graying at the temples. He was fairly
stout and slumped into the chair, the heaviness giving him
the appearance of being short. When he stood up he was tall.
He could have been thirty-five or he could have been forty-
five. John remembered his name was Elwood Fisher. He was
an assistant professor.

"John Thomas . . . Woody Fisher." Bernard made the
introductions.

"Glad to meet you, Professor Fisher." John held out his
hand. The other shook it with a firm grip.

"Not Professor,'" was the answer. "We can be informal
here. Make it 'Woody'."

John smiled and nodded. He was pleased. The height of
informality and friendship in a college was to call a professor
by his or her first name.

Bernard pulled a cardboard box from under the bed,
began to pass out bottles of beer. "Over six-percent," he said.

"Illegal possession again," the football player warned.
He laughed. "One of these days Mrs. Sorenson is going to
find out." Mrs. Sorenson was the house mother who occupied a ground floor apartment in the dormitory, taking kind
and watchful care over "her boys," protecting them against
having women, gambling, or any form of liquor in their
rooms.

Bernard laughed with the football player. He turned to
the psychology teacher. "Don't look, Woody," he said.

Woody slumped in the chair casually, his feet spread straight out in front of him. "I won't," he said dryly. "As long as mine is cold." They all laughed. A faculty member usually was supposed to report any violation of school rules.

Tony sat on the floor near the bed, making himself comfortable. "Sit down, Johnny," he called.

"Make yourself comfortable," Bernard added.

John sat on the floor between Woody and Harry Green, the boy from San Francisco. He leaned against the scumble-painted walls, idly holding an opened bottle of beer.

Bernard went over to the hi-fi. "Waddaya want to hear?" he asked nobody in particular.

"Anything but cool jazz," the husky chemical engineer answered.

"No soul," Tony countered good-naturedly.

"How about Stravinsky?" Bernard asked.

"Aw!" It was the football player. "Longhair doesn't go with beer."

"Do you have any Gershwin?" Woody asked.

"For the honored Doctor," Bernard answered, "we shall compose some Gershwin." Laughter again. He opened a Gershwin album, started the music, then sat next to Tony with his bottle of beer.

Woody gulped on his bottle. "It is cold," he smiled.

"Leave it to Bernard."

They all drank quietly. It was warm and good-natured, and if John had had predisposition to wonder about these people, he no longer did. They seemed to be just nice ordinary people. He didn't move into the conversation quickly with the flip rejoinder or the occasional joke. It didn't matter. He enjoyed himself quietly. Tony lost himself in conversation with the fellows by the bed. Another boy entered, a short red-headed boy who spoke with clipped phrases. John had seen him before on campus, but they had never met. The newcomer settled himself next to Bernard with his ration of beer. Gershwin continued to play in the background.

John talked to Harry Green. He felt stiff, but not afraid. It was just talk—about their economics course, about theatre, about music. The psychology professor remained silent, listening to them at random. John noticed him watching and tried to bring the conversation to a higher plane. He found it difficult. Harry was, if anything, even shyer than he. He got lost in syllogisms and became embarrassed. Harry excused himself suddenly and left the room. "Beer always does this," he said apologetically.

The professor spoke first. "You feel a little uncertain?" It sounded casual rather than professional and John reacted the same way.

"Nice place."

"These parties are new to you, aren't they?"

John sensed that the other understood his problem. "First one," he admitted.

"Sit down over here."

John took the chair that Harry had been using and moved next to Woody.

"Known Tony long?" Woody asked.

"About six months. Why?" John wasn't sure of his ground.

"You're a little uncertain about the whole situation, aren't you?"

John started to speak, but the psychologist continued quickly. "I understand these things. You don't have to be afraid to talk to me." He smiled and his manner was gentle.

"No, I'm not afraid." John felt that he would like to talk to him.

"There's always fear in something new, isn't there, John?"

"Yes."

"Of this party?"

"Yes." John wanted to say more, but somehow felt that he would have to wait for Woody to lead him.

"And of other things?"

"I feel good about it, but I'm not sure this is all right." John dragged the words out.

"This?"

"The party . . . and . . . " Woody waited for him to continue. "And even sometimes Tony."

"You're afraid of Tony?"

"I'm not really afraid of him," John answered. "Really, I'm less afraid when I'm with him."

"You're afraid of other people?"

"Yes." John blurted the word, then spoke easily, the important point already told. "I feel they look at me. I feel they laugh at me and shun me, as if I were something queer and different."

"Is this something new, John?"

"No, I guess not. It's always been like that. Only now I feel guilty about it. I was only sorry for myself before." He thought a moment. "Isn't that a funny thing? I'm not sorry for myself anymore."

"You're happier with yourself?"

"Much. While I'm with Tony, that is," he added quickly. "But sometimes I still feel guilty, like I'm doing something I shouldn't. But how can that be? If that were so, then I shouldn't be happy. But I'm happy. I guess there's nothing really wrong."

"Some people find happiness in tying tin cans to little dogs' tails," Woody offered.

John pondered a few seconds. "You shouldn't have said that," he said sadly. "I thought I had begun to settle my doubts."

"Is your happiness dependent on hurting little dogs—or anybody else for that matter?"

It was a new light for John. "No. No. It isn't." He smiled. "Just being different is not bad," he said, half a statement, half a question. Woody gave him no answer. "It's when you hurt people by being different that there is reason to be guilty about it," John continued. He laughed. "Maybe I'm being too philosophical rather than practical."

"Do you think so?" Woody tossed the idea back at him.

"No," John answered immediately. "I understand that much about philosophy. It is practical." He mused again. "So there's nothing to be afraid of, really. Or to be guilty about. Just something to adjust to. As long as you're happy. As long as you're not hurting anybody else."

"The psychologist is just as concerned with man's hurting himself," Woody suggested.

Again it was a new idea for John. "How does one tell?"

The psychology professor shook his head. "It's not simple. I suppose dissatisfaction and unhappiness are the basic symptoms. Usually at times of crisis. I wish I knew an easy formula." Woody threw a final notion to John. "But this self-hurt does exist. And it must be considered."

"I'm not hurting myself now," John thought out loud. "At least I don't think I am." He paused a moment. "So it's only a case of adjustment. I'm happy." He paused again, looked at the other, knowing he should add something more. He said it confidently: "When I even begin to feel sorry for myself again, with Tony or without, then I'll know it'll be time to seriously worry."

John watched the psychologist's face, waited for an answer. He was relieved as Woody reached out his hand and grinned broadly. It was a smile affirming a mutual principle.

The party grew. More people arrived. John was introduced to them all, new faces, some; others who he had seen or met briefly before. During the course of the evening he managed to speak with each one, if only for a few seconds. It was a good feeling and as the room became crowded he became more relaxed. He met them all on a common ground and felt an unconscious bond of belonging. He was sorry when the beer bottles began piling up empty and one by one and two by two the guests made their goodbyes. Some had homework to do, others an early class to get up for, others, couples, simply said with a laugh that they wanted privacy.

John had made his place and the little details were unimportant. He didn't feel that he had to make an impression of any kind or measure any action by someone else's judgment of right and wrong. He sat next to Woody, only now on the floor by the desk. The red-headed boy had fallen asleep in the big chair. The football player was on the floor next to them, stretched out, his head in the lap of the chemical engineer. The talk fluttered from them and only an occasional serious note broke the frequent laughter. He was reluctant to leave when, at one o'clock in the morning, Tony patted him on the shoulder. Tony sensed his reluctance.

"There'll be more parties, Johnny-boy," he said. "Let's leave before it gets too late."

John got up, shook hands with those remaining in the room and responded in kind with generous bear hugs to those who he had gotten to know. He purposely waited till the last moment to say goodbye to the psychologist.

"So long, Woody." The hand grip was firm, then Woody initiated a strong hug. "Thanks for the talk," John said.

"No thanks necessary. I hope you've found the understanding a little easier."

"I have."

"Just remember that 'should do' is often just imaginary morality in an amoral or immoral society. No guilt feelings where they're not necessary." He winked at him confidently. "See you again," Woody said, and went back to his seat and another bottle of beer.

John felt Tony take his arm and he followed him out of the room. They walked to the street silently, then toward the apartment without a word. John's face was set thoughtfully. It was not a silence of sadness, but of satisfaction. They were almost home when Tony spoke to him.

"It turned out the way I said, didn't it, Johnny-boy?"

"Yes." John didn't feel like talking. He felt as though he was surrounded by a bright sunbeam, shutting out the disagreeableness of the outer society and allowing him to keep the luxury of the hours just past.

"You see," Tony continued, "that there is a place for us. It may not be out in the open with a brass band, but it's there. And it's something we can enjoy, just as the others enjoy their pleasures."

"Uh-huh." John didn't want to lose the floating feeling. He smiled to Tony, letting him know that he knew all this now.

Tony opened the apartment door with his key. John moved inside wearily, threw himself on the couch-bed. He was glad they had opened the couch before they left. He was tired.

"I'm glad we're here," he said.

Tony stopped, barely having closed the door. He smiled broadly. This was a welcome surprise. Usually John waited, let Tony go in first, get in bed first, as if John needed the other's reassurance. Now John was taking the initiative.

"That party did do you some good," Tony said.

"A lot of good," John answered. "We'll go to some more, won't we?" He started getting undressed. He knew they would.

"We sure will." Tony walked to the bed, took his coat off, sat down next to John. "But we really don't need them, do we, Johnny-boy?" he suggested very softly.

John looked up, saw Tony's sharp dark eyes suddenly seem soft and his tall thin body appear to be hard and yet pliable at the same time.

"No, we don't," he answered. He sat up, moved closer. "Come on, Tony," he said. "Let's not waste any more time. Let's get to bed."

In finding he was not alone, John did not need to draw so heavily on Tony for assurance any longer. That first party had set up for him a bulwark against the stings of the little fears. His need for Tony was still strong, but the dependency that had been a weakness was less so. He allowed himself the weakness only because he was satisfied and comfortable in it. They went to more parties, some with new people, some with the same ones he had already met. Invariably he looked for Woody and when he found him he talked with him delightedly, not as to a counselor but as with an old friend in whom he could confide. Actually, he found there was less and less to confide, and the conversations simply revolved around his own stability and happiness. And he was happy. The world outside didn't bother him. It was set away into a mental corner of whatever uncertainty might remain always in a person who deviates from the majority norm, as a necessary inconvenience in any existence. The ever-increasing closeness to Tony far overbalanced this small inconvenience.

The musical was completed and they found their spare time free. They went on picnics with others of their group— they had made a place in the then-closeted society of Des Moines—drives in the country—one of the fellows had a car—and listened to their ever-increasing music collection. Once every two weeks they made it a point to shop around and buy an album or possibly two. It was, in all, a good happy time.

Tony submitted several of his songs to New York publishers and along with the rejection slips came an occasional

encouraging letter suggesting that he continue his composing. He did, buoyed by the presence of John, exiling the
outer-imposed emotional discord and finding the platitudes
of security necessary for steady composition.

John didn't write. He wanted to and talked about his
ideas and plans with Tony, but somehow he never could
quite actually get around to it. He could not totally leave
the dependence he had cultivated and when Tony sat at the
piano, sometimes for hours picking out a melody and writing down the notes slowly, often laboriously, John sat on the
couch silently, listening and feeling that he was inexorably
tied with Tony's creations and unable to work independently.
He had become an addict and Tony was his opiate.

Spring came and the musical was produced. It ran four
nights at the college auditorium. There were praises from
all quarters, including excellent reviews in the Des Moines
newspapers. The music was singled out; it was noted that the
lyrics and book were also good. John was not slighted. Tony's
success was praise enough.

On the final night of the production the customary cast
party was arranged. This time, because of the large number
of people involved, two parties were planned—one with
the drama club members, a tight little island of actors who
dominated the department's presentations and fiercely protected the glory of their theatrical achievements within their
narrow society. Tony and John decided against this party.
The enjoyment there, they felt, would become too personal,
a made-up sophistication marked by elitism, even sarcasm,
at the expense of those who would not be at the party. They
accepted the invitation of the second party, at the home of
one of the young women who had worked on the costumes
for the show. She had become popular backstage because of
her attempts to be popular. She was brash, loud and forward,
sometimes to the point of annoyance.

Her name was Hester Balch, a young woman of twenty, small, stout. She was unpretty, her face matching the bigness of her body, with chiseled hard features instead of the softness that usually makes a plump person pleasant to look at. She wore thick-lensed glasses and varied them with a number of different shell frames, alternating green, red, yellow and multi-colored patterns, depending on the particular outfit she wore. She was given to loud, over-dressy clothes. Her lips were made too wide with thick, vivid lipstick, her hair cut short but fluffed fully on top of her head, giving the appearance of having never been combed, as if she had just climbed out of bed. She always wore perfume and always to excess. Everything about her was overdone. Even her voice was loud and unceasing. She pushed herself to the center of every group and strived mightily for attention. It seemed to be always necessary. She worked with the theatre department for this reason. Theatre is a highly cooperative enterprise. It gave Hester the opportunity to work closely with many other people, particularly the male members of the casts and crews.

Her father was a doctor, rarely home, devoting almost all of his time to the hospital where he was a staff member. Her mother, in her turn, spent all her time with clubs and societies. Hester was an only child and a lonely one. Her home was in a suburb of Des Moines, a restricted residential area called Walton. It was named after the contractor who built and sold the two-story houses, becoming the founder and, by virtue of the many mortgages which he financed, the virtual owner of the town.

Hester's family life had never been stable and when she grew up she desperately sought the companionship she never had. At first, when she was younger, this manifested itself with girls. But she soon likened them too much to her mother and when puberty arrived she turned to boys. She felt sorry for them. She felt sorry for her father and wanted to give to the men she met a love she felt they deserved. Being quite unpretty by accepted standards, no matter how flawed, she found it difficult to attract males. In her struggle she pushed her physical attraction beyond the norm of acceptance and consequently pushed herself into a society where she refused the friendship of women and men refused hers. At college she tried even more desperately and by occasionally spending the night with a male student at one of the nearby no-tell motels, she found a temporary companionship. It was all too infrequent and in order to meet the growing compulsion to be near men she made friends with the homosexual groups on the campus. Though the physical relationships did not exist, she did find herself surrounded by males. She ran through life furiously, absorbing as much outward contact with men as they allowed her, as much personal relationship as she could give them, hoping that enough of it coming in unceasing waves would compensate for her inner emptiness. She was, by this time, caught up in unbridled nymphomania.

To her party came mostly men, some from the circle that Tony and John knew, a few with dates, and others who simply went for the free liquor and, if drunk enough, a quick turn with Hester. They left the school in several cars, Tony and John riding with a young man who had been the show's stage manager. He drove, a young woman who was a dancer sitting in front with him, John and Tony in the back seat. They remained silent, unconcerned with the driver's one-handed control of the wheel, his other arm reaching around the shoulder of the woman next to him.

"Maybe we ought not to go at all," Tony whispered, as the car sped along the flat streets, toward the outskirts of the city.

"Why?"

"That gang of Hester's is too womanish," Tony answered. They kept their voices low. The drone of the motor kept the couple in front from hearing. Tony and John sat back deep against the car pillows. The girl in front was too occupied to listen, trying to make herself small and close next to the boy so that his arm could reach completely around her.

"Those fellows are so damned insecure," Tony continued, "they make fools of themselves trying to show everybody, including themselves, that they've found a happy society. They go over the top. Flamboyant. Queens."

John nodded in agreement.

"They make the whole thing seem damned immoral and abnormal," Tony said. "People see them and think that all of us are like that. They make it bad for the rest of us."

"Yeah," John complied. He didn't like to talk about it. He would rather just feel and be.

The car pulled up at a white stone house, standing out from the other houses on the street by the brightness of its lights shining from every room and from the porch overlooking the driveway that led to the rear. They parked in the street in front and went in. The first floor contained a large living room, starting at the front door and circling the left side of the house into an adjoining dining room. The kitchen was next to it, on the right. Upstairs were three bedrooms. As long as Hester could remember, her father and mother had had separate bedrooms.

Most of the guests had already arrived. They were seated conventionally around the living room, some drinking, others talking. Two sofas faced each other from opposite walls of the room, a number of straight-backed chairs completing the circular link between. Two large easy chairs were at the far end and several small chairs placed here and there by the people using them. The room was crowded with perhaps thirty people. It was well lit, with the only hint of darkness coming from the dining room. Talking could be heard from there, but nobody could be seen. Hester stood by one of the easy chairs, wearing a wide, flowing black and yellow skirt, the colors alternating in large square patterns much like a checker board. She was concentrating her attention on a tall, extremely thin fellow of about thirty-five who, after many unsuccessful years of trying to find a place in the business world, had decided to return to college and study art. His name was Nevin Martin, a quiet person who made friends with difficulty and who, although attending all parties and gatherings, contented himself with being alone with his observations and a full martini glass. He was often incisive about people who disturbed his contemplations, and Hester, albeit the hostess, was no exception.

Tony and John made their way through the crowd to the kitchen. They got drinks from Hester's mother who, strangely enough, had decided to stay home that evening and help by mixing and distributing the drinks. More and more, in these years that her daughter began to bring home to parties older and older young men, she had made it a point to be present in some manner at the parties. She remained in the kitchen, listening eagerly to the conversations outside and particularly in the adjoining dining room. She perked up considerably as the young men came for drinks. With but a minimum of urging, she would have joined the party. Otherwise, she was forced to be content by merely observing. She was not old, not much over forty. She was thin and attractive, prettier than her daughter, although she relied heavily on makeup and form fitting, well-cut clothes. John and Tony returned to the living room, sat near Nevin's chair, where Hester sat balanced on the arm, her hand on his shoulder.

"You're an artist, I bet." Her voice was low and false with extra sweetness.

Nevin's voice was deep and very cultured. He looked at her as though he had been frightfully insulted. He emphasized each of his words as he spoke, as though they were more important than anything anyone else could possibly say.

"My artistry is not a matter for speculation." He sipped his martini, not looking at her.

Hester tried again. "I'll bet you're a good artist," she insisted.

Nevin turned his glance toward her. "I am an excellent artist," he assured her coolly, not caring whether she heard him or not. His tone was of ice. "If I had a bucket of shellac I would immediately paint you out of my sight."

Hester would not be put off. "Not if you knew me better," she told him.

"If I knew you better, I would unhesitatingly paint myself away."

"Don't be so cold, Nevin," Hester said. "You're very nice." She put her other hand on his shoulder and moved closer to him.

He glanced at her from under his eyelids, the only thing about him moving. "Young girl," he said with measured annoyance. "Would you kindly remove your grimy paws from my suit? I am not a bear trap."

"Well, you needn't be so haughty," Hester said. The pinpricks began to show. "I don't like your attitude."

"Good."

She stood up, took her hands from his shoulders.

"Are you going?" he asked hopefully.

Hester became angry. "You're a wise guy, aren't you?"

"I'm quite talented," Nevin replied.

"You think you're pretty smart."

"Without doubt." He was beginning to enjoy this now.

"Why don't you find a nice muddy lake somewhere and lose yourself if you hate people so much," Hester said slowly, trying to match his attitude.

"I don't hate people," Nevin said. "They hate me."

Those sitting nearby laughed. They were attracted to the conversation now, and Hester, knowing it, was embarrassed. She was upset by her inability thus far to come out even.

"It's easy to see why," she answered to his last comment.

Her voice changed from the husky haughtiness to an almost uncontrolled high pitch.

"I'm glad you have no trouble understanding it," Nevin said. "It's fortunate it's so simple."

She couldn't go any further. She laughed. "You poor boy," she said purposefully loud for all to hear. She flicked at her skirt as though she were brushing away the entire incident. "I feel so sorry for you and your intolerable attitude." She walked away.

Nevin's last words reached her as she disappeared amid the crowd at the other end of the living room.

"My attitude is a state of mind, my dear," he said. "Which is a great deal more than you, unfortunately, can lay claim to." He lifted his eyebrows, put the glass to his lips and finished the martini. "Is there any more of this vile stuff?" he demanded. He rose from the chair reluctantly, shrugged, and went into the kitchen.

Hester busied herself with the few people who contin-ued to arrive, helping each one find a place to sit, managing to spend a moment or two in the lap of each male she had made comfortable, adjusting a tie or eliciting a hostess's good evening kiss. She avoided the area where Nevin sat and when-ever she passed from the living room through to the kitchen she kept her head high, her eyes straight ahead. Nevin had salvaged the evening for himself and was soon immersed in a discussion of art with a young man who had designed the setting for the musical.

Tony and John sat and watched, drinking and talk-ing, letting the noise and people move by them. They soon decided to leave early. The party was a loud and not homogeneous one. Some of the men who had brought women with them either held them on their laps on a single chair and made furtive attempts at amour, or disappeared with them and their respective glasses of liquor into the back yard where the attempts were opportunely less furtive. Many of the men who had come alone were boisterous and extroverted, the ones Tony had spoken about in the car. They split into small groups of twos and threes, ignoring everyone else, although they themselves, open and sometimes frenetic, could not be ignored. Two bulked themselves into a corner of the couch, close against each another, their sexual relationship not duplicating the purview of male-female pairs, but nevertheless loud in voice and without subtlety in action.

"It's as if they feel they are doing something wrong," John remarked, "and have to do it with much ado to convince themselves that it isn't wrong."

A group of three stood in one corner of the room laughing shrilly, their hands darting out at one another, provocative screams punctuating each lurch. Like children in a dark alley who for the first time have discovered the unlightable thing called sex. Other pairs disappeared to the cars parked out front, returned in minutes time, reevaluated themselves into new pairs and disappeared again. One of the men, a tall blonde with a receding hairline, laughing incessantly, went from group to group, pulling one, then another after him to the upstairs rooms. Hester followed him doggedly, her face pained, and went upstairs every time he and a companion did. John wondered what she did along with them.

"Nothing, probably," Tony told him. "That blonde fellow, Jerry, used to take her out a lot. Now that he's gone all the way, he won't bother with her. I suppose she gets some kind of vicarious pleasure in watching. They don't mind. She's become, with some of them, like a third part of the family. They know how important it is to her."

John felt a revulsion as he contemplated Tony's description. He lost himself in a semi-consciousness, the pattern of what was happening surrounding him like a wildly moving series of pictures spinning one into another, each frame pushing into the next going around and around, without any idea of finding a track that would make the pictures move along in a comprehensive pattern. Each item of forced pleasure or hectic enjoyment crowded against the next and it disturbed him because, in a small way, the same picture presented itself on occasion in his relationship with Tony. It was as if he were trying to grasp at something before it got away, without judging whether it was something good or not. A heavy hand on his shoulder woke him from his reverie.

"Hi, Johnny. Having a good time?"

The voice belonged to Jim Borson, a big raw-boned young man from Oklahoma who had come to Des Moines because, to him, it presented a big city and at the same time a small school where he could combine the new experience of a large town with the security of the small environment he had known in Oklahoma. He was a good-looking man, open and free, almost to the point of naiveté. He made friends with men, up to the point of a good poker game. He attracted women, but let himself go much, much further with them.

"Good show, Tony," he said. "Damned good show." He looked around him and laughed in his deep voice. "Good show here, too."

At either side of him stood a young woman, both of them small and slender, almost dwarfed by Jim's big physique. He put an arm around each. "Okay, sweethearts, don't get impatient. Poppa will be with you soon." He kissed each of them, turned to Tony and John. "Glad you came," he said. "Hope you have a good time." He snuggled the girls closer to him, his long arms reaching far around their backs, the tips of his fingers touching the edges of their bosoms. He herded them to the kitchen. "Let's get something to drink. Do you good."

"That's really an operator," Tony observed.

"I like him. Seems like a nice fellow," John said.

"He is. Pure clean-cut American boy." There was no sarcasm. "A big man with the girls. He doesn't make any bones about it and that's good. Some of the others are too smug." Tony looked to see that he hadn't returned. "I like him because he's not a hypocrite," Tony continued. "He knows about most of our crowd and is friendly with them, though he isn't interested otherwise. Live and let live, he says, and doesn't look down his nose."

John was for the moment caught up in the enthusiasm. It was too rare that someone from the other world didn't take a stand of superiority.

"He's a good friend if you ever need one," Tony said. He put his hand on John's.

John acknowledged the touch. "I've got a good friend," he smiled.

Jim Borson came back to the living room. The young women trailed behind him. Hester ran to him, threw herself in his arms.

"Jimmy, my lover boy."

He held her tight, winked broadly for anyone who could see his face, ran his hands once up and down her body, lifted her off her feet and kissed her.

"Oh, Jimmy." She clung to him, her voice becoming a moan.

He put her down. "Later, sweetheart," he said. "I met your beautiful mother and I promised her first." He laughed. Hester sighed and walked away. Jim turned to Tony and John.

"Make 'em all happy," he said. "That's my motto. And anyway," he confided, "I think I do prefer the mother." He laughed again and went back to the kitchen.

Two newcomers walked into the party, both of whom they knew. Tommy Colton, small, thin, dark-complexioned, was editor of the college newspaper and known as the brilliant young man on the campus; and Arnie Wakefield, a tall, thin, willowy young man, with well-defined features and actions, a dancer who had graduated from Des Moines the year before and now performed for private parties around town. They had known each other for about a year and by the superior intellectual and artistic positions they held in relation to most of the others, acted with a studied quietude, proclaiming their superiority by not being in any way obvious about it. They didn't belong to any of the so-called "crowds" and kept to themselves most of the time. They had not been associated with the musical, but came to the party at Hester's request. The moment they entered, Hester lost the ebullience and over-playing and became studiously reserved. Her relationships to Tommy and Arnie were strange ones. Tommy had always been a quiet boy, alone and afraid. When Hester met him, by giving him her friendship she obtained his nearness at the same time. Then Tommy met Arnie and found a more fitting companion, esthetically and intellectually, and their relationship grew into a sexual accord. Hester quickly resented Tommy for abandoning her. At the same time, Tommy felt a gratefulness and closeness to Hester, continuing to like Hester perhaps as much as he liked his new companion. But it all remained inside. He could not take any positive action in regard to her.

Hester, in the meantime, had grown violently in love with Arnie, and the complete frustration of her life reached a peak when she realized that Arnie had no interest in her whatsoever. The triangle was completely unusual and unusually complete: Tommy loving Hester, unable to make it known; Hester disliking Tommy and loving Arnie; and Arnie's energies all going to Tommy. The triangle was constant, the three more often than not together. Each suffered the company of one to be near another. It went round and round intolerably, growing more incisive, stifling any possible growth of the three and twisting their neuroses even further.

The three, arm in arm, went to the kitchen together. The crowd itself, knowing the situation, for the moment grew quiet.

John knew, too, and he was disturbed. "There's something terribly wrong if it leads to this kind of thing."

"They just don't know how to channel it," Tony said.

"And we do?"

Tony was concerned with the question. "Don't we, Johnny?" His tone was sharp. He smiled and then John smiled back.

"It's getting hot in here," John suggested. "Let's go or let's get another drink." Then he added, "Okay, Tony?"

They got some more drinks. The party continued to revolve around them and apart from them. Nevin Martin and themselves, John thought, were perhaps the only sane ones there. The party became more frantic, everyone running faster and more excitedly, as if they were trying to ride the merry-go-round and at the same time beat it around the circle.

Once it was John's turn to fetch fresh drinks. He found Hester and her mother in the kitchen and big Jim Borson with them. Hester's two companions, Arnie and Tommy, had walked away from her and, apparently desiring only each other's company, had gone for a short drive in one of the cars.

"This is Mrs. Balch, Johnny," Jim said, introducing him to Hester's mother. He had one arm around the woman, one holding a glass of liquor. His face was red with lipstick. John looked quickly at Hester; her lipstick was untouched. Mrs. Balch nodded an acknowledgement of introduction, then let herself be tucked further into Jim's arms, pulling his shoulders forward toward her with her hands. Hester pressed against Jim's free arm, rivaling her mother for the coveted place. Jim pushed them both away as he saw John looking for the proper drink ingredients.

"Something important to do," he muttered. "Here, let me fix it, Johnny," he said. He did.

John thanked him, took the drinks. He felt a little weak in his stomach as both mother and daughter went back to Jim, crushing him against a corner of the wall. Jim laughed, enjoying himself immensely with the incredulity of the situation.

The weakness in John's stomach condemned this kind of male-female relationship. He pictured his own mother in the same situation and the ugliness repelled him, giving him a solace for the male-male manifestation that was going on in some of the rest of the house. The picture in the kitchen was an immediate antidote for any questioning he might have had about his and Tony's relationship. The proof of the righteousness of their kind of existence was further strengthened a moment later when Jim emerged from the kitchen with Hester's mother and bundled her quickly up the staircase.

Hester came into the living room much disturbed, asking about Arnie and Tommy.

John and Tony decided to go outside for some air.

"A little walk, another drink, and then we'll leave. Okay?"

"Okay."

They passed the parked cars on the street, the occasional outline of couples stretched out on the back seats, shoeless feet pressed against the window pane. Tony nudged John as they passed one car about a block away. "Tommy and Arnie," he whispered. John looked, saw only darkness, and they walked on. They returned a half hour later, in time to see

Jim come downstairs with Mrs. Balch. Her face was newly lipsticked. Tony nudged John again. "Different dress," he observed. John noticed that it was.

The house had become a continuing bedlam. Although the noise had somewhat abated, the emotion had grown, and the sounds approximated the high-pitched constant whine of a motor whirring faster and faster. Jim and Mrs. Balch went into the kitchen. He came back a moment later, now with Hester. He winked at John and Tony as he passed, taking Hester with him up the stairs. She clung to him, her fingers entwined into the lapels of his tieless shirt.

"I'll show you how they do it in Oklahoma," Jim whispered.

Arnie and Tommy returned. Arnie busied himself, as if by agreement, with some of the people who had flowed into the still darkened, but now crowded dining room. Tommy looked for Hester. He had to wait twenty minutes for her and grabbed her arm as she came downstairs with Jim. She wore the same dress, but it was no longer starched and flowing. The black and yellow squares were criss-crossed with hundreds of small creases along the back and sides.

Jim went to the kitchen, came back with his jacket thrown over one arm. On the other clung one of the young women he had initially come with.

Nevin was discoursing on his philosophies of art to a number of young people gathered about him.

"Goodbye, old boy. Watch the intellectual waistline.'

Nevin looked at Jim and smiled an acknowledgement without pausing in his talk.

Jim shook hands with John and Tony. "There's nothing more for me here. I'll be shoving off." He turned to the door. "C'mon, sweetheart," he called. The young woman followed him out.

Hester and Tommy had begun arguing, first quietly, then with passion. They stood by the stairs where Tommy had pulled roughly on her arm as she came down a few moments before.

"It's none of your business what I do," she said. "You live your life and let me mind my own business."

"If you can't take care of your business like a lady, someone has to do it for you." His voice had risen almost as high as hers. It was the only release for his anger. He was unable to find any for his jealousy.

"I don't like you, Tommy, and for my part, you can leave this minute."

"If I do, I take Arnie with me." This was his weapon.

Hester's frustration, only so recently physically satisfied, stumbled on its intellectual counterpart. "Bastard," she spit at him.

He smiled, then close to her face whispered as loud as he could, "You're a bitch." He turned. "I'll wait for you in the garden." He turned toward the rear of the house. She stood a moment, waited until the people who had overheard went back to their own conversations. Then she followed him.

The liquor and heat of emotions and the tired hours of the early morning had taken hold and, straining their limit, faltered, and gradually the party began to die down. Mrs. Balch had come into the living room, settled herself on the floor near one of the couches with a drink in her hand. Nevin had left his patriarchal chair and gone over to her. He sat next to her, discoursing on the difference between moral good and evil. He seemed satisfied to have a mature face to talk to. She agreed with every word he said, not out of understanding, but because she was too happy and satisfied at the moment to break the spell by doing otherwise. Hester returned and as she passed looked spitefully at her mother. Her mother smiled condescendingly, in the smugness of having accomplished something her daughter had been unable to, as though they were perpetual rivals for whatever presented itself. She had garnered the larger portion.

Tommy was involved in a political discussion in the kitchen and Hester found Arnie again, as if by agreement, waiting for her alone.

"Walk with me," she said.

"Okay."

She pointed to the staircase.

"Like hell," Arnie answered.

"I'll keep Tommy here," she threatened.

"Outside," Arnie compromised. They went quickly out the door.

"I love you," she began to say as they left. He snorted and walked gingerly.

Someone called for Arnie.

"He went with Hester."

"They'll be back in a few minutes," someone else offered.

They were. A few of the people began to leave.

"Had enough?" Tony asked.

"Let's go," John answered. "This is pretty awful."

"It happens all the time." Tony tossed it off.

"Then maybe we're in the wrong company?"

"We are," Tony said. "You see how the other half—or the other quarter—lives."

"They're not all like this," John suggested.

"No. But some are. These are. You can see how good our relationship is."

John agreed. He was eager to leave, for Tony to lift him out of this place and into the shelter of their apartment. They started toward the door.

One of the fellows stopped them. "Wait a minute, we're going to ask Arnie to dance."

Tony looked at John, smiled as if to say that it would be worth a few minutes more of their time.

"It's the high spot of the evening," the fellow said.

"All right," John muttered.

"Come on, Arnie, how about a dance?" someone called.
The others took up the chant. "Dance, Arnie . . . dance, Arnie
. . . dance, Arnie . . . ."

"Is he any good?" John asked.

"I've never seen him," Tony muttered. "They say he is.
Interpretive dancing."

Arnie stepped to the middle of the living room, walked
off a large circle, the people forming the perimeter of it three
deep, giving him the full area of the center of the room.
Hester pushed forward, sat on the floor part of the inside edge
of the circle.

"What'll it be, Arnie?" someone asked.

The dancer began to take off his shirt, then his undershirt. His chest breathed in and out heavily, testing his wind.
He flexed his arm muscles. He was not husky, but sinewy.
The muscles were hard and flexible and as he made them
move up and down his arm they contorted in their own interpretive dance.

"The Bolero," he said softly. He was intent and serious.
His face became hard and his body tense as though this were
the most important moment of his life. There was scattered
applause when he announced the number.

"This is a good one," John heard someone whisper.
A moment later there was the pounding sound of Ravel's
"Bolero."

Arnie began to twist, at first in one spot, rhythmically
with the music. Then, using his arms to their fullest advantage, he moved gracefully about the circle, reaching his hands
out and clutching with his fingers, figuratively entwining all
whom he passed.

His body moved faster. His face had become a mask,
lost with himself in the music. It was as though he had put

himself in a trance, his eyes staring wide, but in a blur, at
nothing. His mouth tightened into a thin closed line. His
body seemed to detach itself from everything else and move
of its own accord, only the music penetrating into whatever
consciousness it retained. The sounds of the "Bolero" began
to pound and his body responded, thrusting itself sharply in
and out with each beat.

John felt the music reach him and unconsciously began
to sense the rhythm of Arnie's body attach itself to his. The
sensation became strangely a part of him, as if he were one
with the dancer. The blood began to rush through him in
heavy waves in time to the music. He had heard the story
of the "Bolero," that it had supposedly been written as an
empathic response to sexual intercourse, with the rhythms of
the music corresponding to the rhythms of the body in the
rise and crescendo of the orgasm.

As the music grew more violent, so did the dancer.
He threw himself lengthwise onto the rug on the floor and
started to squirm and move along on his stomach, digging
himself into the rug, his mouth opening wide and gasping
heavily. The breaths grew louder and merged into a continuous moan. It was as though in reality he were at that moment
in the midst of the sexual act.

The room was stilled, everyone transfixed, their entire
selves hypnotized by the dancer who moved now more and
more violently. He tore at an imaginary shirt, ripping it from
his body. He reached for his stomach, pushing away from
it, then digging into its depth, trying to free himself of the
pounding and pressure within. He pulled at his trousers,
twisting and turning wildly on the floor. He was like a crazed
man, outside of his world and his mind, and yet a man who
somehow had a full knowledge of where he was and what he
was doing. His total existence was the music and the dance.
The inner feeling loosed itself and came into the open, a

purge of the neurosis within his being, making him free to meet the world on the only level he knew.

Hester sat on the floor at the edge of the circle. Her mouth was open, breathing heavily, her eyes wide and staring. Her hands clutched at her thighs, pulling them apart. Her insides reached out toward the man moving violently on the floor.

The music grew louder and quicker, moving from peak to higher peak. Suddenly Arnie stretched his body outward, straining it, shook uncontrollably, the interpretive dance becoming one with his own inner release. He grasped at his trousers again, pulled them off, his hands moving like an automaton, flung them aside. Hester grabbed them, pulled them to her. The dancer moved and shook more violently, in sharp spasms, each movement melting into the next, trying to find fulfillment.

He grasped toward his stomach again, tore at something that wasn't there, then taking his shorts between his fingers, pulled them off. His body buried itself into the ground, then alternately flung itself toward the sky, reaching to a freedom that it couldn't seem to find.

John shook. He grabbed Tony's arm. "Let's get out of here."

Tony turned with him, pushed John's elbow in front of him to the door. They hurried out.

"Christ," John murmured. His breathing was wet and his throat quivered. He wiped his hand across his forehead, flecked his fingers with sweat.

As they walked down the street the music suddenly stopped. There was a moment of silence and then the sound of applause. "More," somebody said loudly and then repeated the word again and again frantically. It sounded like Hester's voice. They walked out of earshot. They weren't sure whether the music started up again or not.

## Chapter 8

They didn't talk about the party again. It was put into the back of their minds as though it hadn't happened. A nightmarish dream that settled into their imaginations, not to disturb their consciousness. They did not see the irony in their attitudes: non-conformists in society rejecting non-conformists in society.

The days and weeks and months followed, some happy, some with an occasional quarrel. It was an averaging out process, the good and the bad added, subtracted and divided into the median of life's reasonable pace. John sought the average, although it was not always willing to accommodate him. Little things happened—on campus, in a drugstore, in the library. He would meet someone or see something or hear some word having to do with so-called normal relationships of people, it didn't matter what, and he was sensitive toward its possible meaning, building it into a self-problem to be presented before Tony and himself. It was not a purposeful thing on John's part. It was part of his constant need to know that he was living in what was for him the best of all possible worlds.

He sought reassurance from Tony, blaming himself for any doubts, accepting self-censure for being unstable or at times, even as he put it, womanish. Tony's long talks, the slow, calm realizations of satisfaction with Tony, and the ever-present liquor to make it all seem smooth, obviated any serious questioning. When he let himself be happy it was a wondrous thing.

On rare occasions Tony's patience would snap and he would threaten dire consequences, going so far as to tell John to break their relationship if he wished. John would leave fitfully, spend the night in his old room, where only the bed remained, and return in time for breakfast the following morning. A few minutes of coldness, an apology from John, a similar regret from Tony, and everything would be as it had been before. This happened once a month, sometimes twice. Most of the time life moved at its uneventful pace. Above all, to John, there was the security. He had a surety of relationship to the one and to the many, he felt he belonged, and he had fulfilled the immediate need of his life.

The semester came and went, and then another, and finally the snow melted once more and the trees lining the campus began to grow green and the leaves blossomed and it was spring. The classes, for many students, became relatively unimportant. They did as much of their studies as did not interfere with the rest of their existence. They managed to pass their courses with average grades and this was sufficient. Other things now, like the coming of spring, were more important.

John heard the shutter of the window slap against the faux-brick ledge siding, pulling his consciousness away from sleep. He lifted the blanket quietly, not to disturb Tony, and got up to close the shutter. It was warm even for April and the window was open wide, the shutter detached to allow more air to reach the room. He felt the sweat on his bare feet

cling to the varnished floor near the window where the rug
ended. It annoyed him and he shivered at the stickiness. He
breathed deeply, closed the shutter, exchanging the air to be
rid of the cracking sound of wood striking against brick-like
wood. He slammed at it hard, angry at the window. He felt
uncomfortable, felt that maybe he should be disturbed, but
didn't know why. He lay back on the bed again, this time
over the covers. Tony grunted, twisted half around to the
other side of the bed. John closed his eyes tightly, tried to
force the blackness into sleep. The more he tried, the more
the consciousness of purposeful sleep bothered him and the
more awake he became.

He thought about himself and Tony and the thoughts
became part of the months past and the months present and
the months to come, riding quickly along on top of torn
calendar pages caught up in an unceasing wind. It was April
and April led into May and May followed into June and there
the pages of the calendar suddenly stopped and fell weightily
to the ground, carrying John along with them. In June Tony
would be graduating from college. He, John, had another
year left. He opened his eyes and looked over at Tony. It
was inconceivable, he thought, that two months hence or at
any time Tony could be anyplace but where he was at that
moment. But John knew that would be. He forced his eyes
tighter together, trying to shut out the thoughts, and turned
over on the bed, trying to find sleep. Finally he got up,
walked to the kitchen and, shading the light with a piece of
newspaper to keep the glare from the living room, sat down
at the table.

He sat for a long while. The problem was not new. It
had come up before, but it had always been remote. Two
years away, then one year away, then six months away. Now
it could be measured in weeks. It was something not to sleep
over, something to think about again and again. In the span

of a lifetime it was, at the moment, the most important thing that seemingly could happen in an entire age. He let the ideas come, sought a solution in them, but no solutions came. He could only think of Tony leaving, and the idea was too terrifying to allow rational thought. The white porcelain of the kitchen table squinted up at him, the small black strips on the top making patterns, and out of the patterns of half sleep seemed to come an invention that he would not find in the waking hours. It was as if the unconscious creativity of his mind loosed itself and forced its way out, pulling outward into a dark half-awakedness that could not choke his creative urge, either by peopled morality or literate objectivity. He lay his head on his hands, close to the table. He began to visualize in words the solutions to the problem, strange things he could not think of in the clear light of daytime, but which seemed so opportune now. The words danced in front of him, striking him as a pattern of genius. He felt relieved in his discoveries. He could not tell that they were as much make-believe as was his conscious world of that moment.

For a second he wondered why it was so important. He thought of the several times he had questioned his entire relationship with Tony. But only for a moment. He knew what he had with Tony. He remembered what it had been without him. He would continue in his security with Tony. He raised a hand, reached for the words that had come to him so brightly, trying to put them together into a cohesive whole. As he reached they seemed to dance faster and whirled away from him. He tried to catch onto a syllable, even a letter, but he couldn't. The solutions that had seemed to come so quickly went away just as suddenly. He thought hard and tried to remember.

Something about a boat. Tony and himself on a boat, sailing to South America and writing musicals. Impossible, he decided, and rejected it. The solution had been something logical and real. A big estate and an old woman, perhaps. A patron to support them while they worked and lived. But where and how? This too, he rejected. He damned himself for not being able to remember. He got up and walked back and forth in the narrow space between the table and the refrigerator, cursing himself because he had found an answer in his half-dream and so quickly had let it slip away, back into the nothingness from whence it had come. He sat at the table again, closed his eyes and tried again to find the key to the knowledge he had grasped, almost held, and lost. It didn't come. He sweated, the sliver of air slipping into the room making him shiver. He forced a mental image of Tony and himself two months from then, conjuring means of keeping the time from moving except in the same pattern, holding both of them together for the months and the years afterward. But the more he tried to think, the less he thought about, and the thought image became a white blob against the closed eyelids. He opened them to see the black cracks on the porcelain table and hear Tony's voice from the other room.

"Johnny! Are you all right?"

"I'm okay," he answered after a moment. He adjusted himself to the real-life world again.

"What the hell are you doing up at this hour?" He heard Tony fumble for his wrist watch on the small table next to the bed. "It's four ayem," Tony called.

John walked into the living room, sat on the edge of the bed. "What's going to happen in June?" he asked.

Tony turned over on his side, pulled the sheet over his head. "The swallows'll come back to Capistrano," he said. "Go to sleep, willya?" He turned his face into the pillow, remained buried for a moment, then twisted around clumsily to see John still sitting there.

"In June you graduate," John said. His voice was soft and he was sad in his questioning.

Tony was angry at having been awakened. "So I graduate. Go to sleep." He pulled the blanket up, turned into the pillow again.

John remained motionless. "What's going to happen? I don't want to stay here all alone." There was no inflection.

"I'll be around," Tony muttered.

"You won't be around. What will you stay around for?"

Tony was angrier. "Well, if you've already decided, then don't ask me."

"I've been thinking about it," John continued in a monotone. "I can't find an answer."

Tony hesitated, then decided John was in another period of depression. He assured him. "I'm not going anyplace. I'll stay in Des Moines. Maybe at home, maybe here, but I'll stay. You won't be alone."

John smiled now. "You sure?"

Tony reached over and put his arm on John's shoulder. "Sure I'm sure. There's nothing to worry about." He took John's arm and pulled it toward him. "Get some sleep now."

"Okay." John smiled in thanks, got under the covers. He closed his eyes, felt an untroubled drowsiness come. The picture of the boat and the old lady with the estate came to him again. He reached for them, but they faded away again. He didn't care now. He felt Tony's arms move around him and he moved into him, warm and close. He had this security. The shutter on the window suddenly banged open again and cracked against the sill outside. This time nobody heard.

They had worked the past months on a new musical and spent the early weeks of April working on some last minute revisions. Rehearsals had started and the show was scheduled for early June, the week before the graduation ceremonies, with a final performance in the evening following the ceremonies. The music was exceptionally good. John's lyrics weren't too bad. The book was fair, comparable to an average college musical. They only talked once more about Tony graduating.

"I'll stay here till next year, when you graduate," Tony reassured John. Then we'll go off together, New York, Hollywood, Chicago. It doesn't matter. Anyplace where we can work and live together." That seemed to settle matters.

For the graduation exercises Des Moines College had invited back a number of now-famous alumni. Gerald Stearns was one of them. He had never graduated. He was expelled after his second year because he was unable to meet scholastic requirements. At that time he had wanted to become a teacher. In the process of trying to make a living, he went into show business and now, fifteen years later, was a well-known Broadway lyricist, having written the book and lyrics for a number of successful shows. His alma mater was recognizing him, finally, with an honorary degree of Doctor of Letters.

The whole idea was funny to Stearns. He was the kind of man who regarded with a biting sarcasm all forms of hypocrisy and he felt, in this instance, seeing it in action would be a big joke. It was a serious affair to the college authorities. Successful people in show business often made a great deal of money, and in view of the high tax rates they often donated substantial tax-deductible amounts to educational institutions. A college is a big business and the Trustees felt that the exchange of an honorary degree for a possible monetary gift was a good investment. The ceremonies were held in the afternoon. Stearns had decided to stay overnight in Des Moines and went to the college musical that evening against his better judgment. He was never satisfied with mediocrity and remembered from his own stay at college how amateurish these shows could be. He was a short man with close cropped hair, a tight fitting suit that looked as If he wore it perenni ally, and a thin strip of a necktie. Even in this dress he looked precise and sufficient unto himself.

After the first act he was pleasantly surprised, changing his pre-performance plan to leave during the first intermission. He marveled at the music and looked at the program several times to remind himself of the name of the composer. It was the kind of music that he would be happy to write lyrics to. And he considered it seriously. After the performance he went backstage.

"Where can I find Tony Jordan?" His voice had a nasal quality and came in short, commanding bursts, as if his small stature was insufficient to give him the strong sustained vocal tone he desired. Someone finally recognized him and, with undue obsequiousness, led him to Tony. He found Tony alone in the prop room, gathering together his sheet music.

"Are you the composer?" Stearns asked bluntly.

"That's right." Tony was equally blunt. The man in the cap and gown whose talents he had admired that afternoon did not at all resemble the little man who stood in front of him now.

The little man smiled, somewhat impressed with the other's independence. It reminded him of himself. "I'm Gerald Stearns," he said. He was pleased when Tony reacted with excitement.

"I'm glad to meet you," Tony said. Inside he was excited. Wondering why Stearns had sought him out was more pressing and he remained calm. They shook hands.

"I want to talk to you," Stearns told him. "Let's go someplace out of here."

Tony hesitated. "I have a friend waiting for me."

"I don't want to quibble, I want to talk," Stearns insisted. "Someplace where we can be alone. The Owl's Head Bar is still here, isn't it?"

"Still up the street," Tony answered.

"Then let's go. I spent more time there while I was in college than in class, anyway," he smiled.

"The fellow who wrote the book and lyrics is the one who's waiting for me," Tony said tentatively.

"I don't want to talk to any lyric writer. I want to talk to you." Stearns was insistent.

For a moment Tony resented this man who had suddenly taken command of the situation. He was used to being in command. Stearns started to leave.

"Okay," Tony said, "Let's go."

At the stage entrance Tony stopped one of the actresses in the show. "Rosie, will you tell Johnny Thomas that I was called away? Tell him I'll meet him at the apartment later." The girl nodded and hurried away.

As they walked toward the Owl's Head Bar, Tony asked, "What do you want to talk to me about, Mr. Stearns?"

"Wait until we get a drink," was the answer. "It's too damned hot to talk. We'll cool off first."

After a few beers and forced small talk, Stearns told him. "I like your music. I like the professional sweep and at the same time the naïve patterns. Almost like a syncopation that you aren't quite sure you're doing."

"But I know what I'm doing," Tony protested. "Four-quarter beat off-time . . ."

"I don't give a damn if you know it or not," Stearns interrupted. "It sounds like you don't. It's good commercial stuff. Not just musical comedy, but the Hit Parade kind of music. The stuff that makes money today."

"Thank you . . . " Tony began. Stearns again didn't let him finish.

"I want you to come to New York next month and work on a couple of numbers for a musical revue I'm going to do." It was not a request, but more of a command.

"Well, I . . . " Tony wanted to think about it. Stearns didn't give him time.

"Well? Yes or no?"

It was sharp, as if he would suffer upon Tony the extreme penalty if he refused. Tony didn't want to refuse. This was the opportunity that came once in a lifetime, the most important break of a career. But he thought about John. "Give me a minute?" he asked.

Stearns looked at his watch. He was a precise man.

Tony wondered whether John would understand. At once he knew that he wouldn't and at the same time knew that he would have to. The opportunity was too big to leave him any choice. He didn't take the full minute.

"I can't tell you how grateful I am . . ."

"Yes or no?"

"I'll be in New York whenever you say."

Stearns swallowed his remaining beer. When he looked up the brusqueness had disappeared. So did Tony's growing dislike. Stearns spoke softly now, as if he had consciously decided there was no longer a need for the sharp command.

"Good boy, Tony," Stearns said. "You've got a lot of talent. With my name and lyrics, you'll make out fine. I'm not being facetious. New York works that way."

"I know. Thanks." Tony smiled, relieved that the decision had been made and was past.

"With the contacts I'll get you, you'll be able to go ahead on your own after a while." Stearns held out his hand for the first time since he introduced himself. "Go ahead, shake," he said, "I'm not going to bite you." They held their hands clasped together for almost half-a-minute, both smiling warmly. "We'll celebrate," Stearns said. He called the waitress and ordered champagne. It took her ten minutes to find a bottle. She put it down on the table, puzzled that anyone from the college would order champagne. Stearns noticed her open-mouthed expression.

"Is there something wrong with it?" he demanded.

"No, sir."

"Then pour it and let us talk in private." He was harsh. "You'll get your tip." The waitress stammered a "yes, sir," poured the champagne and left hurriedly, glad to be away from Stearns' disagreeable attitude. She was to be shaken even more a moment later when he called her back and handed her a twenty-dollar bill "for your service."

They sipped the champagne slowly, Stearns explaining more fully what Tony's plans and duties would have to be. Tony would come to New York by the fifteenth of July. Stearns would locate a small apartment for him—"that's another thing you can get in New York only through contacts," he said—and advance him some money against future salary or royalties if he needed any. "This isn't businesslike or usual," Stearns had him understand. "I'm taking a long shot with you. But I think you'll pay off."

The likening of himself to a piece of business property disturbed Tony. He let it pass, concluding that this was, after all, just Stearns' manner of speaking to people, covering up perhaps something he himself lacked. Tony was told that he would work on perhaps half-a-dozen numbers on a trial basis. If one or two of them clicked, then Stearns' investment would be a success. If not, then they both would be losers. He talked, too, about the music writing business, about the composer's role in the entertainment business and, as he repeated several times, "the rat race that they call New York."

It was two o'clock in the morning when the champagne, the entire bottle, was finished and Tony glanced at his watch. Stearns seemed to have said all he wished to at that time, anyway. There was no talk for a minute, both sitting silently.

"Perhaps I'd better go soon," Tony said.

Stearns looked at him directly for a long second. "To your friend, the lyric writer," he said pointedly.

Tony felt his face flush. He wanted to say something, couldn't, and simply nodded. He grew angry at himself for feeling so small and overwhelmed and, as he knew, inadequate in dealing and talking with Stearns.

Stearns acknowledged the nod.

"Good friend?" Stearns asked.

"Yes." For a moment Tony felt like he was reliving something that had happened before. Almost three years before with the concert pianist. He looked inquiringly at Stearns, not quite believing now everything that had been said. He himself might have used this same approach with a younger, inexperienced person to achieve his own desires and needs. It occurred to him that this was in a sense what he had done with John. He looked straight at Stearns now, determined to find out if his suspicion was correct and, if so, to find the means of meeting the situation on a stronger plane.

"A very good friend," Tony said, his words slow and purposeful. He brushed at his hair several times nervously, the black lock nudging his forehead.

"Must be, at two in the morning," Stearns observed with the same definite tone.

"He is." Tony bit into the inside of his mouth and ran his tongue up and down the gums. Stearns noticed it.

"Don't worry about it," the latter said. "I understand." The words were still without an inflection of meaning.

Tony still wasn't sure. "I'm glad you understand." He said this purposefully, as a question begging for an answer.

Stearns got up without a word. Tony followed him into the street. It was dark except for the single street lamp surrounding them in a precise circle of light. Tony looked up toward where the street sloped toward the "hill." The trees were deep and dark, the secretive forest of two years before.

Stearns watched him, waited until he turned back. Then he put out his hand, shook it tightly. He held on to it. Quickly Tony wondered what his own answer would be. He was almost certain now that his suspicions had been correct.

"One thing you ought to know, Tony," Stearns said.

"Yes?"

"A man's personal life is his own. I don't pretend to interfere with it one way or another." Then, softly, the measured words lending emphasis. "My main hobby in life is women." He turned quickly and walked up the street toward his hotel.

Tony stood there. He felt like a child who had just been given a lollipop and a pat on the head. He wanted to be angry, but he couldn't. He somehow had to admire Gerald Stearns. In his own way, he wished to be like him.

John was awake when Tony returned to the apartment. The lights were on, both in the kitchen and the living room. An empty ice tray was on the kitchen table, a half empty bottle of bourbon on the end table by the couch. John was sitting there silently, a glass in his hand. Stravinsky's "Firebird Suite" played discordantly and too loudly. John didn't say anything, but watched Tony closely as he took off his jacket, his shirt, went into the bathroom, returned a minute later, sat on the edge of the couch. Tony began to speak, hesitated, went over to the piano, tinkled a moment with the keys. Then suddenly he stopped, turned away from the music and stood in front of John.

"I've got good news, Johnny-boy."

"Oh." John wasn't angry. He was silent because he was afraid. The evening had been a severance from Tony, the first like that they had known without having had a quarrel, and this was sufficient cause for fear.

"Good and bad," Tony amended. He broke it quickly. "Gerald Stearns offered me a trial job to come to New York and write some music for a new show he's doing."

"And . . .?" John shivered inside. He knew by Tony's attitude that this was the beginning of one life coming to an end without promise of reincarnation.

"Well, of course I took it. It's a good chance for me."

"Good for you. Bad for me." There was no emotion. It was as if John had been prepared for what had come. In his fear he had expected something like this for a long time. He felt that it was the pattern of incompleteness and insecurity of his own life. It was further proof that he was never meant to find a normal, stable happiness. "So that's the end of everything. You go to New York and I stay here and rot." He said this matter-of-factly, without emotion.

"It's not like that," Tony said. He was surprised for the second time that evening. He had expected John to be emotionally upset; that, he knew how to handle. But a quiet, unemotional John was another thing. "It's the chance of a lifetime for me," he continued quickly. "It'll only be a little while apart. Next year when you finish school you'll come to New York. And we'll just go on as if nothing had happened at all." He paused a moment. "We'll keep in touch with each other," Tony added.

John began to shake now. Until Tony mentioned "keep in touch" he was trying to remain steady. But the prospect of knowing each other now only long-distance was too clear and too much to take. His hands trembled and then his whole body. He threw himself against Tony, pulled him close to the couch and buried his head in his lap. "Don't, Tony, please don't go. Please don't leave me."

He hated himself for his weakness. But he couldn't help it. He felt Tony's fingers run over his hair, comforting him. He moved away, the trembling stopped. He wiped his eyes, was glad to find that they were dry. "You won't go, will you, Tony?" he pleaded.

Tony no longer had to be gentle. John was completely dependent now and there was no necessity for any compromise. He thought of what Stearns might say.

"I'm leaving for New York July fifteenth. You finish school and next year you'll join me there." The words were crisp and hard.

"I'll leave with you now," John offered.

"I'm going alone." Tony repeated it. It was final and definite.

John leaned on his knees at the edge of the bed, looking up at Tony.

"Please," he began.

Tony didn't wait for the rest. He turned, walked toward the piano, stood looking mechanically at the keys. John ran after him, grabbed onto his arms, digging his nails into the flesh.

"I won't let you go, Tony. I won't, I won't." His voice rose until it was almost a scream. Tony grabbed John's wrists, pulled them away, then, half-pushing, shoved John roughly onto the couch. He stood in front of him, the giant willing the fate of the lost little man.

"I tried to tell you calmly," Tony said. "But you have to act like a woman." His tone was bitter. He held the word "woman," letting it out slowly. He knew it would hurt more now, but he decided it was time to hurt. "I told you what my plans were. If you don't like them, then all I can say is for us to call it quits for good." Tony felt strong with the words. Like Gerald Stearns might handle the situation.

John didn't want to call it quits, even for the moment. He still hung on. "It's that Gerald Stearns, isn't it? It's because of him you're going." He felt like the jealous lover

Tony had just accused him of being. He didn't care. "It's that, isn't it?"

Tony laughed, first a low snort, then a loud booming sound. John stared at him, angry now. He wanted to scream at him, but somehow managed to hold it back.

"Do you know what Stearns told me?" Tony said, still laughing. "He told me his major hobby in life was women. I thought maybe he was going to proposition me and he told me his only interest was women." He stopped, looked down at John and squinted his dark eyes. "You poor god-damned stupid fool," he said.

John got off the couch, choking back the tears before they reached his cheeks. He opened the window by the piano, looked out into the back yard. It was empty. Dark and lonely and empty. Like himself. It made him feel less alone. He stood there a minute, maybe two, staring without thinking until the salt taste in his mouth disappeared. There was nothing more for him to do. He turned back into the room.

"I'm sorry, Tony," he said. He forced a smile. "Let's have a drink to celebrate the beginning of your success." He walked slowly to the kitchen to get another glass as Tony stood silently watching him.

John spent the next few weeks moodily, comparing himself to a condemned man waiting for the final day of life. Tony began to pack his clothing and personal belongings, transferring them to his home in Belleville. John watched their gradual removal, hurting as they went, as if part of himself was being taken with them. Soon the apartment on Academy Street was empty of Tony's things, leaving John the furnishings and the music system and albums. This was, John told himself bitterly, his legacy.

John decided to stay in Des Moines for the summer. He hated the thought of returning to Cleveland in his depression. Home would make his mood that much worse. He enrolled in two classes in summer school. He gave up his own room completely and moved everything to Tony's apartment, now his apartment. He pushed his clothes to one side of the closet, leaving it half empty. He filled only half of the bureau drawers. There was a morbid satisfaction in living in only half of an apartment. It let him know at a glance that something was missing, that he was living only half a life.

Tony stayed at the apartment in the evenings and often at night. But there were so many things for him to do: buying new clothes, packing, writing and receiving instructions from Stearns (the latter had obtained a sub-lease on an apartment for him on Barrow Street in Greenwich Village). Little time remained and that sped by quickly. Tony was pleased with John's apparent conciliation with the future and they made the most of what time did remain. When Tony could not come into the city, John would go to Belleville, sometimes for dinner, sometimes just to spend the evening in the music room, with Tony playing piano, or the two just sitting and drinking and talking.

John met Tony's father briefly. The latter seemed never to have time for anything but clients and eternal pinochle games. He saw Tony's sister, Carol, more often, but also briefly. He had met her before, when as a commuter to the college she occasionally stopped in at the Academy Street apartment. But he paid little notice to anyone or anything but Tony. The brief time allotted allowed concentration only on the latter. The nervousness and strain that he had experienced at first became a lethargy of acceptance, and though there was an occasional argument or irritation between them, John feared to let it strain too far. Now he had hopes only for the future and he feared to endanger them. Tony was helpful, the very fact of Tony's departure taking itself entirely out of their conversation as though the situation did not even exist. Only when he was alone was it perpetually on John's mind.

Then came the last night, with the final argument and the
bitterness that wasted into acceptance. Tony left and John
was left alone. For the moment.

When he saw Carol the following night it was with only
a vague sense of being. And when he asked her to come with
him to the college dance it was with even less understanding
of doing. One life had departed and the murmurs of his reincarnation into a new one were not yet conscious ones. In some
way the sense of his future did occur to him. When he left
Carol that first evening he had a presentiment that something
would happen to him.

But he didn't know what or how much.

# Chapter 9

The new life for John Thomas adjusted itself slowly. Conceivably, it might have happened quickly, but it didn't. Not at all friendly and clear like the multi-colored rainbow brightening up of the sky after the summer's rain. It was at first antagonistic and muddled.

The loneliness of the apartment following Tony's departure weighed more heavily than any other time John could remember. The rooms seemed bare, silent, empty, crying out to him with each minute of the hours and months when it had been otherwise. He tried to make it full with music, playing album after album. But this became tiring too quickly—too much symphonic music, good or bad, was like too many strong drinks taken one after another. It made his head swim and his mind noisy. That was the first day.

The second day he got up early, took a cold shower and felt better. The previous evening with Carol offered a lightness for him. The heat of the night had helped keep him awake and he was aware of the bed empty beside him. He went to his class, for summer school had begun, came home, did an hour's studying and took another cold shower to wash the sweat away. He returned to his books, this keeping him occupied the rest of the afternoon. Although inwardly his body continued to urge him to wait expectantly for Tony to open the door, outwardly he was for the most part composed. After supper, when evening came, there was nothing more with which to occupy himself, and the gnawing began again. It knotted up inside of him, crept through his stomach, pushing him back and forth in long circles across the apartment, unable to find a straight line to take him out of it. He sat down finally at the piano, played the single notes from the lead sheets of some of the last songs he and Tony had written together. For a moment it brought him closer to New York, and then the reminder was too strong and he hurriedly grabbed the music in a bundle, tossing it face down on top of the piano. Carefully, he closed the keyboard cover. He paced across the room again, stopping in the kitchen. For a brief moment he intended to go to the liquor. Then he decided in favor of his self-imposed martyrdom and left it alone.

His typewriter was open on the kitchen table. He had re-copied some class notes earlier and had been so glad to be finished with them that he left the machine, not bothering to put it away. It stared at him now, like an animal waiting for the trainer's command to do tricks. He sat in front of it idly, without purpose placed a white sheet of paper in the rollers and began to write. Still without direction, he spelled out his own sadness. He read aloud what he had written.

"John sat at the table, trying to busy himself by writing, but all during that time his inner self was fixed on the front door, wondering if Tony would miraculously walk in, yet knowing all the time that he wouldn't." He scratched the last line off quickly with a pencil and rewrote ". . . waiting for Tony to walk in and wondering." It made him feel better. The meaning wasn't so entirely hopeless. He reread it several times. And then a strange thing happened.

He suddenly realized that this was the first thing he had written for himself and not for Tony since he had met Tony. Even these few words gave him an odd kind of confidence. His actions that followed seemed natural enough at the time, but thinking about it later he wondered at the seeming unimportance of what proved to be his new beginning. He sat down at the typewriter again and, taking up from where the last line left off, continued to write.

Then another thought floated quickly by him, almost before he could grasp it, the possibility that perhaps Tony had not been the correct answer in the first place. This writing might be, after all, simply a purgation of his now-returned fears and insecurities. By writing about Tony and himself, he was somehow bringing Tony back and at the same time taking him physically away while keeping him close in memory. There was nothing wrong with this, he told himself. Indeed, he decided, his reason for writing was not important as long as it gave him the impetus to do so. He re-read the pages carefully, made notes at the margins for revision and correction. The prospect of extensive writing solidified his own feelings and was in essence a putting together again of what he felt was a shattered existence. He decided to change the names, the locale, but use the same people, those he knew and himself and all his experiences and put it into a novel. It was the novel he had been thinking about writing all his life, the one that had been waiting for him and that he had finally caught up to.

He slept little that night. Thoughts of Tony did not torment him in the same way as the night before. He did not push the remembrance aside. He reached for Tony; he knew how much he needed him and it was unnatural to suddenly not need him any longer. But Tony now had been, in part, transferred from the empty sheets to the full page on a type-writer, and this gave Tony at least some kind of existence.

Tony had been the crutch and the crutch was no longer a vital
necessity. John felt he could stand by himself. As small as it
was, this sudden self-reliance was a remarkable achievement.
It was a changing pattern of life, thrust suddenly at him, and
he couldn't help but be afraid. The crack in the armor loomed
large and recrimination poured through. It was too quick
a change for John to accept. He slept past his class hours
and awoke early the next afternoon. Tony had begun to slip
even further away and the crack in the armor widened. John
tried to close it, but the more he pushed the more strained
it became. "I can't let this happen," he said to himself aloud.
"If I lose Tony, I lose myself." Out loud it sounded more
emphatic.

He sat at the typewriter again that evening and the writing came easily. He tried to stop it, for the more he wrote
about Tony, the more objective he became about him. He
stopped typing, trying to come to a decision over what was
happening. It was something not to be decided. It was simply
a thing that was happening, for good or for bad.

He knew full well that this beginning, these buds of
doubt that he could not live without Tony, could not be
stopped. But at the same time these buds threatened a
catechism that had been the cornerstone of his existence for
more than two years, and when the first crack in the foundation begins to open it is only reasonable to expect that the
buds will push their way upward until the flowers struggle
for air and the pressure breaks the concrete vise open into the
freshness of that air. Nature had never yet been stopped.

He didn't write further on the novel that evening. He
had almost decided to forget about it, to let it lie in a corner
of the bookshelf and gather dust, or to burn it, like the self-
styled Puritans ridding their souls of the prejudged evils in
man or matter by throwing the object of their fear into a fire.
He went to bed after midnight. It was hot again, too muggy

for the usually dry Midwest. The humidity drained over
him and wet him with swollen globules of perspiration. He
tossed in the bed, throwing the sheet off, then finding it and
pulling it back over him as if the protective covering might
shut out everything else and allow him to find the peacefulness of sleep. He was almost asleep when the noise of a party
upstairs awakened him. The floor vibrated to pounding feet
and he could hear the sound of loud, fast, rhythmical music.
Occasionally the music stopped, a low voice would speak a
few words, and then a roar of laughter, the approval following
a good joke or a jovial dedication. John pulled the pillow over
his head, half smothering himself in his insistence to force
sleep. But the feet were stronger and continued to pound
back and forth, shouting down from the ceiling with each
step.

He looked at his watch. Two in the morning. He tried
to think more about the novel and about Tony. It was too
stifling to do it clearly. He found only the dichotomy of need
and rejection. How terribly he wanted to write and how
much better he felt about Tony when he put his thoughts
down in words rather than letting them hurt so much inside
of him. At the same time he realized how much he needed
the reassurance of the life that Tony had given him. What
terrible things must certainly await him, he reasoned, without Tony as the symbol of security.

At five o'clock in the morning the pounding upstairs
had stopped, the music was gone. Half awake, he heard the
unhushed voices on the staircase outside and the pointed
high-heeled shoes digging with sharp gasps into the linoleum
stair treads. He had not solved his problem; but the voices
and movement and the half-grey light coming through the
window let him know that life did not stand still but moved
inexorably forward, for better or for worse. He got up out
of bed, washed his face in the cold water of the wash-basin,

went into the kitchen and sat down at the typewriter and began to write.

The week passed and the writing continued. Not too much, but enough for John to know that soon his novel would begin to crawl under its own power and, after that, to walk. The book became an entity unto itself and inasmuch as Tony was in it, Tony became clear again in his mind. He was in full bloom, only now the thorns didn't prick at John. They only reached out toward him.

The evening for the dance he had asked Carol to arrived. John dressed gingerly, not quite sure of what he was doing or why. He shaved carefully, too carefully, nicking his face several times. He tried three different ties, matching them to his light brown gabardine suit, finally chose what he felt would be the right one. It took several attempts before he tied it to his satisfaction. He made sure the collar of his white shirt had been pressed just right and he shined his shoes until they were smooth, without the usual cracks and rough edges. He had never gone to such trouble before in dressing and it was a great deal of trouble because he could not understand why he was being so meticulous. He felt a twinge of anxiety in his stomach because he wanted all the effort to be worth something. He decided it was the making of a proper impression and this worried him because he wasn't sure what the proper impression should be or why. Even after he was all dressed and ready to leave, he wanted to talk himself out of going. Yet, he felt that for some reason he must go. It seemed that somehow this was tied in with the whole new concept of existence he had been forced into since Tony left. With the premonition of the extra-sensitive person who has begun to understand subjectively his relationship to society and people, John felt that something important was about to happen.

He walked slowly after he got off the bus in Belleville. He was tempted to pick the green leaves from the bushes, but he didn't. He told himself that he didn't want to get the green fuzz into his clean fingernails or onto his hands. Actually, he tried not to succumb to his nervousness. In compensation, his fingers twitched and his index finger dug at the torn edge of the cuticle on his thumb. He stopped and bit off the ragged skin. He felt better. Carol was dressed and waiting when he rang the bell.

She opened the door quickly and he was struck again by how much she looked like Tony. She stood in front of him and the light in the hall made her black hair shine even darker as it hung down across her shoulders, reaching to the top of the off-the-shoulder bright red gown. When she went to the closet, put a cape around herself, he remembered that he should probably compliment her on her dress. He did, a little hesitantly.

She laughed. "Just like Tony," she said. He followed her around the side of the house, to the garage. "We'll use Dad's car," she told him. "You drive, don't you?"

He mumbled that he did. "What do you mean 'Just like Tony'?" he asked her. The reference bothered him.

"He never noticed my clothes, either. Till all of a sudden he remembered he ought to be polite and mention how nice I look." She laughed. "That's a silly custom. Sometimes a girl doesn't look so nice and it would be better for nothing to be said."

John silently thanked her for understanding. He backed the new Dodge out of the garage onto the street and started toward the college. They didn't speak for a while and in the silence John began to wonder at the incongruity of the moment. The more he thought, the more uncertain he became, and the misgivings he had felt a few hours before returned. He told himself that there was no reason to be frightened. The car frightened him. The wheels of the car speeding along the black-tarred highway reminded him of the ride three years before and the girl in the tavern. That was the only other time he had been out with a girl. This time, he wondered, would it be any different? He knew that rationally there could be no comparison. But he was nevertheless afraid.

But he was not afraid of dancing per se. He thought he'd be able to dance passably well. He was not really even afraid of Carol. She was too much like Tony. It was the people that frightened him. The people at the dance that he knew and the ones he didn't know. The conversations, the laughing, the little amenities that he had never had to do and would encounter that evening—all these were fearful. He determined to try to enjoy himself. That's what Tony used to say. Enjoy yourself now and worry about it later. This relaxed him for the moment and he turned and smiled at Carol. She smiled back. He was grateful that she had allowed him to remain silent and think it out. Suddenly, the fear of the unknown came back to him. Who would he meet and what would he have to say, and would he be able to say it? What would he have to do and, even knowing, would he be able to do it? The wheels of the car spinned faster and hummed louder and the knotting inside of his stomach began following them around in a circle.

Carol watched him closely, not understanding what was bothering him, but knowing that he was troubled. That he was shy and afraid, she suspected. She didn't know why.

"If you don't feel well," she suggested, "we can turn around and spend a nice quiet evening at home." She touched his arm lightly. "I really won't mind," she said.

This made him feel better again. It was funny, he thought, how she could make him feel better so easily. He decided that he would go to the dance and that he would try to enjoy it, too.

"I guess it's just a long time since I've been to a dance, so I'm a little nervous." He tried to be gracefully humorous.

"I guess I just don't know what to do with such a beautiful dancing partner." It wasn't as hard to say as he thought it should have been.

"Thank you, Mr. Thomas," Carol said formally. "If you have any trouble in dancing, just let me know and we'll solve the problem together."

He noticed her teeth as she smiled, white and straight, melting into her cheeks, giving the long narrow bones a gentle roundness and at the same time a physical softness and sweetness that he felt was proper, matching the rest of her.

The car turned onto a bare highway and a breath of air blew in through the windows, making the inside of the car whirl with freshness. John's head felt clearer. Next to him, Carol brushed back a lock of black hair that the wind had blown down over her forehead. It was a sight memory as John glanced at her, satisfied that she would take care of him should anything go wrong.

He parked the car in the parking lot a few hundred feet from the gymnasium where the dance was. Young men and women, arm in arm, laughing and joking, emerged from surrounding cars and seemed to descend like a horde of alien beings on the gymnasium.

"This way, John," Carol said, and led him toward the building, holding onto his hand. They mixed into the crowd of people. He felt like a stranger among the Philistines.

They began to walk in when one of the ushers stopped him. He blushed uncomfortably, hastily took out money for the dance tickets. He was sure everyone was watching him and laughing at his uncertainty. He squirmed uneasily in his collar.

Carol helped him again. "If your collar's too tight, loosen it," she whispered. "I don't mind. And it's too dark for anybody here to see."

"No, it's not that," he assured her. "I guess I'm just not used to a dance . . . the tickets, the people, the whole responsibility . . . " He stopped at the word and smiled at his own inadequacy in making something important out of what was really only trivial. It was not a small thing to him, however, and the very word "responsibility" made him feel uneasy. Since he had met Tony, there had been no need for him to assume any of it. He looked hard at Carol, then took her by the arm onto the dance floor. He wouldn't worry about responsibility.

The music started and they danced. "You'll have to excuse me," John apologized again. "It's been so long since I've danced." His only dancing had, in fact, been during the past year in the apartment as he and Tony tried out some pop dance music. He lost the beat of the music now and skipped several times, trying not to step on Carol's toes. The band played a slow fox-trot. He found it easier to follow.

"You dance all right," Carol tried to assure him. She compared him to her brother and suspected that John, too, was uncertain in the social graces, even such a small one as dancing. She felt that there were perhaps many outward graces he lacked. But she felt, too, that there were many things inside that were deep. She wanted to help him be comfortable. After several numbers she found it easier to follow him as he gathered the sweep of the music and the pattern of the beat into his step. The first set finished, the band turned to fast music. Along with dozens of other couples, they left the dance floor. Again John apologized.

"I'm sorry, I can't dance this fast music at all. I'm not particularly fond of it, either."

They sat on one of the benches that lined the edge of the dance floor. The lights were low and the shadows covered them. People passed and others sat near them, but all melted into the semi-darkness and it was almost as if they were all alone.

"You don't have to keep apologizing to me, John," Carol said when they were seated. "I'm really having a very good time."

"I guess I just feel sort of foolish," he said. "Do you mind if I tell you something, Carol?"

"No."

"This is really the first time I've ever been dancing at a real dance." He felt embarrassed saying the words, then knew it was all right. He wanted to say more, but the music stopped and the lights came on. People hurriedly got up from their seats and walked toward the exit.

"Just a twenty-minute break," Carol explained. "There's no smoking allowed in here, so everybody heads outside every time the band takes a break." She stood up. "Want a cigarette?" she asked.

"Sure." He got up, took her by the hand and led her through the crowd to the outdoors. They found a concrete walk around the edge of the building, followed it, and half-leaned, half-sat against the stone outer sill of a street-level window at the far side of the gym. John offered her a cigarette, took one for himself, lit them. They puffed the smoke out contentedly, remaining silent for perhaps a minute.

Then, very calmly and softly, Carol moved close to John, spoke to him. "Why are you so tense, John?" She liked him and wanted to help him relax.

He was taken aback for the moment by the bluntness of the question. But he felt she was serious and honest about it. It gave him an opportunity to resume talking to her. "I guess I am, a little," he admitted.

"You seem frightened of something," she said gently.

"I am," he answered, telling part of the truth. "Like I said, this is the first time I've ever gone to a dance and as a matter of fact the first time I've ever gone with someone . . ." He spread his palms upward to transfer his stuttering into mime.

"I shouldn't have asked." She flipped the half-smoked cigarette out toward the grass, watching it stain wet with the night dew. She turned to John again. "I just want you to know that you don't have to act formal with me. We have known each other, in a way, for two years now, so we can be friends, can't we?"

John nodded his head and smiled, letting her know he understood and that he was happy she did, too. The music had started again and they could hear it softly from around the corner of the brick building. John took her hand and started back, leading her this time along the narrow brick pavement, finding his way through the darkness by the outline of the wall a little bulkier than the rest of the blackness around him.

Inside again, they began dancing, talking but little, mostly just moving along slowly and easily with the music. As they danced, they passed people John knew and, meeting their glance, he answered their greetings with a nod of his head. The first few times he was embarrassed and tried to avoid the eyes of people he recognized. But as he met more and more, he began to enjoy the pleasure of being a recognizable part of this group and played a game with himself of keeping on the watch for acquaintances, anxious to dance into a position where he might exchange greetings with them.

"You're more popular than I imagined," Carol said finally.

John hesitated. "I met them through writing the musicals with Tony," he explained modestly.

He was rather surprised at the number of people he knew. These were not close friends, the ones from the dormitory parties or the crowds he and Tony had circulated in. They were classroom acquaintances, those who nodded a friendly hello on the campus, some from the drama club. These were new people in his social milieu and he began to compare them with his own group. They, too, seemed to be searching for something and, it seemed, in almost exactly the same way his close friends did. Only here there were a great many more of them. He studied the long somber faces of some of the men and the stony features of their female companions, dancing hurriedly as if they were trying to finish the dance as quickly as possible so they might rush home to bed, to the back seat of a car, or to a formal kissless, thankless goodnight in front of the women's dormitory. There were smiling faces, some who seemed to be enjoying themselves almost too much, as if they were trying to insist that they were having a good time instead of, as they really were doing, forcing themselves to comply with the conventional norms of the social atmosphere they wished to be in. Some couples just danced, friendly and relaxed. John imagined he and Carol looked like one of this group.

He noticed one girl in particular, a large stout red-headed girl, her hair tied tightly at the back part of her head with a huge black velvet ribbon, the red strands sprawling aimlessly down over her bare back. There was much of it to cover. Each time he saw this girl she was dancing with another man and each time she would be roaring with laughter and her steps would be light and quick and high. He decided that he should feel sorry for her, for her apparent difficulty in forcing herself to enjoy conformity. He smiled and thought that by the same token he should be sorry for himself. But he couldn't really be, for although this was not the society he belonged to, and he had found security in another, he felt pleasant and relaxed and did not feel that he was forcing himself any longer.

He asked Carol who the red-headed girl was. "The one who seems to be having so much fun."

Carol looked. "That's Helen McCall," she said. "She always has a lot of fun." They danced a moment more. "Would you like to meet her?" Carol asked.

John quickly answered in the negative. "I was just curious," he explained.

"It looks like you have no choice," Carol said. The red-headed girl had left her partner and was coming towards them. John stiffened and felt Carol's reassuring squeeze on his hand. "Relax," she whispered. "She's a very nice girl." She wondered a moment about John's behavior, then dismissed it as an unaccountable shyness.

The girl came up, put an arm around Carol's shoulder and surveyed John.

"Who's the handsome new boyfriend?" she inquired. John shifted his feet uncomfortably. Helen noticed. "Don't mind me, "she laughed. "I have no manners whatsoever."

Carol introduced them. "You worked with Carol's brother on the musical, didn't you?" Helen said to John.

"Yes." John hoped she would leave quickly. Everything had gone so well, he didn't want anything to upset it.

"I've never danced with a songwriter," Helen said. "Do you mind?"

She was looking at Carol. Carol looked at John helplessly, not knowing how to spare him the predicament. Without waiting, Helen took John's hand and moved herself close against him. John looked at Carol, felt a little better by her reassuring smile. Fretfully, he began dancing. The girl's manner suddenly changed.

"I hope you don't mind me taking you away from Carol like this," she said. She spoke softly and sweetly. John sputtered in surprise.

"No . . . no . . . of course not."

"I don't have a date for tonight," she confided, "so I sneaked in and I'm going around dancing with all my girlfriends' boyfriends." She was interested in talking. John nodded and let her go on. "Too many people take these dances too seriously," she continued. "I think they're just a place for people to get together and enjoy one another's company. Not a formal thing where somebody expects something of somebody else and everybody walks around looking like they're performing a duty. It's just a place to have fun."

They swung across the floor quickly and brushed up close against the bandstand, in the overlap of the spotlight where the other couples could clearly see. John didn't mind as much as he thought he should have. He was particularly interested in how well he was dancing. He had made only a few mistakes in his step.

"So I come to have fun," Helen said as they danced back into the crowd and the semi-darkness of the dance floor. "I think that's what life is for. To do what you want, what's best for you as a person, and as long as you're not hurting anyone never mind what anybody thinks. Most of those people who object to other people being like that usually have something to hide, anyway."

They had crossed the dance floor again, to the side where Carol was. The music stopped and Helen left John's arms. Carol came up and put her hand into his.

"Thanks for the dance," Helen said. "And for listening." John thanked her in return. "I'll see you again," she said. She straightened the velvet-wrapped tail of red hair and trotted off to another couple she knew.

"That wasn't too bad, was it Johnny?"

"You know," he mused, "she's a very nice girl."

They danced again, and as the evening moved along John found more and more pleasure in making his feet adapt to the music. He shied when Carol attempted to show him the steps for the rumba, gradually tried out the movement, and when the next rumba was played found himself pleasantly surprised in being able to dance it.

"And quite well, too," Carol encouraged him.

They laughed and they danced and with each dance John felt Carol's body coming closer to his. At first he attempted to push her away, not roughly, but with an automatic rebelling. She moved away, hiding her embarrassment. Later on, during the slow numbers, they came close again and John did not rebel. Mentally, he thought that there should be some kind of ugliness in his closeness to a woman's body. Physically, for some strange reason he could not determine, it was not so distasteful.

They went outside for another cigarette, then came back in.

"I almost forgot," Carol said.

"What?"

"The chaperones."

John didn't understand. "They have some rule about not letting us poor innocent college girls go to dances unescorted," she explained. "They're afraid all kinds of dire things may happen on a gym floor. So they get some of the faculty to come to each dance as watchdogs. We ought to go see them before we leave."

"Is it necessary?"

"If they saw us here and we didn't say hello, they might not be so friendly in class. Good politics for good grades."

John agreed and they walked toward the far side of the building where a number of chairs had been placed along the wall. Several were occupied by the older faculty who were talking with each other, seemingly oblivious to everything else. The rest were empty, but Carol recognized some of the teachers nearby, dancing or standing in the vicinity, ready for the unhappy duty of the reception line.

John shook hands first with the Dean of Men and his wife, young looking people who were more concerned with getting back to dancing than with the greeting. The Dean smiled at John, acknowledging an unspoken rejection of the formality. Then John shook hands with a large portly man who, Carol explained later, was head of the physics department. His wife, if anything, was even larger. He was gruff, over-bearing, and his condescension so open that there was no doubt he felt he was doing the students a favor by being there to shake their hands. John decided he didn't like him. They were greeted by several more faculty members. To his right, before he turned to go, he heard a familiar man's voice call his name. John turned and saw who it was and wanted to run. But he waited until the man came over. He shook hands with him, his own hand suddenly sticky with sweat.

"Don't tell me you were going to pass me by, John. Even psychology professors go to dances."

John started to say, "Hello, Woody," remembered where he was. "It's good to see you, Dr. Fisher." He wondered what Woody was doing at the dance, even as a faculty member. He seemed just as out of place as John thought he, himself, must seem to Woody. He introduced Carol.

"Carol and I are old friends," Woody said. "From a freshman psychology class, wasn't it?"

"You have a good memory, professor."

"All professors are supposed to have good memories—and bad bank accounts," Woody answered. They laughed with him. "Are you enjoying the dance?"

John knew the question was directed to him. Carol answered in the affirmative. John hesitated, still embarrassed. He finally muttered "Yes."

"That's perfectly normal psychology," Woody smiled. John knew again that the words were not flip, that they were meant for him. Their eyes met and John remembered what Woody had once told him: "Be yourself." Woody spoke again. "As long as you have a good time. That's the important thing. Am I right, Carol?"

"I'm certainly enjoying myself," she answered.

"And you, John?" Woody had asked him before; now it was a suggestion.

John smiled and accepted the suggestion. He had thought at first that Woody would look somehow disdainfully upon him, on his doing something that might seem abnormal to the society in which they had first known each other. He knew differently now. "I'm having a very fine time," he said. He tried to judge his own strength. "Carol is Tony's sister," he said slowly.

The psychologist looked at him, momentarily surprised, then smiled broadly. "Tony and John are both friends of mine," he explained to Carol, hiding his surprise at John's statement of a thing that might have been otherwise accompanied by deep feelings of guilt. He was pleased that John had ventured the association. "Tony's been in New York for a while now, hasn't he?" Woody asked.

"A few weeks," John said quietly.

"Have you heard from him yet?"

"No."

"I imagine he'll be interested to know that you two are having fun together," Woody said purposively.

"I haven't written him about it," John said quickly.

"It doesn't matter," the psychologist advised. "I wouldn't worry about it one way or the other." He shook hands with them again. "I'd better get back to that greeting line. Anything to make the administration happy." He stopped, turning back to them. "Stop in and see me at my office some time, John."

"Thanks, Dr. Fisher." John smiled and felt better.

"I didn't know you knew Dr. Fisher that well," Carol said.

"Oh, I thought he mentioned. I met him through Tony." That was all.

They returned to dancing and after the last number was played, at one o'clock in the morning, went out to the car. They were tired, but in the tiredness they seemed to lose any tenseness they might have started the evening with. John's ups and downs of mood, which had begun with depressions of guilt and moved pleasantly into acceptance of the situation, had reached a feeling of satisfaction and even pleasure.

The drive home was nice. They rolled the windows down and let the early morning air whip against the car, splashing them with its coolness. John watched the patches of wood and concrete and brick construction flash by and then concentrated on the forms of the woods as they reached the outskirts of Des Moines. He felt like the shadowy trees, comfortable and secure, hidden within their own little islands of darkness, not worried about the morning or what the light of day would bring. The road was empty and he drove easily, the car almost driving itself.

He parked the car, then walked with Carol to the front steps, almost forgot himself and walked inside with her as he had done with Tony on many an early morning in the past.

"I can't tell you what a really wonderful time I had, Johnny," she said before he could speak. "I know that's what's usually said, but I really mean it. I hope you had a good time, too."

Suddenly he began to feel a choking in his stomach. It was time for saying goodnight and he hadn't thought about it. It was, again, something new and unknown and he was not prepared for it. He wanted to mutter a quick "good-bye" and start for the bus. But he didn't have time to think about it or about what other procedure he should follow.

"I had a good time," he said, the words coming out automatically, strange to his ears, as if his lips were moving but the words were coming from someplace else. "And perhaps we can go to the next dance together?" These words were even more astounding and even as he said them he wanted to call them back. But he was glad, too, that they were said. He held his breath, trying to accustom himself to the strangeness. He took her hand quickly, held it loosely, then squeezed his fingers around it, feeling the softness and warmth of the skin, began to shake it, then slowly let it fall from his hand.

"The next dance would be fine." Carol was smiling. He nodded and started to turn. Carols' voice called him back. "Johnny."

He looked at her.

"Remember, you're not a stranger here," she said. "You're welcome to come over any time." She turned quickly and went inside.

He remained for a moment, staring. Then he walked to the bus. The walk, the bus ride, the few steps to the apartment passed by quickly as if they had not even occurred. He was thinking deeply, trying to fit the circumstances of the evening into a pattern of life where heretofore they would not have been even admitted for consideration. He was relaxed and satisfied and this disturbed him. The successful conclusion of what he imagined would prove to be a failure in his social experiment disturbed him. The people he had seen during the evening, the diversification of security and insecurity of the hundreds on the dance floor being no different from that of the ten or twenty in a dormitory room party disturbed him. His own adjustment to a situation that he had never been able to face before disturbed him. He wondered how that could be? He did not feel that he could really find a security on two planes, as the facts suggested. Did it mean that he really didn't have a place in either? he asked himself. Or did he fit into both? Had he, by what had happened that evening, proved himself an apostate to the one society and, more important, to Tony and all that he stood for? There had been too much goodness with Tony to forget. He got a drink for himself and sat with the one glass in his hand on the opened couch and felt that there should be two glasses full, one for Tony. Then he would have someone to solve his

dilemma. But it was hardly more than a wish; there was not
the deep depressing aching of a few days before. He drank
from the glass, put it in the sink, put a sheet of clean paper
in his typewriter still open on the kitchen table, and wrote
Tony a letter. He wrote about school, about himself. He asked
about the various things he thought Tony might be doing
in New York. He wrote how he had felt when Tony left and
reminded him of their promise to be together again the following year. He stopped there. Now there was only one thing
more to write about: his date with Carol. He put in one line:
"I spent a few hours with Carol; we talked about you." He
wanted to write about the surprisingly good time he had at
the dance. But he didn't. He hoped Carol would not write too
much to Tony about the dance. He closed the letter, sealed it
in an envelope and left it on the table, ready to mail it first
thing in the morning.

He felt a bit relieved, but the problem had not been
solved. It was too difficult to think about and, besides, he
was too tired. He would just let it work itself out. He turned
out the light and got into bed. A feeling of guilt reminded
him of the evening again. He should have written Tony that
he had enjoyed himself. He felt that he had done something
wrong. At the same time, his thinking turned to the next
dance that he would take Carol to and the thoughts were
relaxing and calm. He kept these thoughts as he closed his
eyes.

He slept well that night.

# Chapter 10

John saw Carol often. By the end of the summer he was with her almost every evening. His afternoons were spent writing, his mornings at class. He was pleased with the progress of his novel. What had begun as a rebellion against the frustration of his immediate existence developed into a full scale revolution. His writing became a positive action.

He didn't shy from the house in Belleville as he had two months previously when Tony had left. Dinner and conversations with Carol in the same rooms where he had spent so many hours with Tony bothered him no longer. The memories were not pressing. Sometimes he and Carol would drive onto the open highway, going no place in particular, melding into the flat, plate-like countryside, becoming a part of the fields and the shadowless vista. Other times they drove to the rim of the city, alone except for the gold-lit dome of the State Capital striking out over the low-flat houses of Des Moines. Each time he saw Carol he found more of a relaxation with her; the relaxation soon became indispensable and he desired her closeness. He found he could talk to her—no longer was Tony a necessary part of their conversation—about himself, excluding the two years past, about his childhood, his schoolwork, and now about his novel. In turn, she talked to him about what she felt and wanted and she read the pages of his manuscript and gave him her opinions and he valued her suggestions and used them. He found that he could give of himself and receive from Carol in a calm, peaceful manner on an equal basis.

Sometimes he felt so close to Carol that he vaguely thought about a continuing relationship, but pushed it out of his mind. When a physical sensation presented itself—when they danced together or walked holding hands or when she sat close to him in the car—he unexpectedly enjoyed it. Not the sharp vivid staccato he had known with Tony, but a warmth and fullness of not only give and take but of belonging, a favorite word he had used in his relationship with Tony, only now it had a different meaning. It was not a conciliation to a new lifestyle, for he was bothered often with thoughts of distrust—distrust of his own feelings of rationality that permitted him to be part of the kind of relationship he had always disdained. He had not yet dared to kiss Carol and at first had no inclination to do so, but after their summer months together the feeling that not only he should, but that he wanted to, grew stronger. He did not understand what was happening to him, but he did not deny it. And he did nothing to try to stop it.

They parked one evening on the treeless concrete drive that runs southwest of the city, a bare ribbon that tries to slope upward, then gives in to the natural flatness of the area and settles itself on an even plane. They were far enough from the city to catch its panorama. The lights of the streets and the business places and the shadowed rooftops of the cramped buildings of the interior and the shining dome of the Capitol Building and the yellow bulbs of the porched and windowed houses of the suburbs mixed together into an impression of a large city. The car was parked on a concrete shoulder that jutted off the road from the main highway, built, perhaps, by a sympathetic contractor who expected that young people would welcome such a place to park. Other cars were parked nearby.

Carol looked out at the city. She leaned back against the seat cushion, her hair blown, her face clean and fresh. John, too, felt free and alive, helped by the tingly clear wind that had blown in on them as they drove.

"You feel as if you can almost reach into the city and grab a handful of everything and hold it in your hand," Carol said.

"Sometimes you can if you want to," John answered.

"Do you want to?" Carol asked him. John looked at her, trying to find a right answer. He let her eyes catch his, hold on to them.

"I've never had that kind of confidence," he said slowly.

"But that doesn't mean you never will," she said to him. She moved closer to him, her eyes never wavering from his. He felt his stomach begin to quiver and his chest pound. His palms felt wet as he closed them. Her face was very close to his and the black hair that sprayed in a lock over her forehead touched against his cheek. He shivered and then stopped, not moving. Not altogether willingly, because willingly he might have gone away. There was no other choice; it seemed that what was happening was inevitable. He would not fight it and could not. He looked from her eyes to the city and knew that whatever his destiny would be, this must be part of it.

"I am holding the city in my hand right now," he said, the words barely audible. "The city and everything in it and everything beyond it." The words were strange to him, spoken. These were words he had before only written, for only in writing had he heard the silent sounds of his creativity. Now that he had heard them aloud he knew that this, too, was part of his creation.

He lifted her head and held it close to his and kissed her, first gently, softly, barely touching her lips, and then strongly, feeling full of her lips and of her body pressed equally close against his.

"The city, the world is mine," he thought to himself. He was afraid that when he let Carol go it would go, too. But it didn't. Even as they drove back to Belleville his body remained keyed, continuing its euphoria on the bus back to the city. There were no cracks in the sidewalk as he walked to his apartment.

Back in the apartment he tried to understand what had happened, just as he had almost every night for the two months past. Only this time it was more important to understand because what had happened, albeit only the closeness of a kiss, felt like the confirmation of a new existence. He had met on even terms that which he had so long feared, the female relationship, which for so long had been a woman on horseback. The sudden disappearance of that fear both excited and puzzled him.

He tried to rationalize the situation between himself and Carol. He told himself that he was attracted, at first, because of her resemblance to Tony. This was no longer true. She was a person unto herself, distinct and different from Tony. She was gentle and kind, understanding, intelligent in her ideas and beliefs, incisive in her appraisal of his work, encouraging to him. Mentally she gave him a strength and confidence he had not known before. It was not a full confidence nor was he sure that it was a lasting one. Physically he found in her a beauty and an aesthetic attraction. He evaluated calmly; he thought of every factor. But the word love did not yet enter his calculations.

He knew that his intensity of feeling toward Tony had been gradually diminishing. He wasn't sure whether it was because Carol had absorbed this feeling, but he knew that what had once been an immutable dependence was no longer there. He could not deny that some dependency still existed.

He could not yet be fully objective toward Tony. He could not totally accept the idea that the role Tony had played in his life for two years was no longer required.

With Carol he would occasionally let his mind and body drain into inaction and trust her to carry him and give him strength. He knew this and it worried him that Carol might know it, too. He wanted it to be otherwise with her. It was at these moments that he especially could not dismiss Tony from his need.

As John's novel grew, so did his affection for Carol. When he didn't see her, he found it difficult to write, and when he did see her it was with a combination of inspiration and remorse. He wrote well and he worried more. Worried whether he could complete the relationship with her that was gradually coming to a head. Worried whether he ought to. Woody Fisher tried to explain what was happening to him.

"Your need before was in something, someone who shielded you from your insecurities, your childhood fears. Tony gave you that security. A person upon whom you could be dependent. With him you found the answer to the inner need that enabled your body and mind to do what was required for daily living. With Tony gone, you needed security again. You took the closest substitute, Tony's sister. Only she proved not to be a substitute but a reality in herself and the reality is not one on which you can lean completely as you did before, but which encourages your growing self-confidence and self-assuredness. Whether the security you find now is less, the same, or greater than that you found with Tony is something only you can determine."

John sat attentively in Woody Fisher's office. Woody looked a long time at John. "Does this sum up what you've been telling me?"

"I think so. But it somehow doesn't seem right."

"Your worry now that you are doing something strange, something different, is natural," Woody continued. "You feel that because you were happy in one life, somehow you shouldn't be happy in another. You live in the environment of the moment that you are happiest in, insofar as you can control your environment. Even groups know this. That is why new ideals are made and how revolutions occur. You try to achieve your own self-determination within your society or societies, present and possible."

John nodded that he understood.

"You were normal in one world," Woody continued, "now you feel normal in another. Sometimes there's a division and you find yourself torn between both. This does not seem to be clear in your case. Perhaps someday you shall find you wish to return to the first kind of society you knew, or to be part of both, but right now you seem to feel that you belong to the second. Do you understand?"

John said he did.

"I should warn you," Woody said. "You were weak with Tony. This was obvious from the first day I knew you. Now you have to be strong. That you are not yet, I know. I can't tell you how to be. All I can say is that you will gradually have to find the way. If it doesn't come about, then maybe you will undergo another upheaval. We'll just have to wait and see."

John thanked him and turned to leave. He had one more question. "How much shall I tell Carol, Woody?"

"Sometimes it's psychologically wise to instruct a patient to follow the old adage of 'what they don't know won't hurt them.' I advise it in this case, providing it doesn't hurt you. You can judge if it seems to."

John thanked him again. Woody walked with him into the hall. They shook hands warmly. "Don't worry, Johnny,"

Woody said. "Whatever happens, I think you'll come out all right."

John felt better and the dichotomy of his feelings didn't disturb him as much. The important thing now, as Woody had told him, was his gradual building of confidence into a real strength. It was during one evening with Carol that he had the opportunity to find some of that strength. The incident in itself was just one of many relatively unimportant happenings in most peoples' lives, but it gave John an opportunity to solve a problem that in other circumstances he would have run from or left to someone else, like Tony. The solution was now solely in his hands.

They drove to a town called Dexter, some twenty miles west of Des Moines, a small village whose entire existence seemed predicated on the number of bars and saloons whose services it offered to young couples and some older people who preferred to escape from their own little towns and cities for entertainment. They stopped at an inn near the center of Dexter, a clean, neat brick building outside of which were parked some twenty or so cars, giving evidence that, if nothing else, the beer was probably good. A sign over the entrance to the inn announced a band and dancing. The inside was divided into two parts, a set of tables at the left filling in completely every spare inch of space and a dance floor at the right at the far end of which was a small platform occupied by a five-piece band. It was not a nice place in the sense of middle-class propriety, in the manner that the corner pool parlor is not a nice place compared to the game room of a country club. Most of the men were in shirt sleeves, some in white tee-shirts. The women wore simple blouses and skirts, a few in low-necklined brightly colored dresses as flashy as the imitation jewelry they wore. It was a hot night and the heat of early October, lingering heavily as the residue of a late summer, made the evening too sticky and humid for the uncomfortable pretension of ties and jackets.

A number of the men there without dates were a bit too full of liquor and made nuisances of themselves on the dance floor, cutting in on some of the dancing couples. Nobody seemed to mind too much, however, and John and Carol, watching, decided that the inn was probably frequented by neighborhood people who knew each other and tolerated each other's eccentricities. Some of the women without male companions followed a parallel procedure, moving from table to table where men sat alone. John and Carol sat at a small table against the far wall, away from the crowd. Carol drank martinis. John still preferred bourbon and ginger ale. It was a sweet drink, hiding the taste of liquor which still disturbed him, but strong enough to give him the warmth and giddiness of alcohol satisfaction.

"We don't talk about Tony as much as we used to," Carol said suddenly. John looked up cautiously, knowing by now that she had a purpose in mind with that sort of comment.

"Is that bad?"

Carol didn't answer.

"We've found other things to talk about which seem to be more personal," John suggested.

Carol smiled. "I've been thinking about it a long time," she said. "I didn't want to talk about it, but I think we've reached the place where maybe we ought to." She waited for John's nod of agreement. "I know you were first interested in me only because I was Tony's sister."

"That's true," John said soberly. He reached across the table and took her hand. "Not anymore," he assured her.

"I want to be sure," she said. "There was such a closeness between you and Tony, almost an abnormal . . . "

She stopped as John looked up at her quickly, his face anguished. "Is anything wrong?" she asked. She didn't know. She had used the words without specific implication.

"No, nothing. Go on, Carol."

She continued. "I wonder, even now, even in some small way, if I'm some sort of replacement." She opened her fingers and squeezed his hand. "I'm not saying this to make you upset, Johnny. It's important that we talk it out."

"It is important," he agreed. "I've thought about that, too. At first, maybe, and even later I was afraid that maybe . . ." John stopped, looked intently at Carol.

"I know. I know you're afraid of a lot of things and you're shy and you're uncertain," she said. "But I also know you're honest and intelligent. There's so much goodness inside of you. I've got to know. You understand what I mean, don't you, Johnny?"

"You're you, Carol, and nobody else. If I had never known Tony, I would know you anyway, any time, any place."

"That makes me happy," she said. She paused a moment. "One more thing I want to ask you."

"Go ahead."

"I know you depended a lot on Tony for things. And from what you told me of your childhood, I can understand why. I also see, sometimes now, that you depend a lot on me for things. Is this a transference of some kind?" Her voice became stiff and objective and she caught herself. "I don't mean to be clinical about all this," she explained. "And if it makes you feel bad talking about it . . ."

"No," he said quickly. "We ought to hear this out."

"You know what I mean, Johnny?"

"I know what you mean. It's something in my life that I have to overcome. There are a lot of decisions I leave to you, I know. But it's been better than when we first met. Remember that first dance, when you had to lead me everyplace."

Carol smiled, letting her hand slip back into his. "This bothers you a lot?"

"Enough. Because I want to get everything right and straight between us." He paused a moment. "But in any case I'm not transferring anything from Tony to you. I want you to understand that." He wasn't sure it was entirely true, but he wanted it to be, and that was enough. "Don't worry about it."

"I'm not worried," she said. "I'm never really worried about you." She stood up. "Let's dance while the music is slow."

The music was not good, but for the most part the musicians played together. John and Carol danced. The band took a break and they sat down again, sipped their drinks.

"Tired?" John asked.

"A little."

"Want to go?

"After another dance," she told him.

They waited for the band to return. They didn't talk about Tony again that evening. Mostly, as in recent weeks, it was about John's novel. They didn't seriously enter their own conversations. They never got around to the future. Usually when they talked, in the car or at Carol's home, they did not hide their liking for each other and they relaxed in laughter or silence over something that pleased or displeased them together. But there was no talk of love, of marriage, of the things that young people who go together even for a few short months invariably get around to. Unspeaking, they both knew that the future existed and they both felt inextricably tied up with one another whenever either one of them thought about it.

The musicians returned to the stand and they danced again. The floor was not crowded and John delighted in broad steps and sweeps. He had learned to dance fairly well by then and Carol moved quickly and easily in his lead, making it easier for him to maneuver. They glided to the far end by the bandstand and then started easing slowly through the several couples on the floor back to their table. They didn't get there. A large man in a white tee-shirt, the paunch of his stomach punching the shirt out in front of him, making it seem a soiled yellow in comparison to the rest of the whiteness, stepped in front of them.

"How about a dance, baby?" he said to Carol, his voice unexpectedly soft and high for a man of his huskiness. He put a hand on John's shoulder, half leaning, half standing, facing Carol. He repeated the question. The staleness of the liquor on his breath was strongly unpleasant. John pushed away from him, danced back on the floor with Carol. Other people hardly noticed. It was a common occurrence.

The man followed them out onto the dance floor, walking heavily with uneven steps. He stopped them.

"What's going on here?" He slurred the words, and they wobbled like his body. "I said I want a dance with the dame." He put his arms out toward Carol, jogged a step by himself to the music. "C'mon, baby."

She attempted to move away with John. "No, thank you."

The man caught her arm, pulled her toward him. His arm wavered, but his grip was tight. "What're you givin' me? You ain't no different from the other dames and they dance with me." He tried to snort and sucked in the spittle that came to his lips. "C'mon and dance." He pulled at her arm.

Other couples stopped dancing and turned to look. One woman in a bright red dress lifted up the shoulder strap that was dangling low over one shoulder, laughed, and resumed dancing. Some of the people at the tables were interested now.

Carol pulled fiercely, but the man retained his grip. She looked at John. He felt the emptiness in his stomach of not knowing what to do. The man was much bigger than he and

if he should fight him there would be no match. He heard
Carol call "Johnny" and his immediate reaction was a physical one. He put his hand on the wrist that held Carol's arm
and tried to pull it away. The man held on.

"The lady is with me," John said, making his voice as
deep as he could. He felt it quiver and wished, quietly, that
the man would go away. The wish died.

"Go away, sonny boy." The man pushed at him with his
free hand, breaking his grip on the wrist. The voice reached
almost to a falsetto at the end of the sentence as it reached for
more breath. "I said I wanna dance and I'm gonna dance." He
lurched further onto the dance floor, pulling Carol after him.
He sang, his voice reaching a ridiculously high pitch. "Baby,
won't you dance with me!" Carol pulled back suddenly and
the man almost stumbled, then stood up straight and glow-
ered at Carol.

"Gratitude," he mumbled.

A crowd had gathered around them, watching. John
wondered why they didn't do anything. He knew they
wouldn't. They were waiting for him to do something. She
was his girl.

A woman giggled and a man whispered to another,
"Looks like maybe we're gonna have a nice little fight."

The people looked at John, waiting expectantly. He
felt like the sea lion at the zoo, all eyes waiting for him to
perform. It frightened him even more than the drunken man
did and he walked toward him, the one fear overshadowed by
the other.

The bartender locked the register and came out from
behind the bar and began walking slowly to the group. He
was still some thirty feet away. John couldn't wait for him.
He didn't decide to do anything, he just knew he had to, and
he did.

Without thinking, he went toward the man again. This
time he grabbed the whole body, one hand pulling the upper
part of the man's arm away from Carol and the other pushing
against his hip, spinning him around. The man stared at the
unexpected attack and swung a fist toward John, almost losing
his balance. Without stopping, John moved in toward him
with the same motion, pushing against his fat middle with
both hands with all his might, his hands doubled up into fists.
The man was big and the push itself didn't disturb him. But
in his drunkenness the further surprise did and he couldn't
keep his balance, his feet tripping him backward, sliding him
across the floor, slipping and falling on his backside. The male
onlookers laughed and some of the women giggled.

"Sonofabitch," the man snorted. Then he yelled it like an
angry bull who has been kicked by a rabbit. "Sonofabitch." It
sounded through the inn. He pulled himself to his feet. The
bartender began to step forward.

Another man stepped in front of him. "Leave them finish
it," he said.

John wanted to run as the man slowly came toward him.
But he couldn't. Everyone was waiting. Carol, too, was calm
now, watching. The fear opened a passage in John's brain for a
moment and he wondered whether it was fear or expectation
or both. For a split second he wished Tony was with him, to
rush in and give him the crutch he had always offered in the
past. But Tony wasn't there. For another moment he wanted
to rush to Carol and bury his head against her breasts and be
safe and protected. But it was not he who needed Carol now.
It was Carol who was depending on him.

He didn't move as the man reached him. Suddenly he
shifted to the side as the man swung a fist at him, moved
around the arm and tried to push the man in the stomach
again. But this time the drunk was prepared and a closed

fist struck out from the other side. John ached from a sharp blow against the bridge of his nose. He suddenly felt sick to his stomach and his eyes began to water. The man hit at him again, this time the fist landing on his cheek. He felt himself stagger backward, held his balance for a moment and struck out blindly with both hands at the man's face as he struggled to keep his feet. He felt one fist hit the man sharply across the head. The man almost slipped again, but this time he laughed as John, losing his balance, tumbled to the floor. He heard Carol scream.

He looked down and saw a blotch of red on his white shirt. He felt his nose, and his hand came away smeared with blood. He stood up quickly, listened to the laugh of the drunk. Some of the people in the crowd laughed and he began to get angry. First inside, at himself, then at those in the crowd who were laughing at him, and then at the large drunken man who had made all this happen. He wanted to make all their noses bleed. Then he laughed. He realized something funny. It didn't hurt. Only his dignity had been hurt. And he wasn't afraid. If the worst that could happen to him was a bloody nose, then there was no reason to be afraid.

He felt Carol's arm on his, pulling at him. "Let's get away from here," she pleaded. "Let's go, Johnny."

He pushed her arm away, gently but quickly. John laughed again. He mused. If all he had to fear was a bloody nose, why, then, he already had that. And he didn't need Tony or Carol or anyone to help him. He could help himself.

The big man was still laughing when John's doubled fist pounded into the soft flesh of the man's stomach, followed by the other fist crashing against his face. John didn't know why he hit him that way; it just seemed the thing to do at that moment. He remembered the action from movies he had seen of prize fights. The man's mouth opened and his eyes closed in disbelief at what was happening. He didn't slip or slide this time. He went down heavily, slumping to the floor in a heap. He had stopped laughing. Only his mouth remained wide open. John turned toward the dozens of faces circled about him. There was no laughing this time. A man in the rear timidly clapped his hands in applause.

John took his handkerchief, wiped his nose and face. The bleeding had stopped. He almost wished it would continue, the red wetness a symbol that made him feel strong. For the first time in his life he felt really confident in his strength. He took Carol's hand now, without a word slipped through the crowd. They hurriedly opened a path for him. The bartender was pouring a glass of water on the drunk's face.

"C'mon, get up, ya bum," he said. "Always pickin' fights, ain't you? You had it comin'."

John and Carol moved out the door, walked to the car. Carol walked quickly, her hand pulling him along. He held her back. Now that it was over he began to feel frightened again, but he forced himself to walk slowly. He stopped and looked back at the inn, half expecting to see the drunk come out of the door. The satisfaction of his accomplishment had been so great he would have almost welcomed meeting him again. They got in the car and drove away. They didn't talk all the way back to Des Moines. Carol just held tightly onto his arm and leaned her head against his shoulder. He looked at her and was satisfied. He shifted in his seat to let her move even closer to him. Every few minutes he looked down to see her smiling and he smiled back. She was happy in the thought that, for the first time, she felt she could really lean on him. He was happy for the same reason. His entire body felt fuller and stronger and his mind felt clearer, as if a heavy weight or worry had been lifted from it. Before he had needed protection and, in a way, Carol's protection. Now he could protect her. He thought of what had happened and some minutes and miles away from it thought again that, after all, what had happened wasn't as important as it seemed. He didn't care whether it was or not.

When they got to the house in Belleville he held Carol for a long time, kissed her heavily and then, without the hesitancy of the past, held her even closer. He kissed her fully and he felt that it was she, now, who quivered. He held her tightly until suddenly she pulled away, then let herself fall into his arms again, this time more gently.

"I'm sorry," she said. "You were almost hurting me."

"I'm sorry."

"No," she told him. "I liked it."

He smiled. "I did, too."

"I'd been waiting for you to hold me that way. And yet I was afraid."

"Are you afraid now?"

"No."

"Neither am I," he said. "And that's good."

She said nothing. He waited a moment. Then he laughed. "You're supposed to ask me why that's good," he said.

She laughed with him. "Why?"

"Because it would be kind of silly, from here on in, for a girl to be afraid when her best beau passionately holds her."

She looked at him softly for a long time. "You are my best beau, aren't you?" she asked. "Seriously?" she added.

He stopped smiling. "Seriously."

He was not unhappy when the door closed and Carol was safely inside the house. Sad because he would not see her any more that evening, but not unhappy. He walked lightly with a quick step to the bus. He had forgotten about the dark red spots dried on the front of his shirt. He smiled to himself as people glanced warily at him, noticing the blood stains. He was somehow proud that they noticed.

John, finding this new facet in himself, used it advantageously. In his studies he became not content to learn merely by rote, but began to analyze each new thing according to its strength and weakness and interpret it openly. He accepted a confidence in his own opinions and occasionally voiced them even in contradiction to his professors. Whatever ideas came anew to him he did not inhibit them any more out of fear and joined in discussions with his classmates. It was a freedom for him, in the sense of self-confidence, and though he was by no means ready to carry a world on his shoulders or lead a people—nor, indeed, was there any thought that he ever would—the basic strength that lies within every person began to overshadow the basic weakness.

His contact with the "old group" was for the most part gone. He spoke with them on the campus and when they asked why he no longer came to their parties he carefully avoided a direct answer. Soon they stopped asking him. He saw Woody Fisher often and in their talks would apprise the latter of his feelings and development. It seemed that in all respects Woody avoided advice and simply gave him encouragement in his own decisions.

Gradually John began to enter the society of the majority of the students, the one away from the closeted minority. He did not reject his former world-apart-from-a-world. Indeed, he remembered it and what it had meant to him and, for what it had given him, he respected it. Simply, he did not feel that he any longer particularly needed it. In a philosophy class he got into an argument with one of the students about the role of society.

The student, Tom Hiller, was from Connecticut. He had, as John had heard the story, gone to a college in New England, left at the end of a semester and had enrolled at Des Moines. He was fairly popular although rather easily annoyed and annoying in social situations. He was an above-average student. He was always striving for something, in class and out. Where he was running to no one seemed to know.

The philosophy professor, a tolerant man as John knew, had been teaching at Des Moines for more than thirty years and was considered one of the leading philosophy instructors in the Midwest. He had been speaking on the particular day in question about the plurality of societies: how the American society, in its conception of mores and morals, was a minority compared to the majority of peoples and societies in the world. He had presented the thesis as a sociological statement preparatory to a philosophical interpretation of morals per se. However, Tom Hiller objected to the thesis.

"But there is one best society and one accepted code of morals," Hiller said confidently. "And this is the code we must all follow, regardless of what the pre-historics of other countries want to do."

"Pre-historics is an incorrect designation, first of all," the professor said. "Before we can discuss your opinion, we must understand that some of the peoples in other lands are more advanced culturally and, in many senses, intellectually and philosophically than we are."

"And whose opinion is that?" Hiller asked brashly. He found it difficult to have his points listened to in class, not because of his quick belligerence but because of the smugness that went with it. "Not in my opinion," he said. "Not in the opinion of people who count." He explained what he meant without having to be asked. "The best people in the country. The highest economic and social strata in the country. This country is without a doubt on the highest plane of living in the world. Therefore, to follow the logic through, it is these people who should know."

"They may know in their society," one of the other students suggested. "But not for all people."

"They are the elite," Hiller retorted.

"In their society they are secure," someone else said. "But they wouldn't be in others, just as other people wouldn't be in theirs. Then their judgment, I bet, would be no better than the next fellow's."

"Sure," said Hiller. "But that's got nothing to do with the fact that their society is still the highest and best."

"The best for whom?" came a question.

"For anybody," came the answer.

"Then why isn't everybody in it so that they can have the same right to judge that you say your so-called elite have?"

"That's a stupid conclusion," Hiller said. He began to be angry now and when he became angry he relied on authority rather than on logic for his arguments. "Everybody doesn't belong there. Foreigners and"—he hesitated—"well . . . and others. Those who live in slums, for example. You can't compare them. They're lazy and don't want to be anything."

"Whose fault is it that some people have to live in slums?" another student demanded.

"Maybe it's really all one society," someone else said. "The people in the slums and the people in the penthouses. The world is one big society and we're all part of it."

"Yeah, and maybe we're all living in one big slum and some of us don't know it," came another voice. "If one of us is poor, then we're all poor."

Hiller snorted. "That's ridiculous. I know how some people live and I know how some others live. You've got to be pretty stupid not to know which is best."

The students looked to the professor to say something. He remained silent. The discussion, he realized, was going far afield and, in many respects, very illogically so. But he was pleased that it had at least taken a controversial turn. As an old professor he had grown sick at heart during the few years past. The free discussion he had encouraged for three decades had slowly become decimated, he felt. He had witnessed nonconformity used as a reason for the suppression of individuals. As a philosopher he knew that only non-conformity and new ideas would keep a culture alive. The students he had been getting were more and more like machines, hesitating to speak honestly and freely for fear of peer-pressure disapproval. Any discussion was now satisfying to him and he folded his hands on top of his desk and bid the debate go on.

Hiller continued talking. "Sure, I know we've got slums and crooks and perverts and every damned thing else under the sun. Because we've got them doesn't mean we have to accept them. Just as we don't have to accept the lesser societies of other countries. We should stick to the best. What we ought to do with these dirty people, these homosexual queers and all the others is to throw them in jail or take them out and shoot them and improve society that way."

John had not spoken. Now he felt he had to object. He did not draw back at the identification with homosexualism. The specific context made him feel he had to take a stand. He waited a moment.

"Maybe we ought to shoot those at the top, instead," someone suggested to Hiller sarcastically, "so that those at the bottom could get their money and have the same chances they have."

Someone whispered the word "communist" very loudly and then Hiller continued quickly. "Sure," he said, just as sharply, "let's have everybody become homos and perverts." Then, soberly: "They're immoral, abnormal, and amoral, and the only thing to do with that kind is to get rid of them."

John interrupted before anyone else could break in. "What makes you think homosexuals are immoral and abnormal?" he asked.

"What kind of question is that?" was the answer.

"I'm just asking, so I can understand what you're driving at," John said quietly.

"Okay," Hiller answered. "Because they're sexually abnormal, of course. They don't act as they should, they're different from the norm. They corrupt children," he concluded with obviousness, striking what he felt was the emphatic and empathic example.

The rest of the class quieted and let the discussion move between these two. They anticipated a good word battle.

"Maybe what they're doing is normal for them," John said. "It's not a matter of choice. In the larger society they have to build their own world and society. In that society they're normal. Just as monogamy is normal in some societies and polygamy, for men and women both, in others. There are many societies."

"Does that make it good?" Hiller asked, almost laughing.

"Not necessarily. But it doesn't make them enemies of the people or any less good than any other society. All these minority groups are people who have to be understood. Because they have been rejected by your . . . by our majority groups. If our society were that good, then it would find a place for all people regardless, not only for some lucky ones who might come from Connecticut." He was sorry he said these last words the moment they left his mouth.

Hiller stood up angrily. "Are you making this personal?"

John tried to stand his ground without continuing on the false basis of personal background. "I'm sorry," he apologized. He could find no other words. He wanted to quit the argument, to let Hiller have his way now.

Hiller stood silent for a moment, then softly and slyly: "Are you a homo, Thomas?" There was a movement among several of the students. They knew or suspected that they knew.

John flushed, for the moment regretting that he had allowed himself to be placed in that position. He could easily

deny it and save himself from embarrassment. In another
moment he knew that what he had gained in personal
strength would not let him. He would continue to argue for
the principle.

"I don't think that has anything to do with it," he said
slowly. "It doesn't make any difference if I'm a homosexual or
not." The class buzzed suddenly and just as quickly became
quiet. "I don't think that's any of your business," he said.
"But I'll tell you this much: I believe that all people are entitled to be what they are. If society considers them something
detrimental to society then there's something wrong with
that society and there's nothing to say that these minori-
ties are not as right or even more right than the majorities.
If their larger society can't give them the security they need
in it, then they are entitled to their own society and own
normality."

Hiller started to speak, but John didn't let him.

"Until society helps them, each and every one of them,
whether crooks or homosexuals or people of different economic or political standing or black or white or women, and
guarantees them the same rights and securities as the people
in the so-called best society, then they have the right to make
their own society, whatever they desire it to be. And in fact
if the larger society is that prejudiced to begin with, and I
repeat myself, it might not be a bad idea if they re-made the
whole society."

John sat down now and as he did he thought he noticed a
smile on the face of the professor. He was a little disappointed
in himself because he hadn't been able to express himself
the way he felt inside. He wasn't quite sure that everything
he had said was clear and understandable to the others. He
had not thought all this out clearly before and verbalized its
meaning. He could have written his thoughts much better

than he had spoken them. He felt that he might very well
have made a fool of himself.

He knew that he hadn't when Hiller began speaking
again. The latter did not argue at all with what he had said.
John was too wrapped up in his own effort, worrying about
its efficacy, to pay attention to everything that Hiller said and
he knew that he had not any more to say or answer back. But
he caught some of Hiller's words. ". . . Guys like you belong
in jail with the rest." When this level of language is used,
he knew that the user has no more sustainable argument. He
was unnerved by what he had done and his belly felt empty,
divested of the responsibility of belief he had assumed and
discharged. But it was not altogether unpleasant. The bell
rang and the class was over. He thought that the professor
was still smiling at him when he walked out. An appreciative
smile. A moment later, in the corridor, one of the students
congratulated him on his stand and shook his hand. He felt
good. Almost the same kind of pride he had felt that night
some two months before when the people had stared at the
dried up blood marks on his white shirt.

He argued more frequently in class after that first big
attempt, only now with less excitement and with a great deal
more forethought. His novel, too, seemed to grow with him.
As he developed, so did his characters, taking words from
him but using them in a life of their own. By Christmas the
book was half finished and at Carol's suggestion he put aside
his notes and began to rewrite, reorienting himself with the
story line and the character analyses. The extra work helped
and he found in his second draft a better work. He showed
it only to Carol and with her encouragement moved steadily ahead. She was enthusiastic about his writing, insisting
that his talents were more than pedestrian. Exceptionally fine
literature, she called it. So close was he to the writing, it was

difficult for him to judge it, but he liked to think that perhaps Carol was right and, thinking so, worked even harder.

One of his characters was not as clear as he wished. That, of course, was the interpretation of Tony. He had not heard from Tony as often of late. In the Fall, letters and phone calls had arrived twice and even three times a week. Now it was on the average of once every two weeks. It was just as well for John. He had little time to answer. When he wasn't writing, he spent as much time as possible with Carol.

Tony had done well. The musical he had written with Gerald Stearns had been successful and two of his songs had found their way to the Hit Parade. He was New York's rising new composer and in the columns of the Sunday <u>Times</u> John occasionally found Tony's name mentioned. Tony had also done well financially and had moved. The address was still Barrow Street, but it was a different house and a full-sized apartment. In his letters and calls he rarely mentioned his personal life. He was still too excited about the people he met, the big names which he repeated again and again to John. He told about New York: The places of interest, then the restaurants, then the night clubs and, soon, the lavish penthouses and the East Side high society townhouses.

John wondered about Tony. He was glad that their personal relationship had disappeared from the letters, although it was something he did not want to forget. It had been too important and too deep. Yet, he doubted that what had been happening to him had also happened to Tony. He wasn't sure why it worried him. Perhaps he was disturbed because he knew that the time would surely come when he would see Tony again and, not knowing what Tony thought now, he grew fearful of what he must do or say. He didn't tell Tony about Carol and himself and, as far as he knew, Carol in her communications to Tony had elaborated no more than that they had become good friends.

Carol's friendship became the greater part of John's life.
He saw her every evening now. At the beginning of the
spring term, in order that they might be closer together, she
had taken a room in the woman's dormitory on the college
campus. They could spend the entire day, each and every day,
together until the dormitory ten-o'clock curfew. It was just
as well. John had the late night and early morning hours
to write. On weekends they either attended college events
or borrowed Mr. Jordan's car and went for long drives. This
was what they really enjoyed most. Even the same paved
roads and the same squat fields of grain or green-and-yellow-
limbed acres of corn were something exciting. Each new field
or road or town gave them the feeling of seeing new things
and doing new things together. It was a rediscovery of the
world, no matter how small, on a common ground. As spring
blossomed into Des Moines and the people walked a little
lighter and trees reached a little higher, John watched the
flower buds grow and open wide with the satisfaction that he,
too, was doing the same. He was happy and fresh and free and
he wished that the springtime would last forever.

During that spring he went with Carol and her father
one Saturday afternoon to the small cemetery on the other
side of Des Moines to visit the grave of Carol's mother. He
hadn't particularly wanted to. Even in his closeness to Carol,
he felt that he did not yet belong. But she asked him to and
he went. Mr. Jordan, used to John's presence over the three
years past, treated him with full acceptance as one of the
household, although without any indication of like or dislike.
He seemed to welcome John's presence at the cemetery, however, perhaps as an added detraction to take his mind away
from the unavoidable duty of paying homage to his dead
wife. They had placed flowers on the grave, just in front of
the small white tombstone. His duty finished, Mr. Jordan
had gone back to the car. Carol remained, her eyes dry but

her voice stopped, choking back lumps of dry air. John watched her, standing to one side; he wasn't sure whether he should try to comfort her or not. Suddenly she began to choke audibly and started to cry. She dabbed at the tears with a handkerchief, thrusting at them as if that could make them stop. John walked to her, stood hesitantly in front of her, wanting now more than ever to help her, but still not knowing exactly how. He had always been gentle and soft and kind with her. It seemed that something more than sympathy was needed now.

Carol didn't look at him, her eyes remaining focused on the flowered earth. The crying abruptly ceased and her body began to tremble, as if the tears had emptied and were drowning now inside of her. John watched all this for a moment, then, conscious of her need for help and his need to help her, took her arms from in front of her face, held her tightened fists in his hands and pulled her close against him. He put his arms around her and held her tight. She buried her head against his shoulder, trying to make herself small to fit into the protection of his body. She began to cry again but now made no attempt to stifle the tears. She stayed close to him for a minute, perhaps two. They didn't speak. Then suddenly she moved away. There were no more tears. Her eyes were red and her cheeks seemed about to crack with the brown-stained redness. But she was smiling.

"Thank you, Johnny." She said it quietly.

"Feel better?"

"Much better. I didn't think I would, but when you took me and held me I knew I wasn't alone." She added: "I'm sorry I cried."

"You cry any time you want to," he said.

"The second time the tears made me feel better, not choked up inside. I felt like there was a terribly big thing that had just become light inside of me. I think my mother was the only one who had ever really loved me."

John looked at her, holding her all in one glance.

"I love you," he said, very slowly and very quietly. Then: "We'd better get to the car. Your father will be waiting."

"Yes."

He took her hand and led her back through the small mounds of earth, past the wild tattered grass and disturbed weeds and the proper, cared for, soft-hued flowers. They found Mr. Jordan in the car. They drove back to the city, the three of them in the front seat, Mr. Jordan driving. Carol sat in the middle. John could feel her hand holding onto his arm, tighter than it had ever been. She seemed closer to him than she had ever been before.

# Chapter 11

It was June and the heat had descended once more on the Midwest as if the tall rows of corn, struggling to free themselves from the earth in order to grow higher and higher, generated the waves of warmth that moved upon and enveloped the entire countryside.

John ran hurriedly from the bus stop in Belleville the two blocks to the Jordan home. He pushed through the front gate, let it bang against the iron fence post, raced for the front door. Only then did he stop, take a handkerchief from his pocket and wipe the sweat from his face. He felt the presence of habit, took his comb and quickly brushed back the brown waves that wouldn't stay put. He did it carefully and laughed to himself, for even though the actions were the same as when he had come to meet Tony, the feeling was completely different. He rang the bell, followed with a fast rapping on the door. Carol's footsteps moved quickly along inside; in a moment the door was opened. John kissed her as he brushed past, grabbed her arm and pulled her after him into the living room. She followed, first amused, then protesting at his brusqueness. Then seeing the excitement he had brought with him, she let herself be pushed roughly onto the couch, waited while John, his face broadly smiling, went to the small cabinet and poured a drink for each.

"A toast, my darling." He lifted his glass.

She wanted to ask him what had happened, but she held her curiosity, seeing how long he could hold whatever news it was he had. "Another?" he asked, finishing the drink. He was like a schoolboy who had just learned that summer vacation would start two weeks early. She watched as he pulled an envelope from his pocket, opened it, and took out and ran his fingers caressingly over a letter. He held it in front of her without unfolding it.

"All right," she said finally. "I give up. What is it?"

He leaned over and kissed her lightly on the cheek. "From Harmon and Johnson," he announced with much ado, "New York publishers extraordinary."

"Let me read it," Carol said, reaching for it, as excited as John. He pulled it back, his face even wider in a smile.

"I'll read it," he said. He walked back and forth across the living room, trying to be as matter-of-fact as possible.

"'We are in receipt of your manuscript, *The Vineyard*,'" he read. "'We have read it with great interest and believe that this novel shows more potential merit than any we have had in some years.'" He stopped, purposefully clearing his throat.

"Go on," Carol urged.

"'On the basis of what we have seen, we are willing to offer you a contract at our standard rates. Your manuscript at this point, we feel, is not yet ready for publication. There are some revisions we believe should be done. We would like you to complete this work in conference with one of our editors in New York. We will offer you a $1000.00 binder now and a $5000.00 advance against royalties when the work is ready for publication, at which time a final contract, including financial arrangements, will be completed.'" John concluded: "'We hope this offer is satisfactory to you.'" He stopped, held the letter out for Carol to read. "Etcetera, etcetera, etcetera," he finished.

Carol took the letter, read it herself. John stood in front of her, waiting. She jumped up from the couch, threw her arms about his neck and kissed him. He held her tight and kissed her for a long time. Then she suddenly withdrew, apprehensive.

"You accepted, didn't you?" she asked, as though there might be some doubt that he had.

John laughed. "I called them immediately. I told them I'd be on my way to New York as soon as they let me know when they wanted me."

They kissed again. She stayed close to him a long time. When he relaxed his hold and she moved away she was much quieter.

She hesitated to ask. "What about us now, Johnny?" She didn't want him to feel any obligation that might hold him back from this wonderful success he was about to have. But she had to know.

He looked at her tenderly, began to speak, then let the words become only a smile. He took her hand. "Let's not talk about it now," he said. "I wanted to tell you about this first. Now I'm going back to town. I've got some things to do."

Carol tried not to show her hurt. "It's important about us, isn't it, Johnny? It's important what happens to us?"

John kept his smile, kissed her on the forehead. He took her hands, pulled her close against him again. "Not now, Carol. I'll be here at eight o'clock tonight and we can talk about it then. Okay?"

"Okay." She walked with him to the door, closed it behind him. She tried not to think about it. She felt mixed up and unclear over John's refusal to talk about their future. She would wait until evening.

The afternoon hours passed too slowly. In the evening they stood outside on the small stone front porch of the house. Carol watched John's face close to hers, the small flickering strains of light across it making it soft and nervous at the same time. Her eye caught the glint of the lamppost light as it seemed to blink and waver as the shadows of a thousand moths deflected its light into tiny ripples across the street.

John was nervous. The first time he was really so in many months. His hand moved around in the pocket of his jacket, opening and closing on the crumpled edge of a cigarette package, giving him a release from the nervousness. He shielded Carol from the lamplight on the other side of the street. The leaves of the trees reflected around her onto the wall of the house, surrounding her face as a bower, making it seem even warmer and gentler than he had ever seen it before.

"Carol . . . " He started to speak, then stopped.

"You can tell me, Johnny," she helped him. This was so much like the boy she had known a year before, not like the one of the last few months. He had needed her then and he needed her now. Only she needed him now, too.

"I'll be going to New York in a few weeks." His words came slowly and they were most difficult for him to find. She gave him all the time he wished. "And in a few months after that I ought to have the book revised and finished." He stopped again. She waited, let him catch his breath and search for more words. She wished she could do more. She held her hands loosely, let him take them into his. Her heart pounded, just as she could feel the same pressure inside of John.

"I'll have enough money then . . . " John stopped, not knowing yet how to say it.

"Say it any way you want to, or you don't even have to say it at all," Carol said softly.

He looked at her and his face grew long and the round softness of the young man disappeared for a moment. He

spoke quickly. "Before I say any more, Carol, I think there's
something you ought to know about me."

She didn't understand. This was something unexpected.
A secret from the past? A squaring of accounts that he felt
must come to light? It wasn't important.

"I know everything about you that I want to know," she
told him. Her voice was steady. "There's only one thing you
have to say if you want to, Johnny. You know that."

He stood watching her, studying her face. She began to
feel uncomfortable. What felt like minutes was only seconds.
The sharpness of his face eased a bit, but not yet completely.

"I want you to marry me, Carol. I want us to be engaged.
Right now." The sharpness had disappeared.

She smiled, then as an afterthought asked him: "Is that
all, Johnny?" He was still the boy, half-way between the past
and the present. She wanted him as of now.

"All?" he asked. His face had unstiffened and the soft
lines began to pour out. She didn't say anything and he
watched her smile grow wider. Suddenly his lips broke and
he joined her. Staring at each other they started to giggle and
then both laughed. He pulled her closer.

"I love you, darling. I love you very much. So much that
it would take all the novels I could write in a lifetime to tell
you." He stopped, pushed her out at arm's length, holding
tightly to her shoulders.

"And you know damned well you didn't have to ask me
to say it."

"I know," she said.

"Then you will marry me?" he said firmly, more an order
than a question.

Her eyes grew wet although she didn't want them to. She
pulled herself back into his arms so that he wouldn't see her
tears.

"With all my heart," she said.

He fumbled in his pocket, brought out a small box and opened it. "This is why I didn't want to talk about it this afternoon. This is what I spent all afternoon doing," he mumbled. He took the ring from the box, a square cut diamond in a gold band. Without a word he slipped it onto her finger. It fit snugly.

She didn't care that her eyes were wet now. She could see the glistening, too, in John's. He brushed her lips, her face, her hair, with his mouth. They stood without speaking, close together. A car pulled into the driveway next door, hitting them full with its headlights. They broke quickly and walked inside the house into the living room. They sat on the couch holding tightly and fully to each other.

They didn't know how long they stayed that way. It was already light when John left.

# Chapter 12

A month later they were in New York. John had wondered for a time about the propitiousness of Carol coming with him, even for only a short holiday before returning to her fall semester studies. The prospect of seeing Tony again alone and explaining his new feelings made him nervous. With Carol along, finding an opportunity for this explanation would be even more difficult. What concerned him, too, was Tony's not knowing of their engagement. He wondered how great the problem would be, but felt he could deal with it. He doubted that Tony would accept his decision. He felt some of the butterflies of old return to his stomach and though he chose to ignore them they nevertheless remained. He watched the tick of the cab meter and his concentration on its changing numbers kept his mind from thinking about Tony.

The cab driver left them off in front of a two-story brownstone house with windows that seemed to reach to the ceilings of the rooms inside. There were no steps leading up to a first floor. They had been removed and modernized into a small, white, street level archway leading into the ground floor. They went inside, walked up to the first floor apartment

and knocked. John's stomach fluttered as the door opened and
he caught the emerging lump in his throat.

Tony watched John closely as he came in. If he expected
any sign other than friendly recognition, he was disappointed. He shook hands with John and then turned to Carol,
kissed her affectionately.

John looked closely at what he saw. It was the same Tony,
only in a different setting. The expensive house robe, the
modern blonde mahogany furniture and, at the far corner of
the room in front of the windows, a baby grand piano instead
of an upright. There was the same personal aesthetic thinness,
the lock of hair that threatened to fall over his forehead, and
the deep, dark eyes. Even as he looked, the face seemed to
change and it was something John did not know as well as he
thought he should have. It was someone he had not known
before. Maybe another John Thomas had known him, but not
this one.

Tony waited until the greetings were over and looked
again at John and again he did not find the recognition
he sought. The intangible strangeness about the meeting
disturbed him. There was a sense of irresolution about the
whole thing he could not understand. It disturbed Tony. He
had looked forward to seeing John again, feeling that what
had been between them could no doubt be resumed. He
had found many relationships in the year past, but the basic
elementary one between himself and John was still the most
important. It gave him a security of control and understanding that he wanted again.

John walked over to the piano and examined it. Carol,
looking over the living room, started for the bedroom.

"Not in there," Tony called quickly. For the moment he
had almost forgotten about Larry. "It's awfully messed up
right now," he apologized. Carol sat on the couch, took the
drink that Tony made and offered her. John came over to

them. Tony stood by him and extended his hand again. They clasped hands.

"Good to see you, Johnny." Tony tried to catch John's eyes again to ascertain what was missing. Their eyes met and held together for a moment. John's didn't waver. They both looked aside at the same time.

"Don't be bashful here," Tony said. "My house is your house. Mi casa es su casa—or something like that. I just finished some music for a Latin dance," he smiled. Their hands remained clasped. Like two old friends trying to hold on to a long lost moment that has since slipped away. Tony felt a steadiness in John's hand that he had not known in the past. It was sticky, but not wet. It was only the heat.

"Relax, Johnny, relax," Tony said. He meant it for himself. John sat on the couch. He was smiling. He knew that Tony's words were self-commanding. It was a strange feeling, having so much control of himself when with Tony. He looked at the latter and then at Carol and then suddenly felt the tightening inside when one is caught in a lie. Yet the tightening didn't devour him, but only warned him. His only concern now was to go through with this first meeting without Carol finding out their secret. He didn't know what Tony might do when they told him, as they must, that they were engaged.

There was an embarrassing lack of conversation for several minutes. It was Carol who broke it. She got up from the couch, took each of the others by the arm. "Let's not be so formal," she said. "Nobody died. Let's act like we're at least acquainted."

"Okay," John apologized. "The excitement of having come to New York has left us kind of blah, I'm afraid."

"Okay," Tony said. "Let's make it like old times. That's the way it should be." He glanced at John as he said it.

The new alignment of differences between them was becoming more obvious. Tony tried to check it. He poured some more drinks. "Things haven't changed at all, have they?" he suggested again. It was up to John to answer.

"Some haven't," John said. He ran his hand along the liquor cabinet. "Furniture has," he said.

Tony was disappointed in the answer, but joined in the laugh. He declined to carry it any further. He hadn't anticipated this at all and didn't want to become involved in subtle word games. Tony patted the top of the cabinet. "Pure blonde mahogany. One thousand four hundred and fifty bucks worth."

John whistled in appreciation.

"It pays to be a composer in New York," Tony said.

"For about how many?" Carol asked.

"For about me and six other people," Tony laughed. "Oh, well, somebody's got to starve," he observed without meaning. "All of us can't have everything."

"We can try," John said.

Tony walked quickly into the kitchen. "Why doesn't someone invent a permanent ice-cube," he protested, changing the subject. "I'm always fighting ice-cube trays, it seems like."

"Drinking a lot?" Carol asked.

"No more than usual." He came back with a hammered-aluminum ice-bucket full of ice cubes. "Despite what you read in the novels, it's no easy life in New York for any artist, particularly musicians. I've been lucky." He spoke about the show he had done and the new one he was working on. Carol sat on the edge of the couch, interested.

John slumped down comfortably at the soft side of the couch. He noticed Tony looking at him. Settling into a soft deep part of a couch or a chair was what he had always done when he was afraid and need protection. He pushed himself up hurriedly, leaned forward.

Tony noticed and stopped his account long enough to remark about the couch. "Foam rubber," he said. "I like soft couches, don't you, Johnny?" Perhaps this would break the coldness?

"It gives you a chance to relax and think about things," John answered.

"What things?" Tony asked quickly. He tried again to crack through the invisible wall.

"About making a success in New York. Tell us more about it, Tony."

Tony laughed and resumed his account. It was small talk and he told it almost by rote. When people in the profession were there it was shop talk and he could speak in technical terms and with understood passion. With outsiders it became less technical and personal and was merely small talk to amuse and instruct.

"Funny thing about a show in New York," he advised. "You can be the most terrific actor or writer or director or singer. If the show's lousy for any reason, you're lousy. But if it's a hit it doesn't matter how good or bad you are. Jobs from then on."

"Are you good?" Carol teased.

"I better be either that or lucky or the finance company gets all this furniture back," Tony laughed.

John smiled agreeably. The purposelessness of the visit was dragging on too long. He was becoming uncomfortable. In some situations, like this one, a smile lasts only as long as you can keep your face screwed out of position. "From the looks of things you've got plenty of fans—or some rich ones, anyway," he said. The others laughed with him.

Tony acknowledged the reverse pat-on-the-back. "I've made more friends in just a year in New York than in a life-time in Des Moines."

John looked up. That was good, he thought. If Tony had found a fullness and satisfaction in New York, when John had to explain about himself and Carol there would be less danger of a disturbance. At the same time he was glad, unconsciously, that Tony was worried. His pride appreciated it. Tony watched John and half-guessed what he was thinking.

"But not as good friends as the few I had in Des Moines," Tony added pointedly. There was no reaction from John.

"I thought for a moment you were forsaking your home town," Carol said jokingly.

"I forsook the place years and years ago." Tony was not joking.

"Even us?" Carol smiled.

"Never, Carol," Tony assured them. "Neither you nor John, even if they gave me the Empire State Building on a silver platter." He sat on the edge of the easy chair across from the couch, dangled a leg over the arm. "That's enough talking about me," he said. "Let me hear about you." Hastily, he added: "Dad okay?"

"Wondering when you were coming to that?" Carol said.

Tony was hurt for the moment. "Now, Carol . . . you know."

"Yes, I know."

Tony shifted in the chair to better balance himself. "I've got nothing against Des Moines. Nobody every understood me, that's all. Not even Dad. So why go out on a limb for no reason?"

"All right, Tony," Carol said. "You don't have to explain to me."

They sat silently again, each searching to find the words that always seem to elude the tips of the tongues of people who meet after not seeing each other for a length of time.

"I'm pretty excited about what you wrote about John's book," Tony said finally. "Whoever thought he'd become a great writer so soon?"

"No confidence in me, Tony?" John offered, smiling.

"All the confidence in the world," Tony answered. "But how many people so close to each other both make out so well? I got a big break. It's almost like an act of the gods that my luck didn't stop yours."

"John's got a lot of talent," Carol interposed. "The publishers think he could become a really fine author. I guess he wrote you about it?"

"There hasn't been any horn-blowing in Johnny's letters. But he was always shy, weren't you, Johnny?"

"Compliment?" John asked.

"Statement."

"I guess you're right," was John's answer. He didn't want to banter about something unimportant.

Tony was insistent. "You've always been bashful about a lot of things, don't like to talk about what's happening to you, what has happened to you . . . "

John interrupted. "Anything in particular you'd like to know?"

"About the novel. How does it stand? What's it about?" Tony was quick to find the way out. John seemed arrogant. Tony decided quickly not to seek an answer then to what he really wanted to know. He would wait until they were alone.

"The same old stuff you read every day," John said. "People who are lost in the world." He hesitated, decided to take it one step further. "About two young men who can't find a place in society and in order to achieve a security try everything—normal and abnormal."

Tony didn't even blink. "How do they come out?"

John looked directly at him. "In the way that's best for both of them."

"I understand that. But you haven't really finished it yet. Carol wrote me you have some revisions to do," Tony said.

"Only to make things clearer and more definite," John quickly added. The sharpness of dialogue had become electric and even the pauses of silence were balanced carefully between them. Carol got up from the couch, walked across the room, stood near Tony.

"I may as well tell Tony the big secret." She looked at John.

"Secret?" Tony put his glass down, interested.

John felt his face grow red. He didn't want to, but he couldn't stop it. "We can wait if you want, Carol." He thought the words but didn't say them. Instead: "May as well now as later." John wanted to sink back into the cushions until it was over. It was a feeling not of fear, but as if he had done something undercover when it should have been done out in the open, and now it was going to come out.

Carol took from her left hand a white glove she had been wearing, held the hand out to Tony. At first he didn't comprehend, looked at the ring disinterestedly. He was about to comment on the loveliness of the diamond when suddenly it made sense. In a split second he was on his feet. He laughed and then they all laughed. John watched as Tony's tongue worked hurriedly against the inside of his cheeks, making them puff like rubber balls, and he brushed back the lock of hair from his forehead even though it had not fallen. John stood up. He felt taller and bigger than he had a few moments before, although he was still not sure of what might happen. Tony came to him, his hand outstretched, and spoke quietly.

"So that's the secret," Tony said. "A wonderful secret." He kissed Carol. "Congratulations," he said. "Congratulations to you both. Another drink, this time a real toast." They drank. It tasted bitter to Tony. He had not in the farthest reaches of his imagination guessed at this, and even with the preparation of John's coldness since he and Carol first arrived it was a surprise. He thought about it a moment and it became almost a ludicrous joke. He was hurting inside and in his whole year in New York he had made it a point not to be hurt. He had grown stronger and more commanding in his relationships than even in Des Moines and the sudden hurt was almost too impossible to be accepted. He had had little doubt of his control over John and the sudden prospect of this basic strength being shattered stifled him. Not that this alone hurt him; there was more that he did not yet admit. He looked up from his drink to see that the others were staring. He smiled quickly.

"I've been deliberating," he said. "This calls for a real celebration. I'll take you both out tonight to do up the town."

John tried to understand what Tony was thinking. He was relieved that there had been no sudden argument. He knew the tone of easy superiority that Tony could call up to hide his real feelings. He knew that he had done that now. How easy or difficult it had been to accomplish he didn't know.

"When I left, you two hardly knew each other," Tony said. Then with the slightest trace of irony: "Big things must have happened."

"They did," John said. The dark eyes, now burning angry black again, met his and an old memory was there. He forced the memory away.

Carol noticed the sense of difficulty between them. She thought perhaps that it was a natural adjustment between two good friends when their relationship has been changed. She took up the conversation and tried to give it an informal tone. She told about the fight in the tavern when John's nose had been bloodied. She made it as humorous as she could. "But you should have seen that other fellow. He was completely knocked out."

"Never knew you to have that much strength," Tony observed.

"Something new," John told him. "All of a sudden, this past year, I've gotten stronger than I ever have been before." He flexed his muscles so that the words would not seem too obvious.

Tony knew what he meant and didn't ask again. Carol continued from there, bringing Tony up to date about John and herself.

John wanted to leave. If they were going out that evening he wanted to get to their hotel, wash up and rest a while. He wanted to get the day over with so that he could make arrangements to talk to Tony alone. The first step was taken now and he wanted to settle it. He looked at his watch. Almost one o'clock in the afternoon. Another few minutes and he'd suggest that they leave.

Carol walked over to the piano, looked at the open music. "I remember this," she said, pointing to the song that Tony had been playing earlier that morning before they arrived. "From the first show you two geniuses did at Des Moines." She acted surprised. "You're not stealing your own stuff for Broadway, are you, Tony?"

"No, just reminiscing over old times," he said pointedly.

Carol sat at the piano, played a few bars. "It was a really good song," she said.

"Thank your fiancé for that," Tony said. The emphasis was on the word "fiancé". Tony had taken another drink and the liquor had allowed the bitterness to begin to flow. John felt that they had better leave soon.

Carol came back to them. "How about some of your new music, Tony?"

Tony went back to the piano with her, picked out a piece from inside the piano bench.

"For a show Gerry Stearns hopes to get together some time next spring." He played and sang the number. He took a

few lead sheets from the bench. "Here, Carol, you try them."
He walked back to the couch, sat down next to John.

Tony's voice was sharp and precise, but low enough not
to be heard except by John. Carol's music drowned out any
more volume.

"Let me have it straight. What happened?" Tony asked.
It was an order.

"Carol told you." John was calm but just as direct.

"That's not what I mean."

"I know what you mean," John said. Inside of him the
butterflies began running from net to net. It disturbed him
for a moment, then something else tightened inside and the
butterflies were gone. "I don't want to talk about it now,"
he said firmly. "We'll talk about it later." The softness in his
voice became hard.

Tony hesitated, almost stuttered as he tried to answer
back quickly and angrily. Always before, when he had talked
to John in this way, commanding or ordering, John had been
his. Now it was different and he felt weak and dependent. He
couldn't allow himself to be brushed aside and, from what he
had seen of John now, he hesitated, afraid to risk a complete
rejection.

"Whatever you say, Johnny-boy." He spoke as sweetly
as he could. "I just didn't think you could have forgotten all
there was between us."

"This isn't the place to talk about it," John insisted.

"Where is the place?"

"Nor the time." John began to get annoyed.

Tony spoke quietly, trying to control the conversation.
"When is the time?"

"It's over, Tony." John tried to make it clear. "If you want
to talk about it, we will. But not here or now." He held his
breath, waiting to see what Tony would do. He had bluffed,
gambling that his own insistence would stop Tony. He had

tested his strength and apparently he had won. Whether it was tactically wise, he wasn't sure.

Tony didn't feel by any means that, as John had put it, "it was over." His own pride and strength and confidence would be seriously hurt if he allowed it to be, and his need to retain these—by the obvious continued satisfaction of his need for John—was necessary. A few hours before, when there had been no doubt in his mind, it almost did not matter. Even during the many months past, when he neglected writing to or calling John, it was not important. He had been sure of himself. Now that he wasn't, the insistence of his ego intended that he win again with John as he always had. He wasn't in love with John. Not really, not any longer, he told himself. His own philosophy denied the permanence of this kind of relationship. But he couldn't bear to see anything taken from him, especially something that had been so completely his.

"Johnny?" he questioned. It was almost a plea.

"What do you want, Tony?"

"Only what's right. Nothing that isn't right."

"Things change," John said. He looked over to the piano, where Carol had begun playing another number. He picked up his glass, drank from it. Tony watched him, gulped quickly from his.

"Later or not at all," John said quietly.

"I don't understand you," Tony insisted. The voices were hard whispers.

"You do."

Carol stopped playing, came back to the couch. "That first one is a great song, Tony. It ought to be a hit."

Tony got up, started to walk from the couch. He faced John, his back toward Carol. His lips formed the words "Later, Johnny-boy." He smiled. "Hope so," he said to Carol, acknowledging her compliment. "It's a good commercial number."

John looked with much obviousness at his watch. "It's after one," he said. "If we want to get some rest before our big evening, we'd better get to the hotel."

Carol agreed. "I'm tired. That long train ride."

Tony phoned a cab company, ordered a taxi. "It'll be here in a few minutes," he told them. A few minutes later a horn honked loudly outside. Tony walked with them to the door. He opened it, held it a moment, sucked against his cheek.

"Johnny doesn't have to go to a hotel," he said quickly. "My invitation for him to stay here still goes."

John became angry inside, protested graciously. "I have the reservation. I wouldn't want to take advantage of you here." He didn't know what else to say.

"My invitation for you to stay while you're in New York begins right now. You take Carol to the hotel, cancel your room, then come right back here. I'll have everything ready for you."

"No. Thanks anyway, Tony." John started out.

Carol stopped him. "Why don't you, Johnny? It'll save you money and you'll be more comfortable, I'm sure."

"I have enough money."

"If you say no, I'll feel hurt," Tony insisted. "As I said, my house is your house."

John looked at Carol, then at Tony. He didn't want to argue too violently. He wasn't sure of Tony yet.

Carol continued the pressure. "The cab's waiting. I'll go out and hold it while you and Tony make arrangements."

Tony let the door close as she disappeared. "Are you afraid of something, Johnny-boy?"

"We don't have time to talk about it now," John said. "Maybe tomorrow or when Carol leaves."

"You didn't answer my question. Are you afraid?"

"Should I be?"

"I don't know."

"I'm not," John said.

"What's happened, Johnny, what's happened between us?"

"I'll explain it all later. I'm sorry, Tony, but there's no use trying to settle it all on a dime."

"I'll expect you back, Johnny."

"No."

"Please." Tony held John's hand, grasped it tightly.

John pulled his hand away, opened the door. For the moment he was undecided, caught in a conundrum of something he could not understand. This was a different Tony, a different situation entirely. Now he, John, was in charge. It was an interesting realization and it was a good one inasmuch as it was the culmination of something he had been wanting to happen for a long time. At that moment, when he became aware of what was happening, he was undecided. He was reluctant to leave his advantage.

John saw Tony smiling at his hesitancy and became angry at his own indecision. He wanted to get out of there quickly, but now the inner force that told him otherwise was laughing at him, and not very gently at that. Tony smiled more broadly. Somehow, he knew.

"We'll talk about it later," John said, the urgency gone from his voice, and he walked slowly out of the room. Tony was still smiling as John closed the door behind him and went to join Carol in the waiting cab.

# Chapter 13

"I thought I'd have to stay in there forever." Larry tiptoed gracefully out of the bedroom in Tony's Greenwich Village apartment.

"Enjoy yourself listening at the door?" Tony said sharply. His suspicions were confirmed by the answer.

"Why Tony . . . " the tall thin man protested, his lips beginning to quiver in feigned hurt.

"Yeah, yeah . . . I know better than that." Tony finished the protest sarcastically, turned away and walked to the high windows by the piano, twisted open a slat of the venetian blind, watched John get into the taxi with Carol and waited until it pulled away. Satisfied, he adjusted the blinds, letting thin strips of sun into and across the room. He turned back. "You'd better pack up, Larry," he ordered.

It didn't register for a moment. The other man rejected the absurdity of the words and then they formed into a meaning.

"What!" Larry's high-pitched voice was almost shrill. "What . . . what are you saying?"

Tony spoke steadily and with authority. "You'd better pack up. You're leaving."

"Why? What for?" He was bewildered, tried to find something he had been guilty of, a crime for his punishment. "You mean leave for good?" he asked, still not believing.

"For a while."

"Why? What did I do?"

"Nothing?"

"Well then, why?" Larry insisted.

"No reason. I just need the space." Tony said all this matter-of-factly, as if he were turning out a stray cat after having satisfied his conscience by giving it a warm bed and a bowl of milk.

Larry tried to steady himself, dropped his voice as low as he could get it. It melted from a soprano into a forced tenor. "I don't get it. You need the space for whom?"

"For an old friend," Tony answered.

The other man suddenly understood and began to smile. "For whom?"

"For the friend who was here this afternoon," Tony said quickly. "He's going to be in New York for a while and has no place to go and is going to stay here." He turned away, satisfied that this was the end of the matter.

But it wasn't. Larry possessed a secret and he felt secure in it. He walked to the liquor cabinet, idly poured himself a shot of whiskey. "He's going to stay here, Tony?" he questioned, denying the words even as he spoke them.

"That's right." Tony's words were angrier. He didn't want to play word games.

"You sure?"

"Sure I'm sure." Tony flushed. "Stop that God-damned nonsense and do what I tell you."

Larry dangled a leg over the edge of the easy chair, sat sprawled on the arm. "That's not what I heard." He caught himself and shrugged his shoulders. "So I was listening." His pattern of speaking had slowed down. It was his way of making a point.

"What you heard and what's going to be are two entirely different things," Tony told him. His voice was harsh and steady. "He'll be here. Maybe not today, but he'll be here, soon." He was aware that Larry's interest was one of revenge by proxy. Tony watched his own harshness growing as Larry sipped a drink. Tony walked over to the armchair, pulled the glass abruptly from Larry's hand and slammed it on top of the cabinet. Larry grabbed for the glass, lunged to catch the back of the chair to keep from falling over.

"Tony, I . . . " He didn't finish.

Tony's words grew louder with each syllable. "I decided he's going to stay here." The increased tone of the words countered his own uncertainty of what really would be. "You go and he stays and that's the end of it." He looked hard at Larry, convincing him as well as himself of his seriousness. He was fully in command at that moment and he held the superiority for several seconds, enjoying it. Then the authority became mixed with doubt about John and he softened. He had to leave the door open.

"It isn't permanent, Larry," he said. "Just for a little while. Then you can come back."

Larry was shaken by the sudden anger and the equally sudden gentleness. He was like a little child looking for a mother's hand that reached out, but only to slap. He was rebuked for his attempt to slap back. He knew Tony meant what he said. He didn't doubt, even though he had overheard the conversation between John and Tony, that the latter would somehow get what he wanted. But even understanding all this fully, he found his own leaving difficult to accept. This had been his home and breast-milk for many months. It was easy to understand, but not to accept.

"Please, Tony, I don't want to go." It wasn't a plea yet, only a statement. It was in a monotone, said out of necessity.

Tony tried to be kind, but he was becoming impatient. "There's no choice, Larry. Why don't you go now without any more trouble and make it easier all the way around."

Larry walked to the piano, ran a finger over the keys, stood with his face down rubbing the finger back and forth over the shiny white of the ivory. "I don't want to go," he sulked.

Tony walked up to him, was about to place an arm on the hunched shoulder, decided against it, and stood straight and tall, towering over the other man's bent figure. He looked at his watch. "I'll give you fifteen minutes," he said quietly. He turned and walked to the couch, sat down and lit a cigarette.

Larry watched him, raising his head little by little to follow his actions, trying to hold back the collapse of his insides. He went slowly to the couch, stood in front of Tony, eager for another pat from the master. "Please, Tony, I have no place to go."

"I'll find you a place," Tony said without inflection. "I'll call Jack Wyler."

"I don't want to be with Jack Wyler. I want to be here with you." Larry was almost on the verge of tears. "I want to be with you," he begged.

"Maybe later. Not now." Tony looked at his watch again. "Ten minutes," he said.

Larry pleaded, looked down into Tony's open palm, saw his own life held there. "Don't throw me away, Tony."

"Don't be melodramatic," Tony said in an unwavering dull tone. "It's not that important."

Larry tried to speak, his voice caught, but when the words finally came out they were louder and sharper. "What was between us all these months not important! You can't know how I feel and say that." The voice became shrill.

He sat on the edge of the couch near to Tony. "Let me stay, please. Find another place for your friend, but let me stay, please."

Tony moved away from the couch, feeling full advantage of and at the same time soiled by the other's weakness. "Maybe I'm being hard on you, Larry, but this whole life is hard and you damned well know it. If we could make it permanent or make it legal or satisfy our needs like everybody else satisfies their needs, then maybe it would be different."

Larry lunged at him, trying to grab at his waist and stop him from talking any more. Tony moved quickly away.

"Don't interrupt me," Tony said. "You'd better listen because I'm saying this now and I'm not going to say it again." He walked back and forth across the width of the living room. Larry had sat back on the couch, waiting.

"There is something you'd better understand sooner or later," Tony continued, "and since you don't, now is as good a time as any." Tony pressed out one cigarette, lit another. "As real as this may be to you or to me, it's not real to anything outside of that criss-crossed venetian blind on the window. Those lines of sun coming through are bars, our bars. Outside they have their rules, but they won't let us live by ours as they live by theirs. So we run and we scrape and we take what we can get and we understand all the time that as real as it is, it must be at the same time unreal. It's no more than passing, and when something is over it's got to be quick and easy. And if it isn't easy then it's got to be hard. But it's over either way." He paused, puffed deeply from the cigarette. "And if you can't follow these rules, you get hurt." He listened to his own words and they sounded like enemies. He thought of John and he knew that he was violating his own logic. He, Tony, was exempt from the rules, he told himself. And even as he made the mental reservation he wondered whether some day he himself would be hurt and how badly. He turned back to Larry. "Do you understand me?"

"Sure I understand," the latter said. "Nothing means a damned thing to you. Life or faith or love. Nothing." The words were soaked with bitterness.

"You don't understand," Tony said. "There's no use talking any more."

"You're wrong, you're wrong," Larry screamed. "If what we had meant anything to you at all, then it still does."

"It did mean something," Tony said. "Otherwise you wouldn't have stayed here and I wouldn't have supported you all these months. But it doesn't mean anything any more." He held his watch up high to look at it. "Five minutes," he said.

"I've got a priority," Larry demanded. His voice screeched through the apartment. "I've got a right to stay."

"In our life there are no priorities. There are no rights." Tony tried to avoid the words because, again, he knew that his own salvation of security and pride was demanding the priority of John's return.

Larry continued yelling, his last resort. "You think it's a joke, all this. You think you can throw me away so easy. Well, I'm not going. I won't go." It was as though he were shouting for all the world to hear, for some echo to catch the words and give him help. "I'm serious, Tony, I'm serious."

For one moment Tony's voice matched his in answer, reaching to drown out the other's intensity. "I know you're serious, God damn you, I know you're serious." Then it was quiet. Tony barely whispered. "That's the hell of it, Larry. That's the hell of it."

They stood looking at each other, the one man with the deep dark eyes, stern and straight, the blackness of hair matching his temper; the other, tall and thin, the body bent with futility. For a brief moment they caught a former mutual confidence, but only for a moment because they could not remove the mantle of darkness that had covered it. There was the realization that this, like the entire transcendency of life, sometimes lasts even less than a moment.

Tony walked away, stood by the piano, his back to Larry. "Get out of here this minute," he said slowly and clearly, "or I'll make it permanent." He didn't turn. He would give no more.

Larry knew it and knew that it was over. There was no more to be done. He twitched, his hands moving back and forth, one into the other and out again. He tried to smile. He couldn't. He wanted to spit. His hands clasped and they steadied themselves. He turned and with quick steps walked to the bedroom, packed his few belongings in a suitcase and came out minutes later. He found Tony standing in the same place. The cigarette had burned almost to his finger tips.

"All right," Larry said. "I'm ready." The bitterness was gone. His voice held its normal lightness and was steady. There was no answer and he walked to the door himself. He stopped and turned.

"Tony?"

"Yes?"

"I'll be back sometime?"

Tony hesitated. "Yes," he answered.

Larry started and again stopped.

"Tony?"

"Yes?"

"Will you call Jack Wyler and tell him I'm on my way?"

"I'll do it right away," was the perfunctory answer.

Larry stopped again.

"Nothing?"

"Nothing."

Larry opened the door, stepped out, closed it behind him. He turned around and looked into the closed door.

"Bitch," he said, and walked away.

# Chapter 14

In the taxi Carol and John rode silently, the latter again fascinated by the ticking of the meter as if it were a new toy he had just found, and he adjusted each tick to the flash of the telephone poles that sped by along the streets of New York's Tenth Avenue. He leaned back comfortably against the leather seats. He was tired.

Carol watched, and wondered at the sadness of his face. He had suddenly lost the freshness she had seen gradually grow within him during the year past. Now, for some reason, he was disturbed. She did not ask; if it were important, she was sure he would tell her.

She, too, was tired. Her face was tired, its thinness accentuated by the faint lines crossing from the edge of her eyes outward and deepening downward to the tips of her lips. She wondered, absently, how she would look in ten years, past the thirty-year mark, when a woman's face begins to line and look tired by accepted artificial standards. She passed over it. Female beauty was too much a vanity that had never been quite as important to her as it might have been. Beauty to her was what the person was inside, not what they looked like. John felt that way as well. Certainly, he had told her she

was pretty and, with the warmth of love, that she was beautiful. It was not in the casual terms of glamour or sex or in the
heat of passion. John's feelings were truthful and real and
Carol was grateful for this understanding and closeness that
existed between them, that reached within and drew them
together.

Carol watched the flashes of the sun strike the cab, pour
onto their seats as the taxi passed each cross street. The flashes
lit John's face, reflecting onto hers. It outlined gentleness,
calm, and certainty, and even the momentary lines of worry
did not let her doubt that what was good would be lasting.

The buildings thinned out on the left as they rode
uptown and the long streets of low warehouses and docks
took over. The sun was steady now as it rushed over them.
John moved, bathed in the yellow light, and Carol wanted to
move close into his arms, warmed by the heavens and by love
at the same moment. She relaxed, feeling all this, her fancy
making the sensation almost physical.

John turned toward the patches of blue that the Hudson
River flashed at them between the brick and wood of the
buildings and piers. Across the river he saw the Palisades of
New Jersey, the high-wooded cliffs almost like another world.
Through one window, on his right, were the concrete statues
to industrial progress, the living machines; through the other,
on the left, a disappearing skyline of nature and naturalness,
where people might still be their basic selves, at one with
their natural environment. He looked at Carol, her head back,
her eyes closed now. His thoughts had been so loud in his
head, he wondered whether they had filtered through his lips
and whether she had heard them.

He looked again at nature and at the city. On equally
large square feet of ground, on one side the green and blue
growing world and on the other the concrete canyons that
converted humans into their own images. He looked up to

his right and toward the high buildings and imagined large-bosomed dowagers and bald aristocrats leaning from their castle towers twenty and thirty and forty stories above him, pointing out their windows disdainfully toward the Palisades and chanting in unison: "To hell with nature."

He sat up quickly, half expecting to hear the words screaming down. He put an arm around Carol, pointed toward the river. "Where Henry Hudson was set adrift by his crew."

"I know," she said, opening her eyes. "I took American History, too." He smiled. "So much history in New York," she offered.

"Despite the city itself," he said, not knowing why.

"Don't you like New York?" She was surprised.

"No!" He hesitated. "I guess maybe I do," he said, not very sure. "I just really haven't seen it yet. The first time you become overwhelmed by something," he decided, "I guess you immediately feel you don't like it."

"I think I like it," Carol said, "because it gives a person so much to see and do, with others and with themselves. It's a challenge. It sort of makes an adult out of a child."

"Or a child out of an adult." John didn't know why he said this, either.

"What's wrong, Johnny?" Carol asked gently.

"Is something wrong?"

"You don't sound like John Thomas," she smiled.

"I guess I'm tired," he apologized.

The cab stopped for a light. They straightened up in the seat.

"You can lie down on my lap for a while," she offered, "while we ride."

"In a cab?"

"We're engaged."

He laughed. He put his arm around her shoulder again, pulled her so that her head rested against his shoulder.

"You're just as tired as I am," he said. He noticed the taxi-driver's face through the rear view mirror, smiled at him. The latter looked away as the light changed, turned the cab to the right and started through the traffic toward the mid-town hotel.

John knew he was upset over the last few minutes with Tony and it bothered him all the more because he had let himself become so. He was no longer afraid of Tony and no longer needed him as a pillar. This was an achievement he was proud of. However, he had seen a complete turnabout and now, it seemed, Tony needed him. In this moment of glory of his command, John had felt himself becoming caught in the four walls of the past, melting into a sympathy he had tried to avoid. He insisted to himself that his love for Carol was now his only love and that what he had learned and found with her would remain strong and, in fact, grow even more. What was disturbing was the duplicity of feeling, the understanding of the past that verbally was the dried swallow of something dead, but emotionally kindled a spark that still remained. Whether he would have to fight it anew and whether such a fight would be difficult he was not yet certain. He was sure that he was willing and capable of winning such a fight. Or so he told himself.

He looked out the cab window and watched the people hurrying along the sidewalks, pushing against one another, past each other, quickly, anxiously, trying to find the security of being able to pause for a moment after reaching their immediate goal, only to rest so that they might begin rushing again. He was certain they were not happy with this situation. He laughed to himself and compared his own life to theirs. Because the world seemed sometimes to be an unalterable confusion and uncertainty, he felt he was falling into the pattern of being afraid to acknowledge his own beliefs and convictions and tempered them with doubt. This was, he thought, what he was doing in relation to this new situation with Tony. He told himself that his concerns were of no consequence. And yet, he thought further, if they were of no consequence why would he continue to think about them?

The driver of the cab suddenly yelled and brakes squealed, throwing John and Carol to the other side of the seat. The driver apologized, cursing at the same time at a pedestrian who had been too much in a hurry to wait for the light. The taxi started again. Carol was open-eyed. She had not seen what had happened.

"Nothing but a careless jay-walker," John assured her.

"Nobody hurt?" she asked.

"Nobody."

She snuggled back against his shoulder. "I almost fell asleep right here," she said, closing her eyes again.

He thought further about the people on the sidewalks, about himself, about Tony, and about the decision that is everyone's at some time. "You were right about New York," he told Carol. He was not running from himself now. "It is a challenge. I can understand how people who come to New York to visit say they wouldn't live here. In their own home towns they're big fish in little ponds. Decisions are different ones. And there are fewer of them. In New York they're suddenly thrust into a big pond and become little fishes and their decisions are part of and interrelated with those of millions. I suppose most people haven't got the confidence or understanding to become part of this big pond. So they just go back home."

It was a long thought, but it made sense to him. He thought about the people he had imagined before, leaning out of their ivory towers. He was certain there must be a way to make them understand the problems and needs of all the others. To understand others is to understand oneself. Just as

he, he conjectured, now understood Tony and, in doing so,
better understood himself. He stopped deliberating.

"You're not unsure of New York now," Carol said, com-
menting on what he had said. "You're not going back to Des
Moines."

"Huh?" John was startled. He had forgotten he had given
his thoughts aloud. "No," he said. "I'm going to finish the
book and then . . ."—he paused, looking for the right words
to see whether Carol's reaction would be the same as
his—". . . then we can sit on top of the whole city in an ivory
tower just built for you."

Carol's answer was the right one.

"I don't want an ivory tower," she said. "I just want to
be me." She saw his smile. "We'll just be ourselves." She held
onto his hand and squeezed it tightly. They were both happy
knowing this.

The cab pulled up at the hotel. John paid the driver,
went into the lobby, Carol preceding him. The front of the
hotel shone with highly polished colored marble, the hotel
name in large three dimensional gold letters on a black
marbled plaque. The inner lobby, plush and rich in color, was
even more brilliant. It was a palette thrown onto a canvas
without purpose, a paean to someone's interpretation of
abstract modern art. It made its effect.

John laughed. "People have fancier places to stay when
they're away from home than when they're home." He looked
around. "How phony can you purposely be?" he suggested.

They got the keys to their respective rooms and took the
elevator. Their luggage had arrived from the station and had
been taken up.

They walked down the narrow hall on a floor marked
with a big number 9, passed a dozen small, silver-tinted
doors, turned the key in one marked 947. This was Carol's

room, a bed, bureau, small desk and an adjoining closet-like affair for a bathroom. She flopped down onto the bed.

"I guess some people would think it funny that we're engaged but have separate rooms," she said.

"And some people would think it scandalous if we didn't," John responded.

"In this day and age, almost the 1970s . . . " Carol began.

John cut her short. "If you want us to sleep together . . . ?"

"Of course I do. And I know you do, too. But we agreed. Your upbringing . . . I don't want you to feel any guilt. And I guess me, too."

"I feel like a hypocrite," John said.

"Pretense would be hypocrisy. Better frustration for a while more than paranoia! I'm tired," Carol yawned.

"Me, too."

"Only I can take a nap while you've got to get back to Tony's."

"Oh, didn't I tell you?" he said casually. "I'm not going."

She sat up. "I thought you arranged it."

"No. I've decided to stay in the hotel."

She came up to him, put a hand across his shoulder. "What is it, Johnny?"

He laughed. "What is what?"

"I don't know . . . "

"Because I'm not going to Tony's?"

"Well . . . " She hesitated.

"I've decided it'll be much easier this way," he said. The tone was soft but solid, indicating an end to the discussion.

Carol waited a moment, then turned back to the bed. "Okay. It isn't that important."

"You take a nap, get showered and dressed," John said. "I'll take a cab, pick up Tony, and we'll both pick you up here."

She was a little confused at the arrangement and John hastened to explain. "I don't feel like sleeping, so I might as well spend the time talking to Tony." The explanation was flimsy, but it was the only one he could think of. He felt it was important to see Tony and try and straighten out things before they saw Carol again. He must make certain that there would be no slipup. Carol raised no objection and he kissed her before leaving. "Suppose we make it for six-thirty," he said.

"All right." Carol had begun unbuttoning her blouse, stopped long enough to kiss John again. He was smiling as he walked out.

## Chapter 15

On the way to Tony's apartment from the hotel later that afternoon John tried to formulate his plan of action, the words he would use and how he would say them. He had phoned and told Tony again of his decision not to stay with him. This was to make it all final. He wanted to make it as easy as possible for he had no desire to hurt Tony. At the same time he wanted to make it quick for he did not want to hurt himself. As the cab went down Seventh Avenue, getting closer to the Village, the anxiety about his own position grew. It was strange, the decision lying in his hands. Once it was over with Tony there would be no more decisions to make. He began, for the moment, not to trust himself to give up the power he could keep by holding on to some relationship with Tony.

When he entered the apartment he found Tony waiting for him, dressed in a dark blue double-breasted suit, prosperous and successful looking. He was well-poised again, as if he had readied himself.

"I'm sorry you decided not to stay here," were Tony's first words. "But there's no rush. We can talk about it."

John wanted to make it clear right then that their talk was to be of more important things. Instead, he kept himself calm. "We don't have too long," he said quietly. "We're going to pick up Carol at six-thirty."

"Whatever you say," Tony agreed. "We never do seem to have too long, do we, Johnny?" he said. He pointed to the couch. "Sit down and make yourself comfortable." He sat next to him. "Drink?" he offered.

John refused. He did not want to become comfortable or relaxed. He wanted to avoid any of the pattern of the past; it had all but disappeared entirely, remaining only like the image burned into the screen of a television set, vague shadows that melted completely as soon as the next picture came clearly into view.

"We'll make it quick and simple," John said. "What was between us is all over. I'm sorry, and for your sake I wish it weren't, but it is and that's the way it is."

Tony stood up, walked back and forth in front of the couch, trying to find the right thing to say. John continued before he could speak.

"We were both upset earlier today," John said. "Things weren't put across too clearly. I hoped, with time to think about it this afternoon, you'd understand."

Tony walked slowly back to the couch, stood close to John, barely not touching him.

"One thing we both should understand," Tony said. "Relationships like ours never change."

"People change, so do relationships," John countered.

"Not with us, Johnny-boy. Ordinary relationships, yes. God knows I know that. But not ours. It was too strong. It's like an escalator. It may go up or down but it never stops."

John got up now and faced him.

"You're wrong, Tony. I've found something new in life. Just like I found something new when I met you. It changes everything." His voice quickened. He didn't want to have to explain again what he had said before.

"You think Carol fulfills something for you?" Tony said. "Like I did?" He knew what he wanted John to say.

"Yes." John clarified it. "Only even more. If anything I feel more complete than I ever did before. I'm going to marry her and have a normal life."

Tony jumped on the answer quickly.

"The other life disgusts you now? You want to run around waving a flag, screaming about immorality?"

John angered at this, but held himself in check.

"Not true," he said. "The other life simply doesn't fit me any longer. Or rather, I don't fit it." His tone was definite. "That one is over, the new one is here to stay." He walked over to the piano, came back and faced Tony squarely. "That's it in a nutshell. Shall we go pick Carol up now?" He hoped the argument was finished.

Tony did not give in. John had controlled his emotions and a new trick was necessary. Tony knew he could threaten to tell Carol about them. He was certain she didn't know. However, he realized that by doing this he would lose John entirely and completely and maybe Carol, as well. That would accomplish nothing. He had to be careful to make sure he retained the main chance. It had to be another way.

"Don't you think, Johnny," he suggested, "that whatever you feel for Carol is just a compensation for what was missing after I left?"

"No," John said. "It may have been at first. But now it's real and normal. I know it's difficult for you to realize, but what I feel is the true thing."

"What you feel isn't normality," Tony protested. "It's abnormal because it really isn't you. I know you, and what you feel now is the abnormality of a corrupt society that isn't even true to its own stinking corruption." His voice had risen, making the words seem even more important than they might have otherwise.

"Don't talk all these principles to me, Tony, because there's no sense in trying to confuse what society is with what you feel my place in it is. I know where I stand. I don't fit there anymore."

"You're the same person. You're no different," Tony insisted.

"That's what you don't understand," John told him. "I am different." His voice had grown heavy with definity.

Tony knew that John was right, but he did not want to believe it. He had to continue his argument.

"Was there something wrong with our relationship?" he asked, almost apologetically. He hoped to work on John's sympathy. He was beginning to be seriously afraid that John could really finally resist him.

"Nothing wrong with the relationship."

"Were you afraid of me?"

"Sometimes," John admitted. "But that's not the point," he added. "I'm not afraid any longer and I don't need you any longer. Maybe that makes sense."

Tony sat back on the couch, trying to find his next step. John had indeed taken over now and he knew it. Now it was his need that was the greater.

"We had a great need for each other," he reminded John, "and we fulfilled that need. It was a good thing. The need is still there for me. It's still there for you, isn't it, Johnny? It is, really?" He almost pleaded.

"No, Tony, it isn't. My need is with Carol. Not with the world we knew."

Tony jumped to another idea. "Is it sex?" he asked. The mental picture was discomfiting to him. The word sounded long and ugly.

John was beginning to feel very sorry for Tony. He understood that the other man was talking with desperation, even though he tried hard to conceal it. John decided to settle it now. He didn't worry any longer over the outcome.

"I don't exactly understand your point, Tony."

"If it's just sex," Tony quickly grasped the opening, "that could change easily." He didn't have time to put his thoughts together as he searched for a telling point. "You remember the dormitory at college. A man may have gone out with a woman every night, had half a dozen mistresses and patronized every whore house in town—but sometimes he found he fulfilled his needs in other ways, too. Isn't that right, Johnny?"

"What has that got to do with me?"

"It means you don't have to break up our relationship," Tony said.

John laughed. "You're trying too hard." He was sorry he had laughed. He knew it was cruel. There seemed to be no other way. "My mind is made up, Tony, you can't change it." He waited a moment. This was the time, he felt, that Tony could play his trump card. It was here that he could threaten to tell Carol about everything.

It entered Tony's mind again for he knew that the rope was almost at its end. But, as before, he knew that this would accomplish nothing. For a moment Tony thought he might bluff it. "About Carol . . ." Tony began to say and then shut it off.

John spoke quickly. "What about Carol?" He waited, but no answer came. "You know that it would do no good, don't you, Tony?" He understood, now, what Tony had decided and guessed the reasons. John acted as if he had known all along. "Both Carol and I would be gone from your life. You know that."

"I know," Tony said simply.

"You see that what I'm doing is right for me and for
Carol, don't you, Tony?" John tried to comfort him, to speak
with friendship in his voice.

Tony looked up quickly, grabbed at John's arm, held
onto it tightly. "Don't end it like this," he begged. His voice
cracked and the black lock of hair splashed against his forehead. He didn't bother to brush it back. "Please stay with me,
Johnny. At least for a little while."

John remained quiet. He was angry at himself for letting
the situation go so far. He let Tony talk, sorry for him, thankful that it was not himself in that position any longer.

"Why don't you stay here, at least until you finish the
book? After that, if Carol comes, then okay. But for now,
for a little while." Tony waited for John to speak, saw that
he wasn't going to, and continued. "You did your best work
with me, on the musicals. I'll help you with your writing.
Please, Johnny."

"No, Tony."

Tony stood up now. He straightened his suit jacket, tried
to find himself again, embarrassed and ashamed for his own
weakness. He did not understand it. It was something he had
never thought would happen to him, this terrible thing he
had seen happen to so many others.

"I'm working on a new show, John." He spoke evenly
again. "Frankly, this last year, without you, I've had someone else here. Now that you've come, I sent him away. With
you I'll do my best work. I'll write the best music I've ever
written." He was begging and he felt sorry for himself and he
knew more clearly what Larry must have felt only a few hours
before. He didn't care.

John looked at his watch. "It's after six," he said. "We'd
better be going."

Tony remained silent, catching his breath at the final
rebuff. He was not nervous. He accepted, finally, John's deci-

sion—for the time being. "One thing, please, Johnny-boy?"
he asked.

"What's that?"

"Next week after Carol leaves, would you think about
what I said, about staying here a while? At least think
about it."

John was ready to leave and knew there was no point in
discussing it any further. He smiled at Tony and in the other's
sadness felt a little of the compassion of old. There was no
more to be gained in being verbally cruel. "All right, Tony,"
he said. "I'll think about it."

# Chapter 16

The week in New York was good to Carol and John. They were excited and they were tired. They were tourists on a spree. Even for Tony it was interesting. Though weary guiding them, he nevertheless caught sight of many things he had not yet seen in his year in the city. They went everywhere, saw everything that was big or old or tinseled. They overtook themselves in their rushing, stopped and laughed at the incessant running that had joined them with the tourists they had once mocked. From the Cloisters to the Metropolitan Museum of Art to the Statue of Liberty to the Empire State Building to Rockefeller Center, they felt like they were on a constant merry-go-round and, in fact, made a point of riding on the one in Central Park. In the exhaustion of their eagerness they sometimes wondered whether it was all worthwhile. After a full meal and a refreshing shower and the soft comfort of sleep they were ready to begin all over again.

"It's a wonderful place to live," John said one evening as all three, he and Carol and Tony, were eating in one of the many small French restaurants along New York's Lexington Avenue. "But I certainly wouldn't want to visit here."

Tony laughed. "That's just the opposite of what every-body else says who comes to New York." He had been in a good mood during the week. He had tentatively accepted John's decision and was waiting now until Carol left before attempting anything further in that direction. The subject had not even been mentioned.

"Visiting New York is too much of a rush and you're too tired to really appreciate anything," John explained. "Living here, you can take your time and see the sights and enjoy the city gradually."

"Some people live here forty years and never see any-thing, I'll bet," Carol observed.

"At least here they have the opportunity for its culture," John countered, "even if they don't take advantage of it. It's kind of thrust upon them whether they have the time for it or not."

A waiter came up wheeling a small cart on top of which were heaped dishes of varied garden vegetables, greens, and spices. "Self-mixing salad," Tony told them. "You just choose what ingredients you want and he makes it up to order right here."

With child-like eagerness Carol and John pointed out the components and proportions, watched fascinated as the waiter mixed them with artistic deliberation and flourish. Tony, too, watched with delight. He had participated in their pleasures of discovering New York and he had taken a pride in leading them. It gave him back some of the superiority that had failed him: his choice of artistic and cultural places and events; his location of the ethnic sections of town; even his knowledge of the subways, an impossible task to master in a few days or a few months, that made the others, to that degree, dependent upon him. But his decisions were by no means complete or binding. It was John at the Museum of Natural History who took Carol's hand and led the way to

the various exhibits that caught his interest. In the past it
was Tony who would have made the choice. It was John, after
they had dressed for a night club visit, who suggested they
go to Coney Island instead and they boarded a subway and
headed for Brooklyn. It was John who showed no bashful-
ness in asking directions, who became friendly with a man
standing next to him on the crowded subway train, who got
a bored taxi-driver into an animated conversation about New
York's newest baseball team, the Mets, giving a new lease
on life for former Brooklyn Dodgers fans, freeing themselves
from a continuing dependency on the Dodgers and furious
at their former heroes for abandoning their followers and
moving across country for the sole purpose of even greater
monetary gain.

Their table in the French restaurant was pressed against
the near wall, part of a long line of tables down either side
of the establishment. Leather padded benches jutted out in
a continuous run along the walls and the tables could be
moved as the diners wished. For parties of more than two the
waiter disappeared into a room at the far end and brought out
small stool-type chairs to be placed against the table down
the narrow center aisle of the restaurant. The atmosphere was
informal, the food apparently good because the restaurant
was crowded. There were occasional snatches of conversation
in French. Both walls were decorated with identical maps of
Paris, the Eiffel Tower in the center of the illustrated dia-
gram, the streets branching out to drawn facsimiles of the
other wonders of the French capitol. John stared at the map
of Paris, caught in its suggestion. His enthusiasm over the
largest city in America had whetted his appetite for more.
Carol saw the glow.

"When you finish the book and start collecting all that
money in royalties," she said, "we'll go to Paris."

He smiled back seriously. "Yes, we will."

"And Tony, too." It was Tony who added this, joking.

John smiled at him. "And Tony, too." There had been no bitterness in Tony's voice. It was only said as something for John to think about.

Tony took the check after the dinner was finished.

"You've been paying for everything," Carol protested.

"Nonsense," Tony said. "I consider it a privilege." He excused himself, went to the front desk.

"It's very sweet of Tony to go to all this expense for us," Carol said.

John nodded agreement, smiling.

"I'm so glad you two were friends, such good friends," Carol said.

"Yes." This time there was no smile.

"Or we might never have met," Carol added. John took her hand, held it tight as they walked to join Tony at the front desk.

At the desk, as Tony turned to go, a young man appeared seemingly from nowhere and came up to him. He was quite young, no more than twenty. The boyishness of his face was accentuated by bushy blonde hair that hung in haircut-needing wisps over his ears. By the smoothness of his light-complexioned skin he apparently rarely needed to shave. He wore a tight fitting brown sports jacket over white flannel trousers, too dressy for New York's late summer. He reached for Tony's hand, grabbed it and held it tightly between both of his as if he were afraid that Tony would run away. The people near the door looked up as the boy's high-pitched voice announced his presence, apparently heedless that he was not alone in the room with the other man.

"Tony, it's so, so wonderful to see you again. Where have you been keeping yourself?"

The people stared for a moment, shrugged, and went back to their eating. Tony glanced at Carol and John, obviously embarrassed. His friend didn't seem to notice.

"When are we going to see each other again?" the blonde boy continued. "It's been such a strain, you know." Each word was accented beyond normal projection.

Tony fidgeted for a moment, was about to say something, thought better of it.

Carol noticed his uneasiness, put her arm into his as she reached him, just as the boy had begun to speak again. The boy stopped, his mouth dropping the words in mid-air. He stared at Carol, then at Tony, confused, then inquisitive.

"My sister," Tony explained hastily. He made the proper introductions, introducing John as his "very good friend." The boy was visibly upset.

"I'm Carol's fiancé," John said quietly.

This relieved the blonde young man. He inched away from them back toward his table, understanding now the discomfort he had thrust upon Tony and feeling sorry for it all.

"It's a pleasure to have met you," he said to Carol and John. And then to Tony, "Let me hear from you, will you?" He stopped, looked at Tony directly. "Will you?" Then he was gone.

"Strange person," Carol observed when they were outside.

They walked down Fifth Avenue, looking at the glamour of the shops after dark, absent the distraction of the afternoon shoppers.

"Met him at a party once," Tony explained. He was still a little upset.

"I really didn't think he was a good friend," Carol observed. She didn't very seriously care, but wondered about it idly at the same time.

"Not really," Tony answered.

"Certainly not like the friends I knew," John said. He hadn't wanted to say anything and he didn't know why he did. It was simply the taking advantage of a difficult situation. He knew that he didn't have to resort to such opportunities to prove his status anymore.

Tony took up the remark as a challenge. "We have many lives," he said pointedly. "In the friends we meet, in the things we do, in the ideas we have. Even in the way we live."

"I guess we do," John agreed. "And I guess we're all entitled to the lives we choose."

"Or those that are given us," Tony responded quickly, challenging John's point "Sometimes the ones we pick out are not the right ones." John let it go without an answer.

Carol changed the subject as they turned onto the promenade of Rockefeller Center, lined with fountains and flowers, the large statue of Prometheus holding the life-giving flame open to humankind forming a gold background, brighter in the night shadows, gathering in the benches along the promenade full with men and women, some embracing, some scurrying looking for mates, male and female.

Carol stopped and looked over the scene. "It seems to have a life all of its own."

They began to talk about Rockefeller Center and the incident of the blonde boy was not mentioned again.

During the week Tony found himself alone with John only once. It was on Friday night, the evening before Carol's leaving. He had not attempted to talk to John about what he felt was John's promise, the reconsideration of his, Tony's, need. Except for the brief moment after the episode in the French restaurant they had not exchanged any significant words. It hurt him, the position he had been put in and the expectancy of having to beg again for John's favor. It was a harsh medicine, but Tony rationalized it into a prescription for health. His weakness now with John was only a step toward the cure, and once the cure was accomplished he hoped he might find himself in the position of command

he had held before. He used the word "hoped" consciously
because he was not quite sure.

Only once before in his life had he felt this way, his own
complete subjugation to fulfill a need. That once had been so
many memories into the past that it was now relegated out of
present reality and was only a shadowy thought, to refer back
to when he wished. Only with reverence did he, occasionally,
try to recall the name of the musician from New York who
had been responsible for that first time and who had given
him the key to his existence. Even now he couldn't remember the name. If he had, he might have attempted to look
for him, like the student looks for the former professor to
say, "look at me, look how I've grown, look what I've accomplished." But that was gone and John had taken his place and
it was with John he had reached a maturity and it was for
that reason he knew, no matter what the cost or the difficulty,
that it must be to John he returned: the return to the bosom,
even if it were once removed from the womb.

They were, that Friday night, in a nightclub called Vic's,
a Greenwich Village club that featured jazz music, better
known than most of its similar contemporaries because of its
larger floor area and top-flight musicians—as well as a less-
publicized substantial minimum charge.

The three, Tony, John, and Carol, sat without talking for
a long while, listening to the music, to the vibrating sounds of
"Tin-Roof Blues," to the solo trombone vying for volume with
the beat of shoes on the floor and the sometimes abortive vocal
accompaniment of the rhythmic screams of twenty-somethings
crowded around the bandstand. It was an exciting moment
when the band reached its peak and they could feel the music
coming out of the inner feelings and emotions of the musicians,
into and out of the audience, transferring from the mechanical
instruments across the room into them and out of them and letting no one be free from joining in the furious tapping of feet

upon the floor. It was an expurgation, letting loose whatever inhibitions and knotted desires there were inside the body and soul. John felt that way and as he looked across the table he saw Tony, too, caught up in the wild rhythms, his mouth opening and closing with the blare of the trumpet. It was an involuntary response and when Tony saw John looking at him, he stopped. While Tony had applauded the technical construction of jazz, his feelings toward it had had been a rationalization. Jazz came from too many souls and common feelings. It came out of the people themselves. Tony, put aside by the people into another world, rejected what he felt came from their majority emotions. John had felt that way, too. Now he felt free and part of that music. Thinking this, John watched Tony again slowly begin to join in the beat of the music. Even in his conviction he could not escape society, John thought.

The number was over and Tony turned to them. "Do you really like this music?" he suggested, making the words a self-apology for his own involvement.

John remembered that Stan Kenton's cool jazz had been one of the Tony's favorites and judged that this seeming turnabout was a message aimed at him. "Why not?" John asked?

"So damned common. Like a comic book compared to great literature."

"It gives me a good feeling." John added slowly, "a feeling of belonging."

Tony held back his sarcasm. "To what?"

"To society."

"What kind of society? A false society?" Tony insisted.

"To some it is."

"Isn't it to you?" Tony asked.

"Not anymore," John said calmly.

Carol listened with interest. Aware that she was disturbed over their sharp words, the others stopped. A piano player had taken the place of the band during the break and was softly playing musical comedy numbers: Gershwin, Coward, Rodgers. The customers seemed to regard it as the intermission signal to drink and few paid attention to the pianist. "That's more like it," Tony grunted, nodding toward the piano.

Carol excused herself, went to the ladies room. Tony moved his chair closer to John. He hadn't intended to talk with John until Carol was gone, but the conversation of a moment before lent impetus and carried him forward.

"You're kidding yourself, Johnny," he said hurriedly. "This isn't your life, this razz-ma-tazz hustle-bustle. You belong in the world of music he's playing now. You understand what I mean, don't you."

"Let's not get involved in this now, Tony." John tried to stop him.

"Just for a minute."

"All right. Just for a minute," John conceded. "I enjoy jazz music just as I enjoy any other. Why limit yourself?"

"Some things you only think you enjoy. But they're impressions of the moment. They're not real. It's like throwing yourself into a maelstrom where you don't belong." He caught his breath and let his feeling roll out. "Quit it, Johnny. The apartment's waiting and empty. Fill it."

"We better not talk about it now," was the answer. "I told you I'd think about it."

Tony felt a rush of frustration, then chose not to fight it. "Okay, Johnny. I'm just trying to help you, to do what's best for you."

Carol returned and there was no more opportunity for discussion. They stayed at Vic's until early in the morning. Carol enjoyed the crowd, the first time she had been to a jazz club. John enjoyed the music, caught up in its inner expression and feeling good about its release. Tony sat silently, drinking far over the minimum check.

The week together in New York ended too quickly for Carol and John. It had been a happy time, almost like a honeymoon, seeing and doing the things that people do on a wedding trip to the city. Their hotel rooms remained separate. The culmination of sex remained, a promise between them that would add to what they already had in understanding and companionship. Neither had expressed any fear or disavowal of pre-marital sexual relations. It simply was that the opportunity for it, for themselves, had not pressed itself forward and they were satisfied to let it wait. The mental image no longer bothered John. He could talk about it.

That Saturday morning, following their evening of jazz, the occasion came to talk about it. They were seated on one of the couches in the lobby of the hotel waiting for Tony to pick them up. Carol was packed and ready to return home and when Tony arrived they would go to the train station. The week had been so wonderful and the excitement and enjoyment had been to Carol almost complete. As she watched John's face, sad with the thought of her leaving, she wondered why they should not make it complete.

"You look in a deep dark sadness," she told him. She leaned over to take his hand.

"Just thinking about things." Besides Carol, he was occupied with thoughts of Tony. As soon as Carol left he knew he would have to face him again and their argument would resume.

"Me?" Carol smiled.

"Always about you."

"Can I help you be . . ." she fumbled for the right word ". . . happier?"

He looked at her, then smiled. "Just looking at you makes me happy."

"And is that all?" He didn't understand. "There's such little time before I leave," she said. She pushed the words and moved closer to him, needing his protection for her thoughts. "There's so much we can still do to be happy."

He still did not see the point.

"What?"

"Don't you know?"

He did and for the moment it frightened him. He smiled. The incongruity of the hotel lobby made it seem odd. Then, when he looked at her, he was disturbed no longer. The slim darkness of Carol melted into him and he felt then what she, too, must be feeling. He had gotten to know her physically, but it had been limited. Kissing her and holding her tight and close had been part of a gentle rather than passionate relationship and, as such, remained gentle itself. He had, in time, desired her, but he did not rebel against the frustration and rather welcomed it, for it made him feel that he had become more of his new being. He had known that she felt the same thing, something warmer than just friendship when he had stopped the car on the unlit drive outside of Des Moines or when they had remained silent in the darkened living room of her house long after they had no more need to talk. He had let his hands move over her body, getting to know her entirely as he knew the lines and softness of her face. She, too, watched him grow stronger and as he grew reached for the strength of flesh and muscle within him. But it had been gentle, warm, yearning, never explosive. There was a contentment in the reality of a soft love.

Now, about to leave each other, they felt the need for an even greater closeness. This was, if ever, the time.

John said simply, "I know what you mean."

"And?"

The decision would have to come from him, he knew.

"I'm not afraid," she said.

"Nor am I." After a moment: "I do love you, Carol."

"I love you, Johnny."

He could not seem to find an answer or, if he knew the answer, the words were not clear. "I know so much of you," he said after a moment, quickly as though the time had suddenly grown short, "and yet there's so much I don't know."

She, too, felt as if there was no time left. "I'll be gone for so long."

He held both her hands, their eyes meeting and holding, the lovers who want to tell each other how much in love they are, but because words seem inadequate they push each other's entirety into the other and know without needing words. They stayed like that for a minute, sober, without moving, the most important problems of the universe written on their faces, their minds full with the purity of love, their bodies anticipating the mercurial passion of its consummation.

Then, without warning, John's lips began to twitch and his mouth melted at the edges, bursting into a broad smile. Carol was surprised. Then realizing, as he did, the ridiculousness of their seriousness, joined him. The smiles grew into laughs and, their eyes still not moving from each other's, they roared loudly, the notes coming from deep inside. They were conscious of people staring and their mouths closed, holding back the tinkling sounds that still remained within. It was a strange and wonderful feeling for both, this lightness of understanding, the seemingly important thing taken from its pedestal and made a common possession to laugh about together. It was the first time they had felt it in just this way and it was a good feeling.

The implication of what they promised came down to a level of naturalness, of complete informality.

"Now who is supposed to be convincing whom?" John said, still holding back the laughter.

"You agree?" Carol asked.

"Of course." There was no doubt.

"Well then, am I being formally propositioned?"

The question was with feigned innocence.

John carried along the lightness.

"I think we have both been propositioned," he said.

"Then, with such overwhelming odds . . . " She stopped, waiting for John to finish it. But she didn't let him. She had to say again, "I do love you . . . so, so much."

They looked at each other, confident in their decision. The turn of events, the conversation itself they both knew had been so unlike them, so new and yet so much like the warmth and understanding of their love.

"We've got a little while," John said. "If Tony rings my room, we'll just let him wait."

Carol got up, straightened her dress as if she should present her best appearance. They held hands, not having to speak, and began walking slowly to the elevator, faster with each step, the anticipation pushing them. One elevator closed and started up just as they reached it. They anxiously waited for the next. It arrived, the doors opened and a woman came slowly out, taking up what seemed to them an eternity, pulling after her a small boy who was intent on remaining with the elevator operator. They started to step in, finally, when they heard Tony's voice. Tony had come too soon. Hours and days and years too soon, they both thought.

"Hey, there you are." Tony ran up to them, puffing.

Hesitating, they stepped out of the elevator. They wanted to do something, but there seemed nothing that could be done. The smiles stole their way out of them and their stomachs became empty.

"We'd better hurry," Tony said, "if we want to get some lunch before we catch that train."

They stood motionless. John held Carol's arm and she moved closer to him as he tightened his grip. It was as if to say, "What can we do?" Then they looked at each other and smiled. Slowly they followed Tony down the lobby. There was so much they had to look forward to.

At Penn Station they walked along the platform toward the front of the train. The conductor's monotone repeated, "Sleeping Cars Forward." Carol and John, arm in arm, stepped along quickly. Tony followed behind. "Pittsburgh, Cleveland, Chicago, Iowa City, Des Moines." The travelers heard the announcement somewhere out of the noise of the goodbyes, the scraping shoes, the silent kisses, and they hurried a little faster.

John helped Carol into a seat near one of the doors, pushed her suitcase onto the rack above. People brushed past him, trying to find seats by windows before they were all gone. John sat in the seat next to Carol. Tony stood by, bent down and kissed her.

"Be good, sis." He patted her on the top of her head affectionately.

Carol laughed. "Sure you're not being sweet just to get rid of me."

Tony's smile faded just the slightest bit, then was full again.

"I've been here a whole week having you spend all your money on me," Carol continued. "I wouldn't blame you."

"Good trip, Carol," Tony said. "I'll wait for you on the platform, Johnny." He walked the few steps down the aisle, out of the car. They watched through the compartment window as he walked around the side of the train. He waved at them. Carol waved back. Tony leaned against one of the iron posts, right outside the window. He said something that Carol couldn't make out, the tightly shut window barring conversation between the two sides. He propped himself against the post.

John looked at his watch. "Only a few minutes left," he muttered. He felt hollow and empty inside. He knew he was very much in love with this woman who was about to leave. The hurt showed on his face.

Carol saw it. "Don't make me cry, Johnny," she said, her voice as low as his.

John moved closer to her, took her hand and clasped it tightly as if doing so he wouldn't have to let go when it was time to part. Something to hold on to and keep until the rest of her returned.

"You look so sad, it makes me want to look sad, too," she said. "It's bad enough to feel that way."

"I'm sorry." John sat up straighter. He forced a smile and leaned over and kissed her. He saw Tony standing outside looking at them. It made him feel just a little resentful that he was being watched. He held Carol closer and kissed her again. It was for a long time.

"I feel better," she said after the kiss. "That's the way it's always going to be." She sat up now. "It won't be very long, will it, Johnny?" Her eyes shone into him and they reflected more than just the question.

"As soon as I finish the book, then it'll be," John told her.

"You work hard on it, Johnny. Make it quick." She stopped herself abruptly. "I don't mean to push you," she apologized. "I'm just impatient."

"No more than I am," he assured her. "It'll be real soon."

They sat, not speaking, both wanting to say something, listening to the seconds move by. The pressure of trying to find words in order not to waste the remaining moments kept them silent.

"When you only have a little time left, you try to find important things to say to make the time important," John said. "But I don't know what to say."

"It doesn't matter," Carol helped him. "We both know what we want to say."

Passengers filled up the few last vacant seats. A man
with a large suitcase stopped by them, looked at the single
piece of luggage on the rack above the seat, looked down at
them, waited a moment. They didn't say anything. The man
shrugged his shoulders and walked away. Outside the window Tony was waving at them again.

"Are you going to stay with Tony now?" Carol asked. "If
not, I'll want your address so I can write."

"No," he told her. "I'll get a room someplace and let you
know as soon as I do."

"It seems a shame not to take up Tony's invitation. It
seems like the logical thing to do."

"I'll write better alone," he explained hastily. "The sooner
I get the work done, the sooner you come here."

The issue of Tony's apartment wasn't important enough
to take time to talk about any further. "Whatever you decide
is best," Carol agreed.

The conductor came up the aisle, went to the train door
and leaned his head out toward the platform. "All aboard."
They could feel the vibration of the motors beginning to
start beneath them. John tightened his grip on her hand.
The conductor came back into the car, glanced at the single
ticket in the slot of the seat in front of them. "Train pulling
out, sonny," he said in the same monotone he used to call the
route stations. He passed without stopping, without even
looking at them.

John let her hand slide out of his and stood up. "I'd better go."

Carol stood with him. Her eyes were wet. She forced a
laugh.

"I can't help it," she said.

She pressed into his arms and he held her close. He could
feel all of her against him. It was warm and good.

"I love you," he said. It was almost a whisper, and then, as though it weren't enough, he said it louder: "I love you."

"I love you," the words came back. He kissed her hard, felt the wet from her cheeks move onto his. He started to wipe his eyes, stopped. Instead he let go of her, walked quickly away.

"Soon," she called.

He stopped, turned and looked at her. She stood with one hand balanced against the seat, as if there were not enough strength left to sit down. His mouth formed the one word, "soon". He caught her smile and walked out of the train onto the platform.

Carol sat down and watched John's every action, saw him move toward Tony, stand with him by the post, looking at her. He waved, she waved back. Tony joined him in making some signals she didn't understand. She answered by putting her hand to her mouth and blowing a kiss. John did the same. She wondered why the train didn't move and wished it would hurry. She pressed her face close to the window, held back the choking feeling in her throat and laughed for them. She could see John laughing back and it made her feel better.

She remained that way, close to the window, for a few seconds longer. Then came a rumbling sound across the tracks, then the screech of the wheels starting to move. The noise increased, the window began to blur and move slowly, then more quickly down the platform. Carol waved as the window moved past John and Tony. They walked a few steps, following it, keeping Carol in sight. Then the window was gone and Carol had disappeared. They stood a moment, waited until the train had entered into the blackness of the tunnel, and turned back.

"Give me a cigarette," John demanded.

Tony took one out of a pack, gave it to John, lit it for him. John puffed deeply, rapidly, exhaling as soon as the smoke reached the roof of his mouth.

"Feel better?" Tony asked.

"Yeah. Feel better." John dropped the cigarette on the concrete, stamped it out. "Let's get out of here," he said.

They walked without talking, up through the waiting room, into the main corridor and up the escalator out into the street. They stood on the corner for an interminable time. John let the fresh air cool him. Already he was beginning to feel an anxiety much like that he had felt when Tony had gone to New York a year before. He was alone again. Then he had turned and found Carol. Now, as he turned, next to him stood Tony. It was a grim thought, the cycle that thrust itself on him, one event beginning where the last had left off and then repeating itself. He belied the comparison. He had long since gotten off the merry-go-round; he resolved not to be caught up in a never-ending circle.

Tony was smiling and John knew it was because of his own seriousness of face. He forced a smile and asked for another cigarette, smoked it while he stood there, thinking. He watched the people pass, letting them carry his mind away from his own thoughts. He thought nothing particular about the people except, as always, wondering where they were all hurrying to. Tony finished his cigarette, flipped it into the gutter, looking around to see if anybody was watching him.

"Can't drop them on the sidewalk anymore. Police campaign. They give a ticket to anyone they see littering the sidewalks with cigarette butts." Then he added as an afterthought, "Gutter's okay, though."

John grunted an acknowledgement of the information. He didn't feel like talking. Yet he knew that this was the time Tony had been waiting for. He was being tolerant, his tolerance only a prelude to something else. John made up his mind that it was as good a time as any to settle it. "Let's get a drink," he said.

Tony looked surprised. "That's more like it." He anticipated what John wanted and prepared himself for it. He judged how John felt, with Carol having just gone and deduced that the offer of a new companionship, the enjoyment and security of what he would offer, would most likely at this moment have the optimum effect. He would have to take advantage of every opportunity. He realized that it was no longer his game to play as he wished, that there were two of them holding the cards and that John held too many aces to be bluffed. "Let's walk to 39th Street," Tony suggested. He put a hand on John's shoulder, tentatively pointed the way. "There's a quiet little place there where we can talk."

They crossed the street, walked past the shops without noticing them. Tony with a long step, briskly, in a hurry to get there. John walked more slowly, almost automatically. He stepped back quickly as they were crossing Lexington Avenue when a car turned into the road. Tony pulled him onto the curb.

"Come out of it, Johnny, you don't want to get hit by these crazy drivers."

"Yeah."

"Thinking of Carol?"

"That's right." His thoughts were not altogether about Carol. He was thinking about Tony's apparent good humor and expectations and he was thinking about himself, his own depression at the moment. In his moodiness he didn't want to begin to feel sorry for himself. Any weakness on his part would make it that much more difficult in dealing with Tony. He knew Tony.

"Don't worry," Tony assured him. "Everything will turn out just fine." His voice twinkled as he said it.

They walked to 39<sup>th</sup> Street, entered through glazed glass doors into a small café. They sat down in a narrow booth across from the bar that lined one wall of the room. John moved onto the bench first, Tony sat across the table from him. It was comfortable, the seats red-leather cushioned with enough slope between the backrest and the bottom to lean back upon. The wall, deep brown, extended out on both sides of each booth, giving the customers privacy for their own company and privacy from any other.

"Nice place," Tony commented. "The Green Lantern, they call it. Don't know why. Maybe it's because the glass doors are green?" John didn't answer. "You're all alone at your table and nobody bothers you," Tony continued. "The waiter brings your drinks and leaves you alone. You can talk in comfort."

"It is a nice place," John agreed. He felt he ought to say something. He wanted Tony to say what he had to so that he could answer, finish the argument, and leave. The whole tenor of things seemed to be going so slow, the conversation sounding as though it were coming out in monosyllables. He felt sluggish and wanted to rest. He wished Carol were there to lean against, to be comfortable with. The thought of leaning against anyone else disturbed him, the transference going involuntarily in his mind to Tony. He wished everything would hurry up.

Tony ordered drinks. John began playing with the book matches on the table. He tore out, one by one, the cardboard matches, tore each one down the middle, formed little strips of evenly matched rectangles.

Tony watched him for a moment. "No need to be nervous, Johnny-boy," he said, his manner indicating that he would willingly take care of John's disquiet. John hastily pushed the match ends together into one pile, dumped them into the ashtray. He picked up his drink and began to sip it slowly. It tasted good. The moodiness of a moment before passed quickly. The warmth of the liquor helped give him a stability. He opened the match book again, pulled out a few more matches, only this time he was less deliberate. He wasn't nervous. The momentary lapse had settled him. He was marking time, waiting for Tony to speak.

"It's just like old times," Tony said confidently. "We won't worry about anything," he said. "We'll enjoy life, just like we used to and let things come as they may." He looked at John and smiled. John smiled back. Tony mistook its meaning. It was a smile of pity.

"We're ready to settle it, aren't we, Tony?"

Tony was expectant. "All ready. It'll be good between us. Like old times," he repeated.

John put the matches down, spread his hands on the table. "There's no point in going over it again, Tony. We can be friends if you want. But only friends. The rest is finished." He said it slowly and calmly so there would be no mistaking the words.

Tony's face drew in, the cheeks sucking against his teeth. Perhaps he had misjudged the moment. "You're upset now, Johnny-boy. We'll skip it for now and talk about it later."

"We came to talk now and that's what we'll do," John told him. "We'll settle it here and now." His voice remained calm.

Tony stammered. "But you promised. You said you'd think it over."

"I have thought it over. My answer is still the same. I'm not going back to the old world."

"You don't really mean it, Johnny."

"It's changed, I'm changed, and there's no point in going over it again." John gulped the last of the drink. He hadn't expected it to be so quick and easy. He started to get up.

Tony's cheeks began to quiver now and he bit his tongue, trying to keep still its irritations. "No, Johnny, don't go. I thought . . . ." He stopped and the words became long high-pitched sounds, each one a plea unto itself. "I thought this was going to be like old times. Don't leave so soon. Let's talk about it."

John was up now. "I've talked. You don't understand. Maybe it's best if I just leave quickly." He tried to be kind.

Tony got half up, held onto John's arm. "Please, please don't." The sound of his voice became still higher as though he could find what he wanted by yelling for it.

John moved away. Heads darted out of other booths to look and he was embarrassed. These were strange faces and they discomforted him. He felt lonely among them. He felt lonely in New York and for an instant wished that somehow he could go back with Tony. And as though he were afraid he might do just that, he walked hurriedly to the front door. He heard Tony call to him again, then heard the bartender's voice and he knew Tony had stopped at the bar to pay the bill. He walked more quickly. Tony's voice screamed after him. "Wait, Johnny, please wait. Please don't go without me."

He got to the door. A stout woman sitting at the corner of the bar, her scraggly long dirty blonde hair dipping its loose ends toward the glass of beer she held in her hand, looked at him and said, "God-damned queers."

The green glass doors closed behind him and he heard Tony's voice calling his name. He began to run down the street.

# Chapter 17

John felt cold as he ran down the street. He felt a shivering as though he had escaped a great fright. The people he passed mopped their foreheads, struggled with stifling girdles, unloosened their ties. John wanted to fold his arms to shut out the chill. He stopped running and looked behind him; no sight of Tony. He began walking urgently toward his hotel. He made up his plan of action quickly. In the hotel lobby he bought a copy of the <u>New York Times</u>, folded it to the classified section as he took the elevator up to his room. He sat on the bed, spread the paper out and carefully ran his fingers over the "apartment to rent" ads, checked off several with a pencil. He looked at his watch. Two o'clock. He hoped he would be gone before Tony decided to look for him at the hotel.

He called the first number, thanked the voice that told him the apartment was taken, called a second, asked the rental price and said that it was too high and hung up. The third call brought him the information that he could rent the available apartment cheaply, providing he was willing to pay a substantial sum for the few pieces of furniture that the tenant "reluctantly" had to leave behind. He didn't bother to

thank this one and called another number. In twenty minutes
he had tried all his rental-range possibilities in Manhattan
without success and began checking the Brooklyn vacancies.
The story was the same: either rented, too expensive to rent,
or requiring an unofficial, albeit substantial, payment for
"services rendered."

Under "Furnished Rooms—Brooklyn" he found an
ad calling for a single man. There was no price listed. He
wasn't sure whether the voice that answered was a man's or
a woman's. It was a hoarse voice and for the first few words
sounded like that of an old man's. Then it cracked and the
higher-pitched female tones came over clearly.

"You want the apartment?"

"Yes, ma'am. I'm single and interested in a small furnished place."

"The ad said furnished room," the voice repeated.

"Yes, ma'am."

"You sound like a nice educated boy." The voice paused a
moment. "You an educated boy?"

"I got out of college a few months ago." John was disturbed by the odd questioning.

"Good. I went to college myself, you know."

For a moment he was tempted to put the phone down,
but decided to go along with the conversation. "Oh, is that
right?" he asked with interest.

"Yes. I'm a nurse," the voice continued. It stopped. John
could hear the sound of the person drinking something.

He waited a moment. "About that room . . . "

The voice was low again. "It's really an apartment," the
woman told him. "A living room with a studio couch, a small
kitchenette, and a bathroom." There was a pause. "One hundred a month." After a pause: "rent controlled."

The rent was fine with John. Cheap for an apartment
with a kitchen in New York, even in the 1960s. He could

save a great deal on meals. "May I come over and see it?" he asked.

The voice began to say something, then hesitated.

"Do you drink?"

John pondered a moment. Ordinarily he would have replied that he didn't. The sound of drinking again on the other end of the phone changed his mind.

"I'm not averse to an occasional drink," he said.

"That's good," the woman told him. "I wouldn't like anybody here who didn't like to have a little fun once in a while. I had fun when I was a girl. I went to college, you know."

John smiled. "Yes, I know."

"You come over to 194 Congress Street in Brooklyn. IRT subway to Court Street. Come up to apartment number five and ask for Mac."

"Mac," John repeated. "That your husband?" he asked.

"Hell, no," was the answer. "That's me. My first name is really Florence. Florence MacDougal. When you see me you'll know why nobody calls me Florence."

"I'll be right over," John said. He could hear Mac laughing at the other end of the line as he hung up.

He packed his suitcase, glancing at his watch every few seconds. If the telephone rang, he decided he wouldn't answer it. He reasoned that Tony might be at the hotel by this time, certain that he would try to find him again. He checked the bureau and the closet, satisfied that he had everything, gripped the suitcase and his typewriter case and opened the door to go. The phone rang. He closed the door behind him. He waited until the phone stopped, then walked down to the other end of the corridor and remained there for five minutes under the assumption that if it were Tony he would go away thinking he was not there. He went downstairs, checked out, told the clerk there was no forwarding address, and walked through the lobby, his head low as if by not looking at anyone in the hotel lobby, no one would see him. He hailed a cab outside and gave the driver the Brooklyn address.

"That's just over the Brooklyn Bridge," the cabbie told him. "Pretty nice section. Near Boro Hall."

"Good," John muttered. He settled back in the seat.

The driver noticed the luggage. "You visiting there?" he asked, trying to be friendly.

"Hope to get an apartment there," John answered.

"Hope you get it," the cabbie told him. "Yup, good location."

The cab ride was expensive, but with a suitcase and a typewriter and but scant knowledge of New York's subways, John felt it was well worth it. The hotel bill had been more than he had expected and John made a mental note to be extremely careful from then on with his money. His family had supported him through college and when his graduation came his mother insisted he return home. When he refused to do so, she threatened to cut off all monetary aid. When this did not convince him, she accused him of turning on her, being ungrateful to her, and threatened all kinds of dire reprisals.

His parents did come to Des Moines, briefly, for the graduation exercises. On top of everything else, it had taken all his courage to tell them of his engagement. Strangely enough, on this score there was no immediate argument. His father congratulated him heartily, expressing an unsaid sense of relief. He had never dared to interfere, but always secretly hoped that John would someday find his own independence in life. Marriage seemed to be it. His mother, already angry at his decision to be a writer and to go to New York, looked on the engagement as a last possibility of salvation. A marriage, she thought, would now make it impossible for him to go to New York. He would have to settle down, make a living and, she expected, return to Cleveland. The girl would be with him, true, but she could abide the girl as long as he remained close.

When he made it clear that the engagement did not change his plans, his mother was furious and she returned home with hardly another word. She ignored the whole idea of marriage from then on, as if the very act of not acknowledging it would somehow make it not happen. John felt sorry for her, but the cord had been cut and he had no intention of returning, in any manner, to her control. He did not want to argue with her over the merits of the government savings bonds he had received as gifts from her and his father over the years and hoped that redeeming the bonds, along with the advance from the Harmon and Johnson publishing firm, would last him in New York until the book was published and royalties began.

The trip to Brooklyn took forty minutes, the cab screaming through traffic as if the other vehicles weren't even there. Except for Canal Street, where bumper-to-bumper traffic doubled the time that the trip should have taken. John watched the tenement houses, cramped against the view of the tall buildings of Wall Street, as the cab rode over the Brooklyn Bridge. He thought he should remember the anachronism to use in a book sometime. The thought drifted away as the land below melted into the waters where the Hudson and East rivers met. There were small boats everywhere and against the docks larger boats with specks of people moving about on them and assuming odd shapes as they carried cargo on and off. The cab reached the crest of the bridge and John remembered the story of Steve Brodie. He tried to, but couldn't imagine anyone feeling bad enough or crazy enough to jump into the waters that were now so far below. Without wanting to, he wondered for an instant how Tony was feeling. The taxi passed the center span and darted down toward the Brooklyn side and the thought of Tony disappeared.

Number 194 Congress Street in Brooklyn was a small
apartment house. It would look like a tenement except for the
fact that it was on one corner and instead of being part of a
pattern of similar attached buildings was almost unique, with
windows on three sides instead of just the front and back. It
was an old building, red brick, now dirtied, and the entrance,
once perhaps enviable for the two tall silver-glassed doors,
now had the pane of one missing and the wooden borders
badly in need of fresh paint. The front hallway was dark and
a marble design on the floor worn away until it was barely
discernable. The row of buzzers at one side of the hallway had
an old style inter-apartment telephone communication system. The names, those that were not too worn to make out,
pleased him. It was much like a token of the melting pot he
had imagined New York to be. Bronson, Walker, Antonelli,
Carrol, Spiros, Braunstein, Jones, De Winter, Chiotti, McCa-
rthy. There were sixteen apartments listed on the panel. He
walked outside again and looked up. Four floors, four apartments on each floor. He went back to the hallway and looked
for Apartment 5. He found the name P. MacDougal. He
pushed the bell and after a moment got an answering buzz.
"Hello, hello." He spoke into the small telephone on the
panel. There was no response. He concluded that it was out of
order. He went inside and walked up to the second floor and
found Apartment 5.

He knocked and after a moment heard the heavy step of
a large person approach the door. It opened and if he hadn't
been completely sure by the appearance, he could tell by the
voice that it was the woman he had spoken to on the phone.

"You're the young man who called," she said. She didn't
wait for his nod. "Come in, come in."

He followed her inside, down a short narrow foyer. She
was a big woman, almost as tall as he was, and extremely fat.
She walked easily, as though she had become accustomed to

her weight and didn't worry about it, carrying it with her as she would an article of clothing. She wore a faded blue housecoat that left plenty of room for her body to hang loose. The folds of fat hung over the low cut slip above her breasts and the seams at the shoulders seemed about to burst. The hem was short and her legs bulked below her, the blue veins making their thickness stand out even more. Her arms were loose and chunky. She had a red face, as fat as the rest of her, and without makeup it was lined with wrinkles, not those of a really old person, but of one who had given up trying to control the wrinkles and no longer had reason to try to make them an acceptable part of her features. Her hair was musty blonde with patches of real yellow blended with strands of dark grey.

"I'm fifty-three," she said, without being asked as they passed through the foyer into the living-room. The room was immaculately clean, the furnishings bright and loud, all of it shining like a newly painted picture. "I don't look it," she said, referring to her age, "when I really get dressed up. I'm not dressed up now, but when I do, I don't look it. I used to have a lot of boyfriends in college, you know. What's your name?"

John caught his breath in sympathy with her winded speech. He was amused and the same time didn't want to become involved in any complications. Certainly this woman didn't appear to him—he hesitated to use the word—completely normal.

"Don't be afraid of me," Mac told him. "I just like to get talking sometimes and never stop. It's so lonely here that I drink a lot and sometimes just like to get talking. What's your name?"

"John Thomas."

"Would you like a beer?" As she spoke she went to the kitchen, returned in a few seconds with two opened bottles of beer. "Here," she said, giving one to John, "it's good for what ails you." She sat on a chair opposite the couch John had settled himself in.

"You can have the apartment," she said suddenly. "I'm not the owner, I just take care of it for the owner. He lets me do anything I want." She gulped from the beer bottle. She leaned toward John, as though she were telling a great secret. "I know something about him that he doesn't want anybody else to know," she whispered, "so I do what I want around here. Been living here fifteen years."

John took a drink. He didn't particularly like the taste of the beer, but the day had caught up to him and he was hot and the beer was refreshing. "Nice place you have here," he said, feeling he ought to make some conversation.

She got up, nodded for him to follow her. "I'll show you the rest of the place." She led him through the two bedrooms, the kitchen, and a small sitting room. They were all spotlessly clean and although furnished with an indiscriminate taste for color and form, neatly and precisely arranged. She seemed to be getting a great pleasure in explaining the apartment to John and he felt sorry for her apparent loneliness and he wondered whether she had ever had any visitors besides the bottles of beer.

She put her finger to her lips as they entered one of the bedrooms. "Pushie is sleeping," she told him. In the corner of the bed, lying comfortably on top of a white, silk-slipped pillow was a small bulldog. As they walked in, one eye of the dog opened, watched them for a moment, then closed again. They returned to the living room where Mac drained the last of the beer and promptly got another one.

"I don't look fifty-three," she said. "Not when I'm dressed up. You'll have to see me dressed up sometime. Me and Mac, that's my husband, sleep in that bedroom." She pointed to the one where the dog was. "Pushie is sweet, isn't he? I love him like a baby."

"Very sweet dog," John smiled. He began to wonder when he was going to see his apartment.

"Helen lives in the other bedroom." Mac smiled knowingly. "A good girl," she said, "and she likes to have fun. That's why her husband left her. But you really can't blame a girl for having fun. You'll have to meet her."

"Yes," John agreed. He finished the beer, looked for a place to put the empty bottle, but Mac quickly got up and took it to the kitchen.

"You went to college?" she asked, as if he had not told her before.

"Yes."

"What do you do now?" She took a comb from one part of her hair, pushed it into place in another.

"I write. I expect to have a book published soon."

"Wonderful," she said. "I read a lot. Went to college, you know. For a whole year. I was real smart. I'm educated, too."

"Good. We can talk a lot," John ventured. It was the right thing to say. Mac's eyes lit up like she had just gotten a wonderful present. She sat on the edge of the chair for a moment, then slumped back.

"I talk too much," she said matter-of-factly, without apology. "If I ever talk too much and bore you, you just let me know."

"I will," John assured her. "But I don't think you will." That pleased her. John wondered again when he was going to get to see his apartment.

"Don't let that 'P' on the mailbox downstairs confuse you," she said, catapulting into an entirely different subject. "That's for Peter. He's my husband. But we all call him Mac. He's not around much. Works a lot. He doesn't like my drinking," she confided. Then: "He's a big, strong man, husky, like me." Again, a little sadly: "But he doesn't like my drinking so much. Come on, I'll show you your apartment."

She led him across the outer hallway to a door, took a key from her housecoat pocket and opened it. The door opened onto a good sized living room. It was papered a light grey, reflecting the sunlight that poured in from the two windows at the right of the room. A studio couch was at the side of the wall nearest the door, to the right, and across from the couch a small faux-velvet chair. At the far wall, between the windows, stood a dresser. The apartment was clean.

"I've been taking care of this place since Helen moved out," she said. "Helen's my roomer, staying with me since her husband left her. A good girl. Likes to have fun. You can't blame her, can you?" Mac insisted.

"No," John assured her again.

A small archway divided the living room from the kitchen, a much smaller room with a single window at the right, a small table and two chairs in the foreground and an apartment size stove, a refrigerator and a sink against the left wall. They went back into the living room. At the left of the front door John noticed the bathroom. It was a good apartment. The taxi driver had told him that it was only twenty minutes from the center of Manhattan by subway.

"I'll let you get settled now," Mac said. "John. That's a good name. I like you. You take the apartment and I'll tell Morrissey, he's the landlord, that it's rented. And you don't worry about anything. If you have any trouble here at all, you just tell me and I'll take care of it. You're a nice boy and I like you."

John got his suitcase and typewriter from the hallway under Mac's watchful eye.

"There's not too much furniture here," she said. "But I have a lot of things I don't need, so I'll just bring you in some things. A little cocktail table and a couple of bookcases." She took him by the arm. "Come on," she decided, "you get them right now."

He protested mildly at her gifts, then followed her back to her apartment and gratefully accepted the furniture. She helped him carry it back.

"I couldn't have carried it myself," she advised. "Got bad feet. Used to be a nurse and my feet got bad walking too much. You wouldn't believe it, but I was really beautiful as a girl. Then I started drinking and I got fat. Mac, my husband, he don't like my drinking."

"What about the rent?" John asked after she had supervised his putting everything in their proper places.

"I'll phone Morrissey right now and tell him it's rented. He can send one of his collectors over in the morning." She walked to the door. "You just make yourself at home and if there's anything you want, you just tell old Mac." She emphasized the word "old," then added: "But I don't look fifty-three, do I?" She didn't wait for an answer. "You're a nice boy, John. A real nice boy. I won't bother you any more now. You want to get settled." She closed the door as she left.

John smiled to himself. He shouldn't laugh. This was a good woman. Perhaps not so according to some standards, but so very good compared to so many of those who would judge her. He thought he would like it in this place. He went to the windows, looked out on a series of wash lines, some dipping with clothes, others bare, connecting to window frames like his from one building to another. This was the rear of the house and it met the stare of the back parts of similar houses on the next block. He opened his suitcase, started to unpack, then changed his mind. It was still light out. He decided to take a walk through the neighborhood, to see where he was, what it looked like.

At the corner he turned left and walked past several more small apartment houses, much like the one he lived in now.

Then came some old brownstones, some well kept and fronted
with small gardens and whitewashed steps. Others were a
little less varnished and the small areas of ground in front of
them had either been filled in with concrete or were merely
patches of unblossomed dirt. On the street in front of several
stood large, new automobiles. In front of others were wound-
worn smaller models of considerable age. On the next corner
he passed a large Catholic church. He could see no other
places of worship in the immediate neighborhood. In the
street in front of the church some boys were playing stickball
and with them, his face flushed with exercise, a young priest.
It reminded him of a Bing Crosby movie and he smiled.

He crossed this street of houses into another and immediately felt an uncomfortable insecurity. The houses were
dingier, real tenements now, one against the other, the red
brick having lost its lightness, an unstable mixture of black
and grey. The brownstones struggled to remain independent,
the few that remained on this block, but the chipped stoops
and dirt fronts whose only buds were scratched silvery-tin
garbage cans melted into one another and became one continuing patch of brick without any individuality. More children appeared, seemingly out of nowhere, and little boys and
girls, most of them in worn clothes, some tattered beyond
repair, were blocking the sidewalk, playing in front of him.
He wondered, idly, why these children were not playing with
the priest. They obviously needed adult interest. A woman
struggled up the front steps of one of the old brownstones,
her arms heavy with a basketful of laundry. Another, her hair
unkempt and her flesh hanging loose in a single thin dress
covering, walked toward him and passed by him, several children following her, one barely able to walk holding her hand
and another, an infant, in her arms.

Children on the block were playing with toys that were
broken, he noticed, and he saw several little boys playing

catch with a rolled up newspaper around which they had tied
a piece of string. The buildings' apartments, as much as he
could see of them through an open window or an open hallway door, looked worn. There were so many more children
than in the block before. He wondered why these people,
obviously with no material wealth, did not at least make
the landlords fix up the places they lived in. It was an idle
thought and without reason it carried him back to earlier that
afternoon when he had been calling for apartments and had
been lucky to find one without having to pay a substantial
amount of graft for the privilege. It answered his other
question.

He crossed Atlantic Avenue and walked toward what he
remembered from the cab ride would be the general direction of the Brooklyn Bridge. The houses began to grow
newer again and there were fewer children. There seemed to
be a disparity in this for John. The children who lived in the
poorer houses were thin and undernourished. The children
who lived in the nicer houses were well-dressed and more
than adequately nourished. There should be some kind of
equalization some place, he mused. What made one child less
deserving than another?

A peculiar looking house with a flat front and a low roof
on the next block caught his eye and he walked faster to it,
letting the thought about the children go. He found that this
house was really a people-occupied garage, the large front
entrance now with a center door, and small windows on both
sides covered with white lace-like curtains. He was puzzled for a moment because this seemed like a fairly well-off
neighborhood. Then he saw hanging above the front door two
old-fashioned gas lanterns. This had been, of course, a carriage house at one time, serving the surrounding brownstones
which probably had once been a mecca of Brooklyn society.

He noticed now, on that block and on the next, a number of
converted carriage houses, reincarnated as fashionable homes.

Most of the brownstones were like the ones he had seen
in photos of old New York, with a flight of steps leading up
to the first floor. Some had undergone a renovation, the steps
having disappeared and modern-looking stone arch entrance-
ways taking their place, leading right into the street floor.
Like the one in which Tony lived. He tried to glance inside
the first floor windows as he walked along and in most of the
houses saw what seemed to be beautiful furnishings, ornate
chandeliers, large paintings and tapestries on the walls. Those
that he could not see into were protected by rich-looking
draperies.

When he reached the corner he found a number of small
shops, the sign on one of them reading "Brooklyn Heights
Pharmacy." The name Brooklyn Heights was familiar to him
and after a moment he remembered having read about it.
It was where Washington had made his headquarters during the early part of the revolution just before the Colonial
troops had been driven out of Brooklyn. This had apparently
been one of the early residential sections of the borough, he
thought, probably with many well-to-do families. Some of
the luster, even after almost 200 years, still remained.

The more he walked, the more he became sure of his
conclusion. With each block the houses became more elegant,
most of them rebuilt and redecorated outside. Finally, the
old houses disappeared almost entirely and were replaced by
modern, sleek apartment buildings. These were beautifully
built and in front of many were doormen. It was clear that
the well-to-do element had not disappeared. The old houses
that did remain stood forth with distinguished supercilious-
ness, frowning on the modern invaders. John searched for
open windows to see inside of these houses and there was no
doubt that here one could still observe an aura of majesty,

even if in no other way than through a lorgnette while clipping stock and bond coupons.

A few blocks further John reached a boardwalk overlooking the freight landing piers on the Hudson River. A metal sign, brightly polished, announced that this boardwalk was appropriately named "Brooklyn Heights Esplanade" and added the warning: "No Peddlers Allowed." The promenade was built at the rear of a number of old and new houses, each with a small garden and each, except for the new apartment buildings, covered with ivy that might have begun its growth more than a century before. Wrought-iron gates and fences separated the walk from these back yards, offering a vista that compared with the pictures John had seen of old New Orleans. From the promenade, out over the short stretch of the Hudson River, John saw the postcard skyline of Manhattan, the close-set stretching fingers of Wall Street and downtown New York skyscrapers. The promenade was several blocks long and John walked the distance slowly, staring at the skyline, feeling elated in its bigness. It gave him a feeling of confidence, being able to look at it and hold it visually in his palm. It made him feel that whatever it contained was somehow within his grasp and could be his. He didn't regard this as more than a feeling. The people of the tenements and the emaciated children with the bloated stomachs a few streets away had this same view, too. It didn't seem to have done very much for them, he thought.

He leaned across the rail guard of the walk and looked below, a hundred feet or so beneath, and across to the docks and warehouses. A small shed stood apart from the buildings. Dozens of men crowded around it, other men walked back and forth aimlessly in the vicinity. They seemed to be biding their time and simply waiting. A fewer number of men were visible beyond the beginning of the first pier, carrying loads of various shapes and sizes from a ship.

To his right he could see the Brooklyn Bridge. He picked out one of the specks moving across the span and wondered if an hour or two before someone else had stood on the promenade and had picked out the speck that was his taxi and followed its course to Brooklyn. The dots came and went and as he watched grew more numerous. They were unending. There were so many more specks in New York, he thought, than any place else.

To his left, across the water, was the Statue of Liberty. He would have to visit it soon. The sun came down hard from across the river, from New Jersey, splashing into the river and reflecting up again, the rays gilding everything in its sight. The towers of Wall Street and the tenements of Atlantic Avenue were etched with the same unbiased sunlight. It was five o'clock and the promenade was almost empty now. The mothers wheeling baby carriages and those keeping close watch on playing children had hurried home to get ready for their husbands' return from work.

John started back, too, feeling good as he walked through the now crowded streets of rushing people. He passed a subway exit and the people emerged as a wave, almost engulfing him. He didn't mind. He had walked by himself, seen and begun to understand the new world that he was in and, finding that he was not afraid of it, was relaxed. He checked his billfold, then entered a small restaurant for dinner.

It was dusk when he came out. The streets looked prettier now. In the half-light, half-darkness they seemed to go back into history and he could almost feel Washington and Howe and Hamilton and Lafayette riding on great horses over the cobblestones or rock-filled mulch and the old Dutch and English burghers lighting the lanterns over the carriage houses as they made ready for an evening's outing. It was a sensation to remember, he noted, and something for him to put into written words some day. He walked in reverie, lost in the romantic past.

As he came closer to his street, the dream suddenly shattered. The imagined cool of an 18th century evening became drenched with sweat and the streets crowded with the people of 20th century apartment houses, out to find a breath of fresh air, something so much more difficult to get here, it seemed, because there were so many more people for the air to be divided among. The windows were open and the smells of the evening meals came through to him. In some blocks they all smelled alike. Poor people can't buy much variety, he thought. In other blocks, especially as he crossed Atlantic Avenue and the rich smells of Arabic and Middle-East cooking reached him, he sought the scents of different ethnic and national foods. As he walked down the two blocks of Congress Street to his apartment house, lights in the apartments facing the street began flashing on and he remembered that he had forgotten to have his own gas and electricity connected. He had better start thinking of these little responsibilities, he told himself. He wanted light that evening, particularly so he could write to Carol. It would be nice to find a letter from him not long after she got home. Perhaps he could finish one before it grew completely dark. He rushed up the steps, thinking about her. It would be so good if she were there with him now. He needed her. It was a healthy need because he knew that he could wait until he was ready for her. He reached his door and smiled foolishly. He had forgotten to get a key from Mac. He knocked at her door. A man answered it, a big man, much like Mac, only larger and fatter.

"Is Mrs. MacDougal in?" John asked cautiously. The man grunted, went inside, and his wife appeared at the door a moment later.

"That was Mac, my husband," she explained. "If he was rude, don't mind him. He's always rude to my friends." She was dressed up now, in a bright, yellow-flowered dress, her hair combed, her face rouged and powdered. The fat, somehow, had been caught and pulled inside and John, looking at her, understood that as a young woman she must have indeed been attractive. She had the key to his apartment in her hand and walked down the hall with him. "I knew you'd be coming for it."

"You certainly don't look like fifty-three," he told her, trying to find some kind of compliment. She smiled. "You look like thirty-five," he added, then hoped that the lie had not been too overdone.

"I'll take forty," she answered. She was pleased nevertheless. It gave her a reason for talking although, in fact, she needed none. "I was really good looking when I was a girl," she said. "I was quite something. I went to college, you know." She opened the door and pressed the wall switch. The lights went on. "I had the electric and gas men from Con Ed over while you were gone," she said. "I knew you forgot it."

John thanked her. He thanked her again when she told him she had called the phone company and arranged for one to be put in.

"I know an educated boy like you must have a lot of friends and that you'd want a phone." She stayed and watched as he unpacked his suitcase. He was kind of glad to have her company. She sat on the couch and talked as he put his things away in the dresser.

"My husband don't like me drinking. He's got a good job. With the bus company, as a manager. Makes two hundred a week. Been with them thirty years. Good money." She talked on and on and John let the words pass, acknowledging them with an occasional nod or murmur of "yes."

"Oh, I forgot to show you the closet," she said. "It's right over here next to the bathroom." She jumped up and opened it. "I'll get you some hangers." She started for the door. "Want a bottle of beer?" she asked. Before John could answer she was gone.

She came back a few minutes later, hangers over an arm and a bottle of beer in each hand. A young woman of perhaps twenty-two followed in slowly behind her. Mac introduced her.

"This is Helen, the girl I told you about who lives with me. This used to be her apartment. Helen's a good girl. A real good girl. Likes to have fun, but we all like to have fun, don't we?"

Helen smiled, acknowledging the introduction as if she had heard the same one many times. She didn't speak. She seemed to be shy and quiet. She was blonde, her body a bit chunky, perhaps like Mac's had been some thirty years before. But her chunkiness was not obvious, fitting well into a well-formed figure, with sharply outlined hips and with pointed breasts standing straight out from her body making her physically attractive. Her face was smooth, without makeup, her eyes blue and large, her lips thick and wide as though she were in a state of constant anticipation, waiting for some surprise. When she smiled her mouth was full and round.

She sat on the couch next to Mac, not speaking as the latter talked. John sat on the faux-velvet chair and joined them in drinking the beer. After several minutes Helen spoke, having waited until Mac had paused at the end of a thought.

"I better be getting back," she said. Her voice was child-like and came in high-pitched slow syllables. "Pleased to have metcha."

"Pleasure was mine." John stood up, politely. Helen left. He wasn't sure whether she had come with Mac simply to see the new neighbor or whether this had been meant as a formal introduction.

"Nice girl," Mac said. "Likes to have fun, but we all do sometimes. It gets lonely sometimes and we got to have something to do."

John finished the beer, handed the bottle to Mac. She took it and stood up. She seemed to be talked out for the night and now had to rest up for the morning.

"Have to get back to Pushie," she said. "Mac don't like dogs. Don't know why, but he don't and I have to take care of Pushie." Then, a bit sadly: "He's the only one I have." She paused a moment. "I'm a nurse, you know. I went to college. If you need anything, just let me know and I'll help you."

"You've helped me so much already," John told her. "I don't know how to thank you."

"Don't thank me," Mac said. "That's what God put us on this green earth for, to help one another. I'll see you in the morning." She left.

John wrote a short letter to Carol. He told her what he felt were the necessary things: how he missed her and how much he loved her. He mentioned briefly the apartment, Mac, and his walk. He would go into more detail in the next letter the next day. He started to open the couch, realized that he hadn't brought any sheets with him. He didn't want to bother Mac anymore and left the couch closed. He didn't mind sleeping on top of it for one night. It was warm and he didn't need any covers. He undressed, wadded up some underclothes for a pillow. He turned off the light and the darkness felt good. He got up again, took his typewriter case to the kitchen, took out the machine and placed it on the table and next to it a sheaf of paper and some of the manuscript of the novel which had been stuffed into the case. The good feeling was too good to let go. Tomorrow, fresh and early, he would put it into his writing.

The sun had barely begun brightening the room when
Mac awakened him with a sustained knocking on the door.
Sleepy and angry that his pleasant sleep had been disturbed,
he slipped on his robe and walked to the door. He was no
longer angry when he saw that it was Mac. She was dressed as
she had been the previous afternoon, her own person untidy
and hanging through the thinness of the old housedress.

"Just finished my cleaning," she said, "and came to see if
you want some breakfast. You can come and have breakfast
with me." John could smell the faint tinge of beer-odor as she
spoke.

"What time is it?" he asked drowsily.

"After eight," she answered, as if this hour was a surprising one for anybody to still be in bed.

John accepted her invitation, washed, dressed, and
in a few minutes crossed the hall to her apartment. He
looked around idly as he followed Mac into her kitchen. She
answered the look.

"Helen works in a bar during the day. A waitress. Pretty
girl, isn't she? I was pretty like that when I was young." She
looked at him and there was a knowing smile on her face.
John was embarrassed. His silent inquiry about Helen had
been unintentional. He didn't have the slightest idea why he
had made it. Fresh bacon crackled on the stove and he didn't
think about it anymore.

The pattern of his first days at Congress Street was the
same. Each morning he ate breakfast with Mac, listening
attentively as she repeated over and over again the incidents
of her life. The late mornings and all afternoons were spent
writing. First, before anything else, he would finish a daily
letter to Carol. Then came the novel, slow careful work, taking parts from the raw manuscript that he was not especially
fond of and rewriting, cutting, expanding. Within three days
letters had begun to arrive from Carol and he waited

anxiously for the mail each afternoon. This was the bright spot of the day.

In the evening, when he no longer felt like writing, he read. He invested in a small radio from one of the downtown Brooklyn department stores and soon learned quickly to dial stations WNYC and WQXR for good music. He didn't get a television set, not only because of its expense but because everyone he knew who bought one for the first time told him of an immediate addiction to it for the immediate future that superseded virtually everything else that they should have been doing. The hi-fi and albums as well as his books still remained in Des Moines, stored at Carol's house. The evenings were inordinately long and he used the radio a great deal, even listening to the news broadcasts, something he had done only rarely before. Strangely, he found them interesting and, after a few days, important. There was so much in the world he didn't know about.

Each evening, long after supper, Mac would come in, a bottle of beer in each hand. He welcomed her visits and after a time even began to get used to the taste of the beer. Every few days, for no apparent reason, Helen would come in with Mac. She rarely spoke, but would sit or stand near the older woman and after a few minutes excuse herself. After a couple of weeks John got to expect her. Involuntarily, he began to play a mind game with the clothes she wore. Each time she was dressed differently, but each time her costume seemed to make her body more sinewy and projecting and her breasts more predominant, more and more difficult for John to keep his eyes away from.

When he was fully settled in the apartment, he called and confirmed an appointment with the publishers, Harmon and Johnson. It was for the date they had originally suggested he come to New York, October 1.

He found their offices in a new skyscraper on Manhattan's Madison Avenue. The receptionist in the plush outer office took his name into one of the smaller rooms inside. He looked over the titles published by Harmon and Johnson on the shelves lining one wall of the waiting room. He imagined his name on one of those books in a few months. It made him feel proud and he wondered whether the people who were already in the room and those who had entered the office after him realized that he, John Thomas, was one of these authors-to-be. He tried to act with a sense of casual accomplishment befitting the position he would hold. He was still contemplating his success when the receptionist called his name and ushered him to a small office closed in by a partition of glass brick.

A short man wearing a drab, dark blue conservatively cut suit, complete with a neatly brushed and fob-chained vest, greeted him inside. "My name is George S. Staffall," he announced. "I'm one of the editors. Sit down."

John sat in a straight-backed chair at the side of the man's desk. The man did all the talking. He spoke quickly in a hurried voice, rushing through what he had to say, it seemed to John, so that he could get back to more important matters of business. After every sentence he pushed his eyeglasses back up the bridge of his nose; when he began talking again they slipped down once more.

"You have a good basic manuscript," Staffall said. "One of the most promising I've seen in a long time." His face was stony, without a twitch or a trace of smile. We want to publish it. We expect to give it proper publicity and marketing and can almost guarantee a sale of twenty thousand. You'll get a five thousand dollars advance against royalties and ten percent of the net sales. On a ten dollar book we expect you to earn a minimum of twenty thousand dollars minus, of course, the advance and the thousand dollars we sent you to come to New York."

John nodded to everything the man said, his seriousness of manner making it pertinent to agree with him.

"That offer, as you may know," Staffall continued, "is a very fine one for the publishing business today. Unknown authors who make two or three thousand dollars for a book in this day of television can consider themselves quite satisfied."

The man continued. "Our contract will give us first option on your two subsequent novels. You know, of course, that if this book is a success, it doesn't matter much what you write afterwards. The public will know your name and they'll buy your works. Which does not mean that you should be content with writing second-rate material. No, indeed, not with the talent you show in this manuscript." He patted the top of the folder on his desk. In it was the original copy that John had submitted.

The compliment was the first nice thing John had heard in this office and it relieved him a bit from the tenseness of the business conversation. Staffall reached for a cigarette box on the desk, offered it John. He declined. Staffall lit a cigarette, smoking it in short puffs, tapping it onto the ashtray every time it left his mouth. Finally, he reached the end of his speech.

"Enough of our financial arrangements. If they are satisfactory." He squinted a smile.

"They seem all right," John said.

Staffall reached into his desk, took out a note pad. "We'll have a contract drawn up immediately." He found a sheet on the note pad with a series of numbered notes, referred to them by tapping his finger on each one as he spoke about it.

"First, you will have to cut down on two of your characters. The boy and girl, Jack and Martha, who take second place of importance in the book. You make them too important. They detract. It's too difficult for a young writer to handle more than his main characters on a full-drawn scale."

"How do you suggest . . . ?" John started, tentatively.

Staffall anticipated this. "Cut out some of the description of their past life and background and tie the ends together. Now . . . " he ran his finger down the note page ". . . one satisfactory note I have here. I'm not particularly pleased, but I am relieved by the absence of any particular social comment. Don't write any in. A writer has to be extremely careful today. We must be orthodox. Readers are afraid, reviewers are afraid. We can't afford to hurt our book sales."

He stared at John as if the latter was expected to ask for a fuller explanation. John gave him no sign and Staffall felt obligated to explain for his own self-satisfaction. Staffall leaned forward. "Hangover from the "50s," he said, as if he were delivering confidential information. Even years after the Senator's death, people hesitated to openly discuss the legacy of McCarthyism.

Staffall adjusted his glasses and found another note. "Oh, yes, your relationships, intellectually, are very good. But physically they are incomplete. You should have more graphic sex. The commercial seller today must be a quick and exciting read. Sex is the excitement that sells best. I feel it unfortunate that it is so. It was not always so, but apparently with television and some of those paperback sensation-seeking books, the public is losing whatever taste it might have once possessed. And in order to stay in business we must cater to them. So, Mr. Thomas, a little sex, please." He smiled now, honestly and fully like a man who is pleased that he has found one bright discovery in an otherwise drab and uninvigorating existence.

Staffall went over other details with John and selected from his manuscript the sections to be redone first. "I'm going to be your editor. I hope it will be satisfactory."

John would have preferred a less formal man to work with, but Staffall apparently was highly capable and this was the important factor. He thanked him as he left, overwhelmed by the amount of work he had to do, but nevertheless promised to work quickly, though carefully, and bring in revisions as soon as they were completed. John smiled to the receptionist in the front office as he left, pleased and confident after his first direct person-to-person contact with the publishing business.

He worked extremely hard the next few days and within a week had completely rewritten three of his chapters. He brought them to Staffall. The little man was in a sharp mood.

"It's encouraging," he said without so much as a smile, "to find a young man who can do his work and do it well. I'll keep what you've rewritten."

His routine at the apartment continued as before. One evening he surprised Mac with a present of a case of beer. It was a token payment—he could not think of a better gift—for her kindness. She wiped away a tear of gratitude.

"You don't have to buy me anything," she said. "My husband, Mac, makes good money. But thanks for the present, anyway. Nothing like an educated boy. I went to college, too, you know."

For a few afternoons and evenings after he had seen Staffall he asked Mac not to visit him. He explained his quota of work and she understood. She busied herself with her bulldog, Pushie. It was an ordinary dog, rather ugly, but she treated it like a child, and John himself finally got around to petting it and feeding it the leftover meat from his meals. It wasn't necessary. Mac bought and prepared for Pushie the choicest cuts.

The fever of rewriting lasted little more than a week. The excitement disappeared in the welter of hard work and it became a monotony of work that had to be done. Mac

returned in the evenings now and Helen, in her tight fitting
and gaily colored sweaters, proved an interesting diversion.
Though his interest was still unintentional, John did welcome her, if only as another presence to break the monotony
of his increasing loneliness. He realized, after almost a
month, that he had seen no one to talk with except Staffall,
Mac, and Helen.

He didn't hear from Tony. He expected to, knowing that
Tony would probably write to Carol for his address. But there
was no contact and he contemplated that perhaps Tony had
understood, finally, that his decision was not to be changed.

He began to go to the movies, finding them sometimes
relaxing when they didn't prove too boring. He had become
fed up with the radio programs, the steady diet of bad scripts
and repetitive acting turning him away from them. The movies were a new part of the routine, adding to Mac, his writing
and, most important, the letters to and from Carol. And, of
course, there was Helen. On the nights when he expected
Mac and she didn't show up, he almost wished that Helen
would come in. She didn't talk and he had nothing to talk
to her about, but—and he laughed to himself at what was a
bad joke—he could, at least, always just sit and look at her.
Sometimes, in the tedium of his routine, he almost would
have welcomed a phone call from Tony.

After another two weeks he brought some more of his
revisions to Staffall. The editor kept only part this time, making some suggestions for more work on the remainder.

"This novel is too good to let go without at least
attempting perfection." He also suggested that John try some
relaxation and varying of habit. "It looks to me, young man,
that you've fallen into the writer's doldrums of trying to turn
out something on a schedule, and with the schedule the work
has lost its flavor. Only a few writers can work successfully
that way and you're not Bernard Shaw yet."

John tried to relax and find more entertainment and a
sense of freedom to enable him to work with a fresh mind
on the book. But his attempts were limited to an occasional
Broadway show and a few good movies at the Brooklyn
Paramount despite what to him were high prices. This didn't
help him as much as he hoped. One evening after a few hours
work he re-read what he had written. "Crap," he told himself,
and threw the pages into the wastebasket. He knew he was
pressing too hard. He turned on the radio, stretched out on
the couch, intending to try and relax for a few minutes. There
was a knock on the door and he jumped up expectantly. A
bottle of beer and the endless uninhibited conversation of
Mac that he could listen or not listen to would be just right,
he thought. He opened the door. It wasn't Mac. Helen was
standing there alone, a bottle of beer in each hand.

Without a word she came in, handed John a bottle
as Mac usually did, and sat on the couch. "Mac's out this
evening so I thought I'd come in and keep you company.
Okay?"

"Okay," John agreed. It didn't matter. Company was
company. He sat on the chair. She was visual company anyway, he reasoned.

"I know you like beer, so I brought you one. Okay?"

"Okay."

"You seem lonely here all alone. Are you?" Her voice was
bare, without any sophistication whatsoever. It rose slightly
at the end of each sentence, giving it the sing-song of the
Brooklyn accent popularized in Hollywood movies.

John admitted he was sometimes lonely. He didn't know
what she was driving at, if anything.

"Mac told you I was a good girl, didn't she?" Her words
came slowly with a strange naiveté as though she had learned
them only a moment before and she wasn't sure that she was
saying them correctly.

John nodded.

"So I don't like lonely people, see," she explained, now speaking more quickly. "So you were lonely, so I came over to keep you company." She waited a moment. "You don't have to sit over there, you can sit over here by me." She patted the space next to her on the couch.

John smiled and walked over to her. "Mac has told me you're a very good girl. But you don't have to carry hospitality too far."

"Oh, I'm not carrying it too far," she replied. Her eyes opened wide. "Only as far as I want to." She patted the couch again. "Sit down."

John sat. The closeness felt comfortable.

"I like you," Helen said. "And because you're lonely I want to do something for you." She said it matter-of-factly, as if it were commonplace. John thought that it probably was. Still, she was being very sweet. She moved close to him and the edge of her sweater brushed against him. It was a stimulating sensation and John wondered how long he could let her stay there before he would want her to leave.

"So what're you waiting for?" she asked, innocently amazed at what she considered his lack of proper attention.

"Nothing. I'm satisfied." He gulped at the bottle of beer.

"So put your arm around me, at least," she suggested. "Mac doesn't know I'm here," she added for no apparent reason. "She thinks you're a real nice boy."

"Aren't I?" John smiled.

"Well, sure. That's why I came in tonight. Because you're nice and you're lonely. So put your arm around me." The last she said impatiently. She put down her bottle of beer, moved closer to John, taking the bottle from his hand and putting it down. She pressed against him and lifted her lips toward his face.

The whole action had taken him unaware although, had he admitted it, he knew what was coming. He sat flatfooted,

watching the girl as though he were watching an unrelated
scene on a movie screen. He didn't know what to say. It was
a definitive reminder of the girl in the house at Lake Erie in
the wild night just before he graduated from high school. He
should rebel, he thought, or at least begin to feel sick inside.
But he did neither. Helen's body was warm and soft and there
was nothing distasteful about it. He began to fill up inside and
a tingling raced through his own body. For a moment he was
ready to welcome this girl as fully as she gave herself. It was
a good antidote for his loneliness. But the next second, as her
body pressed almost full length against him, it reminded him
of Carol and the comparison pushed him away. He stood up.

"Not tonight," he said. His heart pounded and a shud-
der ran over him. But he spoke calmly and gently. He didn't
want to hurt her feelings. He understood what she was doing;
this was to her merely the action of a good neighbor trying
to do a good deed. He searched for the proper words. "I don't
feel well tonight, Helen." He held her by the arms and lifted
her from the couch.

Her eyes and mouth stared, incredulously. "What?" It
was something that had never happened before.

"Not tonight," he repeated. "I thank you for your hospitality, anyway." He wanted to laugh at the simplicity of the
words. But he felt that this was the only reasoning that she
probably could understand.

She picked up her bottle of beer with an angry sweep and
started for the door. "I'm a little insulted," she said. "Nothing like this ever happened to me." She twisted the door
knob, pulled it back. She stopped, turned back to John. "I like
you anyway. So maybe I'll see you another time. So maybe next
time you'll feel more lonely. Okay?"

John smiled to her without answering. She swung her
hips out toward him as she walked out, swung her hips once
more as she leaned in to close the door behind her.

John stood for several seconds without moving, felt a heat all over. He wiped his forehead. "Sonofabitch," he muttered to himself. He laughed aloud and the echo was the sound of a forced laugh. It really was no joke. The four walls of the apartment had become a prison cell and it would have been a good thing for him to have found a release in Helen. He thought of Carol again and rejected the thought. He didn't need Helen, he told himself, he had sufficient independence and control over himself. But the problem still remained. He needed something. He walked to the bureau, took Carol's last letter from the top drawer and reread it. For a little while it made him feel a little better. He went back to the couch, stretched out on it lazily and slowly finished the bottle of beer. He felt a shiver go through him as he thought about Helen again.

He didn't see Helen again for several weeks. Mac had gone for a month's visit to a sister on Long Island. "I know how to live on those Long Island farms," she had told him. "I studied biology when I was in college. I may not look it now, but I was educated. Was a nurse, you know." When Mac left, the apartment grew lonelier than ever. John didn't know any of the other neighbors. They seemed to be all hard-working people without time for visits or parties. They grasped at their few hours' relaxation with their families or with their radio or television sets before they went to sleep and then to get up to start the day's routine all over again.

John wrote more on the novel, but it seemed that the more he tried to concentrate on it, the more difficult it became. His thoughts continually wandered and the hemmed-in feeling upset his stomach after an hour or two at the typewriter and he was forced to leave his work for a walk or for a beer. He knew well that he could not do the proper quality of work without relaxation and he knew, too, that he had not been able to find the right way to relax. He felt more

and more hemmed in, in this psychological cell, and became
more and more lonely as there seemed no way out.

He called Staffall at the publishing house and told him
he had struck a snag and would not be in for another couple
of weeks. It was more than a month now that he had begun
writing in New York and he had not finished half of what he
had expected to. Once, on a particularly lonely evening, his
apartment quiet and a bleak, thin rain slapping against the
windows, he even thought of phoning Tony. He got as far as
picking up the phone, intending to spend just a few minutes talking and then return to his work, and he dialed the
number. But before it could be answered he angrily slammed
down the receiver, opened a bottle of beer and switched on
another murder mystery on the radio.

One afternoon, returning from one of his frequent strolls
on the promenade, he entered the lobby to find Helen walking up the stairs just in front of him. It was the first time he
had seen her since the abortive evening. She turned to see
who it was.

"Oh, lover boy," she said with attempted sarcasm.
"Hello." She started to walk up the steps when she stopped
and looked at him again. This time her voice was soft, as
though she had just remembered she was supposed to be a
friend. "Mac hasn't come back yet," she said, making obvious
conversation. "She'll be away another week."

"Hope she's having a good time," John said.

"Yeah. How about you?" Helen asked.

"I'm getting along."

"You feeling lonely enough yet?"

The question hurt and he wanted to say yes. She could
tell from his hesitation and put her hand on her hip and
opened her mouth in what she felt was the proper enticing
smile. John scuffed his foot against the stair tread and almost

tripped trying to hurry past her as if he was not disturbed by her offer.

"Not yet," he said.

"Okay," she told him without animation. "You just let me know when you do." She smiled broadly again and walked up the stairs in front of him, shaking her hips meaningfully with each step.

John paced the room till late that afternoon trying to force out of his system the knots that tied and folded him into himself. He thought about Helen and the thoughts were purposive and the visual contemplations began to ease him until they grew too direct and tightened him up even more. The typewriter was open on the kitchen table and the manuscript scattered in several piles around it. He looked in on it several times, but he could not bring himself to write and continued pacing. There had been no mail from Carol that day and that made him feel even worse. He almost wished he were back in Des Moines; at least he would know somebody. New York was such a lonely place. In New York he really knew only Tony and he tried to keep him out of his mind.

Still restless that evening, he decided to go for a short stroll. As he walked down the hall he stood a moment outside of Mac's door, not with any reason, but in the strange speculation of what he might do if Helen suddenly, perchance, opened the door. But the door remained closed and, a little disappointed, he went downstairs.

He passed a small café-bar on the next corner and after a second's hesitation went in, ordered a shot of bourbon at the bar. He heard a voice behind him, a little girl's voice calling.

"Hey, I'm over here. Hey!"

It was Helen, sitting in one of the booths at the far end of the bar. He had half-wanted to see her a minute before when he stood outside her door, but now that he did see her he didn't know whether to leave or to join her. The bartender brought his drink, he paid for it, then making up his mind, paid for another one, took them both to the table where Helen was sitting alone. He sat opposite her.

"Thanks," she said. "I was wondering when you were going to come in here."

"Were you expecting me?" he asked, wondering, perhaps, whether she too had anticipated their meeting that evening. His heart began to beat heavily, as if before some important event. He tried to dispel the feeling but it wouldn't go away.

"Why should I expect you?" she asked. "I just said it's about time. It's a nice bar. Don't you like nice bars?"

"Sure," he answered. He sipped the drink and some of the tenseness went away.

She watched him drink, waited a moment, then put both her hands flat on top of the table toward him. She looked him up and down carefully. "You feeling lonely now?"

The feeling of the pickup in a bar, the feeling, again, of the girl in Lorraine five years earlier vied with his feelings of loneliness. Even as he ached from the emptiness of being alone, he wondered whether there was a place within him for Helen. He avoided her eyes, staring straight ahead into blankness. He nodded his head slowly.

"So there's nothing to be bashful about feeling lonely," she assured him. "A lot of people are lonely." She touched his hands. "Right now, for instance," she said, "I'm lonely."

"I'm sorry," he muttered. Things seemed to be happening too quickly and he couldn't seem to stop them. He didn't want to.

"So what for you gotta be sorry? We're both lonely. It's better than just one being lonely, isn't it?"

"I guess so."

"So it is or it isn't. What's the matter, you can't make up your mind?"

"Yes, it is," he admitted.

She smiled and took her hand away. She swallowed her drink, coughed and stood up. "Leave the girl a tip." She nodded toward the waitress. "I work as a waitress. It's not an easy job. Let's go."

John followed her out of the bar, walked silently next to her to the apartment building.

"Silent John here," she observed. "Say, that's a good one, isn't it? Your name really is John." She laughed at her own humor. She looked at John. "So at least you might smile," she said, a little hurt.

John turned the key in the door mechanically. Walking with this girl to the apartment, going inside with her, and whatever would follow seemed to be the thing to do simply because it had to be done. There was no premeditation or rationalization. Helen closed the door after they were in, fastened the lock. She stood by the couch, waiting for John to do something. He remained near the entrance to the room, watching her.

"A girl wants a little privacy," she complained, a little annoyed.

"Sure." He understood and went into the kitchen. He sat at the table, waiting for the next word from Helen. Everything moved slowly. Like the steady ticking of a clock, the words, the actions, the time, carried him along with them, giving him no control whatsoever over them. After not much more than a minute Helen called, "Okay." There was no excitement in her voice. It was all matter-of-fact.

Each step measured, he walked to the living room. He kept his eyes low and the first thing he saw were the woman's clothes folded neatly on the seat of the chair. Then he saw Helen lying on the couch, her blonde hair bushed against the palm of her hand, her elbow propping her up on one side. His eyes moved quickly down the length of her body, as open and wide as her mouth and eyes. He wanted to turn away, not because what he saw displeased him, but because he knew that the lust within him was not founded in honest emotion. But his eyes remained, choosing carefully the areas of soft sloping flesh; they rested on her breasts and if he had any thoughts that the well-filled sweaters were not of herself they were dispelled. He was caught in the trance of a rising passion within him and he would have come to her, slowly, in the patterned somber stops of the ticking seconds, had she not spoken again.

"So what are you waiting for? I don't bite." The voice was squeaky and sharp and it startled him. It was so unlike the softness and invitation of the body. He suddenly felt awake and angry. He closed his eyes and he saw Carol in front of him on the couch. He opened them and it was Helen again.

"Get out of here," he said. The words started deep down in his throat and came out slowly, painfully. "Get out of here." They loosed themselves from his insides and came out strong and loud. The time, slowed down to a crawling pace, began to gallop and he felt as though the words ran from his throat. "Get out." The room took on moving shapes and it, too, began to run in patterns of crazy circles.

"I said get out." He felt himself begin to shake all over.

"So what's the matter?" Helen was half-frightened, half-confused. She wasn't angry, only startled by the apparent impossibility of what was happening. She stared at him a moment, trying to understand this strange, insane man who was literally kicking her out of bed. She got up.

"So okay, so who's crazy, so who's losing out!" She got dressed, calmly but quickly. John stood and watched, his hands at his sides, still trembling.

"So maybe you weren't so lonely as I thought." She walked to the door. "Thanks for the drink." The words sounded bitter now. She unlocked the door and walked out. There was nothing left but the slam.

"God damn. God damn." John heard the voice fill the room and only after a moment did he realize it was his. He started to talk to himself, mumbling aloud, trying to break the spell of what had just happened. "Why do I always have to get into situations I can't get out of? Why did it have to be her? Why does it always have to be something like that?" He laughed aloud, waited for the sound to echo off the wall back to him. "Why couldn't it have been Carol? Why isn't it Carol?" He fell onto the couch and tried to chase away the confusion and bitterness. He was too tired and lonely to really care. He wondered whether the drops of wet he began to feel on his arm were really his tears.

## Chapter 18

John was awakened the following morning by the ringing of the telephone. He was startled by his own condition, fully dressed, lying on the unopened couch. His face felt dirty and stained and the blotches of sunlight through the window had none of their usual clean freshness. They were ugly and he was ugly. He remembered what had happened the evening before. He had fallen asleep on the couch where he lay after Helen had left. He hurt when he thought about it and his entire body ached. The room was bare with loneliness. The telephone continued to ring and its urgency forced itself on his consciousness and he answered it.

"How are you, Johnny-boy?"

He wanted to put the phone down. Hopelessly, he looked around the room. It was still empty. There was no one else.

"Hello."

"I finally got your address from Carol. I told her I'd lost it. I got the number from information. Do you mind?" Tony's voice was calm and pleasant as if the incident of a month before had not happened.

"No, I don't mind." John said it slowly. He wasn't sure.

"How have you been?"

"Fine, Tony. And you?"

"A little lonely." Tony laughed. "I guess I shouldn't have said that," he added. Then, tentatively: "Hope you've forgotten about that business last month. It was rather foolish."

"I've forgotten," John answered a little too matter-of-factly.

"I guess you haven't," Tony observed. "Well, that's understandable. Right now I'd like to make up for it. I'm having a small party over at my place this Sunday night. Some people you might be interested in meeting."

John didn't answer. He wanted to say yes. He felt he should say no.

"You don't have to tell me now," Tony quickly said, guessing what John's silence meant. "I know you might have something else to do. You can think about it and let me know."

This gave John the opportunity to refuse and still leave the door open. "Right now I don't think I can make it for Sunday," he said.

There was a pause before Tony spoke again. "Well, you see if you can, and if you decide you can make it after all, you call me." He hesitated. "Or shall I call you back?" he asked strongly.

"I'd better call you," John said.

"Okay." Tony was reluctant to leave the phone. "It ought to be a good party, so try to make it."

"I will."

"It's only Tuesday. There's a whole week to see if you can."

"Goodbye, Tony. Thanks for calling. I'll let you know."

"Good, Johnny." Then, anxiously: "And, Johnny . . ."

"Yes?"

"I would like to see you, really." The sound of the click of Tony's phone being put down immediately followed and John

hung up. He walked around the room for a long time, from
wall to wall and back again. He had come to a decision again.
His life seemed to be a perpetual series of rungs of decision, only he had no assurance that the ladder was going up.
Other people have decisions, he reasoned, why did his always
seem to be so complicated? Maybe it was easier for them, he
thought, because they were normal people, whatever normal
meant? He felt he was not. He was a product of one world
who had moved into another and it seemed that he could
not decide whether he belonged in either or in both. He was
afraid to go and he was afraid not to go. Conform to this and
conform to that and never the twain shall meet. The thought
raced through his mind. Dammit, I want to go, he thought.
Dammit, I don't want to go. Is there an alternative? Loneliness is a terrible enemy when you have to live with it.

He had one friend, his typewriter, and he walked into
the kitchen and sat by it. The manuscript was spread out
on the table, pages and pages waiting to be made love to or
divorced. He punched a key on the typewriter, watched the
black mark on the white page. How many of these marks
before the scattered pages would be made whole? He punched
another key and then another and wrote a few sentences.
There was that much less to be done before it was completed.
He picked up some pages from the table, read them, carefully
began to rewrite. It made him feel needed and in turn he felt
less of his own need. He did not have to go to the party. He
had his own choice, his work. He heated the pot of coffee
on the stove. It smelled bitter. It was from the day before. It
tasted bitter, but it made him warm and it woke him up. He
sat at the typewriter and worked. The cup of coffee beside
him got cold.

He wrote feverishly the next few days. He was satisfied
with his writing and only his book was important. He was
not lonely now. He thought about Tony's party. He decided

definitely that he would not go. It would avoid any more difficulty with Tony. And, he repeated to himself, his work had
shown him that he really was not alone. On Friday of that week
he went to the Madison Avenue office to see Mr. Staffall. He
handed him three more chapters of manuscript.

"You look tired," the little man told him, peering over
the top of his glasses.

"I am. Didn't sleep very much the last few days."
He hadn't. He was impatient for Staffall's judgment and
remained silent, smoked a cigarette as the latter read the
pages. He stared absent-mindedly at the cross patterns on the
glass-brick wall.

Finally, Staffall finished. "You worked hard, young man,
didn't you?"

"I did."

"It looks it. When a writer comes in here needing a shave
and some good hours sleep, I know that he's either been
working hard or not working at all. Then I read his manuscript and I'm sure which it is." He smiled, one of his rare
occasions to do so. "You did a good job."

"You like it?" John asked for the definitive answer.

"Very good," Staffall said in his business-like nasal voice.
"Do the remainder as good as this and it'll be just fine."

"Thank you," John told him, not out of particular desire,
but out of politeness.

"Don't thank me." Staffall leaned forward as though to tell
him a secret. "What too many of you youngsters don't realize
is that writing is work. Hard work." He sat back again, looked
in his notebook and checked off some markings on a page.
"You ought to be finished in about another six weeks or so."

"I'll try."

"Keep working and you'll do it." He leaned forward
again. "Remember, a little relaxation is the best impetus for
hard work. You took my advice."

This was not so, but John allowed that he had. It didn't make any difference to him and it would make Staffall happy. John got up and shook the other man's hand. "I'll be back again as soon as I can," he said.

But it wasn't so easy. He had proven to himself that it could be done and, having furnished proof, he had become enervated. The feverish rush into self-companionship of the past few days and its successful conclusion left no room for anything but an anti-climax. He didn't work. The typewriter was a toy to be played with. He tried to write again, but couldn't. What was worse, he knew what the reason was. The insecurity of being alone still rubbed harshly against him. He could not get Tony's invitation out of his mind.

He recalled the episode with Helen. He was sorry now. Deeply and sincerely sorry. But it was too late. The satisfaction of the animal instinct wants no intellectual analysis. He idly thought about getting on the subway, riding anyplace, stopping in any bar and picking up any woman. It was too far-fetched to consider seriously and he put this from his mind. All day Saturday he remained in a suspension of action and only for the fact that the sun rose and set outside of the window there would have been no passage of time. Once he sat down at the typewriter, wrote for about an hour, read what he had written, then tore it up; not because it was so bad, but because he felt he had to make more obvious to himself his lack of satisfaction with his entire situation of the moment. Once he walked to a window and stood a long time looking out, onto and over the rows of windows of the backs of the other houses. People moved back and forth past closed and open and shaded and unshaded windows. They seemed to know what they were doing and where they were going and, most important, seemed to belong there. He did not feel that he belonged. At least there was no satisfaction in his present surrounding. Once, late in the evening, he went to

the phone and picked it up and dialed Tony's number. What
difference would it make, anyway, he thought, if he went?
And thinking this, the answer was clear. He might find a
place to belong and he was afraid of doing so. He trembled,
for he confused fear with weakness. He did not wait for Tony
to answer. He walked to a liquor store a few blocks away and
came back with a fifth of bourbon. By nine o'clock he was
drunk. He fell asleep on the couch.

It was five o'clock the next morning, Sunday, when he
awoke. The sky was tinged with grey, sliced into by strips
of warmer and lighter colors. His head hurt and he took off
his wrinkled clothes and forced himself into a cool shower.
It made him feel less bloated, although the sickening feeling
at the back of his neck remained. It was too early to wake up
and he was too awake to go back to sleep. He got dressed,
decided to take a walk to see what the New York skyline
looked like in the sharp dawn of a November morning.

He turned left at the corner, walking toward the promenade, feeling independent in the deserted streets. Out of the
streets, in the houses, there was security. A strange analogy,
he thought: thousands of people on the inside, belonging;
himself, alone on the outside, more aware of it than ever,
afraid to belong. The buildings on Atlantic Avenue seemed
more awake than the rest, the odors of breakfast pouring
out into the street. From some apartments he could hear
the voices of men, calm and conserved, voices penetrating a
morning hour that on any other day but Sunday would probably have been gruff and aggravated.

On Atlantic Avenue, walking toward John, was a man of
indeterminable age. The man walked slowly along the gutter,
studying it for evidence of a cigarette butt or a coin. His face
was wrinkled, the lines heavy and dark, indistinguishable
from what they really were: dirt, colored by the odor of the
city, or pigment, colored by the constant exposure to the sun

and elements. He wore a blue serge suit, shiny all over, yet
neat and well-fitting. It was threadbare at the elbows and
tattered at the sleeves, but he wore it as though it had been
newly purchased. He had on a felt hat. This looked new. As
he came closer John saw that it was not new, but was carefully brushed and creased. As he passed, John saw the fabric
design of silk on the white shirt and in the strip of tie a metal
pin reflected the light, except in the center where the missing diamond left only an unseeing eye. The man looked up
as he passed John, greeted him with a loud and cheery "Good
morning." John heard the steady tap of his shoes as they
scraped along the sidewalk, magnified in the silence of the
early morning.

Here was a man, John thought, who, in spite of society,
belonged. His world was not the normal world, his difference
was not the average difference, yet he did not shut himself in
a room and drink until his head ached with stupidity nor did
he sit silently and wish that a neighbor would walk in and
offer herself to him and berate himself for being afraid to take
her.

John walked on, coming to the street of the old carriage houses, felt a sudden cool breeze sliding under the
trees that lined the sidewalks as guardians, keeping in what
they wished and trying to hold back what they didn't. The
front door of one of the brownstones opened. In the quiet he
could hear the creak and then the muffled closing. A man
walked down the steps, a small dog at his heels. The dog
strained as the man attached a leash, then pulled the man
toward the curb. John passed them. The small black poodle
was circled with a big halter, a red ribbon fluffed at the side
of its neck and a red leash extending to the man's hand. The
man himself was about sixty, small and squat, his own body
covered with a black suit, a black bow-tie onto a white shirt,
shiny black shoes. In his button-hole he wore a red carnation,

the leaves fluffing as the breeze brushed against the flower and the dog's red ribbon at the same time. John had never seen this kind of match before and he smiled as he passed, thinking that the dog looked ever so much like a Wall Street banker with a red carnation. They were oddities and John wondered whether they, too, forgot their fears and simply belonged.

He sat on a bench on the promenade and watched the sunlight slowly streak onto the tall, silent buildings across the water. At first grey, than the grey changing to blue until it became, finally, a dulled yellow-orange. The sun seemed close and ever growing, to be reached out to and touched. It became brighter as he stared and his eyes watered. The tops of the largest downtown Manhattan skyscrapers, the Woolworth and Singer buildings, began to throw deep shadows over their smaller brethren and they themselves gloried in a vivid, shining yellow. The rest of the buildings then sucked in the sunbeams as the sun rose and they bathed themselves greedily with as much of it as the taller structures had not already used up. They were cleansed now of the darkness of the night, but there was something uncomfortable about them. In the darkness they were soft and placid. Now they were bold and reached higher and seemed more powerful than ever. They frightened John. They seemed gross, a brightness without beauty. He had seen the dawn and sadly turned and walked back to the apartment.

It was seven o'clock and the church bells began to ring. It was an odd sound, the high-pitched little bells of one, the deep slow-breathing notes of another. They blended into one call and here and there, out of houses and around street corners, people began to appear. Some were dressed well, on their way to worship, painstakingly interested in showing off to their neighbors their best clothes. Others were dressed casually, in moccasins or sneakers, in dungarees and sweat-

ers, some for prayer, some to the grocery store for a bottle of
milk or to the bakery for a dozen breakfast buns. He came
to the large church several blocks from his house. The heavy
deep peal of its chimes hurried people along their way, draw-
ing them one by one and two by two into its parlor. The
worshippers stopped for a moment before entering, blessed
themselves with the sign of the cross and then went in. He
noticed, again, that most going into this large and presumably well-endowed and supported church were particularly
well-dressed. The best foot forward in a step toward heaven,
he thought.

A thin small voice in the Brooklyn accent he had gotten
to know said "excuse me" and he stepped aside and let a
young girl brush past him. She looked back and smiled. She
was about seventeen, a small girl with strands of black hair
peeking out from a bandana that covered her head. A bobby-
pin reached out from under the kerchief, trying unsuccess-
fully to pull back one of the strands. She wore saddle shoes,
the white mingling with the black, and dungarees too large
for her that were held up by the stuffing in of the shirt-tail of
a man's shirt and the tightening of a leather belt. She stopped
in front of the church, looked around anxiously as though she
were trying to hide something, half-smiled to John when she
noticed him watching, then hurried inside. John laughed as
he guessed at her secret. It was an early hour for a teen-age
girl to go to mass. If she went at a later hour she would have
to dress up; at this early hour there was little danger that any
of her boyfriends would see her. So her conscience was dutied
with a minimum of effort. Somehow, even in her out-of-place
clothing, she managed to belong.

John turned the corner and started up Congress Street. It
was fully light now and the windows in the apartments and
in the small houses began to open. Women in slips and men
in shorts or pajamas began to parade back and forth. Here

and there he heard the shrill cries of infants calling for food
and he heard the husky voices of those who had long since
been out of the cradle calling in the same way. Above him
a young man about thirty poked his head out of a window,
surveyed the block. His hair was black and tousled. A white
undershirt hung out of the window with him. He scratched
his head and yawned, his mouth opened wide. John could
almost smell the stagnant breath of a night's sleep. Up the
block sounded the chug-chug of an old car. The man leaned
further from the window, stuffed the white undershirt into
his pants-top as it flapped loose about him, looked in the
direction of the car and yelled, not bothering to turn back to
the inside of the room.

"Hey, maw, there's Timmy." Then he turned inside and
yelled it again. "Maw, do you hear me? There's Timmy, and
Ruthie's with him." Apparently she heard, for the woman,
made old by unkempt white hair and a hollow-cheeked
lined face, came to the window and looked out. She waited
anxiously for the car and as it came close she waved. The
young man behind the wheel of the automobile waved back
and smiled and then the young girl sitting beside him did
the same. The young man parked the car with great haste,
the old, square-shaped Ford nestled between the new sleek
shiny-finned monsters. John didn't know these people, but he
thought about them. The mother and son waiting excitedly
in the early hours of the morning for the visit of the younger
son. Whether they had come one mile or a thousand miles,
John didn't know. But he did know that, whatever the case,
they were welcomed and they belonged.

Only he, John Thomas, didn't belong. The thought was
rancid in his mouth. The man in the felt hat looking for
cigarette butts, the dog with the red ribbon, the girl going to
church, even the buildings of Wall Street that had to fight for
their portion of sunlight, all belonged. Ostensibly, he knew

that he did, too. There was Carol and there was his book and
there was the promise of the future. But because they weren't
tangible things in front of him at the moment to hold in his
hands, they weren't sufficient. The walk had not made him
feel better. It made him feel sorrier for himself and lonelier
than before. The promise came too slowly. He could not wait
for it. Even if only for a respite, for only a moment, he needed
something.

He got to the apartment and picked up the phone, dialed
the number and waited for the hollow sound as it was lifted
off the receiver at the other end.

"About the party tonight, Tony," he said. "I'll be there
about nine o'clock."

# Chapter 19

John arrived at Tony's apartment a little after nine. He had taken pains to dress well: a dark gray suit neatly pressed, shined shoes, a clean white shirt, his tie in a Windsor knot. The outward appearance gave him a feeling of confidence. Much like a roll of paper money in a pocket gives some people the illusion of success.

There seemed to be no sound from the apartment and he hesitated before knocking. It might have been, he thought, only a trick of Tony's to get him there. Suddenly a burst of applause came through the closed door. John knocked. In a few seconds the door was opened. John was momentarily confused, almost surprised to see a crowded room. With a quick motion Tony took his arm and led him inside. "I'm glad you came, Johnny," he whispered. "I'm happy to see you here."

They stood just inside the door. The living room was filled with people, on the couch, the chair, piano bench, sitting on the rug, propped against a side of the piano. They circled around a slight man about 40 who was standing in the center of the room, some papers in his hand, reading verses to the interested assemblage.

"That's Monroe Faber," Tony explained, his voice low. "He's a poet by profession, operates a small book shop on Lexington Avenue to make a living."

John listened to the man's words, spoken softly without dramatics in his person or voice. His narrow, thin face seemed even longer because of the hairline that had almost disappeared. Thin wisps of hair combed sideways across the top of his head prevented him from being completely bald. The verse was about fate:

"He would be like Zeus,
decision from within;
But so much stronger
is the force that lies without."

The audience was rapt, almost all, whether or not they appreciated Faber's efforts, at least courteous enough to give him their full attention. John glanced around the room. The strangeness of new and unknown people made him a bit uncomfortable and he looked at each one carefully, trying to determine before he would have to meet them what or who they were, something that would enable him to feel more at ease. On his right on the couch, closest to him, was a young, very tall man who sat back against the pillows, stretching out his legs full length in front of him. They stretched, it seemed, almost halfway across the room. He was very thin. His body curved lithely. He must be, John thought, some sort of athlete, like a basketball player. This man on the couch was absorbed in the poetry, but clearly not overwhelmed by it. He accepted it. He was much unlike the man seated next to him, a short man, bulky, who sat without relaxation on the edge of the couch, his feet barely reaching the floor. He had a glass in his hand but he wasn't drinking. He sat motionless, as though the verses he was hearing were the most important things in the world. He was of indeterminate age, anywhere from 30 to 45. His skin was rough and weathered, like a person who spends much of the day working outside in the wind and sun—or cruising on a sailboat. He had a full face, large mouth, and eyes and nose surrounded by a thick mustache and bushy eyebrows. He was tuned to Faber's every word.

On that man's right, in the third place on the couch, was a bulky man, his legs crossed, in his hand a glass from which he drank sporadically, paying only polite attention to the poet. He was dressed in a dark blue serge business suit. The sparkle of a diamond clip reflected from his tie as did the flash of a gold ring from his finger. He was about 55. Because of his portliness his suit coat stretched tightly across his side. Where it was open in front one could see a vest. His face was fat, the clear skin having few wrinkles, spoiled only by heavy jowls. He had a spotting of dark brown hair plastered in tufts on his head and creeping from his ears and nostrils. John speculated that he must be a banker or a Wall Street broker.

Two young men sat close to each other on the floor, their backs propped against the thick legs of the piano. They were rather nondescript, one in a light sport coat and dark slacks, the other in a dark sport coat over light slacks. Both had full faces, one topped with light brown hair, the other blonde. Both were somewhat thin and probably in their mid-twenties. They sat with arms around each other's shoulders, occasionally exchanging a word and less frequently stopping and giving their undivided attention to the poet. They reminded John of some of the college students he had known at Des Moines.

Above them and just a few feet away on the piano bench was a much younger man, not much more than a boy, perhaps 19 or 20. He was dark complexioned, slender, with deep-set eyes and incisive features to match, thin-lipped, wide-mouthed, a sharp and rather long nose. His hair was black and there was a great deal of it. He looked in a general way a little like Tony. John compared the faces. There was one big difference: Tony's face was half-smiling and untroubled; that of the young man on the bench was deeply serious. The young man stared purposively at Faber, catching every word and phrase of the poet-bookseller. John could imagine him mentally interpreting, choosing, discarding, and evaluating whatever was being recited. He looked like the kind of person who was always being asked if he was writing a book. John wondered if he was.

There was a burst of applause and Monroe Faber thanked the listeners, announced that he had just one more poem he wanted them to hear, and began to recite again. John intended to listen more carefully now, but his attention was distracted by the sudden movement of the man who occupied the easy chair on the left side of the room. He was the only one who Faber was not facing. John hadn't particularly noticed him earlier because he had been crunched far into the chair, his head buried in his hands as he listened. Now he sat up, propped a leg over one arm of the chair and leaned back, painstakingly lighting and smoking a cigarette. He didn't take his eyes off the poet in the center of the room. They were large eyes, deep and full and part of an even larger, by comparison, face and head. It was almost grotesque, completely bald except for a fringe of hair just above his ears. His ears were large and twisted like those of a veteran prizefighter's and his nose was flat and wide, covering a good part of his face. His mouth was round and heavy and his chin shied away, sloping into a thick neck. John stared at him for a long moment. For all its ungainliness, the face seemed gentle. John compared it to the clown who had the wickedest makeup and the kindest heart. The man was wearing a dark brown suit, somewhat shiny, not new, covering a dark brown turtleneck sweater that curled down from the top in several folds. His skin was tanned, somewhat olive. Something about

the man was familiar to John. He was certain he knew him
from someplace, not as a friend, but perhaps as an acquaint-
ance. John continued to stare.

Tony noticed John's puzzlement and nudged him lightly.
"Don't you know who that is?"

"No."

"You should," Tony smiled, as if he had the advantage of
an open secret. "I'll introduce you as soon as Monroe fin-
ishes."

Monroe was almost through and John listened to the last
few lines:

"The cup of gold calls
and in its quest
it fills the bosom
and melts the breast:
The cancer of the people."

The boy on the piano bench moved suddenly, smiled
in broad agreement. There was an audible grunt of dissatisfaction from the heavy-jeweled man in the vest. Faber had
finished and after some applause he turned and walked to the
uncomely-looking man on the chair and engaged in energetic
conversation. The others returned to their drinks and to a
discussion of the poetry. Tony pulled John after him and,
starting on the right, began introducing him to the people at
the party.

"Tommy Carrol," Tony said of the tall thin man on the
end of the couch. "This is Johnny Thomas, an old friend and
budding novelist." Tommy got up. John had been right. He
was tall. He stood well over six feet, towering above the others.

"Glad to know you." He took John's hand and held it
for what seemed to John a long time. "I'm glad you came,"
Tommy said. "It'll give some new life to the party." His voice
was soft, rather high. He spoke in quick syllables and the syl-

lables took on a slight sing-song quality. He didn't talk like an athlete. He sat down. "See you later," Tommy said. It was an invitation.

"He's a dancer," Tony explained. Then in a whisper, "Don't mind him—a little too gay."

The second man, the large man with the dark lined face who looked like an outdoor worker, gripped John's hand hard at the introduction. "I'm Jimmy Daven," he said.

"Jimmy's one of the finest cornetists ever to play in a jazz band," Tony said. John noted the sardonic smile on Daven's face. The muscles settled but the tone of the smile remained.

"Don't play much anymore," Daven said. "But thanks for the compliment." He changed the subject. "Like the poetry?" He was talking to John.

"Yes, I did."

"Wonderful thing, poetry," Jimmy Daven continued. "It takes you out of your own little miserable existence into a world of thought and beauty and lets you forget a lot of not-so-nice things."

He slumped back onto the couch as John and Tony moved on to the man with the vest. The diamond stick-pin shone even brighter from close up. The man didn't get up, but grasped at John's hand after the introduction, barely touched it, and then let go.

"Pleased to meet you," was all he said. His name was George Sturley. John smiled when Tony told him his occupation. He had guessed nearly right. The man was an insurance company executive. John was uncomfortable for the moment. He didn't know exactly why.

The two boys still seated by the piano stood up for introductions. John didn't get their names completely. Harry and Jerry or something like that. Tony mentioned that they were singers. They sat down again quickly. They didn't seem to be interested in much of anything except themselves.

The young man on the piano bench had gotten himself a drink and was standing now by the wall bookcase to the left of the piano, reading book titles.

"How many of these do you know by heart?" Tony asked facetiously as they came up.

"I'm trying hard," the young man answered soberly.

His name was Michael Rozan. The introductory handshake was firm. "Mind if I shed this?" Michael asked of Tony, taking off his suit jacket. "Too hot even for late autumn."

He seemed like a pleasant person and without the formality that John disliked. John felt he might be able to talk with him.

"You're not a writer by any chance?" John asked.

Michael smiled. "I make my living decorating windows in a 34th Street department store."

"Sounds like an interesting job."

"I eat," was the answer.

"Mike is a terrific painter," Tony intruded. "He does excellent work."

Michael was sarcastic. "Some day I'm going to sell my paintings." Then: "You know how? A rich uncle is going to leave me a million dollars, I'll open my own gallery on 57th Street and push my own stuff." He paused. "That seems to be the only chance a young painter has," he added matter-of-factly.

"I'd like to see some of your paintings," John said. He felt a kind of kinship. It reminded him of his own talent, although on a different plane. Michael, too, appeared to be insecure. John thought Michael seemed out of place in Tony's apartment, as much out of place as he himself should feel.

Michael continued the conversation. "Like the poetry?" He meant the question seriously.

"Yes, I do." John repeated the answer he had given Jimmy Daven. He had not heard enough of the poetry to judge. What he had heard seemed okay. "Did you?" he asked Michael.

"What did you like about it?" Michael took a long swallow of drink. He was already warm from the liquor.

John was puzzled for a moment.

"How about the content?" Michael continued.

"From what I got, it seems to make sense."

"It seems to make a great deal of sense," Michael started to explain.

Tony interrupted. "Hold off on the soap-box for a while, Mike."

Michael looked at him angrily. "You afraid of truth today, Tony?"

Tony was embarrassed, for himself and because he thought John might now feel that he was somehow the cause of the altercation. "Wait until the party gets going," Tony said.

Michael smiled. "Okay. Tony objects to some of my social ideals," he explained to John. "Like those that Monroe was reciting, about the cup of gold and it being a cancer of the people." He waited a moment. "Do you understand that, John?"

"I think I understand it," John assured him.

"Good. There's a big world to understand out there and so few of us ever do." Michael swallowed his drink and immediately John could see that the young man, at the mention of ideas had become drunk with them and was about to do the same with liquor.

"I ought to kick myself for getting drunk like this," Michael said. He waved the glass. "I'd like to talk to you, John. Do you know about the world out there? Are you an artist?"

"I write."

"Then you should understand about the world. Not like some people who sit in their own fat and let it roll around in an empty vest." He nodded toward the insurance executive.

John remembered the people on the streets in Brooklyn, the apartments, the windows, the smells, the children in ragged clothes and thin bodies. This seemed to be what Michael meant and he was glad he felt that he understood.

"I'll talk to you about it later," Michael said. "Tony gets upset too easily." He laughed.

Tony, standing next to them, laughed with him and everything was all right again. They moved to the easy chair where Monroe Faber was still standing, listening to the man in the chair talk. John could hear the words.

"It's not only the material," the man in the chair was saying, "but the characters in the material. And it is not only the characters, but the feelings in the characters. And it is not only the feelings, but in the minutest sense why they feel as they do, what it is about their specific environment that has made them feel that way. That is important."

He spoke each word carefully and slowly with a great deal of emphasis. The consonants were pronounced sharply and the vowels rolled fully. It was a romance-language accent, half Italian, half French.

"I don't have this quality?" Monroe asked. It was the student questioning the master.

"You do. Otherwise I should not have wasted my time criticizing your work." He patted the man on an arm. "You have the talent," he assured him.

"Don't you know yet who that is?" Tony asked John softly, holding on to his guessing game. John shook his head.

They went over as Faber was about to leave. Tony interrupted before the man in the chair was quite through with Faber. The man was momentarily disturbed, as was Faber, having had the small compliments abruptly cut off by the newcomers. John was introduced to Faber. The latter stood by a moment as Tony introduced John to the man in the chair, then walked to the other side of the room to discuss his poetry with others.

"John Thomas . . . Mr. Gino Aretti." John knew the name now. He should have guessed from the newspaper photos he had seen. Gino Aretti was a writer, one of the finest to come out of Italy during the past forty years. He had been away from his native country almost that length of time. He had fought the restrictions against civil liberties instituted by Mussolini and after ten years of struggle within left the country to fight from without. He was over seventy now, but his rugged looks and appearance of forcefulness made him seem much younger. His reputation came from the sensitivity of his writing. His books dealt with young people, mostly young men, and their adjustments to their life environment, their relationship to people and things, and the development of their characters. He was always probing and incisive, with a quality of softness and subtlety that gave him a reputation, as one critic put it, for "the peak of sensitivity of feeling on the printed page."

"This is a great honor," John said, shaking hands. Aretti's grip was hard. John didn't know what else to say, although the words sounded quite foolish.

"John is a budding writer," Tony advised. It made John feel self-conscious. He's revising a book now," Tony added with pride, "that the publishers feel is an incipient masterpiece."

"He flatters me." John tried to efface himself. "I'm not a writer yet, Mr. Aretti. I just try."

"We all just try," the other answered. Then he added: "You will call me Gino, yes?"

"My pleasure," John said. He wondered whether he would have the chance to speak with the novelist. Aretti knew what John was thinking. All young writers he met wished to speak with him.

Monroe Faber walked back now, wanting another word with Aretti. He stood at the edge of the group. Aretti motioned to him.

"As soon as I finish talking to Monroe I shall be pleased to discuss writing with you," he told John. And then, before John could answer: "If you wish to spend a few minutes in such talk?" His eyes glistened and his face seemed soft and gentle, not the slightest bit gross or ugly, as some find at first glance.

John thanked him and walked with Tony to the kitchen.

"We need some ice," Tony said loudly. "Give me a hand, Johnny." Tony opened the refrigerator door, then slammed it shut. He stood close against John, half pinning him against the door.

"What do you say, Johnny?" The words came swimming out.

"It's a nice party." John tried to move away. Tony held his arm.

"Whaddya say, John, whaddya say?" He slurred the words in his anxiety to talk. "Will you come back? Will you stay with me?"

Tony surprised himself with what was happening. Somehow it had gone all wrong. He had expected to play it slowly, letting John make the first move. But he couldn't wait and desperation took charge. "It hurts, Johnny, being without you." He repeated the name "Johnny." It made him feel closer than the formality of simply John. "I want you here, please."

John wanted to laugh, to make Tony hear the sound of ridicule. He had been afraid. He had come because he had a need. But for all his need, Tony's clearly was even stronger. It was a turnabout. The satisfaction of his belonging, even for one evening, was to have been relaxation, the thing that would enable him to return to his apartment and write without the knots of loneliness. Now he could not because noth-

ing would have been fulfilled. The anxiety between him and
Tony would still remain and he would still know, anxiously,
that he was needed and that he need only say yes to fulfill the
need, both his and Tony's.

"We'd better get back to your guests, Tony." He heard
the words objectively, as though he were saying them to
himself. Tony's shoulders slumped, the hollows in his cheeks
puffed out. He stared at John for a few seconds, trying to
find words. Then he turned quickly, took the ice trays from
the refrigerator, without a word emptied them into the ice
bucket and followed John into the living room.

Gino Aretti was sitting alone now, fingering a glass full
of liquor. He was twisting it around in his fingers and John
smiled as he saw it. He hadn't done it himself for a long
time, the twisting of a glass. It had been something he used
to do to calm himself when there had been a disagreement
between himself and Tony. As he thought this, he picked up
his own glass, sipped from it, then holding it in his hands
walked toward Aretti. He stopped suddenly, noticed Aretti
was looking at his hands. He glanced down and saw that he
was unconsciously twirling the glass. He did feel anxiety, not
only the physical realization of a nebulous closeness, in some
manner, to Tony again. Aretti smiled, then laughed. The tone
was full and strong, yet light and gentle.

"You too have a nervousness," he said, pointing to John's
hands.

"An old habit," John admitted. "Guess I wouldn't know
what to do if I had to keep completely still."

"Don't apologize," Aretti told him. "I have done this
since I was quite young. A nervous energy. When I am not
writing it is impossible for me to keep still. I must tear bits
of paper or bite my nails"—he showed John the chewed down
cuticles on his hand—"or twirl glasses. Maybe that is why I
have been a success in writing," he laughed. "I have so much

energy that at least some of it must pass through the type-writer to good advantage."

John felt better. There was a friendliness in being able to talk about personal little things. He leaned against the bar by the chair and Aretti turned to face him. "I like to tear apart the little paper matches," John confided, smiling at the same time.

"The American packages of matches," Aretti acknowl-edged. "In Europe matches are almost always wooden and that is too hard for the fingers," he laughed. They both enjoyed the small intimacy. The others in the room looked over at them. Aretti looked back, his face open, questioning their interest. The others turned back to themselves.

"I'm working on a first novel," John said. "The publisher seems to like it, only he's given me a number of revisions to do. I'm finding it difficult."

"And you want me to tell you what to do?"

John was startled by the suddenness. And embarrassed. "Well, I . . ."

Aretti interrupted him. He was not being harsh. "I know the problem and I shall answer your questions." He put the glass down, leaned forward, pushing his palms and fingers together. "You write and you write and begin to wonder if what you are writing is worth the time and effort. So you tear up a few pages and you drink a bottle of beer and you write again and you go to the movies and you drink another bottle of beer and the publisher tells you it's good and you still ache inside of your belly because it all seems sometimes so worth-less."

John nodded. He wanted to ask "how did you know?" But he held the question. Aretti explained.

"I am a writer, I have gone through this. I can tell, as you have walked and talked and acted this evening, that you are going through this problem right now."

John was amazed even further. He kept quiet and let the other talk.

"You try so hard to enjoy yourself," Aretti said, "or at least to give the impression that you are. Maybe you are, but much of it is forced."

"That's right," John admitted. "I didn't want to come." He hesitated.

"Were you afraid?"

"Yes." John hesitated. "Gino..."—he used the given name for the first time—"may I ask you a question?"

"Go ahead."

"Why are you here?"

"Why?" Aretti smiled, concealing beneath it, John judged, a heavy burden. "Because I, too, sometimes become lonely. Even at this advanced age and experience my writing becomes palsied and I want a relaxation. I have lived many years and I have learned to find relaxation among many peoples and in many ways. This way, in this company, is one of them. And so I do this, for when I leave I shall feel better and more inclined to write pleasantly again."

John didn't say anything. He wondered whether he, too, many years from then, would say the same thing. He wondered how involved in insecurity Gino was and whether he, too, would be as much so.

The novelist squeezed his nose, blew noiselessly, clearing a bit of the hoarseness from his voice. He watched John closely, gathered the logical pattern of his thoughts.

"My excitement must come in small doses now," Aretti explained. "I am a bit too old for much more. In some respects it is sad for one to get old."

"I used to know Tony well," John said abruptly.

"I can see that." Gino took his drink and leaned back in the chair. John moved to the arm of the chair, close to the other. "But now there is a division for you," Gino continued, "and you have come here to determine which of the cross-roads is lined with the greener trees."

"Not that. I think I made up my mind. I came only to relax." John knew that his denial had been too quick. He waited for the contradiction.

"If you wish it that way," Gino told him. "However, I must think that you are wondering, no matter what else may have been your rationalization. And this wondering means that you are, somewhere, not certain. It means, certainly, that you are lonely."

"Yes, I am lonely. I don't seem to belong."

"Everyone belongs," Aretti said emphatically. "There are what, four billion people who belong, perhaps in different ways, to different ideas and different feelings and different physical lives. But in the essence they are all one. The differences are small and those of the individual. The group differences are the artificial ones. They must be abolished. You have read my writing?"

"I know what you mean," John answered.

"You are not certain how you belong. You are, let us say, an opportunist now and have not achieved a basic understanding of your relationships. Is that not right?" Gino smiled, knowing it was right.

John nodded in agreement. "And so I feel my work suffers because of this uncertainty," he said. "But at the same time it is much better than it has ever been, even when Tony and I were very close."

"Then take it as a sign," Aretti advised. "Choose your life as it evolves best for you."

"It's difficult."

"Life has never been easy. Note the little things, use them. Signposts make the roads shorter and the hills fewer."

There was nothing more for John to say. He had learned nothing specific because it applied to everyone. And yet he had learned a great deal because it also applied to him. He saw what Aretti was driving at and grasped the importance of the man's incisiveness, that he had a feeling for people and an understanding of them through an understanding of himself and of the world.

"Perhaps you are wondering what all this has to do with writing?" Aretti gave him one last bit of advice. "Simply apply what you learn about yourself to the characters in your writing. There are many paths for a man. If he doesn't understand where he is going or how he is going to get there, he will take any of them or many of them and sometimes discover too late that he has been treading a continuous and unbroken circle. But if he knows his own goal for self-realization and if he understands what the world has to offer and will reject as well as accept, then he will get there more quickly with less pain and, in the final analysis, less struggle. I made up my mind many years ago. My writing was my life. Writing is people. That was my first consideration. It is my being and my belonging. It is that way with many writers. It may not necessarily be so with you. But it may. Think about it."

John wondered whether he belonged in that same way. He knew he didn't yet. He wondered how he was going to get there. He didn't have a chance to discuss it any further. Michael Rozan interrupted. It was just as well. Aretti had given enough personal analysis. A writer devotes so much time to psychology in his writing. Outside, Aretti preferred to limit it, to deal with the non-flexible shades of black and white. It was less trying. Inside, he sought multi-hued images.

Michael was still talking about Monroe Faber's poetry.

"You like it, Gino?" he asked.

"He shows promise."

"What of the content?"

"He will learn a fine line between content and presentation and the art will fuse them both." Aretti disliked talking about someone who was not present.

Michael understood this. Faber was by the couch now, engaged in a discussion with others, at times loud and spirited except for the poet, who listened quietly.

"That's Faber's big fault," Michael said, motioning toward the other side of the room. "He says a lot of good things, but he sits behind his desk in that little bookshop all day and what does he do about them?"

Gino laughed and stood up. "Ah, there are so few of us who can be brave. And yet, in our way, we also serve." He put one arm around Michael's shoulder, the other around John's. "Come, let us see what violent disturbance of minds has befallen our friends over there."

They stepped across to the couch and listened. George Sturley was speaking with the assurance of a man who knows he knows. "A man makes what he wants, he does what he wants. That's what's great about this country. That's why I got a home in the Poconos in the summer and a boat down off the Keys in the winter. Take my word, the man who gets there first gets the most and to hell with everybody else."

Jimmy Daven, the musician, puffed at the stump of a cigarette. His coat was off and his sleeves rolled up now. He continually rubbed his fingers against the side of his left arm. John could see the thin points of small black dots, like pinpricks.

"To hell with me too, George?" Daven was saying. "Don't I belong in your world? I was a musician, a damned good musician, and to pay my lousy rent I work every week, every night and every day and finally I figure I should have a boat in Florida, too. But I don't have a boat, so I get high, and I don't have to give a damn whether I have a boat or not. So what does it get me? A beating by the cops and a year down in Lexington, Kentucky, in a hospital where they take you away from your dreams and make you want them all the more when you get out."

"You're a fool, Daven. A God-damned fool. Who tells you to take drugs?" Sturley pulled down the ends of his vest and straightened up to gulp his drink.

Daven paled, moved away from the other man on the couch. "You're the God-damned fool for mentioning it out loud. It's not a nice thing to mention. You think I want it?"

"Then stop."

"Burn your house in the Poconos and scuttle your boat and cut your throat. It's just as easy." Daven coughed, stood up and walked away, taking his drink with him.

"Damned fool," Sturley repeated.

Daven sat dejectedly in the easy chair.

Tommy Carrol, the dancer, leaned back lazily. "Talk, talk, talk. Where does it get you? Forget about it and enjoy life." He put his hands behind his head, stretched his legs out even further, superciliously bored with the argument.

"Things you should consider, young man," Sturley insisted. "Important things. Necessary for the future." Sturley really didn't care. He merely had to demonstrate what he considered his superior ethics.

"I just have fun," Carrol drawled. "That's all I'm looking for in the future, fun." He winked at John standing in front of him. "Right, John?"

John smiled and nodded agreeably. He looked away and caught the dancer shrugging his shoulders, unconcerned.

"What if you need something and can't get it?" Tony asked the broker.

"If you got the determination you can get anything you want." The answer was unequivocal.

"I used to think so." Tony started to look at John and then, to the latter's relief, let his eyes pass over the faces of all of the others, stopping on John's for only a fragment of a moment longer. Gino stepped in to interrupt.

"Perhaps there is something to consider in Tony's question, my friend?" His speech, deliberate, gentle, and sometimes halting, contrasted with the sharp, quick definiteness of Sturley's. "Sometimes it does prove difficult for the individual to get what he wants, provided he knows what he wants in the first place."

"Then it's the individual's own fault," was Sturley's response. "Any man worth his salt gets there. To the top. Like me. I know what I want. I get it. I wouldn't be here if I didn't know what I wanted."

"Maybe it's something you need? Maybe you should really consider yourself fortunate that you can fulfill that need?" Gino suggested.

"Need. Want. Same thing. I get it." Sturley was adamant.

Tommy Carrol moved off the couch and excused himself. "I'm going to leave you-all to fight it out with your big intellects. I'm going to have another drink with my friend over there." He joined Jimmy Daven near the small bar.

John looked around for the two singers, Harry and Jerry, if he remembered their names correctly. They had been standing by, mildly interested, when he first came over, but they were gone now. He glanced toward the bedroom. The door was closed. It had been open some minutes before. Tony sat in the corner of the couch. Monroe Faber stood at one end, John at the other. Gino Aretti was in front of them all, smoking a cigarette that was almost at the tip, holding the stub European fashion between his thumb and middle finger.

It was Michael who resumed the argument, directing his words to Sturley, "If you get what you want, it doesn't mean anybody else does, too. Maybe it's because you don't let them?" He didn't hold back his thoughts.

Sturley looked at him as he would the scrub woman who apologized for taking so long to clean the floor under his feet. "Are you one of them?" he demanded. The emphasis was on "them."

"One of what?"

"You know what I'm talking about."

"But you don't know what I'm talking about." Michael's words were hard. "I'm one of them." He accented the word 'them'. "One of the four billion people in the world. I'm a human being and it's my privilege to think and act like a human being, freely, the way I want, with the basic rights of a human being."

"I've heard that kind of talk before," Sturley said, treating it of no importance.

"Then apparently it didn't penetrate very far," Michael said. "Open your mind. Did you hear Faber's poem? Listen to it, think about it." He was becoming angry, letting his own clarity become upset.

"Sentimental hogwash," Sturley observed.

"Maybe!" Michael looked around for Faber for verbal support. Faber had disappeared a minute before. He came back now, walking right into the middle of the argument. His face was pale, looking sickly under the tanned bald of his head. A hand was pressed to his forehead.

"Hope you don't mind," he said to Tony, his voice faltering. "I located some bicarbonate in the bathroom. I shouldn't drink so much." He tried to smile, but it was so weak it made him look even sicker.

"You want to lie down?" Tony asked. He pointed to the bedroom.

"It's taken," Faber apologetically said.

Michael ignored his condition. "We were just talking about your poem, the 'Cup of Gold'," he told him. He wasn't going to let anything stop him from making his point to

Sturley. "Our friend here"—he pointed across the couch—"doesn't like it."

"Oh, well, we're all entitled to our opinions." Faber did not want any arguments. He presented his ideas. If they were understood, fine; if not, there was little he could do about it.

"There are certain truths you can't hide. Respect for humanity is one of them," Michael was insistent. "You may disagree with me, but you can't ignore me."

Sturley grunted. "Faber's right, for once. We're all entitled to our opinions." He disliked complicated arguments. If something was good, it was good; if bad, bad. There were no in-betweens.

John wanted to get into the conversation. He felt an agreement with Michael. But at the same time he felt too uncertain about himself in this situation to try to suggest what anyone should think. He was not a debater. He listened.

It was Gino who made the next point to Sturley. "But you, my friend, feel that it is only your opinion which is to be accepted. Thus you contradict yourself."

"My opinion is the right opinion," Sturley retorted. "What I say and do is right. I know from experience." He plucked at his vest again. He was becoming uncomfortable. There were too many against him.

"That's where you miss the understanding," Gino continued. "For all men react in different ways. To the minutest things. Other men may follow the same self-realizations that you follow, but the results are, in some way, always a little different, for better or for worse."

"Philosophical double talk," Sturley protested.

Gino laughed, but not angrily or haughtily. He enjoyed an argument as long as both sides retained a sense of dignity and proportion. But the angry squirming of Sturley retained neither and the novelist was ready to let the matter drop. "One more thing," he said. "You belong to something because it has paid off for you. Or at least you feel it has. But there are many of us who have not received any returns. We do not belong, we are a different species in some societies and thus we cannot adjust. We are taken advantage of and cannot reach the goals you speak of. That does not mean, my friend, that we deserve no consideration, no kiss from the gods. We are human beings, too."

"Misfits. Those not able to take care of themselves. They deserve no consideration." Sturley was red in the face.

"Let 'em eat cake," Michael interjected. "Is that your philosophy?"

"I'm not a philosopher," Sturley replied. "I'm a business-man. And as such I don't give a damn what anybody eats unless I'm selling it." He laughed and felt better. The others, except Michael Rozen, laughed, too. It was a good comeback.

"I have noticed a good many in America," Aretti observed to no one in particular, "who are too complacent in their own superiority. They have created a great many taboos for fear of their position. There are too many here who are forced into a position of not belonging. I am a foreigner. On that score alone I don't belong." He paused a moment. "Do I, George?" It was a friendly question.

Sturley hesitated. He had had enough. "No, you don't," he said sharply. "Not with that kind of talk." He got up. "I don't like this conversation. I'll be getting on." He shook hands with Tony. "Maybe the next party will be without troublemakers," he told him. He buttoned his suit coat and started for the door. He picked up a broad-brimmed fedora from the hall table.

"Good night," Gino said. The others, except Michael, mut-tered their goodnights. Sturley snorted something incoherent and pressed his hand on the doorknob. He didn't look back.

"Coming, Tommy?" he called. Tommy Carrol looked up from his conversation with Jimmy Daven.

"Oh. Sure'nuff. I'm comin'." He gulped down the last of his drink. "Good night, everybody," he said brightly. The tall lean lithe dancer trotted after the lumping, fat, pompous insurance executive.

Tony looked at John, but the latter needed no explanation of that relationship. Monroe Faber decided then that he had better leave also. "I need to get some rest. I'm feeling worse," he said. He made his goodbyes and left.

Jimmy Daven came back to the couch, sat next to Michael Rozan. "I'm glad Sturley left," he sighed. "Makes me nervous. Not angry, just nervous. Guess I can never really get angry anymore. Just feel sorry for those guys."

"Yeah," Michael agreed. "They don't understand anybody except themselves."

"Yeah."

"It would be a good thing if he understood himself," Gino said. "But unfortunately he doesn't. Just as most of us do not. We must be careful with our criticism. If we understood ourselves, we would be better able to adjust to our environment."

"You understand what you are and what you want and need and then go ahead with criticism or action," John summarized. Gino smiled at him approvingly.

"And if you can't?" Tony repeated his question from before.

"Then find the clue, the goal, the reason. Experiment and learn and try to find the enjoyment in doing so and the happiness when you have finally learned," John said, using the statements Gino had given him earlier. "But know what you're doing and interpret it." He hadn't intended to say so much. But the remaining company was a friendly one. He felt at ease with them.

"Interpret." Michael picked up the word. "That's the answer."

Gino summed up. "Keep it in your consciousness until you have enough facts to decide. And if you've observed the little things and felt all things, you shall have your decision." He put his empty glass on the cocktail table. "And with that I shall leave you. I have much work to do in the morning."

"Writing a new book, Gino?" Tony asked.

"Yes. About America. And there is so much to learn about this country. Some things, some people, like George Sturley . . . for a sensitive man like myself . . . so unfortunate."

John shook hands with Aretti for what seemed like a long time. Then spontaneously hugged him. Aretti hugged back. John hoped he would see him again.

"Call me anytime. I shall be delighted to talk with you about your writing." John thanked him and assured him that he would call.

The two singers appeared again as suddenly as they had disappeared and made their exit.

"Met them when I was doing my first show last year," Tony explained. "Just about my oldest friends in New York. Come to all my parties." It was a statement without apology.

They talked for a while longer, Michael, Jimmy, Tony and John. The room was strangely quiet now and the words were whispers. Michael did most of the talking, centering it around political ideologies. John listened attentively. He was enjoying the conversation and, in fact, had enjoyed the party for the entire evening. These were the first really compatible people he talked to and whose company stimulated him since he had been in New York. He appreciated it and was disappointed when Michael and Jimmy decided to leave.

"I've got to get up in the morning," Michael said. "It's Monday and the old time- clock is waiting. Even a Diego Rivera has to live." He laughed.

"Is Rivera your favorite artist?" John asked.

"We'll get into that another time." Michael laughed again. "Perhaps if you come up to see my etchings. You have my address, John."

"Want to come up to my place for a nightcap?" Daven asked the artist.

"I'd really better get some shuteye," Michael begged off.

They both came up to John, gave him big goodbye hugs. "Good to meet you, John. We'll see you again."

"I'm sure you will," John said.

Tony saw them both to door, hugged them goodnight. They left.

Tony and John remained standing near the door. The evening had ended and there was nothing to say. John felt the pleasantness of being numbed with it. It was a belonging to the world again. He dreaded the thought of his own lonesome apartment. He winced thinking of Mac waking him for breakfast, tinted with the odor of beer.

"Will you stay, Johnny?" Tony spoke softly. There was no demand. It was a polite request. It seemed to John that perhaps it might not be a bad idea. As Gino had said, one must experiment with the little things. It takes time to find what is really the right answer, but the application was neither Gino's nor was the idea strong enough.

"I'd better go, Tony."

"Nothing I can say?"

"No."

Tony thought a moment. "Then we can meet again soon someplace?"

That seemed a pleasant enough conjecture. "That should be all right," John answered.

"When?"

"Oh, I don't know." He wasn't fully conscious of the conversation. The words just seemed to come out. There seemed to be nothing wrong with them.

"Today is Sunday. I have to go out to Long Island tomorrow to work with Stearns for a day or two. How about Wednesday?"

"Okay."

"Afternoon? At four o'clock? Just a couple blocks from here. On Christopher Street. It's called the Stonewall Inn."

"Okay."

Tony's voice barely wavered. It seemed to float. "Just be a little careful and not too obvious when you get there. Every so often the New York cops bust in and beat up the patrons. But it's the best place where"—Tony hesitated, looking for the right words—"our special friends can go."

John felt lightheaded, thought about the past few hours and wished that they would continue. "At four on Wednesday," he repeated. He closed the door slowly behind him. As he walked down the darkened street to the subway, he saw his shadow move in front of him, outlined by the flare from the street lamp half a block back. His shadow bounced and he seemed to be walking with a lighter step and with more vitality than he had felt for some weeks past.

In the apartment Tony poured himself a final drink. He smiled as he sipped it. He felt more satisfied than he had in a long time.

# Chapter 20

All the next day John felt he belonged. It was no longer a small apartment on a small Brooklyn street, bounded by a curtain of clotheslines on one side and a dipsomaniac neighbor on the other. It was a place to live. It was part of the city, not outside of it. Part of Gino Aretti and Tommy Carrol and Jimmy Daven and Michael Rozan and even George Sturley. These were people he knew now. He would see them again, as long as they were there and Tony's apartment was there and it gave him something to look forward to and belong to.

The day went quickly. It was a new day with new meanings. He arose at noon, made breakfast, listened to the news on the radio. He began to hear the news in terms of the people it affected. The announcer mentioned war and the atom bomb and starvation and they emerged from the inanimate body of a radio set and became part of the society in both the Congress Street and Barrow Street apartments. Like Gino had said. John thought about what Michael would proclaim and what George Sturley would decide and what Faber would write about it in verse. He could not remember Faber's first name. The poet-bookseller was the type of man who merges into the obscurity of the print on his manuscripts, returning there along with his words the moment after they've been spoken. But he was not of inconsequence. Everyone, even the monotone-voiced radio announcer, was an important human being this day. It all brought John to a vague conclusion, not yet altogether clarified in his mind, that no person should be apart from another, that no group of people should be separated from another. All people should belong. He didn't carry the thought into what should have been a question for himself: Is a person's identity only a reflection of who is around him or her?

Even the prospect of seeing Tony again did not bother him as it had just twenty-four hours earlier. He knew what Tony wanted. But he had no fear. He felt that everything would take care of itself and that it would turn out for the best. He lost the meaning of his resolution and, thinking this, prepared himself with only the words. He thought again about the fullness of the evening before. It was such a terrible thing to be lonely, he told himself. But now, with new friends and the promise of more at Tony's apartment, he decided he was no longer lonely.

He sat at the typewriter and wrote with a new feeling, a new fervor. He wrote and rewrote, paying no attention to the time until he glanced up, saw the darkness through the window, and realized it was night. He could have continued to write, but he felt so good about what he had done and so good about how he felt that he was sure the euphoria would continue and that he could stop, fry up some hamburger to have with a beer, sleep well, and start off the next morning where he had left off that night.

It didn't happen. He didn't resent the early morning knock at his door or the kindness of Mac bringing him a plate of bacon and eggs and toast or the chore of making strong coffee to go with it. It was the smell of beer when Mac entered, the slurring of her words, the too loose oversized dress accompanying her unkempt appearance, its flowered pattern hypocritically out of place with the returned oppressiveness of his immediate environment. Barrow Street and Sunday's party was not only in another borough, but in another milieu. The spell was broken.

"What the hell am I doing here, all alone in this godforsaken place with only Mac to talk to and now not even Helen to look at?" he asked himself after Mac had gone. He tried to eat, but couldn't, and his loneliness, accentuated by contrast with his experience at Tony's party, seemed even more intense than before. He sat down at his typewriter and tried to write. He couldn't. The euphoria was gone.

He paced back and forth in his apartment, counting the steps from the couch to the window, counting the number of loops he would take to cover the room, starting at the perimeter and walking in ever-decreasing concentric circles, feeling even more trapped as he arrived at the end, standing alone in the center. He spent much of the day alternately pacing and sitting down at the typewriter, neither yielding any satisfaction. He drank several bottles of beer for dinner, picked at a boiled bowl of spaghetti, and eventually fell asleep, even in his dreams berating himself for allowing himself to be caught in what felt like an inescapable purgatory. As he fitfully slept, were those the faces of Tony and Michael and George and Faber and even Gino laughing at him and above them, laughing loudest of all, the face of his mother?

The next morning, Wednesday, John continually looked at his watch, waiting for 4 P.M. as if that were a magic hour that would solve his dilemma. Four o'clock was a long way off and he wouldn't have to leave to take the subway to Christopher Street and the Stonewall Inn until almost 3:30. In the late morning John decided to take his usual walk to Brooklyn Heights to relieve the anxiety of waiting for time to pass. It didn't help. Walking alone and, even at that time of day, seeing couples walking together—male and female, male and male, female and female—the latter two combinations very discreetly in the prejudicial social atmosphere of the time—made him feel even worse. He went back to his apartment, showered, dressed and waited impatiently for the time to leave.

John arrived in front of the Stonewall Inn at precisely four o'clock. Tony wasn't there yet. John watched as, moments apart, young men entered the Inn, some glancing furtively behind them as if to be certain that no one was watching. Few shoppers were on the streets, most of them inside the Village stores filling their arms with as many packages as their pocketbooks could afford and seemingly waiting until the four-thirty rush hour before deciding to crowd into the subways.

Tony apologized when he arrived, a few minutes late. "This is one time I didn't mean to be late," he said. His voice was low, trying to find a minimal sound that would allow John to feel that there was no attempt at intimidation. Tony led the way inside. John thought of their previous meeting in a bar-café, and the unpleasant memory prompted him to wonder why he was in one again with Tony. But meeting Tony now was not unpleasant and this realization momentarily disturbed him. Yet, he felt no inner struggle, only the satisfaction of sitting down and ordering a drink and talking with Tony. Nothing positive, nothing negative; a neutral moment of life.

John spoke first. "I enjoyed Sunday very much."

"I'm glad," Tony said. "You seemed a little lonely when you came. You seemed much happier when you left."

'I was."

Tony was hesitant. "I'd like you to come to more parties."

"I'd like to come. Anytime."

This sudden commitment puzzled Tony. He wondered whether he was being toyed with. The drinks came. Bourbon—water for him, ginger ale for John. Tony let the glass stick to his hand as the beads of cold vapor oozed into his palm.

John watched Tony's obvious puzzlement. He felt a strange sense of freedom. "There's nothing to be afraid of, Tony," he advised.

"I'm not afraid. Are you?" Tony caught the meaning quickly and used it.

"Drink your bourbon," John replied, laughing. "A long time ago I was afraid. Of a lot of things. Whether I was doing right. Whether I was in the right society. Whether my relationship to you was right." He thought a moment. He tried to remain sure of what he was saying and at the same time say it as though it was no longer of importance. "I was confused. Because I didn't know myself. And I guess maybe I ran from myself." He watched Tony, waited for a comment. There was none. John felt his own words rebelling and he knew they were not true. "That's a god-damned lie," John said, slamming down his glass.

Tony reached for John's arm, intending to comfort him. He thought better of it, sat back and let John continue.

"I did find myself," John said. "That's the truth. With Carol. But now I seem to have lost that someplace. I've gotten so lonely, so god-damned lonely."

He had held it from himself for so many weeks that when the realization was no longer inescapable it overwhelmed him. He hadn't wanted it that way. "I was god-damned lonely, Tony," he repeated. "At your party I found I belonged again."

John sat back and drank the bourbon. He tried to think his way out of what he had just said. The logic hadn't completely consumed him yet, but the emotional truths were too strong and he couldn't fight them. He knew where they were leading and strangely enough he didn't really care.

"The party was only an appetizer," John said. "It wasn't enough. There's got to be more. I'm so god-damned lonely, I've got to have more." He let the words rush out.

"You want to come back?" Tony asked quietly. There was no cynicism, no "I-told-you-so" attitude in his voice. He was going to suggest that John's need was a complete one, sexual as well as emotional and intellectual. But he realized he didn't have to clarify it that strongly. He needed John. John had weakened for a moment and Tony didn't want to let that moment be lost.

John didn't answer immediately. He looked around him. The leather booth seemed to grow smaller, forcing them closer together. He looked for someone behind the bar to break the spell, but no one was there. Only he and Tony. He felt a little better, having taken a moment to rest his thoughts.

"You want to start all over again, where we left off?" Tony asked. He didn't press the question.

"In a way," John answered. He was calmer. He understood now what was going to happen. He knew what he was doing. There was no purpose in creating confusion through denial. He could not deny the need. He had to belong. Not half-way but for the time being, at least, completely. That was it, simply and honestly.

"I'm lonely. I told you. I need something. I can't continue this way myself. I've got to be with somebody, to share things." He was beginning to feel sorry for himself. It was a terrible weakness he had discovered. He was not self-dependent, after all. He was not even independent. He didn't say this to Tony. He couldn't admit to him how weak he felt. "You're the only one here I know. The only one I know to share things with, the only one I'm not afraid of." Because he could say this and make himself believe it, he felt a surety of sufficient control over the situation to mold it when necessary as he needed and not, as in the past, as Tony needed. Tony looked up at the words and John was glad he had said them. It was well for Tony to know that he was not afraid of him. "So I picked you. I'll stay with you."

Tony smiled. He didn't want to appear the lecherous cat, but he couldn't help the smile. John saw it. "But not for good," John added quickly. "For a while. Until the time and place for a new decision. I've considered all the little things, I've looked at the rocks in the road, and the signposts seem to be pointing one way now. When the time comes that I come to another crossroads, then whichever way the signposts seem to point, whichever road has the greener trees, that will be that way."

"You mean Carol?" Tony wanted to make it clear.

" I'm in love with Carol. As soon as I finish my novel and Carol comes here, then I intend to marry Carol. If this lasts till then, then that's when it ends. If it ends before then, then that's it. I need this now. For the moment."

Tony looked at John and waited for more, finding in his tone of voice too obvious a protest. He was right

"That's what I feel right now, anyway," John admitted.

"If it really is Carol," Tony said slowly, with extra-measured tone, "why don't you call her now? She could help this loneliness." He chanced the suggestion because he knew what the answer would have to be and the answer would strengthen his own position.

"She'd avoid further complications, you mean?" John said.

Tony was surprised by the admission. "Yes," he answered softly, reluctantly.

"Because I'm not ready for Carol. I can't just need her. I've got to give her something, too. When the book is ready, I expect to be ready. Then I'll have something for her. The need won't be one-sided. Maybe it's false reasoning, but you're going

to help me write the book. You're going to bring me closer
to Carol." He spoke without pause, looking directly at Tony.
"You're not taking advantage of me, Tony. And don't try to."

Tony was surprised again. He tried not to show it. He
was disappointed. John was stronger than he thought. Tony
was going to say something about not intending anything
not above board, but John didn't give him a chance.

"You understand that, Tony?" John said, his tone commanding a positive answer.

Tony hesitated only for a second, then offered up his glass
and they toasted the bargain. "I understand. I'm holding you
to nothing and you're holding me to nothing." It was agreed.
A new basis and a new limitation. It was remarkable, they
both thought separately, how quickly and easily it had come
about.

A slender, dark-haired young woman had sat down at
the bar, directly across from the booth. She seemed to invade
their privacy. After several minutes of deliberate glances she
came over to their table.

Though slender, she was well filled out. She was dressed
in a mature business suit, but moved with the spriteliness of
youth. She was trim, yet lacking the neatness of a well-tied
package. She put a foot on the edge of the seat, not bothering
to pull the hem of her skirt back down over her knees. "Mind
if I join you?"

"We're having a private conversation," Tony said sharply,
before she could sit down.

She sat anyway. "Don't argue over me," she said. She
pushed out her dark thick-bobbed hair, fluffing it at her neck
with the back of one hand. "I'm a big girl," she explained.

Tony looked at her condescendingly. "Do you know
where you are?" he asked.

She was puzzled. "That's a strange question," she
answered belligerently. "In a bar, of course."

"Your first time here?" Tony asked.

"How did you know that? Yeah, I live uptown, near 96th Street, and I thought I'd go slumming in the Village." If she thought the slur would get a rise out of her questioner, she was mistaken.

She was now sitting close to John and he moved away, looking at her from the other end of the seat.

"I'm a big girl and can go wherever I want," she said.

Tony winked at John, the girl not noticing. "I can see you're a big girl," Tony said, looking her up and down.

"Is that a crack?" she asked. She wasn't angry. She felt she had been made welcome and picked up the tone of the conversation.

"Just a statement," Tony said. "A compliment."

The young woman smiled. John was not happy with Tony's game. But he did not intend to interrupt it.

She ordered a Manhattan, fished the cherry from the bottom, held it on the tip of the wooden gilt-painted swizzle stick. "To the cherry," she proclaimed with much obviousness. "God's most beautiful and enticing fruit." She was about to pop it into her mouth.

"Don't do that," Tony stopped her. "Save it. Such a luscious thing should be held for the last."

"I don't agree," she said. "I might never finish this drink. Then think of all the fun I might have missed." She gulped the cherry. "See. It's easy. Just like that." Then, lightly throwing the words away, but deliberate enough for someone to catch if they wanted them, like a garter thrown into the audience at a burlesque show: "A lot of things are easy if you want them."

"How do you go about getting them?" Tony asked with mock innocence.

"Why, all you have to do is ask for them," she answered with equal aplomb. "If you asked for something you wanted,

I'm sure you'd have no trouble whatsoever and"—she pointed to John—"neither would Silent Sam there, either." She leaned across the seat to him. "Don't you agree?"

"I never have any trouble agreeing," John answered without expression. He was impatient and bored at the same time, waiting for Tony to finish whatever it was he intended.

"My name's Rita," the young woman said. She hurried on, as if to stop the others before they had a chance to speak. "Don't tell me your names. I don't like to know. Too sentimental." And then, just a bit sadly: "It doesn't make any difference, anyway." She leaned forward across the table toward Tony, almost making him spill the drink he had close to his mouth.

"What do you want?" she asked.

"A lot of things," he answered with forced casualness.

"Lonely?" she asked.

"Sometimes."

"And you?" She turned toward John.

"We're all lonely sometimes, aren't we?" He smiled. He noticed a sudden softening around the girl's eyes, the hardness that had been built to buffer the concrete wall of the world relaxed just a bit. John felt a kinship. He didn't feel sorry for her because he didn't feel sorry for himself. He understood her and he wished Tony and he would leave quickly now. He resented the possibility that she would be hurt. He didn't want anybody to be hurt.

She looked at him a long while and then laughed, her chin up and head thrown back. Her face was hard again, like that of a china doll. "There, you do talk. And you're bright, too. That's good."

"Why?" Tony got back into the conversation.

"It makes things much pleasanter. Conversation is important, you know." She paused. "Where do you fellows live?" she questioned.

John looked at Tony purposefully, letting him know by the glance that he disapproved of what was happening and wanted to leave. The game was too good for Tony to give up so quickly. It was, in a sense, a transfer of the lost superiority over John and he was enjoying it.

She asked again, suggestively. "Where do you live?"

Tony answered immediately this time. "We share an apartment."

"Oh, fine," Rita said. "That makes it convenient."

"Convenient for what?" Tony pretended that he didn't understand.

"Well . . . convenient for keeping both you fellows from being lonely." She was uncertain why clarification was necessary.

"So?"

She was confused now. "I thought that's what you wanted?"

"Who said that's what we wanted?" Tony's eyes thinned out into the narrowness of those of a tiger cat ready to spring for the kill on a defenseless animal.

"You did," Rita said hotly, trying to keep composure. "You said you were lonely."

"Oh, that's right, we did," Tony said, as if he hadn't remembered a thing of no importance. He finished his drink. John's mouth tightened. He pushed his glass down hard against the table and started to rise. Tony saw his anger and knew it would be best to leave. "We are lonely," he told Rita, a little more kindly. "So I guess we better be getting back to our apartment."

"Good," Rita said. She picked up her glass, held it in her hand, about to finish the drink. "Wait for me."

Tony had started to follow John toward the door. He stopped now. He was near the kill and despite John's objection he couldn't resist it. "Oh, there's no need for that," he called, in answer to her request. "I forgot to tell you." He laughed slowly. "We sleep in a double bed."

John's face grew red, he reached the door and ushered Tony out angrily. He turned back, glanced quickly at the young woman. She was glowering at them. The glass was still in her hand, halfway to her lips.

"Fucking queers," she said.

## Chapter 21

Tony sat at the piano. He played a few bars, jotted down a note or two, repeated the melody, changed a note, then played the melody phrase completely through. The blinds were drawn and in the whole world only that room made a sound.

A steel arm twisted upward from a floor lamp and threw a light over Tony's shoulder onto the music paper. Nothing entered from outside. The darkness from the evening street tried to creep in between the edges of the Venetian blind. In the whole world, only that room was warm and light.

Tony sat hunched forward, bending his fingers almost straight down onto the black and white keys when he wasn't reaching for the pencil on the music rack. A black lock of hair hung over his forehead and he let it stay there, not bothering to brush it back. Only occasionally did he bother to adjust the sash of his blue dressing gown. He was too busy being a composer.

John came out of the bedroom. He had some sheets of note paper in his hand, looked at Tony, then continued reading the papers. He licked his lips, satisfied if not altogether pleased with what he read. He flipped a page, read on to the

next while walking to and settling himself in the easy chair,
his back to the piano, the white sheets of paper catching
the yellow light reflection. He stretched his feet out, kicked
off the slippers he wore. They were Tony's, soft and padded
almost too warmly. John wore dark brown trousers and a
loose fitting green corduroy shirt, both Tony's. Good clothes,
the kind the latter always preferred, only now more expensive. John reached for a glass of bourbon that had been mixed
with ginger ale and was waiting for him on the small bar
next to the chair. He tasted the liquor, turned to Tony to say
"thanks," and turned back to his reading without waiting for
an acknowledgement. After a few seconds he turned around
in the chair.

"You shouldn't have done that to that girl in the bar
today."

Tony grunted and continued his attention to the keyboard.

The idea bothered John and he repeated it more directly.
"I didn't like what you did with that girl in the bar."

A discordant echo escaped the piano and Tony straightened up. "I'm sorry. I apologized before. I'm sorry."

John was embarrassed with having disturbed Tony.
"I just didn't like it," he said by way of explanation.

"I was happy and I felt good. When I feel good I like
to have fun. I didn't realize it bothered you so much. Let's
forget it." Tony's voice began to rise under the pressure of
the repeated apology and he stopped himself from saying any
more. He didn't want to argue. He slowed his voice down to
a question.

"Can we forget it?"

John smiled. "Forgotten." He didn't want to argue either.

Tony went back to the piano. John continued reading the
papers in his hands. He read for another minute, then interrupted again.

"Is this your stuff, Tony?"

"Huhmm?"

"This stuff."

"What stuff?"

John sat up and looked around. "Sorry. Didn't mean to disturb you."

Tony made a mark on the music paper, then got up and walked to the small bar, poured a martini from a large glass canister.

"That's all right." He sat wearily on the couch. "I was running out of inspiration anyway."

John held up the sheets of note-paper. "Good poetry. Who wrote it?" He held a page out. Tony leaned forward, couldn't quite reach it, stood up, took it, sat down again.

"It doesn't sound like that Faber fellow's," John commented.

Tony read the hand-written verses. "It isn't."

"Whose?"

"Nobody you know."

"This nobody is pretty good," John insisted. He read another page.

"It's a friend's," Tony responded, answering the question.

Tony tossed the page onto the cocktail table, leaned back from the matter of no importance, sipped the martini. "Fellow named Larry. Used to be around here once in a while."

"You must have known him quite well?" There was no sarcasm in John's voice. He was merely asking.

"Why?"

"Some of the things in these poems."

"We were pretty good friends," Tony smiled contentedly. The smile had more meaning than the statement. John shrugged his shoulders. He resented Tony's reluctance and thought he ought to become angry. Angry, superior, commanding, anything. Now that he was the master, perhaps he ought to do some of the things Tony used to do in a similar situation. But he was too content and let the notion pass. He got up lazily, walked to the couch and sat next to Tony.

"This poem"—he held out a page—"this is really good."

Tony looked at him, a bit frightened that there was purpose in John's action. He saw in John's eyes a roundness and fullness and knew that any seriousness was of a gentle kind. There was no bitterness or jealousy visible.

"Listen." John held up the note-paper and read:

"I tossed upon the seas of life as if a cork,
And I could not find a place to rest my head
Until a wave splashed high and in its wake
Emerged a cushion held in your hands."

"And another:

'Subjected to your thoughts, your ways,
I followed you about as if a shadow.
Blindly, I walked through darkness
For I knew that someday a light would shine
And I would walk toward it . . . '"

"That one wasn't finished," John said. "But at the bottom of the page, the last page, this is almost scrawled, must have been written in a hurry." He read:

"I turned back once again to view
The spot where we stood and made our dreams,
But there was only darkness.
There was nothing left to do but turn away."

"It takes a great deal to write feeling like that," John commented. "That Larry must be quite a fellow."

"Not really." Tony tossed away the credit. "He's rather womanish." He noticed John's raised eyebrows. "Well, really, he is." He felt he had to explain. "Gets upset easily, has a high-pitched temper."

"You seem to know him very well." John was not satisfied with Tony's attitude and he felt he had an authority to satisfy.

Tony laughed now. "All right. I did . . . know him well."

John looked at him, startled at the frankness. He didn't know what to say. He looked at Tony, then realizing the foolishness of their discussion, they both laughed.

"Forget it," John said.

"Forgotten."

They remained silent. After a moment John spoke. "I found them in the dresser drawer as I was putting my clothes away."

"What?"

"The poetry," John explained.

"I thought we were going to forget it." There was a sharpness in his tone.

John let the edge sting him, then bounced it back. "If it doesn't mean anything, why get upset?"

Tony got up, verbally letting his body use the energy he wanted to get rid of. He paced back and forth a moment. "What was, was. What is, is."

"Of course." John was controlled.

"Then don't start something over nothing."

"I didn't think I was starting anything," John said calmly.

"Stop digging into my personal business."

"You're awfully god-damned sensitive," John said. The hardness was measured. He watched Tony's cheeks bulge, saw him push the lock of hair in place, then go through the motion again without purpose. There was a strange satisfaction in getting Tony angry and not being cowed by the anger.

Tony had gone to the chair and was sitting on the arm, rubbing the cold of the martini glass against his palm, nervously. John walked up to him, placed his hand on the other's shoulder. "No need for arguments, Tony," he said, the gentleness of his voice indicating an apology without any compromise of principle.

Tony looked up, grateful. He hadn't wanted anything to go wrong, especially this first night together.

"Forget it," Tony said.

John smiled at the repetition of a few minutes earlier.

"Forgotten," he answered.

They clinked glasses, the little barrier of strain disappeared and they moved together to the couch. Tony reached to the cocktail table, opened a little silver box and with the familiarity of old habit took a cigarette for himself and handed one to John. John took it with a smile of remembrance, inhaled at the proffered flame and puffed deeply. He let out a billow of smoke and watched it as it broke apart into individual strips of thinness, moved across the room toward the windows and then disappeared as it flattened against the lighted bulb of the floor lamp and was sucked into the rounded cone of the shade.

They both remained still, without words. John watched the ash grow on the cigarette. He looked down from the corner of one eye as he inhaled and saw the red glow eat along the tip of the white paper. Each puff moved the fire further along the rim of the cigarette like time drops the passing months off into nothingness. The ashes were the memories. When it was almost gone, he rubbed the cigarette into the porcelain of the ash tray until it was quashed out. Only the crumpled tobacco and the satisfaction of the smoke remained. He felt an ultimate content.

"I'm glad to be here, Tony," he said, his voice very low.

"I'm glad you're here." Tony's words came in whispers too, afraid to break the gentleness of the quiet. They looked at each other, acknowledging a mutual understanding. They sat close against one another. Except for the occasional passing hum of an automobile, there was no sound.

Tony spoke softly, barely moving. "I didn't know how much I was really missing. Should have taken you with me last year."

John formed the syllables on his lips. "Should have!"

Tony looked up. "This first evening is a good one." The words barely reached across the few inches between them.

The sharp lines that had grown into part of Tony's mouth and next to his eyes had softened and almost disappeared. He pulled his arm up, looked at his watch without really noticing it. "Tired?"

"A little." Instinctively, again out of remembrance of habit, John waited for Tony to move. Tony didn't. The realization that Tony was now waiting for him made him feel good. He moved to the edge of the couch and stood up. Tony followed, untying the dressing gown and dropping it onto the couch.

John stretched his arms, yawned, looked at Tony, walked into the bedroom. Tony followed him.

"It's good to be here," John said.

## Chapter 22

John's typewriter sat open on the kitchen table. Only now it was in the apartment on Barrow Street.

John had moved his belongings from Brooklyn. Mac cried a little when he said goodbye. She had hurried into the other room for a moment to wipe the tears away before they became embarrassing.

"You're the nicest tenant we've had here," she told him. "It's been nice being able to talk to someone. To an educated person. I've been to college, too, you know." She brushed away his thanks for her help. "Anytime, you just call on old Mac." When she walked him to the door she was so upset that she even forgot to take along her bottle of beer.

The typewriter remained open for one week. Then one day John closed it. He slammed the lid down on top of it and buried it rudely at the back of the bedroom closet.

This was the first thing. Something unforeseen had happened and John couldn't explain it. The first few days with Tony were tender ones. Calm, peaceful, they fulfilled his need for companionship, they gave him the sense of belonging that he felt he needed to continue his writing.

But somehow he couldn't write. Tony spent a good portion of time away from the apartment. "Gerry Stearns likes us to work at his place. Big house out on Long Island." Reluctantly, he left John alone. The free time gave John a chance to work. The typewriter loomed large. It beckoned at first. Then it annoyed. Finally, it nagged. The inspiration that he felt would come to him did not come. He sat down once and tried, making an unintelligible pattern on the paper and crumpling the sheet into the trash. The typewriter became more and more a living thing, reminding him of what he must do and reproaching him because, even in what he had planned to be the proper set of circumstances, he could not do it. Unable to do it, he shut the typewriter out of sight.

Then he became aware of the second thing. The immediacy of Tony's company, the escape from his loneliness, the fullness of being and belonging was neither the panacea nor the euphoria he expected. He wondered whether it was because Tony was away so much, working with Stearns during the days and even many evenings. He looked forward to Tony's return from his visits to Stearns, but at the same time found himself resenting Tony for leaving him alone so often. He tried to cover his concern when with Tony, but couldn't dismiss it from his own consciousness. The question of whether there was something deeper that caused his dissatisfaction kept intruding, but he dismissed it. One night, only weeks after he had been there, John moved from the bedroom and spent the night on the couch. He told Tony it was the heat.

There were several parties during those first weeks at the Barrow Street apartment. John looked forward to them. He was able to relax, be part of the whole without feeling inextricably tied to it.

Letters arrived from Carol questioning the delay and the final acceptance of his novel, although she didn't hesitate to

assure him of her devotion and patience. John resolved again
to hurry and complete the book. He tried, but once again,
after a few hours of unproductive writing, the typewriter
was returned to its state of exile. He put his frustration into
an angry letter to Carol, berating her with words that were
meant for himself. He let his own torment spill out onto
Carol. And in his awareness that he was doing so, he wondered whether he had been mistaken about his feelings for
Carol. If he really loved her, would he vent his anger on her?
If she came to New York and they lived together, would he
soon find the same kind of dissatisfaction that he now felt
in his relationship with Tony? Perhaps he didn't belong in
either world, neither with Tony nor with Carol?

John realized that he had to do something about it. First
with Tony. His agreement with Tony had been clear. As long
as his need was there, he would remain. When it ended, their
relationship would end. All he had to do was to pack up and
leave. He had not found what he needed, what he thought
he needed. He saw this but could not fully understand it.
He had made the decision to return to Tony, knowing full
well the reasons for it. Was he simply grasping at anything
that might give him a sense of belonging to something? He
searched for answers. Having found none, he decided not to
take any action, not to leave before he found them. He would
stay a while longer.

John remained at the edge of this precipice. Tony did
not see what was happening. He was too content with having John back to think of any kind of dissatisfaction and he
assumed that John must be as happy as he was. John told
Tony nothing. As long as he was still there he hesitated to
say anything, feeling that his inability to cope concretely
with the situation and understand himself would show a
weakness that would give Tony a trump card again. John was
determined to retain his freedom of choice, no matter how far

away or uncertain the use of that freedom might seem at the moment.

He often thought about leaving, but each time he did, he could not decide for certain. He thought of what he would do if he left and realized what his fear was. As dissatisfied as he was at the Barrow Street apartment, the prospect of the loneliness he had known in the apartment on Congress Street was worse. He didn't know what he would do or where he would go if he left. He was caught in a nether world and hung on to the half-a-loaf as better than none.

During the afternoons, when Tony was away, he sometimes became physically ill thinking about the problem. He broke out into cold sweats, got headaches. One evening, just before Tony was due home, he felt a terrible nausea and vomited. After six weeks he could stand it no longer. He paced back and forth across the living room, telling himself over and over again that he must leave. He hoped the words said out loud would help clarify the problem.

"Why do you want to leave?"

"Because I can't stand it here. Because it's not right for me."

"Why isn't it right for you?"

"I don't know."

"What will you do if you leave?"

"Get my old apartment again."

"Will you be happy there?"

"I'll be miserable there."

"So why leave?"

"Because I can't stand it here."

And the questions and answers went around in a circle and he still didn't know.

Then it suddenly struck him. The whole dichotomy of his thoughts became clear and he understood why he hadn't wanted to face it during the weeks past. There was no one, single easy way for him. He had let himself remain in limbo because there was no decision that he could face honestly and say "this is what I want."

He felt he could not remain with Tony. Yet, a nagging doubt remained. At the same time he felt he could not resume what he thought had become his new life. He had become independent of Tony, but he had not become fully dependent on himself. He was not ready to accept the responsibility of marrying Carol. The confidence that had been built up over the year past had dissipated in the months that he had been in New York and he felt that he had been deluding himself, that his hopes and plans for the future had no real foundation. He insisted to himself that he loved Carol. But he had also once insisted to himself that he loved Tony. And perhaps still did.

He was caught between two worlds, unhappy in the one, unable to face the other. Then he thought again, maybe I do belong with Tony? Or with somebody like Tony? He remembered the boy of three years ago, the boy who had no responsibility, who did not pretend to have any strength, who worshipped the young composer and, letting the other take all the responsibility, found happiness. "Maybe I'm too strong for Tony now? Maybe with someone else who's stronger?"

And then he remembered the girl with the dark hair and the warm body and the pride he had in getting his nose bloodied protecting her. "Maybe I should just leave and call Carol and everything will turn out all right?" Then: "But I'm afraid. What if she does come right away, what will I do?" And, after another moment of thought: "But to need her only to take care of me because I'm not strong enough to take care of myself is just as bad. I've got to give her more than that. Where will I find the answers?"

He didn't know. It was an albatross around his neck. He could not carry the burden the rest of his life. He had to know before his relationship with Carol went any further, before his break with Tony was complete and final.

It was dark, the sun bending lower and earlier into the horizon under the November coolness. He put on his tan trench coat and left the apartment. He took the subway to Brooklyn and in less than half-an-hour was on Congress Street. He wasn't sure why. Perhaps it had something to do with the people, the multitude, the strangers. For all his efforts he still did not belong as they did. Maybe among them he could find some answers. Without thinking, he walked toward his old apartment house, stopped automatically in front of it. A big voice sounded behind him.

"Got lonesome for the old place, huh? C'mon upstairs, I'll give you a bottle of beer."

Mac carried two large paper bags in her arm, one dripping at the bottom with the wet of perspiring glass and the other, pressed against her, bulging at the top with the narrow-necked beer bottles. He followed her upstairs. "I'm all alone tonight," she explained. "Mac's out with the boys. Helen's been away for a few days. Got a new boyfriend. A pretty girl like her should have boyfriends."

The little bulldog met them in the foyer of the apartment with high squeaks of barking. It stopped only after Mac put the packages onto the kitchen table, took the dog in her arms and petted and kissed it lovingly. "Isn't he beautiful, John?" she asked, not expecting an answer.

John sat on the low, deep cushioned bright red couch in the living room. He felt more comfortable now, relaxed without the necessity of social duties to perform, no poses, real or forced. Mac brought him a bottle of beer, sat across from him on the green chair, got up as quickly as she had sat down, excused herself, went into the bathroom and returned minutes later.

"Hate to wear a corset," she said. "I'm not as trim as I used to be. I used to be beautiful, you know. Had all the boys after me when I went to college." She took a long drink of beer. "People expect you to look like something you ain't," she observed.

The beer was cold and refreshing, at the same time beginning to spread a warm tingle inside. John remained silent as Mac questioned him.

"You get along with this new roommate you moved in with?"

"Okay."

"That's too bad." John looked at her, not understanding. She leaned forward as far as she could get without falling off the chair. "I'll tell you something, only don't tell anybody I ever told you." He promised he wouldn't. "I was kinda hoping you wouldn't get on with your new roommate, so I've been purposefully keeping your apartment vacant. Landlord doesn't know anything about it." She took a gulp at the bottle. "Damned landlord's got more money than he knows what to do with anyway," she said, condoning her action.

"I appreciate it," John told her. "But you don't have to go to all that trouble for me." He vaguely contemplated returning to the apartment. Perhaps this was, he thought, the unconscious purpose that brought him back to Brooklyn that evening.

"I'll hold onto it another couple weeks anyway," Mac said. "I miss having somebody to talk to."

She continued to talk, repeating the things that John had heard over and over before. John half-listened, contentedly nodding every once in a while to let Mac know he was interested. He let himself become drowsy, the beer combining with the softness of the couch and the warmth in the apartment. The windows were closed and he felt groggy Mac woke him with a high-pitched question.

"Happy?"

"Huh?" He jerked up.

"Happy with your new roommate?" She repeated the earlier inquiry, not conscious that she had asked it before.

"I guess so," he told her.

"That's too bad," she said, continuing the earlier observation.

She whispered again, as if John hadn't heard her the first time. "Don't tell anyone, but I've been saving the apartment for you." She was sadder now. "It's so lonesome now with no one to talk to."

For the first time the individuality of the woman made an impression on John. She was not a caricature. She was a person with problems, the same as he. She was lonely, the same as he. He was awake now to the wish to help, with sympathy rather than passivity.

"There's Helen," he observed, trying to determine whether there really was. He wondered what Mac's beginnings were, where she had come from and in what direction she was ultimately going.

"Helen isn't here much. She has a lot of boyfriends." She absolved the girl from criticism. "You can't blame her." There seemed to be a satisfaction in the transfer of herself into Helen's enjoyment.

"There's Mac, isn't there?" John questioned.

She didn't answer, but holding the empty bottle in front of her walked slowly to the kitchen. She brought back a fresh beer, sat down again carefully as though a perpetual weight that had been propped up into the air had fallen into her lap. She talked with care now, in a monotone voice, as if hearing aloud for the first time the things she was saying.

"Mac and I stopped not being lonely twenty years ago." She put the bottle by the side of the chair and folded her hands tightly into each other. "I wasn't always this way, big and fat. I was a beautiful girl. I went to college. For a year. Then I became a nurse. Worked with some big doctors. Over at Memorial Hospital. You know the Memorial Hospital?" John nodded. "I met Mac there. He was a patient. He was good looking then, too. He made good money. I married him."

She sighed reflectively. This was no torrent of thought or river of words to get lost in. This was truthful remembrance, not pleasant to recall and contemplate.

"After a while, such a little while, I found out I really didn't love him. He wasn't sweet and needy like he was in a hospital bed. He was cross and he was angry. The good times that I liked he didn't like and I had to stay home every night while he listened to the radio or read his newspapers. He was only interested in me when it was time to go to bed." She stopped again to remember. The folds in her face sank deeper and looser, making her older than her fifty-three years.

"I wasn't happy," she said softly. "Not at all happy. I wanted to stay with him and I wanted to have a home, so I thought I could change him. But I wasn't able to. Many times I thought I would leave him. But I was afraid to. I wasn't strong enough for that, either."

She laughed. It was bitter. "You know where my husband is tonight? He's out with some whore someplace. I know it. I never mention it to him, but I know it." The laughing stopped and she was sad again. "Thirty years ago I still had a choice. But I was afraid. Now it's too late to have a choice."

John choked up for this woman. He was ashamed that he had not taken her seriously before. He understood what had happened to her. It was happening to him. "What happened then, Mac?"

He knew there was no need for the question.

She continued talking as if she hadn't heard it. She tried to make it sound unimportant, but she couldn't. "So today

I'm fat and fifty and foolish and he's out with a whore." She looked at John. "What did I do?" John could give her no answer. She repeated the question. "What did I do that was wrong?" She didn't expect an answer. She reached for the bottle and swallowed deeply of the beer, the foam oozing out of the neck of the bottle, forming white beads of whisker on her face. She wiped them away, put the bottle down. Her face had become hardened again, the forced acceptance of life back. She said only one thing more. "I took to drink," she told him.

John remained another hour. He didn't want to stay but he felt a necessity to give her some of the company she needed so much. After a while she talked again, only now it was not reflective. It was the learned phonograph-style repetition of the things he had heard before. He wondered how much of this was the truth, but it didn't really matter. For her, he knew, it was all truth. She walked down the stairs with him. The breeze from the bay blew cold across the streets and the air smelled clean and ripe, dropping tiny hints of winter. John shook hands with her as he started to walk up the street toward the subway.

"I'll save the apartment for you another few weeks," she called after him. He was kind of glad that she would.

Carol's answer to the angry letter he had written arrived two days later. It made him feel worse than when he had mailed it. It was an apology and at the same time an assurance. The years left to them in their lifetimes, she wrote, were not nearly enough for the years they wished to be able to have together. This was the reason for her hurry for his success and for their being together. She suggested that it would be appropriate for her to come to New York at this time. She would work at any job to support herself and she would be near him to fulfill his apparent need for her. Then the waiting would not be so hard.

John read the letter several times, a growing panic with the understanding of what it meant. His angry letter had been a mistake. He knew he could not cope with Carol's coming. He was not sufficient for her or for himself. Her love for him was strong and the kind of love he needed. He wished he had the strength and self-understanding to accept it.

He thought for a moment that he might phone her and ask her to indefinitely postpone her coming. Given time, he might find a solution. But he could not be sure. In his undirected pursuit of himself, he was going in a circle and until he actually found the solution he could not commit himself. Perhaps there would never be a solution and perhaps if there were one it might prove only temporary and his same indecisiveness about his place in the world would occur again and again and again until there would be nothing at all left between him and Carol except the angry words?

He had no one else to turn to. He showed the letter to Tony.

At first Tony laughed. "Like all women," he said. "Getting excited over nothing."

John shut the laughter quickly. "That's too glib, Tony. She'd not all women. Nobody is. No more than you're"—he hesitated—"all men. We're all individuals. When I came here I told you it was only temporary, until the novel was finished and Carol came here. The novel isn't finished, but Carol seems ready to come here."

"You can tell her not to." Tony was afraid now.

John saw the fear. He did not know what he was going to say, but he felt that now was the time to make clear his concern about remaining at Barrow Street. He motioned Tony to the couch, bade him sit. John walked back and forth.

"I came here and thought that would help me. It didn't."

The moment he said the words he felt a sense of relief. It was easier than he had thought. He walked to the window, opened the blind and looked out into the street. It was still light. There was no sun, the early graying of the afternoon striking away the shadows that had been slowly melting into the darkness as it came. People hurried on the streets. Five o'clock, the rush hour home.

Tony tried to reason. "I didn't know you were unhappy here," he said. "I thought everything was all right."

"It's pretty plain to see it's not."

"Is it my fault?"

"No. It's mine," John admitted.

"Is there anything I can do?" Tony was serious. He had gone to great lengths to satisfy his need and would do anything to assure it.

"You've done what you can do. I've been lost. Being here hasn't helped me. I haven't been able to write. I haven't been able to find myself. And I still feel lonely."

Tony didn't understand. "I've been with you as much as I can be."

"Not that kind of loneliness. A loneliness of not really belonging. At this point I don't know whether I belong with Carol or whether I belong with you, whether I belong in one world or whether I belong in another world, whether I belong in both worlds or whether I belong in none. So I feel I've got to move away from everything in order to find out who I really am.

That was clearer to Tony. "Maybe you need a rest?" he suggested. "Maybe you're just tired? I've been doing good composing. I've been feeling great since you've been here."

"I'm not you," John said. "That's just it. It's okay for you, but not for me. You belong here. I don't belong." The thought struck hard at him. He began to get upset and held back his emotion.

"Give yourself more time," Tony said. "It'll work out."

"I've had time." John's voice rose in self-condemnation. "But what I'm looking for I didn't find here." The words, out loud, reassured him of his determination and at the same time gave him the strength to say, "at least for now, Tony. When I find myself. Maybe in the future. Or maybe not."

Tony walked over to John, put his arm around his shoulder. John needed comfort. Tony thought he could help him find the answer. "What are you going to do, Johnny-boy?"

John paused, then gently removed Tony's arm from his shoulder. He knew what Tony intended. "I look weak to you now, don't I, Tony?"

"I didn't say that."

"You're thinking it."

Tony reacted defensively. "You're being foolish," he said. He tried to put his arm on the other's shoulder again, but John walked away.

"It's like a disease," John muttered. "It's crept over me these past few years and it seems like I'm unable to get away from it. With Carol, for a while, I felt well. With you, for a while, I felt well. Alone, I felt unwell. Now I feel sick. Both in my body and my head."

"You're imagining too much," Tony said. He knew that John's words were true. He tried a different approach. "You're caught between two worlds and you're afraid of both, Johnny."

"Maybe I am," John said. "Maybe that's the problem. Trying to make a choice."

"This is where you belong," Tony said. "There's been too much on the positive side to question it. Think back."

"I don't have to. I know what I feel now." He walked to the closet, put on his trench coat and opened the front door. Tony watched calmly.

"You've got a home here," Tony said. "And me. I'm your security."

John didn't stop.

"What are you going to do?" Tony said.

"I don't know." John continued out the door. He started to close it behind him.

"Where are you going?" Tony asked.

"To try to find out what to do," John answered, closing the door behind him.

He walked up Eighth Avenue, through the increasing crowds of people, all of them hurrying, shoes scraping off their tiredness onto the sidewalks. He tried to move past to the inner edge of the crowd, rushing with them and against them, not sure where he was going, but knowing that for some reason he must get there quickly. He stared inconclusively at the shop windows along the way, the ceramic shops with their abstract designs in thin, lace-like colors, the furniture shops with their peculiar uncertain modernistic shapes, the shops with the free-form pieces of driftwood in the window, from lamps to decorative works. Semi-nude pictures of purported dancers and singers hung without glamour on the unpainted signboards in front of several small cafes and night clubs. He turned up 14th Street, bumped elbows and shoulders against the traffic of humanity going in both directions at once. The lights in the apartments above the stores began to make a twinkling pattern of incandescence and large blotches of darkness suddenly appeared to counter them as the stores closed and managers switched off the inside lights and outside neon signs.

John walked down to Fifth Avenue, looked up at the windows in the towering clean-sanded facades of apartment buildings and idly searched the windows for signs of the people who made enough money to pay the exorbitant rents there. He continued past Fifth Avenue, past Park Avenue, and then he knew where he was going. He knew it all the time.

He found Michael Rozan's apartment on the third floor
of an old red brick tenement house above a shoemaker's shop,
just below Third Avenue. He wasn't sure why he had come
to see Michael, except that he wanted someone to talk to and
Michael seemed like a friend who would be honest and who
he could trust.

The apartment was up two long narrow flights of stairs
edged by a banister that wobbled precariously every time
John pressed his hand against it for balance. A small bulb,
the dirt allowing light to escape only from a narrow strip
along the bottom center, hung from a loose wire above the
mailboxes in the first floor hallway. The sockets stared empty
on the succeeding landings. Only the vaguest outline of light
sifted up from the bottom to help him keep his footing on
the stairway. As he knocked on the door he heard the clump
of the elevated train from Third Avenue as it passed over the
wooden ties. The reverberation from the elevated structure
carried to the house, up through the hallway, and the wooden
boards underneath him shook as though they were struggling
to free themselves from bondage.

Michael was surprised when he opened the door. "I'll be
god-damned." He stood for a moment and stared. "I guess
maybe I did expect to see you again." He had just come
home from work and had dressed comfortably, the loose ends
of a white tee shirt hanging over his trouser tops and thin
moccasin slippers on sockless feet. John could smell the fried
warmth of food from the kitchen. Michael led him that way.

"Make yourself comfortable while I throw on another
pork chop." He insisted John have supper with him.

John made himself comfortable in the living room-
bedroom as he waited. The apartment was much like the one
he had in Brooklyn, only much more tastefully furnished.
The room walls were white on three sides, the fourth wall
draped with a maroon weave and the window frame covered

with the same material. There was a desk, a bureau and a studio couch. Two chairs hovered around a square cocktail table. A hi-fi was on the bureau. The top of the desk was lined with books. Along one wall, from end to end, ran a two-shelved bookcase. The furniture was modern, the design something like Tony's except that it was dark, like black mahogany. John was surprised to learn that Michael had made all the furniture himself.

"Most design is too commercial," Michael explained. "Either pretty or useful, but rarely both. And besides, I couldn't afford this stuff if I had to buy it."

On two walls Michael had spaced several of his drawings. John had hardly noticed them when he entered. Now the pin-point of line attracted his attention. There was not much color, but what there was seemed to rise in progressive brightness. Most of the drawings were of people, different kinds of people in different situations and in different jobs. They were intriguing to look at and they held his interest for a long time, making him think about the subjects involved. He was pleased because he had never found much interest in what seemed to him descriptive art.

The kitchen was a new one. Renovated, Michael told him. "The landlord put in a new kitchen, which the apartment needed anyway, and that takes the place out of rent control and so he charges more than twice what it's worth. But what can you do?" He shrugged. "The rent control office won't help you."

Michael told him all this as they ate. The young artist ate without enjoyment, as if it were necessary to finish the food as soon as possible so that he could turn to more important things. Even while he ate, the important things came to the forefront.

"I worked last night until midnight decorating and then had to be at work at nine again this morning. You'd think those bastards would at least give you a day off." He munched on bites of food between words. "I don't get a cent more for overtime. No union. Argue about it and lose your job. Happened to me at one place about a year ago." He put the fork down on his plate, divorced himself from eating so that he might have more freedom for his story.

"We got everybody together at this place to form a union. We even got to the point where we sat down over the table to talk terms to the boss. Well, right in the middle of the discussion one of the guys who had organized with us jumps up and calls a couple of us communists. 'Reds,' he said." Michael shifted back and forth, recalling the incident with a mixture of anger and delight. "Well, that does it. All you have to do is mention the name and immediately everybody stops thinking and starts hiding under their beds. The meeting broke up and those of us who had been the union organizers got fired." He picked up his fork, put it down, picked up the chop in his hand and bit into it vehemently. He reminded himself of an afterthought. "The guy who cried 'red', we found out later, was bought off by the boss. They formed a company union to satisfy some of the guys who were honest, but without any guts. Now their conditions are worse than they were before."

They finished eating. John helped with the dishes. They went into the living room. Michael flipped a switch on one wall, letting into the room a white light of low intensity, evenly distributed, coming from a slender shaft near the ceiling. "Fluorescent," Michael explained. "I put it in and I'll be damned sure to rip it out when I leave. If I leave it in, the landlord'll charge some poor sucker extra rent for it."

Michael went back to the kitchen and returned with two drinks, handed one to John. They sat on the studio couch, nestled into opposite corners. Michael surveyed his drink, tasted it and smiled. Then his thin, dark face grew serious, bringing with it the sharp deep lines along his mouth and across his forehead, wrinkling it into a perpetual frown. The white light sifted onto the top of the unruly shock of hair, casting a shadow that made the rest of his face almost disappear.

"I've been making a lot of small talk and boring you," Michael said. John started to protest, but Michael didn't let him. "I don't think you came here for just a visit, John. Why did you come?"

For a moment John wasn't sure. He thought he had come because he needed someone to talk to, to ask for opinion and for advice. He wasn't sure now that this was the right place.

"Just to talk," John said carefully.

"Not about me," Michael added quickly. "I know about you and Tony." He waited for an answer, then answered it himself. "It gets around, John. I guess that's why you came here, isn't it?"

John was embarrassed that his relationship with Tony was apparently so public. He resented it and his tone made it obvious.

"How do you know about Tony and me? What do you know?"

"I think you've got a problem. If it'll help you, I'm willing to talk with you about it."

The anger disappeared as suddenly as it had come and John felt better. The other's foresight and understanding gave him a respect for whatever opinion he might render.

"You're right," John said. "I came to talk about it and find out something."

Michael spoke with deliberation. "I don't think you came to me to take away loneliness. I think you're dissatisfied with much more. You've got guilt feelings about a lot of things, isn't that right?"

John nodded. Michael spoke again, only this time the words spurted out quickly, half apologetic, half in anger.

"I'm only a kid of twenty-one. Why in hell do you come to me for advice?"

John was stung by the unexpected rebuff and started to get up, to tell him he was sorry and that he would leave. Michael stopped him.

"I'm sorry," he said. "I only mean that I am young and my experiences are my own and they're limited. I can't pretend to be a philosopher or a psychiatrist, though I wish I were. I'm not sure I can give you any worthwhile help."

"You seem to have found some kind of place," John told him. "You seem to belong. I don't. I want to know how you did it."

Michael laughed. He forced it out because it was himself he was laughing at. "Don't let appearances fool you," Michael said. "I only try to imagine I belong. The whole world is cockeyed and I seem to have found a place that's a little less crazy than the rest of it. For me, for the moment."

"You know what you want. You talk like you do," John insisted. "I'm not really sure."

"Oh, I know what I want all right," Michael replied. "But I don't know how to get it. All I can do is try. I found out a lot of things. I found out that the world is twisted. I found that because your name isn't the same kind as the guy who signs the payroll, you can starve to death. For food. And nobody cares. I found that if you don't have the money to buy entertainment and perform the social graces, you starve to death. For love. I found that if you're part of the society that is chosen to provide and not receive, then you don't receive, even if you're bleeding to death right in the middle of Times Square. So again you starve to death. For security. And again nobody cares. Society stinks. I found that out. I tried to fight back. But where did it get me? Out in the street with empty pockets. I tried to find a girl, a woman, to be warm with, to get consideration from, to be secure with. But no dough, no woman, and I was back in the street again, frustrated. I tried to get help, a job, a handout, relief, anything. But it seems that in this lousy jungle a man makes his own way on his own and fights until he wins or until it kills him. I was fighting alone and I'm smart enough to see that one little guy with deuces can't beat the guy with a full house. So I got tired and I got afraid. I ran."

This experience was not new to John. He had thought about it many times, the kind of thing that had happened to Michael, and he understood that it had, in its own way, happened to him. But hearing another person say it made it clearer to understand.

"You either fight or you run away," John summed it up. He looked to Michael for confirmation.

Michael smiled. "There's one other choice, I guess. I didn't want to fight anymore, so first I ran away. Then I met Tony and his friends. They weren't hurting me and because they weren't I neither wanted to fight them nor run from them." He stopped, sipped some more of the drink, got up, put the glass on the desk, began to pace back and forth in front of John. "I thought I could make it with women. I did for a while. But it didn't seem to be enough, like I didn't really belong. The same with Tony and his friends. Yeah, it's fine. I'm accepted. But it seems like I quite don't belong there, either. So I don't know whether I don't belong in any world or in every world."

"I know," John agreed. "That's how I feel. That's why I want to get away until I know for sure where I belong."

Michael thought for a moment. "Maybe I'm not as happy as I want to be," he admitted, "but until the day I find something happier I'll stay where I am."

John sensed futility in his voice. He was sorry for Michael and by the same token felt sorry for himself because he was in the same position.

"It's like this," Michael was saying. "It's kind of like a third sex. Those of us who are not sure we can find a proper place in the conventional world, the so-called straight world, or in the unconventional world, the so-called queer world."

John listened.

Michael continued. "That's where the third sex thing comes in for some of us. It doesn't fight the other two. It has an entity of its own. Therefore, within itself it's normal. Because it isn't prejudiced toward the other two, maybe it's the only one that really is normal. Do I make sense?"

"I think I know what you mean," John replied. "I kind of feel the same way. But the way the rest of the world feels, well, the way most of the rest of the world feels, they make you feel abnormal. Feeling that way, thinking you're alone and separate from everyone else, trying to make a decision, you can't seem to concentrate on anything else. My writing, for example."

"That's because you've not fully accepted who you are. Once you do that—like Lennie Bernstein, if you want a for-instance—you can be as creative as fully as your talents will take you."

"So how do I get there?"

"If I knew," Michael laughed, "I wouldn't have the same problem. Maybe a new set of circumstances?"

"Get away?"

"Why not?"

"To where?"

"I don't know." Michael interjected a thought. "We're playing with words."

John agreed. He would have to decide. In his mind he kept repeating the question. "Get away to where?" There was no point in talking about it anymore.

Michael took the empty glass from his hand, went to the kitchen and returned with fresh drinks. He was smiling now, more friendly and much younger than he had been a few minutes before. "Take off your jacket and relax a while," he said. "Stay and see my etchings." The rising intonation of his voice ended in a short laugh.

John laughed, too. He threw his jacket across the couch and took the proffered drink. He did not want to return to the Barrow Street apartment. "I guess I will stay and see your etchings," he said. They both laughed.

The next day, early in the afternoon, John met Gino Aretti. It appeared as if by accident, meeting him unexpectedly in front of the writer's Central Park East apartment building. Actually, John had been waiting since mid-morning, seated on a bench in the park across the street. It was cold, the leaves of the trees beginning to grow weary of a half year's life and they shivered slowly to the ground, blue and red with the chill of upcoming winter. Few people were walking in the park. The grass, untrampled for the first time since early spring, seemed greener than ever and even the concrete walks were clean in their grayness.

John was chilled sitting there and he wrapped the edges of his trench coat over the exposed portions of his knees, hunched himself forward and passed the time by reading a newspaper. Every few seconds he looked up toward the apartment building, hoping to see Gino Aretti. He had checked with the doorman when he first arrived at ten o'clock in the morning and was told that the novelist was out, but "Mr. Aretti said that if anyone called for him, to say he would be back early in the afternoon and to call again."

So John waited. He had nothing else to do. He read through the newspaper, threw it away, bought another one, read that, and dropped that one, too, into one of the metal-weaved waste cans along the edge of the park. By two o'clock Gino had not yet returned. John tried to find a squirrel or a bird to watch. Most the birds, except for the hardy sparrows, appeared to have gone South, to warmth and comfort. They were smart, not just a handful of them going and leaving the rest to do the work and keep the home fires burning until spring brought them back home, but each member insisting on its share of what nature had meant for all of them. A few squirrels, timid and frightened, scurried from one tree to another, sometimes along the concrete paths to the occasional stranger-human who offered them a few peanuts or a crust of bread. Creatures of a harried and insecure existence, without the means of escaping the winter emptiness, saving their bits of salvation through the good days for the bleak ones to come. And then, when the sun was warm again and the stranger-humans brought food once more, starting the struggle all over again.

John looked up to see Gino turn the corner of 72$^{nd}$ Street and walk toward his apartment building, a new white structure some twenty stories high, each apartment with three paneled windows thrusting out over the avenue and with every set of windows an uncovered stone balcony. The windows were closed now and the wind, moving determinedly across the stone terraces, turned back in flurried beats from the tightly shut framed glass.

John rushed across Fifth Avenue. "Gino, Gino Aretti!" Gino stopped, looked at him closely, undecided for a moment whether he knew him or not.

"Oh, yes," he recalled as John reached him. "John Thomas. You are the writer." He was polite but, caught unawares, without enthusiasm. John was disappointed, felt that he was forcing an unwanted intrusion upon the man and thought he should simply say hello, exchange a few words and quickly leave. But he had waited so long and come this far and he decided he would go the rest of the way.

"I was taking a walk," John explained, "and I saw you." He stuttered for the right approach. "Thought that maybe

I could talk with you. Learn a few things about writing. As you suggested at Tony's party."

Aretti rubbed a large hand across the bare bald head, trying to recall the incident. He smiled. "Of course, of course." He motioned John to walk along the sidewalk with him. "Let us go up to my apartment. I have an appointment in a little while, but I should be happy to speak with you until then."

The elevator took them to the ninth floor and they entered a small but clean and well-furnished apartment. The furniture was of the Louis XIV style, contrasting with the trim, concise plan of the rooms themselves. The living room contained a long, gold-trimmed couch, a large full chair with the same trim, a marble-topped dresser bureau, a dark brown floor radio-music combination. "It came furnished," Aretti disclosed. "It is not exactly what I would put in an apartment myself, but it is comfortable."

John made himself at ease on the couch. "I won't take up much of your time," he said. "Just a few questions to ask you."

Aretti walked back and forth in front of the couch. He wasn't being rude. It was his way of showing that he understood the importance of John's visit.

"I do not think you came to discuss writing," he said. "I have studied people and written about them too intensely and too minutely not to be able to interpret the little things about them." He smiled to assure John that it was all right.

John was satisfied. It pleased him that Aretti guessed. As with Michael, he would be able to come to the point quickly. "You know what my relationship is to Tony, to the whole crowd," he began.

Aretti nodded for John to continue.

"I got away from Tony once and I felt I found a new, better life. I couldn't help myself and came back. Now I feel

I need to get away again." He paused a moment, suggesting the solution. "But I don't know where to go, what to do."

Gino interrupted before he could go any further. "And you want me to help you find the answer?" John nodded in agreement. Gino continued: "I know people and I study people and I can feel their intimate thoughts and reasoning and actions. I feel their smallest sensitivities. But I only write about them. I do not determine them. I am not so wise as to be a literary man and a man of science both, nor to pose as an all-seeing God. I am only a writer who experiences and interprets and reflects. I do not determine."

John remained silent. He had hoped for more than this, something concrete.

Gino noticed his sadness. "There is no easy answer, in any event," he continued. "There is no direct answer. All I might tell you is to follow what you feel within, follow your inner drives and understandings. As long as you hurt no one, including yourself, in the process, what more can one do?" He shrugged his shoulders.

John got up. "I understand," he smiled weakly. "I shouldn't have bothered you. Thank you, anyway." He was not angry. Only disappointed.

They shook hands at the door. "The very best of luck to you," Gino told him.

"Next time I'll come for literary criticism," John said. "I guess I appeared rather foolish today."

"You are honest," Gino replied. "A man is seldom foolish when he is honest with himself. That is why you must find your own way. The final resolution will be that much stronger. I am as sorry as you are that you came with high hopes and are leaving without a solution. Perhaps when I am a hundred years old I will have learned enough to cast a pebble into the sea and see and hear the ripple it makes. Now it is only a silent sound dropped into a whirlpool."

## Chapter 23

The beginning of the resolution of John's dilemma came the following day. Tony was away working with Gerald Stearns. John paced back and forth alone in the apartment. His determination that the time for decision had come was clear two days before. But neither Michael nor Gino had offered him a plan of action. It lay in his hands, waiting. He had to do something, he had to make a move. It nagged at him and he tried to shut it out. But it was not like the radio that he could turn off with the click of a switch. "Go and do, you've decided something must be done, go and do," his conscience screamed at him, and he screamed back, over and over again, "What? What? What?"

He was momentarily relieved when the phone rang. The operator told him it was person-to-person long distance and he wished he had not answered it.

"Johnny," Carol's voice greeted him. "John, darling, I had to call you. I had to know what was wrong."

He wanted to be angry and insist that everything was all right, but the words choked in his throat and a single one squeezed through in a whisper. "Nothing."

Her voice was calm. "You're upset and something is wrong. I want to help you."

"Nothing," he repeated.

He heard the hesitation of forced breathing at the other end of the wire. Carol tried to break through to him another way. "I called your number, but they told me it was disconnected. I thought you might have moved to Tony's, so that's why I called you there."

"I've been here a couple of weeks."

"You didn't tell me."

"It wasn't important." He spoke harshly, as though he didn't want to discuss it. The tone of his voice made it clear to Carol that somehow this was one of the things that was upsetting him.

"How come you moved to Tony's?" She tried to make it sound casual.

"I moved. I just moved, that's all." He wished there would be a reason for the conversation to end.

"You haven't been doing any writing, have you?" she asked.

He wondered how she knew. He was upset and pleased at the same time that she could know. He was truthful. "No, I haven't."

"What is it, Johnny? It's something important and yet it's something you can't tell me. I can tell from the way you talk, from some of your letters. You need me, Johnny."

He wanted to say yes. He wanted her to come immediately and comfort him and lead him and give him direction. But he knew that the direction and the leading had to be his. He would have to make up his own mind. The silence on the phone emphasized the importance of something being left unsaid. Carol waited.

"I'm coming to New York," she said.

John heard it twice. First the words and then, as it made an impression on his mind, a second time. He felt his stomach tighten in an effort to ward off panic. It took him as long to swallow the nervousness as it did for the realization to make sense. He tried to deepen his voice to make it seem steady.

"Don't come to New York, Carol." He tried to laugh, but it was little more than a choking sound. "There's no reason for you to come here. Everything will be all right. Don't come, Carol." He stopped, realizing he was protesting too much.

"I made up my mind even before I phoned," she answered.

"You don't have to come," he insisted.

"If I'm wrong, maybe I'll be sorry. But I don't think so. I think my place is with you. I'm flying in early Monday. To Idlewild. I'll take a taxi to Tony's. I'll see you there."

The connection broke for a moment and the operator announced that their three minutes were up before John could begin to protest again.

"I love you," Carol added quickly. "I'll see you Monday morning."

John felt a shiver over his body. He controlled it long enough to say "goodbye." He put the phone down, not hearing Carol's goodbye. He sat on the chair, a sweat oozing onto his face. He rubbed his hand over his forehead, but it came away dry. It was cold. He tried to think. The roads of indecision were coming to a crossing. He could not wait for a sign or a miracle. It was the moment for action. He went to the bar, took a glass and began to fill it with liquor. He put it back down immediately, stared at it uncertainly for a moment, left it and walked quickly to the bedroom. He took a small traveling bag from under the bed, opened a dresser drawer and filled the bag with some underclothes, socks, and

a shirt. He counted the money in his wallet. Forty dollars.
It was too late to go to the bank. He found twenty dollars of
Tony's money under the scarf on the dresser.

He contemplated the packed bag, felt the money in his
pocket. He was still uncertain. He walked back to the bar
in the living room, stood over the half-poured drink for a
moment, decided against it, walked to the piano, back to the
kitchen, to the couch, to the piano, and back again. There
was not enough room, not enough time, not enough freedom. The walls converged on him like the crossroads coming
together and exploded all about him, shutting him up in a
welter of indecision. He had to get out of there. That was the
first thing. After that, somehow, someplace, the next thing
would be done and the next and ultimately the final answer
would be found. It had to be.

He went back to the bedroom, grabbed the small black
bag, took his trench coat from the hall closet and hurriedly
closed the apartment door behind him. He went into the
street and walked at a fast step. Then he began to run. He
didn't know where, but he felt he had to get there quickly.

He walked along Sixth Avenue, keeping his head down,
mechanically watching the cracks in the sidewalk. He paid no
attention to the people passing, seeing only their shoes and
their legs, funny legs, feet that moved quickly, feet that shuf-
fled, feet that tipped upward, feet that turned in. A strange,
unaccountable conglomeration of feet and legs. It bothered
him that they probably knew where they were going. He
looked down at his feet. They didn't.

At Fourth Street individuals untangled themselves from
the mass as the crowd pushed up out of the subway station
and another crowd pushed down in. Without touching him,
their force moved him onto the stairway. He let himself be
carried along with the movement and went down the steps,
boarded a subway train going uptown. It was crowded and

he hustled himself against a side of the car, shifting with
each stop and with every exodus and influx of these five
o'clock migrants. He found refuge under a strap belt and
lost himself in the monotony of the ride, staring out of the
window at the dull, flashing yellow lights of the dark tunnel, not interesting himself in the multi-colored subway ads
lining the upper walls of the car. A lady rose up under him,
pushed by, and he struggled into her seat. He clutched the
small black bag on his lap. At 125th Street the train began
to empty and for the first time he paid attention to where it
was going. The direction placard read "Inwood-207th Street."
The upper tip of Manhattan just before the Bronx begins. He
noticed that he was on the "A" train. Without thinking, he
hummed the melody of the Duke Ellington song, "Take the
A Train," that he had played occasionally on Tony's hi-fi. It
was a get-up-and-go melody. Maybe he should turn around
and get up and go back to Tony's and play the record and
it would make him feel better? He instantly dismissed the
thought as inane wishful thinking. But where was he going,
instead? He didn't particularly care where. The train stopped
at several stations, lurched into another one. He glanced up.
The station sign announced "190th Street--Overlook Terrace."
The name interested him. It was the first thing that had
really interested him during the entire ride and impulsively
he grasped his travel bag, dashed out of the car just before the
doors slammed shut. He walked up to the street level, taking
the exit that pointed to Overlook Terrace and walked to 187th
Street where the apartment complex looked out over a myriad
of lights blinking on in the uncountable and unending lines
of apartment houses that spread below it. He seemed high
above the city. He started to walk toward where the sun had
almost set. An entrance to a park offered itself at his right
and he walked to it, passed between the two iron gates that
guarded it with the assistance of the white-coated man

selling ice cream from a little cart. The man tinkled his bell
with assurance, as if he didn't know it was already November.

It was a wooded park, the remaining green and increasing patches of brown blending into the grayness of the
shadow of evening. It was after six o'clock. Small groups of
stems, petal-less flowers, separated the thin strips of concrete
walk, and these in turn were surrounded on all sides and from
above by thick tree branches growing half-wild in an entan-
glement of vines and brown bark and autumn-colored leaves.

John followed the concrete strip downhill and was
surprised a moment later to see across the expanse of water
stretching in front of and below him the dimming skyline
of the Hudson River Palisades of New Jersey. It was the
same skyline, comparatively fresh and unspoiled, that he had
studied the first day he had come to New York while driving
with Carol in the taxi on Tenth Avenue. It was too dark to
see any specific landmarks. He could make out only darker
areas that must be trees and somewhat lighter small box-like
areas dotted with lights that must be gently-spaced houses.
They all blended into the darkening blue of the sky and in a
little while the differences in tone between them disappeared
entirely.

The river itself had grown just shadowy enough to begin
to glow with the reflected light from the buildings of River-
side Drive and to pick up an occasional sliver of light from an
overhanging street lamp on the shore.

The concrete and steel was in back of him now. All this
that he watched was the other side of that steep hill of ultra-
modern civilization, away from the city, toward the West,
into the peacefulness of the land. It seemed true that modern
civilization, as New Yorkers pictured it, ended at the Hudson
River.

He leaned against the scrambled pattern of rock that
served as a rail guard, looked down past the stretch of several

hundred yards of wildly growing bushes and flower brambles, all appreciably balding, and onto the white concrete highway of Henry Hudson Parkway where automobiles, at first in large number, then fewer and fewer, moved quickly by, most of them away from the city toward the residential pasture-lands of the crowded East, a few into the city, into the steel and stone carved mountains and valleys.

Some turned off about a mile to his left, away from the bright clean stripe of the highway onto the straight, almost toy-like structure of the George Washington Bridge.

John gripped his bag tighter and began walking toward the bridge. He followed the winding, uneven path. A young girl and boy passed him, the boy pulling his arm embarrass-ingly from around the girl's waist when John approached. He looked straight ahead, as if he hadn't noticed them. He heard a giggle from the girl after he had gone a few yards past them. He passed a bench on which an old man, baldheaded and bareheaded, lay stretched out. The clean-looking, expensive-looking dark brown suit crept up under the man, crumpling the pressed areas and flattening the creases. The man's feet stuck out over the edge of the bench, clad only in socks. A pair of highly polished brown shoes, the laces open, lay on the ground below his feet next to the bench.

He passed a man and woman walking, each with a small child reaching up to their hands, rushing to keep up with the big people's steps. A day-nurse wheeled a baby carriage by with unbridled speed, hurrying to get home in time for sup-per. Two men in overalls, their pants-knees and their hands covered with fresh black earth, walked by, gardener's tools propped against their shoulders, their talk about the weather in serious professional tones. Children playing tag, young men and women walking together arm in arm, hand in hand, old people making their way slowly with canes, and more young couples on the straight-backed iron benches, clutching tightly together, protecting each other from the outer world.

The darkness hurried on, not waiting for John, and the people became a panorama, like the lights of the city, moving into and out of his sight, melting more surely into the darkness. The lights and shining streams upon the water and the red and yellow and white advertising signs flashing on and off, stuttering from across the river, became more the immediate reality.

He reached the bridge. There was no hesitation, although he was conscious that he still had a choice. He could have walked back up to Broadway and taken a subway back to the city. He felt strangely free, although he still did not know where he was going as he walked along the small sidewalk at the right extremity of the bridge and looked into the placid quiet of the water below.

It was after seven o'clock when John reached the other side. He turned to the right as he came off the bridge, toward the north, and began to walk along the edge of the roadway. There was no doubt now that he was running away. He couldn't put it into any other terms and he didn't feel he had to. He felt that running away was part of what was necessary to find an answer. He couldn't find it at home, but he might find it somewhere else. If Carol had not decided to come to New York, he might have procrastinated a while longer. But one day he would have to make a move. Now that he had been forced to, he was glad. He tried not to think about Carol and what would happen when she arrived and found him gone.

He walked for a mile or two. He wasn't sure, losing count of the steps and minutes. The road was shiny new concrete, well travelled, but at this hour empty like the rural highways of the Midwest. But it was not lonesome. There was an air of simplicity and welcome about it. He

walked along the right side, pushing out his thumb to each
approaching car. One passed and then another and still
another. They whizzed by as though he did not exist. He
began to play at hitchhiking, bringing his thumb up from
the length of his arm, swinging it in a huge arc. He continued to walk, doing this with every passing car. Still no ride.
He got tired and stopped, decided to try standing still to see
if that brought better results. The signs on the road pointed
to Albany, Syracuse and Montreal. He didn't particularly care
which way he went. He thought about the possibilities as he
stood there watching the cars drive heedlessly by. The idea
of going to Canada intrigued him. The more he waited, the
more he thought about it, and finally decided that this would
be his destination. It made him feel better having an immediate goal. Perhaps the atmosphere, the change in environment,
the mental adventure of a different country would help to
stimulate him and facilitate his thinking toward an answer.

He was lost in this thought and jumped at the screech
of wheels, realizing that he automatically had his thumb in
the air. He ran toward the new Cadillac that stopped some
twenty feet in front of him. A small man with a moon face,
his bald head making it even rounder and smoother, rolled
down the car window.

"Where you going?" His voice was short and deep. It was
not even a question. It was a demand.

"North."

The man opened the car door, withdrew a chubby hand.
It was smooth, like his face. No hair, not even a freckle. He
would seem incomplete except for the large brown cigar
puffing in his mouth. It stood out, the redness of the lighted
end pointing the way he was going. "Hop in," he told John.
The demand now sounded like a command. John jumped in,
pulled the door tight, barely feeling it shut as the car lurched
forward.

"Where're you going?" the man asked, as if he were dissatisfied with the first answer to the question. "Looking for work?" He held the last word on the tip of his tongue, let it fall down to John as though he were tossing him the syllable out of the kindness of his heart. Immediately, John knew he didn't like the man; it annoyed him to be talked down to.

"Just travelling," John told him as confidently and sharply as he could, trying to keep his pretense of self-determination.

"Nothing for you in the city, huh?" The man puffed a long bead of smoke from the cigar, let it dash from his mouth out of the half-opened window next to him as though it were in a hurry to get away. "Too bad. Lotsa opportunities in New York. Too bad." The words came out gruffly, sparingly.

John didn't answer. His discomfort grew and he hoped the man would have to turn off the road soon. He would not even mind standing at the edge of the road again, exercising his thumb.

"My name is Howard. Ray Howard," the man let him know. "Heard of Howard Associates Manufacturing? No, I guess you didn't. That's mine. One of the biggest clothing firms in New York. Where are you travelling to?" He asked the question again, annoyed that he hadn't been answered properly before. He was a man in a hurry with no time to waste. John half expected Howard to offer the information that "time means money."

John answered him this time. "To Canada." He tried to sound definite. But he didn't. Howard caught the uncertainty.

"You're not sure, huh? Got any money?"

John didn't know how to answer. The question was too strange. He couldn't decide whether the man, after all, was going to offer him some money or was simply seeking some kind of personal satisfaction. He found out a second later.

"Too many young men running all over the country now-adays trying to get away, without resources, without money, without a job. Cluttering up cities and towns and highways." He smiled, satisfied that this hitchhiker had reinforced his personal superiority.

"I have money," John protested hastily. "Enough to travel. I've got no ulterior motives. As soon as I see Canada, I'll head back to New York." His voice was angry. It surprised the little fat man.

"Well, you do look like a clean-cut boy," he offered.

John hoped the other man would be satisfied. He wanted to sit in quiet and watch the dark clumps of houses and trees along the highway and the bright eye-lamps of the oncoming cars and the silver streaks their reflections made along the highway when one car has dashed past and the one up ahead could only be seen by the faint gleam of far-off headlights.

The Cadillac moved forward smoothly, effortlessly. It could have been going forty miles an hour or a hundred. Up ahead, on the road, John caught the tiny unblinking eyes of some animal. A cat or a squirrel or rabbit. It was too dark to tell which. The animal stood directly in the path of the oncoming car, the round slots of its eyes staring ahead, frozen, the animal frightened into inaction by the bright headlights of the Cadillac. The car moved closer and closer, but the animal remained still. John glanced at the fat man driving. He apparently saw the animal, but his foot remained steady on the gas pedal and the car pushed unwaveringly ahead. Desperately, automatically, John pressed his foot against the floorboards, reaching for a brake that wasn't there. He wanted to say something, to tell the man to stop. There wasn't time for words. His stomach began to squirm and he tried to steady himself, preparing for the sickening sound of the bumper hitting and the wheel squashing. The seconds seemed long and divided into black portions of inevitability as he waited.

Suddenly the eyes of the animal blinked, almost under the hood of the car, and in the backwash of the headlights John saw the bushy tail of a squirrel scampering off the road.

The fat man didn't move, neither following John's gaze out of the side window nor shifting the tenseness of his weight into relaxation, as John did. He puffed deeply on the cigar and the smoke whipped out from his lips, rushing toward the open window again, only this time, it seemed, even more anxious to get away.

"What's your name?" Howard asked.

"John Thomas."

"Two first names," he smiled, for the first time obviously satisfied. "That's good. Two first names. Gives you that much jump on being first over the other guy. I've got two first names. Ray Howard. See!" The smile passed as quickly as it had come and he pressed the edge of the cigar against the rim of the opened window pane, the passing wind catching the ash and flicking it into infinite particles through the air. "What do you do for a living when you do work?"

John resented the impugnation of his not working. He had never thought of it before as important. Coming from this man it seemed to be an indignity. He didn't want to tell him he was a writer. He felt that this, to Howard, would be even worse than being unemployed. He was sure Howard felt that way about writers or actors and painters and musicians and any artist. "I'm not doing anything now," John said. "I worked in advertising in New York," he lied.

"Good field," Howard advised him. "Lots of money. Honest field." He dragged on the cigar again. "Get fired from your job?"

"I left to travel," John answered just as pointedly. His frustration was obvious.

Howard smiled again, the round face turning its mouth up at both corners, then twitching slightly as the mouth went back into place. "Ought to keep good jobs. Particularly in advertising. Good money. That's the only thing worthwhile in this life. Believe me." He was certain. There was no room for questioning. "I had my times when I was young," he continued. "Jobs, travelling, running off to find something. Well, I found it. Money. Security. I feel sorry for some of these down-and-outers," he confided, "looking for a light out in the darkness." He paused to let the simile take effect. It was a literary masterpiece for him and he relished any occasional bright word he could find. "Well, they ought to stop floundering in the darkness and get themselves into a good solid business. I know."

The man waited and John nodded. "Yes." He knew the sermon had been meant for him. Little enough payment for the ride, he decided. They rode for about an hour more. Howard told him that he was driving to Tonawanda, his home, "a beautiful place that takes you away from all the rabble of New York." From there John could continue on Route 9, up through Albany and then to Canada, "either west to Toronto or east to Montreal," or he could, Howard told him, if he were smart, "take the next train back to New York and get yourself a good honest job again."

"A good goal does it," Howard said. "Work hard and you will get to the point where you can have a home in the country and a new Cadillac and won't have to be part of the rabble back there." He repeated the word "rabble" several times while talking. He liked to use it with a degrading tone of voice.

The town of Tonawanda, as they drove through, was one long street of brick and stone houses, some with long garden paths in front, set deep away from the road. Others had circular car paths in front, with low, clean lawns stretching far toward the back of the house. They were all rich-looking.

Howard stopped the car at the railroad station. He leaned over to make sure the door was closed as John got out. "If you don't take the train, better be careful," he advised. For a moment it seemed as if the warning were a kindness. "They don't like vagrants"—he stopped, held the emphasis on the last word, then continued, amending it as though the speech had been unbroken—"traveling through this town." He slammed the door, pressed down on the accelerator and pulled away at the same instant.

John watched the car speed away and wondered about the things Howard had said and how it must be to live in a great house in Tonawanda and drive a new Cadillac. Then he remembered the complete indifference of the man toward the possible life or death of the animal on the highway. He quickly turned away.

John went down the main street of the city, looking toward the windows of the homes, catching glimpses of the people inside. He half expected to see them all looking like Ray Howard. He was pleased that they didn't. He found the highway again and continued walking north. It was late, after ten o'clock, and no cars were chancing to stop. After an hour John realized that he would get no further rides that night and began thinking about a place to sleep. He was hungry, too. A sign on the road read "Rest Side Cabins – 1 mile." He walked in the direction of the arrow.

The Rest Side Cabins consisted of a small trolley-car diner a few feet off the edge of the road and a number of small bungalows further back of it. A brightly lit sign on the diner announced to oncoming motorists that there were "vacancies." A small thin man with scraggly hair and an unshaven face to match took six dollars from John and gave him a key for one of the cabins. "You're sure you're alone now?" was all the man asked. "I don't ask no questions here and so you don't need to protect nothin' on that account. If you're alone it's six dollars. If ya ain't it's eight."

John tried the bed, found that he didn't care if it were soft or not, and almost fell asleep as he lay there. He forced himself up, went to the diner and sat silently by himself at the end of the counter as he ate, paying only occasional attention to the truck driver at the other end who continued a steady stream of conversational suggestions to the blonde waitress who parried his remarks without subtlety. He went back to the cabin, fought with the dials of the bathroom shower, trying to keep a steady flow of water as he bathed. He was more amused than annoyed as the mechanical contrivance got the better of him. When he was finished he stretched out under the bed covers. He was thankful that they were clean. He tried to force the quick blackness of sleep, but his mind wandered over the many things he felt he should think about—what must he look for now and how specifically this running away would help him. He knew only that he had to move and seek and that only in that way, somehow, would he find the answer. He buried his face in the pillow, tossed the pillow aside, then took it back again. It was pitch dark and the whirr of the heavy trucks along the highway gave the room its only contact with the outside world. He listened to the sounds of the highway. Then he slept. It was not a peaceful sleep. It was a tired one.

John was up early the next morning. He ate breakfast in the diner. The blonde waitress was gone. A sleepy-eyed, dull-looking brunette had taken her place. He ate quickly and mechanically, in the same manner as the waitress served him the food.

It was eight o'clock, the sun round and bright, slanting the shadows of the trees against him when he got back on the highway. He felt fresh with the newborn day. He stopped

under the large oval sign designating the route, "U.S. 9."
With the mien of an experienced hitchhiker he smiled, thinking of himself as an expert on the road. He reasoned that a
car would slow up a bit to read the sign and, having lessened
speed, be more likely to stop. He was right. Almost immediately he got a ride.

A small red convertible, well polished and shining,
stopped for him. Without a word the young man behind
the wheel motioned for John to step in, waited until he was
securely seated, and started off.

"I slowed up to see the sign and decided it was awfully
lonely driving by myself. It's nice to have company." The
young man's voice was gentle and soft. It had almost a
feminine quality. He was about John's age, thin, and judging from the slouched position over the wheel, fairly tall.
His hands grasped the steering wheel lightly, guiding it over
the small bumps and turns in the road tenderly. "It must be
lonely to hitchhike," he suggested pleasantly.

"It is," John admitted. "Thank you for the ride."

"Travelling alone is like living alone," the young man said.
"It's terrible to live alone." He said it matter-of-factly, letting
his eyes leave the road for a second to look directly at John.

It was a look John knew and although he had never met
the young man before, he might well have. He wanted to
laugh at the incongruity of his position, but yet he understood the young man and, understanding, remained silent.
He offered only his name.

The other looked at him again for a fleeting instant and
then back to the road. "John Thomas," he repeated the name.
"My name is Terry Green. Going any place in particular?"

"Just travelling," John answered. "I'd like to visit
Canada."

"Good," Terry said. "I'm going as far as Syracuse. From
there you should get an easy ride to Canada. Across near

Kingston, by the Thousand Islands." He paused, considered
the words. "They're beautiful. The Thousand Islands. Wonderful to be lost on for a while . . . with someone you'd like to
have with you." He didn't look at John this time, didn't wait
for a reaction, simply satisfied that he had made another suggestion. "Are you coming from Tonawanda?" Terry asked.

"I spent the night near there."

"Alone?" There was a trace of eagerness in the voice.

"Alone," John answered very quietly and very definitely.

They came to a crossroad and the red convertible turned
onto a highway marked "U.S. 11." A sign told them that it
was 149 miles to Binghamton. "After Binghamton, it's about
seventy-five to Syracuse," Terry Green said.

It took two-and-a-half-hours to Binghamton. They drove
rapidly, the speedometer often reaching well over seventy,
rarely below fifty. John said little, mentioning only that he
was a writer and that he was travelling for some experience
for his writing. Terry did most of the talking, telling about
himself. He was a college student, attending Columbia University in New York City. His parents lived in Syracuse and
he was driving home for the weekend. He emphasized the
difficulty.

"It's pretty much hell every time I go home. But I spent
practically all of the summer in New England and I suppose I
ought to visit Mother and Father sometime. Anyway, it's a short
weekend, just today and tomorrow, and I'll be back in New
York Monday. And I won't have to see them again for a while."

They stopped at a restaurant in Binghamton. "Do you
mind if we take some food on the drive? I have a tentative
appointment in Syracuse early this afternoon and I'd rather
not be late." It was all right with John. Terry went in, came
back with hamburgers and two containers of coffee. He
refused to accept John's share of the cost. "You'll do something for me sometime," he said without emphasis.

Terry talked more as they drove, shifting between keeping the steering wheel on an even plane and munching on his
sandwich. He spoke of man's search for happiness, referring
to himself in the third person, an impersonal referent. He
spoke of the intense loneliness one finds when rejected by
one's parents, when one's needs and wants are not understood.
He was impressed, he said, by the struggle of so many others
in the same situation who went outside of parental authority
and other forms of so-called normalcy for their existence. He
was convinced that the need was basic and that it must find
its solution in a basic drive, sex. Terry spoke cautiously, not
too overtly committing himself, but still with the tentative
suggestiveness of a few hours before. He watched John for an
occasional response, but he got none.

They had almost reached Syracuse when Terry began to
slow down, to enable him to turn partly toward John and
drive at the same time.

"Do you have any plans in Canada?"

"None," John answered.

"This appointment I have isn't important," Terry offered.
"If I could drive up with you to Canada, we could have a nice
weekend together." He flipped the words, trying to make
them seem casual and at the same time extremely important.

John did not have to think twice for an answer. "I'm
going to Canada alone, Terry." He said it as kindly as he
could. "I prefer it that way."

"I have the money, if that's what you're worried about."
Terry knew the words were being wasted, but he gave it a last
try. "We could have a real good time."

John smiled knowingly. "I understand. But I'm afraid the
answer has got to be no." He added, not to seem ungrateful:
"I do appreciate the ride . . . and the offer."

They drove silently the rest of the way to Syracuse. It
was a little after one o'clock in the afternoon when they got

there. They skirted the center of town, the business section. Through the connecting streets John could glimpse the hustle and bustle of a city, the people moving quickly and seemingly without direction as they did in New York. But this city, John thought, is probably more like Des Moines than New York. He mentioned it to Terry.

"Maybe all easterners feel they've got to run to see who can be the first one to successfully acquire an ulcer?" Terry commented.

The part of town they drove through was wide and clean with well-kept private houses and modern apartment buildings. Terry drove all the way through the city and onto Highway 11 at the northern end. He turned off the motor as John prepared to leave the car.

"I'll still drive you to Canada for the weekend if you wish." His tone was not insistent.

"Thanks. Again, I appreciate the ride and offer, but it's no go."

Terry shrugged and laughed. "I ought to apologize. I guess I really knew from the beginning that you weren't the type. But you seemed like such an understanding person that I tried anyway. I figure it didn't hurt, did it?"

"No."

"You're a writer. You can always use this in a book."

"Maybe I will!" John smiled back.

Terry started the motor. "Sometimes you can tell about people." He shrugged again, only this time sadly. "I guess I should have known from the beginning." He pushed the gear shift into low. "Good luck," he said.

"Good luck to you. And thanks." John waved as the car sped away. He stood for a moment looking after the car, wondering how long this boy would be able to keep running, driving through life in a red convertible, looking for someone to make the trip a little less lonely. He felt sorry for the young man. He didn't want to feel sorry for himself for the same reason.

He started along the highway again, walking with the traffic, pointing north. A signpost let him know it was seventy miles to Watertown, the next largest city. The word "Canada" was on the same sign, but no mileage was given. He walked.

It was a tiring walk. He sat down several times along the side of the road to rest. He looked at his watch for the first time at two o'clock. Then he looked more frequently, at two-thirty, at two-forty-five, at two-fifty. He alternated walking and resting. At a quarter-after-three he got another ride. The car, a big black Oldsmobile, sped past him, screeched to a stop, then zig-zagged in reverse along the highway back to him.

One girl sat in the front seat, driving. Another sat alone in the back. "Hop in, handsome!" The rear door swung open. John got in and the tires squealed as the car sped away. Both girls were short and chubby, the one in the front perhaps a little less so than the one in the back. They looked alike. Not with the precise similarity of twins, but enough alike to be sisters. Both were dark-haired, cut close, almost in a furry fuzz. Their features were well defined, a bit too sharp with long chins, full cheeks and deep set eyes. They were young, probably no more than nineteen or twenty, but their faces were old, deep circles under their eyes and hard lines streaming down their cheeks.

"Have a beer." The girl in the back seat next to John reached into a box on the floor, withdrew a beer bottle, uncapped it and handed it to him. White foam drizzled down the side. "Come on," she urged. "It's good for you." John took it.

"My name is Janice," the girl said. "That's Wanda up front." She waited for Wanda's "hello," then continued. She spoke in a clipped, fast tongue, the tone high. The girl in front remained, for the most part, quiet. When she did speak, Janice quickly stopped in deference, either to age or leadership or both.

"We're two lonely girls," Janice explained, "driving in our little car papa gave us for our birthday two years ago, only papa is supposed to get us a new one this year. We live in Syracuse and we hate mama and papa, only papa less because he has money, and we hate home because it's so smug and proper, and we hate Syracuse because there's no excitement there. But we love men and you're a man so we picked you up to ride with us." She smiled with a coquettishness that was painful, drank from her beer bottle and moved closer to John. "Now, how about you?"

John was embarrassed for them and would have remained silent if it wouldn't have made the situation even more uncomfortable. He decided to pass it off as lightly as he could.

"I'm a bum, hitchhiking through the country. I have no papa and no car and I'm never bored and because you're both such pretty girls I accepted your invitation for a ride." The words surprised him. Apparently it was the right thing to say, even too much so. Janice snuggled up to him, pushing him against the side of the car.

"Hey, Wan," she called to the front seat. "Did you hear that? Just the man for me. I like him." She turned to John. "I like you."

"Well, just don't be too eager about it," Wanda called back. Her voice was like her sister's, only just a bit lower and somewhat steadier. "He's only one and there are two of us."

"Aw, Wan . . ."

"What am I supposed to do? Just drive and watch?"

"Aw . . ."

John was grateful for Wanda's protest. Janice moved away from him sulkily and drank her beer. He sat back against the seat cushions, on his guard for a while, watching the girl, then he relaxed and drank the beer. They rode several miles before Janice broke the silence.

"Hey, Wan," she called, as if she had just come to an important discovery. "I can have him now and then when he can get it up again you can have him."

John almost dropped the bottle of beer. He had thought that the dialogue before was more bluff than bargain. Now he realized that the girl was serious. She nuzzled to him again, breathing heavily. She seemed about to throw herself bodily on top of him, waiting only for her sister's approval. John was frightened. At the same time he was amused, and now that he understood them more clearly, interested in seeing what they would actually try to do. Wanda thought for several moments as the car continued to speed down the highway.

"That's no fun," she decided. "We ought to have two of them. I'll think about it."

Janice frowned, was about to move away once more, then smiled and snuggled closer. She proverbalized about "the bird in the hand." She rested her fingers on John's leg, moved them artlessly up toward his crotch. He picked up her hand, deliberately returned it to her own lap.

"What's the matter. Am I so ugly?"

"No."

"You're a man, aren't you?"

John didn't answer. He smiled and nodded his head.

"Well, that's all that matters, doesn't it? I'm not charging you anything." She reached for John's hand, placed it high up on her thigh, smiled in anticipation of his approval. He let his hand stay, feeling the softness of flesh, warm and at the same time beginning to shiver under his touch. The idea began to appeal to him and he looked first at Janice, then at Wanda, and wondered whether he shouldn't take advantage of their proposition after all. A demonstration of heterosexual manhood was good for his confidence, he rationalized. He felt a sense of urgency and tingling inside. It was not a familiar feeling, but nevertheless a reminiscent one. But it was becoming unpleasant. It made him feel choked, as if he were beginning to feel like throwing up. He remembered it now: the apartment in Brooklyn with big-breasted, hard-hipped Helen lying on the living room couch waiting for him. Janice's breath panted in his face and he breathed a venereal fear. He pulled his hand away.

"Whatsamatta?" Janice's shrill scream sounded like Helen's. John tried to think quickly.

"Maybe your sister's right?" he offered. "It wouldn't be fair to one of you."

"What do you care?"

"I do. You're both such lovely girls." He kept the sarcasm out of his voice.

Janice picked up the thought seriously and mulled it over. She couldn't accept it. "What's the use of having a man around if he's not going to be used?" she reasoned.

Wanda studied John through the rear-view mirror, glanced around several times to look at him. She half-agreed with her sister. "It might work," she mused. Then, after a few seconds: "Who's first?"

"Me!" Janice fairly shouted in her enthusiasm. "You were first last time. Find a side road and we can park."

John began to decide whether to tell them to stop the car and let him out at that point or to wait a little while longer and see if he could still dissuade them. There was no question about whether he might accommodate them. "Sluts," he thought to himself.

He had no opportunity for decision. A Cadillac, yellow and bright, whizzed by, crowding the girls' car to one side of the road. The Cadillac set a course directly in front of the Oldsmobile, then slowed down, keeping just far enough

ahead so that the Oldsmobile could not pass. John could see
two men in the Cadillac, the face of the driver squared off in
the rear-view mirror, looking back, and the other man, his
head turned to the back window, watching.

"Let's pass them," Wanda said. She pressed on the accelerator, but as their car increased speed, the Cadillac did also.
Wanda pressed harder and the Oldsmobile swerved onto the
left lane, pulled up almost even with the other car. For several
seconds the two cars were side by side. The driver of the
Cadillac, a big man of some thirty-five years, leaned toward
the window.

"Hiya, beautiful women," he cried across the gap
between the two automobiles. "It's too bad you have a
friend." He smiled and the other man waved. Their car
lurched forward and moved ahead. The Oldsmobile moved
back into the lane behind them and picked up speed to stay
in sight.

"Wanda!" Janice called to her sister. It was a squeal of
desperation. Wanda slammed on the brakes and their car
stopped. She turned around to John. "We're sorry."

"That's all right," John answered. He picked up his small
bag and quickly got out, slamming the door behind him.
"Maybe next time."

The gears screeched as Wanda shifted hurriedly into first.
"If we hurry we can catch them," she said. John heard another
squeal from the back seat as the car pulled away. He smiled,
then laughed and continued to laugh even after the car had
disappeared far down the highway over a rise in the road.

He looked at this watch. Four-thirty. He took out a cigarette and lit it, then walked over to a large rock off the side of
the road and sat down. He was exhausted.

His next ride, less than half an hour later, was with a soldier who was going straight into Kingston in Canada. He was

a young man who, in self-explanation, was tired of fighting for a living in the business world and had rejoined the Army.

"My family lived in Clayton, just over the river on the American side. That's why I'm in the U.S. Army even though my parents live in Kingston now."

He was a quiet man, almost shy, and drove carefully and slowly, talking only occasionally and asking John nothing about himself. John was grateful after the thus-far hectic experiences of the day for the comparative solitude. He was content to stare out of the car window and watch the countryside.

The young soldier, in one of his infrequent conversations, was apologetic about the Army. "After the war, when I was discharged, I tried all over to get a job. But I had gone in when I was 18 and had no training in anything but digging foxholes." He laughed lightly, not wanting to presume that he had made an important joke. "It got cold in winter and hungry all year round, so I went back into the service. I got a car out of it anyway, with my savings. Gets me up to Kingston to see the folks some weekends. I'm at Fort Dix now. New Jersey."

They drove along, John accepting a cigarette, smoking peacefully. After a while the soldier found it necessary to talk again, still in the half-apologetic tone. "Anyway," he said, "now I get free meals and a place to sleep and clothes and some money and in twenty years I can retire with a little income. No responsibilities, nice and secure. So much security, I don't even have to think for myself." He paused a moment, squeezed the tip of the cigarette butt between his fingers. "I don't like the Army," he said.

They stopped in Watertown, got something to eat in a small cafeteria in the center of town. It was a small, quiet city and even though it was just six o'clock when they got there, presumably the end of the working day, there were few cars and, it seemed, even fewer pedestrians. They ate casually and it was almost seven o'clock and dark when they got back on the road.

It was pitch black when they arrived at the ferry in the little town of Cape Vincent at the edge of the St. Lawrence River. Cape Vincent existed for little more than the ferry. Small wooden houses lined the main street and as John glanced up the cross-blocks that they passed he caught the reflection of the house lights from larger and more modern structures fanning out from the center of the city. The main street looked like all the pictures of small town main streets in all the magazines. A few people, most of them in sleek rain-type overcoats, walked along the sidewalks.

They stopped before the ferry for customs inspection, signed a few papers, told the inspector their ages, birthplaces, citizenship, purpose, and stated that they were carrying no goods to be sold. The inspector glanced hurriedly through the car, the trunk, satisfied that there was no taxable material, and they were on their way again. It was all simple, taking but a few minutes.

The ferry was small, much like the junior size steam-powered wooden boats that plied the waters between New York City and Staten Island, except that this ferry was more open and flatter, with the automobiles taking up the greatest space and the passengers being left to their own devices, most of them simply leaning up against the thick wooden railings. John was sorry that they had arrived there so late. To his right, to the east, he could see faint outlines of islands, the Thousand Islands that filled books and stories as the romantic idylls of the St. Lawrence River. Even in the dark he felt good in their presence. They were individualities and at the same time an integral part of each and every likeness surrounding them. The soldier explained that this was a shortcut to Canada.

"There's the Thousand Islands Bridge, which most people take for the ride and the scenery. But it's about thirty miles more up the road. I like to do it the easy way."

After a few minutes the ferry stopped and the cars rolled off. "Wolfe Island," the soldier explained. "It's right in the center of the river, between the United States and Canada. Right where the St. Lawrence flows into Lake Ontario." To the left, the distance of water disappeared into an endless blackness. Here and there flashes of light from a boat or a shore house or automobile passing along the road skirting the bank reflected a patch of silvery-blue.

"The Island was named after General Wolfe," the soldier continued as though he were lecturing a pupil. "From the French and Indian War, if you remember your history. Wolfe sailed up the St. Lawrence to take Quebec from French General Montcalm. We have to drive across it to get the ferry on the other side."

John nodded. It was a lovely island, dark now, but the overhanging deep forest at the sides of the clean white road was a nighttime reminder of what must be green lush nature in the daytime. The car moved slowly, the soldier purposely taking the time to allow John to feel the combined simplicity and fullness of the island, even though it was too dark to see it.

There was no hurry. They waited a half-hour at the other ferry gate. It was only a few minutes after the ferry came and took them that their car clumped over the thick boards separating the ferry slip from the dock and they were in Kingston. The car turned up a steep hill, negotiated it with the aid of a quick shift into second gear when they were halfway up. The section was a shabby one, apparently the oldest industrial part of Kingston. There were a few factories, nondescript as to purpose and product, and a number of shack-like houses set in rows where, obviously, the lower paid factory laborers found it necessary to live.

They turned right at the top of the hill and started down
the main street. It was the average street of the average small
town, not too small, not too large, lined with stores of every
description, some new, some old.

John was a little disappointed. "This looks like any town
in America. I thought somehow that Canada would be different."

"I didn't know this was your first time in Canada,"
the soldier said. "I would have explained that to you." He
laughed slightly.

"I was raised in Cleveland," John told him, "but never
got farther north than Buffalo."

"I guess every town, everyplace, is really just like any
other when you get right down to it," the soldier said. He let
John out in front of a corner beer parlor. "I don't know if you
drink," the soldier said, "but they'll at least be able to tell
you where to find a hotel. I haven't been in town enough to
know."

It was too late to travel any farther that day. John decided
he might as well spend the night in Kingston. After all, it
was Canada. He thanked the soldier for the ride.

"Good luck in the Army."

The answer was a grateful smile. "Thanks." He sounded
sad. He waved to John as the car drove away.

John picked up the small bag and went into the saloon.
It was any saloon in any small town. The bar itself was a
long wood-topped structure down the right-hand side of the
already too narrow room. Several tables jutted from the left
side of the room, crowding the space between the bar and the
tables into a minimum. John rubbed past several men and
women who sat at the bar, found an empty stool, ordered a
beer. He had hardly touched the glass when a dark-haired,
plump woman in her early thirties moved from the far end
of the bar and pushed onto the high stool next to him. As

she planted herself on the seat, her brown tweed suit bulged desperately in the places a woman tries not to bulge, her body begging to be allowed to relax. John looked away even as he noticed.

"New here, aren't you?" Her accent was unlike the sharp slur of the New York saloon. The words were spoken neatly, with the faint trace of a French nasal twang the only incongruity in the otherwise precise speech. John looked at her, looked back to his beer without nodding.

"My name is Annette," she said. She twisted a strand of hair brushing the back of her neck, pushed it into the shiny black knot there. "You look lonely. Perhaps you would care for a friend?"

"I'm not lonely." John was curt.

She took the impoliteness politely. "I don't mean to bother you," she said softly. "We don't have to be friends, just acquaintances. Do you care to just talk?"

John was embarrassed by her gentle response. His answer to her question was no, but this time he smiled and tried to also say it gently.

"I am what you think I am," she explained, without ado, "but you don't have to be afraid of me. I'm not going to hurt you."

"I'm not afraid," John told her.

"Of course not," she continued, as if she hadn't doubted it. "I noticed you when you came in. You looked kind and soft and your eyes were sad in a different way from most of the others that come in here. That's why I wanted to talk to you. I'm sad, too."

John looked past her, then seriously at her. He believed her and he felt pity for her. Only it was not the pity of superiority. It was the same kind of melancholy he felt for himself.

"Come on, let's sit down at a table," she said. He hesitated a moment, then followed her. He felt at ease then and

smiled at her, waiting until she smiled back. It made him feel
good to see her smile. It was like a reflection of himself.

"I'll buy you a drink," he said.

"Bourbon," she ordered.

He let her talk. He half wanted to talk, too, but she
had suggested it first and he let her go on. He discounted
her story the moment it began. It was the story of her life.
A sob story, an easy touch, he told himself. But as she spoke
he watched her eyes and they still reflected the sadness of his
own and her voice was still honest and without pretense and
he gradually believed her.

She had been born in Quebec, she said. This explained
her French accent, she told him. In the early 1930s when the
Great Depression hit the Americas, her family moved to
England. "When they were killed in an air raid during the
war, I was still a teen-ager. I was left on the street without
a penny. I wanted to get away from England desperately. I
wanted to come back to Canada and try to forget. So I did
what so many other girls did. They had to live, too."

She drank the bourbon and watched John's face. It didn't
change. He neither winced nor smiled. He accepted her words.

"It was hard the first time," she said. "I wanted to die.
I honestly wanted to die. I stayed in the bathtub for hours
trying to get clean and it seemed that the dirt wouldn't wash
off. I wanted to lie down in the water and let it swallow me.
I wanted to disappear so that only the dirty ring around the
bathtub would be left and they could put it into a casket and
bury it because it would be the same as me. Only I didn't
have the nerve. I cried all night."

"After that I didn't hate myself anymore," she continued.
"Only the men. After that it didn't mean anything. Even the
ring around the bathtub disappeared. After that it was easy."

John waited until he was sure she was finished.

"When you got here, why didn't you get a regular job?"

"I got to Quebec. I lived with an aunt and uncle. Only they wouldn't let me live. It took time to find a job and they wouldn't stop nagging me, so I ran from Quebec and just knocked around. I swore I was through with this. But I got hungry again. I wound up here a couple of years ago."

"You didn't answer my question."

John was feeling warm and lightheaded on the beer now, mixing the thick dark stout with the thin regular beer, giving it a strong kick.

"Why didn't I?" Annette pondered a moment. "No guts, I guess. I got lost and didn't have the guts to fight back for what I knew I really wanted. I didn't think I was strong enough so I took the easy way out. I ran away."

"And you can't go back now?" John asked.

"I don't know. I guess I could. But it's become so easy this way. I just try not to think about it anymore."

"I guess you've got to do quickly whatever it is you got to do, so you don't have time to think too much about it," John muttered. He felt hot now from the strong beer. He had drunk too much too quickly. "I guess you've got to have the guts to do it quick or you're damned."

Annette didn't quite understand what he meant. But she patted his hand anyway. "You're right," she assured him.

John heard his voice rise and he repeated the words. He couldn't control his voice and somehow he didn't care. It went all out of proportion and his words floated and his head floated and the voice dashed away from him and belonged to the world that now spun hazily around him.

"You've got to do it before you're damned." The voice was strong and sure and even though it was no longer part of him it made him smile.

A chair scraped at the next table and a small bent man weaved unsteadily to their table and placed his hand on John's shoulder to keep his balance.

"We are damned," he said, his voice hoarse and cracking from the combination of too much liquor and too much age. He was a thin man with a scraggly white mustache, sparse white hair and white tufts of whisker beginning to show on an unshaven face.

"Hello, Carter," Annette said. She didn't seem pleased by the interruption, but the greeting was cordial. "He's one of the real old timers around here," she explained to John.

The old man shrugged a chair out from the table and sat down. He reached across unsteadily to his table, plucked a bottle of beer from it and plunked it down quickly in front of him. His face cracked into wrinkles and he smiled at his success in transferring the precious burden.

"We are the damned," he whispered confidentially. His unsteady voice was certain of this pronouncement as if this, if nothing else in the world, it was sure of. He leaned toward John.

"That's right, sonny boy," he said, now much louder, "we're damned. Everybody's got some piece of heaven. Everybody except us."

John nodded in agreement and the old man drank from the beer bottle, fortifying his words. They were serious words. They were his only contact now with an existence that had been lost long ago, that was now only a reflection he saw in the dirty mirror back of the bar.

"Didja ever see a grapevine?" old Carter asked. "Huh? Huh?" He didn't care that John nodded. "They hang helpless, little babies those grapes, green around the ears, no place to go. No heaven for them. Just the purgatory of the hot sun blazing down trying to reach them, but the big thick branches keeping all that beautiful blue heaven out. They're like us, sonny boy. They're damned, in Purgatory, just waiting and waiting and waiting."

His voice cracked as it grew louder and he stood up, coughing the hoarseness out. The rest of the people in the

saloon turned to look now. "But then one day, all of a sudden, they get strong and burst out nice and ripe. They come
out and they feel the sun and they see the sky and they're not
damned anymore." Carter stood up, the beer bottle splashing liquid as he waved it in his hand. He squeezed it hard,
putting all his might into the words. They were that important to him. They were his future, his hope, his salvation.

"Even the damned ripen," he shouted. The voice choked
and sputtered. He slapped an open palm on the top of the
table. With a last effort he roared it through the room.
"Ya hear. The damned also ripen." He yelled it with all his
strength. "The damned also ripen." Now all his strength was
gone.

He coughed once, then again, harder. The bottle slith-
ered from his hand and somehow stayed upright on the table.
He bit into his lip, not able to stop the saliva from drooling
through onto his chin. He slumped onto the chair, his head
buried in his arms on the table.

John watched, staring, until the old man disappeared
from his consciousness. Then he repeated aloud the old man's
words. "The damned also ripen . . . ." A shout of laughter
from the bar stopped him. Then more laughter.

"Old Carter's got a disciple," someone roared. Then everyone roared. John looked around, saw dizzy figures and let
them stay in their own moving blobs of space. He grabbed at
his beer glass, filled it, drained it, filled it again with the last
dregs of the bottle and drank it down quickly. He blinked
his eyes hard and deep, trying to keep them open. He knew
he didn't want to stay any longer. He knew he was drunk.
If he were out of there the drunkenness would surely go
away. He reached for the handle of the small bag by his feet,
grabbed it tightly. Across from him, Annette got up. He had
almost forgotten she was there. He wondered vaguely why
she was there. It was all right, he decided. He saw her put

some money on the table and he reached for his wallet, but it seemed too far away, out of all possible reach.

He stared at Annette and the money she had put on the table, decided it was all right, and with one hand balancing himself on the chair turned toward the door. "I'm getting out of here," he muttered.

"Where?" Annette asked.

"My hotel," he answered, surprised that she should ask such an obvious question.

"What hotel?"

"My hotel," he retorted sharply. He was angry that she should not know the name of his hotel. For a second he remembered that he had not gotten a hotel room and the next second decided that this had nothing to do with the situation. "My hotel," he said again. He steadied himself on the chair, then let go and began to walk toward the door. He was pleased that he was walking straight and was suddenly annoyed to find Annette walking next to him, one arm around his waist and the other supporting his elbow. He felt numb and dizzy and didn't argue. They walked out of the bar. He didn't know where they were going, except that he knew they were walking up the street somewhere. He didn't care. Everything began to grow numb and dizzy and dark.

When he woke up the next morning his eyes hurt. The sun shining through the window next to him made them hurt and he shut them and turned away. He sat up. He was on a couch in a living room and he was covered with a thick patch-quilt. He heard someone humming softly. It came from the next room. It was a strange sensation. He could not remember what had happened or why he was there. He felt an inordinate irresponsibility of himself. He stood up, felt the cold floor against his bare feet, slipped them into his shoes at the side of the couch. His clothes were neatly piled on a wooden chair. He looked at the clothes strangely. Even

his shorts and undershirt were carefully folded. He looked
down at himself, still not understanding, and wondered at
the wool nightgown that covered him down to his knees. He
looked around the room, at the small bureau, the magazine
rack, the cocktail table pushed away from the couch, the
easy chair, blinked at the sun shining through the window,
looked again at the pile of clothes, at the bed-made couch, at
his knees sticking out from under the hem of the white wool
nightgown. Suddenly he was awake. He grabbed the quilt,
pulled it around him and marched into the next room, in the
direction of the humming voice.

"Good morning. Have a good rest?" Annette smiled to
him. She lit a match, still humming, and turned up the flame
under a coffee pot on the stove.

"I got drunk," he said sheepishly. He remembered now.

Annette was dressed in a loose black dress, her hair loos-
ened from the bun, hanging soft and silky to her shoulders.
She was much prettier than she had been the evening before.
Much nicer, too, it seemed.

"I must have gotten really drunk," John said.

"It's all right. A lot of people do." She took a carton of
eggs from the fridge. "How do you like your eggs?"

"Up." He had never thought about it before. Nobody had
really ever asked him. Except Carol. Though there wasn't the
slightest resemblance, Annette just then reminded him of
Carol. It wasn't an angry reminder, like Helen had been. He
was rather glad of it.

"You go in and get washed and dressed"—she pointed
to a door at the other end of the living room—"while I get
breakfast."

"How did I get like this?" John pointed underneath the
quilt without opening it.

"That's one of my nightgowns. Not very chic, but better
than nothing, you know."

"Yes, I know." John felt embarrassed, but not upset.

Annette smiled. "Now don't go blushing."

"I didn't mean . . ."

"We don't even have to talk about it," she interrupted.

John turned and walked toward the bathroom. "Very, very strange," he muttered to himself. Yet, he felt good. The strange feeling was good. No tight-lipped morality. He felt free. He wanted to go back to Annette and kiss her for making him feel so good. He washed and dressed and returned to find breakfast on the table, fried eggs, bacon, toast and coffee. He whistled even as he ate.

"You feel a little better than you did yesterday?" she said.

"Much."

"Why?"

He puzzled. "I don't know. I didn't until this morning. But this morning, after I saw you, I suddenly felt like me. I didn't have to pretend anything. I felt clean and free."

"That's a switch," she laughed.

He didn't ask her to explain.

"What happened last night? After I got drunk?"

She didn't answer him. "You must be running away from something pretty cockeyed," she said instead.

He was surprised. But again not embarrassed. "I guess I am. How did you know?"

"I don't know. I'm just guessing. You're a funny boy. You find a place of kindness and suddenly you seem to become happy."

It startled him. It was true. He did feel good. As if it were Carol with him there. The reminder stayed with him and he wished it were Carol. Or like the good times with Tony. Maybe it was the memory of those good times with Tony that made him feel good? The feeling of being free began to grow inside of him. The "open sesame" to the answer that he was seeking. But it wasn't altogether clear yet.

"You're running away from something and at the same time you're looking for something," Annette continued. "You think you perhaps found a little bit of it here, don't you?"

"You seem to know more about me than I do."

"I doubt that."

He thought for a second about what she had said. "I want to say something strange, Annette."

"Go ahead."

"I don't know what happened last night. But I want to stay here tonight. I want to stay with you for a while, if I may."

Annette tightened her lips, looking at him seriously.

"I don't mean to sound patronizing or rude," he hastily assured her. "I like you, that's all."

"It would be nice," she said. She paused a moment. "It would be nice because I like you, too. But no." She continued before he had a chance to protest. "Whatever you're running away from, you're not going to lose by staying here with me. You'll feel good and secure for a while. And maybe I will, too. But you'll be throwing away too much of your life. How old are you?"

"Twenty-two."

"I'm almost forty. Even at best you'd get tired of me before too long."

"I think I'd be very happy here."

"That may be. But I think you'd probably be a great deal happier someplace else. Wouldn't you?"

John hesitated, not wanting to answer. "I could be," he said finally.

"Then be." She pushed the chair out from the table, folded her hands solemnly, forgetting about the food. John listened without moving. "I may be a lot of things," Annette said, "but I am at least honest with myself. I know what I am and I make no pretense about it. I'm not a hypocrite like

most of the people who would snub me and laugh at me. I'll
be honest with you. I ran away from life once because it was
too hard and confused. It was all too easy after that. I got on
the toboggan and kept going and it's been downhill fast like
the proverbial greased pig. If you stay here or if you keep running, you'll be on that same toboggan. Don't run away. Go
back to whatever you're afraid of and fight it. No matter how
difficult. Do what you really believe you want to do. Trust
your gut. Don't settle for second best."

She took a small handkerchief from her sleeve and
sneezed and coughed into it. "I don't mean to be philosophical, but we're all human beings. We're all entitled to the
basic right of living our lives with dignity. Don't ever settle
for anything less." She blew into the handkerchief again, only
this time she used the edges to wipe tears from her eyes. She
tried to smile them away and her eyes sparkled and her face
shone. It was the face of a younger woman, of a pretty dark-
haired girl.

She moved back to the table. "Come on now, dig in." Her
voice was deep again. "See what a good cook I am. Before I
start blubbering all over the place."

John got up from the table and walked over to her and
kissed her gently on the forehead.

That afternoon he was on the highway again hitchhiking,
on his way back to New York.

# Chapter 24

John got a ride that afternoon with a little old lady who asked him many questions and gave him a chance to answer only a few. She asked about his education and was delighted to learn that he had gone to Des Moines College.

"My husband was a professor of English at Drake University in Des Moines," she said. John told her he thought it was a fine university.

He came to Utica to accept a professorship there," she continued, "just a few years before he died." She was driving back to Utica.

"I'm sorry," John sympathized.

"You don't have to be sympathetic," she told him. "I've been without him for three years now. But I was with him for more than forty. I've gotten my bearings now. Not used to it, of course, because I'll never be whole living without him, but I know that life goes on and I've got to go on with it."

"I've been finding that out myself," John agreed.

"That's where I live now, Utica," the old lady said. She hunched forward over the steering wheel of the car, caring for it tenderly and with supreme caution. Both hands tightened over it, keeping it steady and the car on an exact center, bearing down the middle of the right-hand lane of the road.

"I like to take little trips around the countryside, like this one. My husband and I did so much travelling. We enjoyed it, too." She smiled apologetically. "I must be boring you with these little unimportant things."

"Not at all. I admire your courage."

"Not courage. Just the good sense of being alive."

The little old lady drove him all the way to Utica. He was feeling fresh. The understanding he had gotten through Annette was made just a bit more vivid by this widow of a college professor. John knew now that words alone were insufficient for living and that being honest with himself meant something only if he did something about it. He was on his way back to New York. Not with any romantic definitive determination, not with all his questions answered, not with all his torment eased, but with at least a certainly that what he was doing was right and that once back there he would be able to do what had to be done.

They had driven out of Kingston early that afternoon and had taken the long route along the north shore on the Canadian side of the St. Lawrence River. They drove slowly and John was able to indulge the peacefulness of the river, the individuality and concomitant belonging of the Thousand Islands. They drove across the river, high above the islands, on the bright sun-reflecting impressive arc of the Thousand Islands Bridge. The scenery and the river were more beautiful than John had imagined them in the darkness of the evening before. It was fresher and younger than he thought it could possibly be. The green-sprouting island tufts reached up to him from far below and he held onto them. They were life growing. He would never let them go.

It was dark when they reached Utica. It was only six o'clock, but the cold had begun to settle on the city from the

north and the deep thick clouds of evening moved onto it
from the east, adding a heaviness to the enveloping darkness.
The little old lady let him off at an intersection in the center
of town. Road signs were posted at each curb: Syracuse to
the west, Watertown to the north, Binghamton to the south,
Albany to the east.

He took a position by the sign pointing to Albany. An
African-American man was already waiting there, one foot
on the sidewalk, the other on the curb, his thumb ready to
hail any passing car. They both waited. A few cars passed.
None stopped. The night was beginning to send down its
cold and after a while they both began to stamp their feet on
the ground and walk back and forth in front of the sign to
stimulate warmth.

"No joke hitchhiking at night," the other man observed.

John nodded to him. "Too cold!"

"Where are you heading?"

"New York."

"You've got a long way," the man said. "I only go as far as
Albany." He paused. "Any luck up here?"

John puzzled a moment, then understood. "I wasn't looking for a job. Just visiting in Canada."

"I came up looking for a job," the man said. "My wife
is in Albany. Two children." He laughed without humor.
"Guess they're waiting for me to return with the good news."

"Get a job?" John asked.

The man smiled again. "I saw an ad in the Utica paper
for a hospital attendant." He patted a folded-up newspaper
in his coat pocket. His clothes were old, the threads fraying
around the edges, but they were clean and neatly pressed. "I
was in the Medical Corps in the Army and know the job."
His voice fell as he said this.

"No job?" John knew he didn't really have to ask.

The man nodded. "I should have written first. Only I needed a job so bad I took the chance and came up here. They didn't like my qualifications." Now his voice was bitter.

"Not enough experience?" John asked innocently.

"Enough experience. Too much color," was the answer. The man laughed more brightly now, apologizing for making his problem John's concern.

John wanted to answer him, but couldn't' think of anything to say. The relative ease of his own existence compared to the problems of this man was apparent. At least his own problems could be solved on the basis of his own volition to act.

"I've been working since I was a kid," the man said. "Since I was old enough to do something more about getting bread than just crying for it. I never had a chance for an education or to learn a good trade. I thought when I went into the Army to fight for my country it would be different. But I guess I still don't have a square chance."

He smiled again. The bitterness and sadness were gone. A dignity and confidence remained. "A person's got a lot of fighting to do," he said.

A large truck stopped at the intersection and the driver motioned towards them, looking at John, holding up one finger. The other man started toward it and the driver began waving frantically to John. The Black man stopped, looked back. John pretended he didn't see. He heard the driver mutter, "What the hell!" He heard the door open and a second later slam shut. He looked up toward it. The Black man was waving at him from the window and smiling. John smiled back. The truck started forward. "Good luck!" John called. He felt angry and good inside at the same time. Life could be good sometimes, and sometimes, he thought, it could be a bastard.

He got a ride himself just a few minutes later. A woman of about thirty, a thin, small woman with a dark face edged with the blowing softness of jet-black hair that made the face seem even darker and thinner, stopped her car and motioned for him to get in. Before he did, she leaned toward the door, purposely. "I'm not lonely," she said. "I just like company on a drive. Just to talk to." She emphasized the last two words. She spoke loud and sharp, not apologetically, but with an anger that had already assumed her guest had an ulterior motive for hitchhiking. She was not afraid.

John nodded his head in understanding and answered softly. "Yes, I understand. Thank you."

The gentleness of his behavior eased any doubts she may have had and when he was settled in the car she let him know this with a smile. There seemed to be a looseness about her that let him relax, too. She was pretty. He watched her in the intermittent flashes of the street lamps as they drove along. Her face had no secrets hidden behind it. Her eyes were deep set and tired, but showed no fear. She turned out to be the same way.

At first, as they drove through Utica and onto the billboard-lit highway, she seemed different from the others who had given him a lift. She spoke little. Then, like the others, she began to talk. John wondered if all the people who gave lifts to the travelers of the road did so only because they needed to find a stranger to talk to, someone to whom they could tell things they could not say to a friend because after the story was told the stranger would disappear forever while the friend would remain and remember.

Like the others, she reached into herself to talk to John. "People do stupid things in their lifetime. I suppose what I did was one of the stupidest." There was no bitterness of remorse in her speech. It was a statement of fact.

"I married him during the war. He looked good in a uniform and I never had had much to do with men. I was too easy, I guess. After he was discharged it was good for a while. Then I became pregnant. Then I found out who he was."

"You don't have to tell me about this just because I'm not doing much talking myself," John said. It was his way of explaining that he was self-conscious about her confessions.

"Don't feel embarrassed," she said. "I'm not. It's all part of life. You seem like a good person. You may as well hear about this part of life." She continued her story—how her husband had refused to accept responsibility and finally walked out on her, leaving her alone with the child.

"My mistake was going back to him. He came around last year, broke and miserable, and I felt sorry for him. I had been working and had a little money saved. And he promised to get a job and make up for the past." She laughed, trying to cover the disappointment. "I thought that maybe, at last, he had really become the knight on the white horse."

John didn't interrupt, but let her muse for a while until she spoke again.

"Now I'm like all the women who refuse to insist that it be an equal world for men and women. I asked to be stepped on, to be the simple dependent housewife, and so I was. And so are they. He didn't get a job. He just lived off me. And I, like a fool, got pregnant again." She shrugged as though there were nothing more that could happen now. "And so I'm packed and headed for Albany. My mother lives there. My son is staying with her."

She turned to John. His face was tight and dry. "You needn't look so sad about it," she told him. "It served me right for being so weak. Now I know where I'm going. I'll live my own life and not look for shining armor—or handouts, either. I'll raise my children without their father. I only wish he wasn't. Then, maybe someday . . ." She stopped abruptly. Her voice had become low and choked up in her throat.

"Now it's becoming a sob story," she said firmly. "I don't like sob stories." She stepped on the accelerator and the car hurried forward toward Albany.

John felt sorry for the woman and at the same time admired her. She had extricated herself from the web and was moving ahead as quickly as each spin of the car wheels could take her. She was facing the future bravely and strongly. When they arrived in Albany and John stepped out of the car, he too felt braver and stronger.

He found a small restaurant on one of the still brightly lit streets of the city, ate hungrily and contentedly. He counted the money he had left. Thirty dollars and some change. He stuffed a ten-dollar bill into one of his wallet pockets, between the folds of an identification card. He decided now to get back to New York quickly. Carol would be there soon, he knew. He wanted to be there with her, with Tony, and meet the situation. He thought he felt strong enough to make the decision he had to make, and the sooner the better. He asked the waitress the way to the railroad station and with his bag in hand, his trench coat tightly buttoned against the chilled night, started toward the station. He would go as far as his money would let him as quickly as he could, first by train, then, if he were not yet in New York, by hitchhiking the rest of the way. He hurried.

The streets close to the railroad station were narrow, not really streets, but alleys that intertwined between the larger avenues of shops and served them as delivery lanes for the trucks and handcars and as storage for the high-piled boxes of rubbish and cans of garbage.

The alleys were dark. Sunday evening and the stores were closed. An occasional beacon of brightness from a night light in one of the stores sneaked across an alleyway.

A shadow crossed in front of him as he walked, a man hurrying to the station, another from the station. A woman, her coat clutched tightly across her shoulders and folded up around her neck, half running toward the wider, more populated, better lit and presumably safer avenues. A stooped figure leaned against a wall in one of the alleys, gulping from a bottle, spitting its rebellion into the ground and then melting against the brick to shield itself from the cold and to wait for the liquor warmth to do the rest.

John saw the lights of the station across one of the alleys, turned into it and walked quickly, in his eagerness paying no attention to the darkness around him. Suddenly he was startled by the heavy overcoated figure of a man who stepped from the shadows of a doorway, asked him for a match. John put his bag down, reached into his pocket to oblige. He was half-conscious of another person moving up in back of him and, forgetting the matches, reached instinctively for his bag, feeling the urgency to run from whatever was there. The overcoated man who first stopped him moved closer and he heard him saying something like "Get him, quick." His head raced and his stomach pounded too quickly to be sure. He tried to turn away and duck as he felt a hard flat object slash across his forehead. He heard his own voice moan and his throat choke with dryness. He struggled to move away again, throwing his hands up and his arms across his face to protect himself. Something else hit him from the other direction, across the top of his head, and he heard the moan again, only this time much fainter. He tried to straighten out his eyes. They crossed into alternate waves of light and dark and then the black flashes became stronger and his head ached as the blackness pounded in spurts against it, harder and oftener, until the white flashes all but disappeared and the black was all that was left. He tried to move and felt the cold of the concrete street all over him. Without believing that it was really himself, he knew that his body was pulling away from the wet cold and he felt it shivering with the frustration of not being able to. He felt the word "mama" and the words "Carol" and "Tony" come up from his stomach and reach his throat. They tried to come out, but they didn't, and he choked on them and held them there. He pushed his hands tighter around his head and was buried deeper into the concrete. It began to feel less cold and even almost comfortable. Then the blackness took over completely and he didn't know anything.

It was light when he awoke, only it wasn't a clear light but a strange one that seemed to blink with the same feeling he had last felt. This one alternated between yellow and black, but the yellow was predominant and as he stared at the sensation it became all yellow. He rubbed his hand over his face and shut his eyes and rubbed them as he tried to squint away the yellow light, tried to think who he was and where he was and what he was doing. The thoughts floated far off out in space, then gradually became visual objects that drew closer to him and became part of him and he saw the yellow light bulb up against the ceiling and the blue coats of the policemen standing around him.

"Feel better, buddy?"

"Give him another icepack."

A man in a dark grey business suit stood close to him. "You're all right now. "You're not badly hurt. You're in a police station. You're all right. What's your name? Tell me your name."

"John Thomas."

The man applied something cold to the back of his neck and then turned to the others. "He's okay! He'll be all right now." The man walked away.

A policeman held the cold pack against his neck. "The Doc says you're okay. Nothing serious."

"Did I get beat up?" It hurt even to speak the words. He said them again and it didn't hurt so much. The question was unnecessary, but it made him feel better to hear the sound of his own voice.

"We found you in an alley by the station about an hour ago," the policeman told him. "You got a lump on your forehead. That's all."

"Guess I was robbed," John said. He sat up on the long bench he was lying on and reached for his wallet, didn't find it.

Another policeman handed it to him. "We found it near you. No money in it." John took it, thumbed through to the identification card, felt the crinkle of the ten dollar bill still there.

"My travel bag?" John asked.

"Nothing like that."

"I had one," John told them. "It's not important," he added hastily. "Just a few clothes." He tried to stand up, felt dizzy and sat down again. The dizziness left after a moment and he straightened up. The other policeman left, the one who had been holding the icepack remained, took a pencil and notebook from his pocket. John told him, as detailed as he could, what had happened. The policeman promised to let him know if they found his travel bag.

"But don't depend on it," the policeman said. "These things happen all the time. We rarely get any good leads on these petty crimes."

He was left alone then, on the bench, under the yellow light bulb. He was a little angry, now that he had satisfied their questions, that they had left him alone. He stood up and felt all right. He walked to the door of the station house, then turned back and asked for the bathroom. He washed dirt from his face, but couldn't get the dark purple bruise on his forehead any lighter. His coat was torn at one shoulder and altogether dirty. He couldn't do anything about that. He combed his hair, walked to the police sergeant at the front desk and thanked him for the police assistance. The sergeant dismissed it with a wave of his hand and told him again that they would let him know if they got his property back. He left the police station, started to walk again to the railroad station. He looked at his wrist to see the hour, noticed for the

first time that his watch was gone. He decided it would be a
waste of time to return to the police station and continued to
the railroad depot. A large clock in the window of one of the
stores let him know that it was after midnight.

He felt weak walking and the freshness of his determination had worn thin. He thought, "even though I don't feel so
excited, I feel just as eager. Even with my head hurting, I feel
important. Like the time in the café near Des Moines when
the drunk annoyed Carol. I was afraid then, too, but after it
was over I felt good. Like now. Life, strangely, seems to mean
something more. I guess when you come close to risking it or
fearful of losing it, it becomes more important that you don't
want to waste any of it. There is really so little in a lifetime
and it ends so quickly that there is no time to waste." The
words of the thought were not altogether clear. It didn't matter. Thoughts are rarely complete contiguous words one after
another, anyway. The ideas passed through and he understood them. Out loud he said, "I feel good. I hurt, but I feel
damned good."

He walked past the alley where he had been beaten,
stopped, and like a person watching a movie or play, tried to
recreate what had happened. He shuddered at first, but then
it didn't frighten him. It was past. He thought he had called
for Carol or Tony during the mugging. He didn't remember
whether he had or not.

Even standing alone in the darkness he didn't feel alone.
The hurt face and head throbbed a little less sharply. He
turned and purposely walked through the alley. It was bare
now. Was he looking for his assailants? He hurried on to the
train station. Minutes were passing again and he didn't want
to waste them,

Eight dollars got him to New York City. He took the
subway at 42nd Street, mentally helped push it along as it
sped to the Christopher Street station. It was morning and

the crowds going to work pushed in against him and the pressure made his head begin to ache again. When he reached Christopher Street he stopped at the men's room in the subway, found a sink that worked, washed his face, felt better as he poured the cold water across the back of his neck and over his forehead, combed his hair and then hurried to Barrow Street.

The morning was grey. The sun, coming out of an infinite sky, reflected onto the heavy clouds far below, outlining them from earth as dark bundles of enmity. To John they seemed like angry villains conspiring to keep from the ground the brightness and warmth of the sun. He watched them move slowly as the sun trotted higher into the horizon and then they began to break up gradually into smaller shapes and he knew that the sun and the earth would be the victors. Incongruously, he felt a raindrop splinter across his face and he pulled up the collar of the trench coat. The rain started slowly, picked up momentum, and by the time he reached the brownstone on Barrow Street the rain began to fall hard in heavy drops.

He walked to Tony's apartment without a pause. Carol would be there by now. He thought he should stop and comb his hair again and straighten his tie and fidget with his fingernails. The thought was only a reflection and not a reality. He rapped against the door, first hesitatingly, then rapidly. He still hadn't planned what he would do once he was inside. He knew he had to do something.

There was no more time for games. There was no more time for rationalizing. There was no more time for running. There was no more time for hiding. There was no more time for indecision.

The door opened. There was no more time.

Also by Robert Hilliard

*Phillipa*
*Hollywood Speaks Out*
*Surviving the Americans*
*Media, Education and America's Counter-Culture Revolution*
*Writing for Television, Radio and New Media*
*The Federal Communications Commission*
*Television Station Operations and Management*
*Television and Adult Education*
*Radio Broadcasting*
*Television Broadcasting*
*Understanding Television*
*Blue Rock Land*
*Dirty Discourse* (with Michael Keith)
*The Quieted Voice* (with Michael Keith)
*The Broadcast Century and Beyond* (with Michael Keith)
*Waves of Rancor* (with Michael Keith)
*The Hidden Screen* (with Michael Keith)
*Global Broadcasting Systems* (with Michael Keith)
*Beyond Boundaries* (with Melinda Robins)
*Television and the Teacher* (with Hyman Field)